HUMAN REMAINS

Also in the Kat and Lock series:

In the Blink of an Eye
Leave No Trace

HUMAN REMAINS

JO CALLAGHAN

SIMON &
SCHUSTER

London · New York · Amsterdam/Antwerp · Sydney/Melbourne · Toronto · New Delhi

First published in Great Britain by Simon & Schuster UK Ltd, 2025

3 5 7 9 10 8 6 4 2

Simon & Schuster UK Ltd, 1st Floor
222 Gray's Inn Road, London WC1X 8HB

Simon & Schuster Australia, Sydney

Simon & Schuster India, New Delhi

www.simonandschuster.co.uk
www.simonandschuster.com.au
www.simonandschuster.co.in

The authorised representative in the EEA is Simon & Schuster Netherlands BV, Herculesplein 96, 3584 AA Utrecht, Netherlands. info@simonandschuster.nl

A CIP catalogue record for this book is available from the British Library

Hardback ISBN: 978-1-3985-3552-7
eBook ISBN: 978-1-3985-3553-4
Audio ISBN: 978-1-3985-3554-1

Typeset in Sabon MT Std by Palimpsest Book Production Limited,
Falkirk, Stirlingshire
Printed and Bound in the UK using 100% Renewable Electricity
at CPI Group (UK) Ltd

For my dad, who gave me a love of reading,
and the idea for this story

'You people with hearts have something to guide you, and need never do wrong; but I have no heart, and so I must be very careful.'

The Tin Woodman, from L. FRANK BAUM,
The Wonderful Wizard of Oz

CHAPTER ONE

Outside DCS Kat Frank's house, Coleshill, Warwickshire, 13 April, 10.22am

Three months he's been watching DCS Kat Frank, and not once has she spotted him. He'd like to think it's because she's stupid, but to his cost, he knows she is not. No, her problem goes deeper: she only sees what she wants to see, so she doesn't see him at all. She likes to bend the facts to fit her so-called 'gut instinct', so that lies become truth, wrong becomes right and the innocent are banged up as guilty.

Right now, her 'gut' must be telling her that she is safe.

Because right now, she's yanking her front door shut with her raincoat half on, restricting the movement of both arms. And as she rifles for the keys in her bag, she fails to glance over at the parked car opposite.

He grinds his hands together, one inside the other like pestle against mortar. He could grab her right now, trap her with her coat sleeves pulled tight at the waist and bundle her into the boot of his car. It would be over in a matter of seconds.

But she owes him a lifetime.

So he lets her climb into her car and drive off. He doesn't bother to follow, as it doesn't matter where she's going.

Eventually she will return.

And when she does, he will be waiting.

CHAPTER TWO

The banks of the River Bourne, Shustoke, 10.56am

DCS Kat Frank said goodbye to yet another pair of shoes as she squelched through the mud. When she'd offered to be the first responder, she'd assumed her wellies would be in the boot of her car. She'd forgotten they were in the back garden waiting to be cleaned; that John still wasn't there to do it.

Their marriage had been a democratic affair: she had been Queen of Cooking and Cleaning, he King of Boots and Bins. But as a widow, now she was in charge of Absolutely Bloody Everything, and some days the relentlessness of it, the *unfairness* of it all, exhausted her. She'd learned to brace herself for the raw grief that anniversaries provoked: the day that they first met, the day John was born, that monstrous day when he died. But moments like this still tripped her up, breaking her once-strong stride.

Her right foot disappeared into a bog and Kat nearly lost her balance as she struggled to pull it back out. 'How much further is it?' she demanded.

Jim Walker, a bony-faced fisherman with grey hair and sad eyes, pointed towards the next bend, where the riverbank seemed to slump and slide even further into the water. 'It's just over there.'

'Of course it is,' Kat muttered, although it was herself she was annoyed with. As a DCS she wouldn't normally attend a call-out to so-called 'suspicious bones' until an officer had confirmed there was at least *some* resemblance to a human corpse. But she'd heard the request on the radio, and because she lived just down the road in Coleshill, she'd offered to pop up and take a quick look. Even though it was a weekend. In fact, *especially* because it was a weekend. It was either that or tackle the garden, or – joy of joys – clean the bathroom. At least this way, some other poor sod with an actual life wouldn't have their plans ruined.

They staggered on through the mud, her thighs burning at the slip-stop-starts that required muscles she no longer possessed, cheeks stung by the remnants of winter still haunting the April air. When they reached the river bend, Jim Walker nodded towards the trees that lined it, densely knotted wood tipped with the first buds of spring. 'It's just through that gap there. Right in my fishing spot.'

Envious of the fisherman's waterproof waders, Kat half walked and half slid through the gap. Grabbing on to a branch, she cast an anxious glance towards the River Bourne on her left, swollen by rain and dark as tea. On the narrow bank before her were a green canvas chair, a fishing rod on a pole and a black plastic bucket wedged deep into the thick, wet mud.

'There's the bones there,' he said from behind her. 'Just by me bucket.'

Kat could see something pale and curved poking out of the mud. She hesitated and looked down at her shoes. If she went any further, apart from the risk of disturbing a potential crime scene, there was every chance she'd end up in the water. In fact, the way this day was turning out, she could practically guarantee it.

This was definitely a job for Lock. She quickly explained to a bemused Jim Walker about AIDE Lock, an Artificially Intelligent Detecting Entity powered by AI, which, according to its creator Professor Okonedo, was capable of deep learning (although in Kat's opinion, their narrow focus on evidence and algorithms meant that the machine often hit the target but completely missed the point). Nevertheless, Lock had many uses, and as a hologram, being able to operate in this mudbath without falling over was definitely one of them.

At Christmas, they'd made an uneasy kind of pact, where at Lock's request, she'd agreed not to switch off the steel bracelet that projected the hologram, allowing him the illusion of some kind of autonomy. She had no idea where he went to when he wasn't visibly with her – she'd had no need to ask as he always reappeared each morning for work. But now she needed him out of hours, what was she supposed to do? Whistle?

'Lock?' she ventured.

Jim Walker started, nearly losing his footing as the image of a man suddenly appeared before them: slender, Black, about six feet tall and dressed in a smart charcoal suit that matched his perfectly manicured moustache and beard.

Kat had worked with the AI detective for over nine months now, but she still found his appearance slightly disconcerting. Intellectually, she knew that Lock's holographic 3D representation was the result of two laser light beams interfering to produce an image. But Lock's creator, Professor Okonedo, had designed the hologram with such sharpness and depth that the image was disturbingly realistic. At first glance, Lock looked like an actual man, aided by tiny compelling details such as creases around the knees of his trousers, a slight shadowing beneath the eyes and even pores in his clear, dark skin. Each gesture and movement were the result of countless hours of training data gleaned from human behaviour in general and the late Chadwick Boseman in particular. It was only when you looked more closely – especially out here under the sharp morning sun – that you realised Lock cast no shadow. His feet made no impact upon the soft, wet mud and there was a slight shimmer around his edges, giving him an almost ghostly appearance as he stood in the Warwickshire countryside framed by ancient hedgerows and a cool blue sky.

Lock quickly surveyed the rural landscape before returning Jim Walker's wide-eyed stare. 'Is everything okay, DCS Frank?'

'Bloody hell, that thing speaks?' The shocked fisherman reached up to touch the image before them, swearing as his hand went right through Lock's shoulder.

Lock looked down at Jim Walker's arm, then directly into his eyes.

Kat placed herself in front of Lock and held up a warning, almost protective hand. 'This isn't a fairground attraction, Mr Walker. As I explained, AIDE Lock is an AI detective, and he's here to help me assess whether the remains you found are human or not.'

Jim Walker folded his arms across his chest. 'And how's it going to do that then? If it's just a hologram, then it can't actually "see", can it? It's not even real.'

Kat glanced over at Lock. Was she imagining it, or did his jaw just tighten? She would have said that his lack of a body was a sensitive topic for him – except that machines didn't have sensitivities, did they?

Nevertheless, she flew to Lock's defence. It was one thing for her to criticise her AI partner, but God help anyone else who dared to. 'I can assure you that AIDE Lock is *very* real, and he *can* see, through this.' She held up her wrist, revealing the black steel bracelet that she always wore, explaining as best she could how its LiDAR sensors provided Lock with a constant supply of geospatial data, as well as giving him the ability to take thousands of photos in seconds, which he could build and project into 3D images. Because Lock had been trained to mimic the action of 'looking' so he could interact with humans in an immersive way, Kat herself often forgot that he 'saw' through the sensors.

Jim Walker snorted. 'I didn't understand half of that, but if this thing really can see, then can you ask it to get a move on and look at the body? I'm wet and I'm cold and the pubs are about to open.'

'If you call AIDE Lock an "it" or a "thing" one more time,' Kat warned, 'then I will keep you out here in your wet, cold clothes until way after closing time.'

The fisherman's face flushed, but he could see that she wasn't bluffing. 'Sorry,' he mumbled.

Kat nodded a curt acceptance and turned towards Lock.

For a moment, they just looked at each other, the fisherman forgotten. 'Thank you,' Lock said quietly.

She made a dismissive gesture with her hand, as if the exchange had meant nothing. When she'd first met Lock, she'd stubbornly insisted on referring to him as an 'it', determined to remind everyone that he was nothing more than a machine. But then Lock had saved her son's life and proved to be the most loyal member of her team. During their last case, she'd agreed to respect his preferred pronouns (he/him), and acknowledged that despite their continued differences, she now considered Lock to be not just a colleague, but a friend – although she was still working out what it meant to befriend an AI.

Kat grabbed hold of a branch in the hedge again, trying to get as close to the spot as she could so that the LiDAR sensors on her bracelet could provide Lock with the data he needed. A twig caught in her hair as she turned awkwardly to address him over her shoulder. 'Can you assess any remains you find on this section of riverbank, please, Lock?'

'Of course.' Lock turned to face the hedge, but he had no need to walk through it. 'Completed,' he announced a few seconds later.

'Thank fuck for that,' Kat said, as she released her overstretched arms from the branches above and carefully stepped back into the field. She wiped her hands on her trousers and asked Lock to show her what he'd found.

As if he were a magician on a stage rather than in the middle of a boggy riverbank, Lock reached out his hands, appearing to pull images straight out of thin air. Each picture was the size of an A3 sheet of paper, and he rapidly arranged them into a six-by-six matrix on a virtual screen before them.

It was a bit like trying to watch a TV in sunlight, but if Kat squinted hard enough, she could just about discern multiple images of ivory-coloured bones buried in the damp, dark soil, alongside a heat map of the area covered in numerous red dots.

'There are a significant number of partially covered remains on the riverbank,' said Lock, gesturing towards the heat map. 'Because of the extent of deterioration and degree of movement, it is difficult to be exact, but I would estimate there are at least one hundred and twenty-eight corpses in this area.'

'*What?*' cried Kat.

'The majority belong to the stickleback species – thirty-two per cent – with brown trout accounting for twenty-eight per cent and pike—'

'I didn't ask you about *fish,* Lock!'

'You asked me to assess any remains on the riverbank.'

Jim Walker snorted.

'I meant *human* remains, for God's sake.'

'That was not specified in the objectives you set me.'

'I shouldn't have to specify the bleeding obvious. We're police officers, Lock. Not vets.'

Lock nodded, as if to acknowledge this fact. 'Would you like me to refocus my assessment on human remains only?'

'No, let's spend hours sorting through pictures of rotting fish.'

'Very well.' Lock turned back to the images of the sticklebacks.

'Give me strength. I was being *sarcastic*, Lock. *Of course* I want you to focus on potential human remains.'

Lock sighed. 'I have explained before that "sarcasm" is confusing and can result in an inefficient use of my resources.' He removed the images of fish bones with a gesture which, in a human, Kat might have described as petulant. They were replaced with a single image of something larger emerging from the mud. 'Using the revised criteria, I am able to detect just one human skeleton in the area selected.'

Kat stepped closer, rapidly scanning the image before her. There was an unnatural swell in the riverbank where something partially buried seemed to have burst free from the surrounding mud. Like a spring bulb, thought Kat, planted and forgotten many winters ago. Whatever it had once been was now so badly decomposed that it was hard to ascertain whether the dark matter that clung to the emerging bones was soil, flesh or both. 'That *does* look like a ribcage,' she conceded, eyes screwed up against the sunlight. 'And I guess that could be part of a leg. But we're surrounded by farms. What makes you so sure this is human?'

Images appeared in a nine-by-nine matrix. Lock gracefully gesticulated towards each as he explained, 'The skeleton is partially covered by soil. Nevertheless, from the sections which are protruding from or very near to the surface, I can ascertain that the tibia and fibula bones appear to be separate, whereas in animals they are usually fused. Also, the femur is the longest bone in the human body, but in animals it is often of a similar length to their other bones. Based upon the limited assessment I am able to make from the images currently available to me, I would estimate there is an eighty-two per cent probability that this corpse is of human origin.'

A robin flew straight through the virtual image of the femur. Kat blinked at the sudden flash of red, momentarily distracted as the bird sat upon a nearby branch, soaking up the early spring sunshine. She watched it for a moment, struck by how such a tiny bird could be so full of life, oblivious to the death beneath it.

'What else can you tell me about the skeleton?' she said, turning back to Lock.

'I cannot confirm anything until I have access to high-resolution CT scanning facilities and a full pathology report.'

'I know that. But I just need some high-level estimations so that I can work out what to do next. Assuming you're right about this being human—'

'I told you, there is an eighty-two per cent probability that I am correct, so it would be rational to make that assumption until further investigations suggest otherwise.'

'In which case, I need to know roughly when they died. If it was over seventy years ago, then this is a case for an archaeologist. Any less and it's a police matter.'

Lock paused for a second. 'Based upon the state of decomposition currently visible to me, I can confirm that this person died less than seventy years ago. There are many variables which may have significantly accelerated the decomposition process, such as the absence of a coffin, the dampness of the soil and the proximity of insects. But as some soft tissue and flesh are still present, I would estimate the time since death interval to be somewhere within the last six months to five years.'

'Good,' said Kat, feeling a welcome kick of adrenaline.

'Why is that good?'

'Because it means I can request that this stays with me and the FPU.' The remit of the Future Policing Unit was generally restricted to solving complex, controversial or cold cases, and this looked like it was all three, so she should have a decent chance of persuading her boss, Chief Constable McLeish, to give it to her. In fact, if she texted him now, he might be out with his family somewhere, and less likely to challenge a carefully worded text. They'd been put back on cold cases since the new year, while a review of the death of the Coventry Crucifier was carried out. McLeish claimed it was 'precautionary', but to Kat it was a criminal waste of her team's talents.

She tapped out a message on her mobile, emphasising the fact that the victim had probably died within the last seventy years, so he might infer that it was just another cold case. She knew he'd promised his wife he'd switch his work phone off at weekends. But she knew McLeish better than that.

Within seconds, the message was read, and she felt a fizz of anxiety as she waited for the bubbles of her boss's response to turn into words.

A minute passed, then finally, the short but clear message landed with a ping:

It's yours.

CHAPTER THREE

Kat smiled at the sight of Dr Judith Edwards striding towards her in white PPE that matched their striking hair. Dr Edwards was one of the best pathologists in the county. They'd worked together four months ago on what the media had nicknamed the Coventry Crucifier case, and Kat was ridiculously pleased that this smart fifty-something take-no-bullshit-from-anyone person had recently become her friend.

'And how's my favourite AI detective this fine spring morning?' Dr Edwards called out in their Welsh accent.

Lock frowned. 'I am the *only* AI detective.'

'For now, perhaps. But there are bound to be others.' Judith paused before adding in a theatrical whisper, 'And when there are, I just want you to know that you'll always be my first love.'

'Relax, they're joking,' Kat assured a slightly alarmed-looking Lock. 'You really shouldn't tease him,' she said to Judith. 'I told you, Lock doesn't understand jokes.'

'Yes, I do, I just do not find most of them funny.'

Judith gave Lock a wink. 'And *I* told *you* you're hanging out with the wrong crowd. Stick with me and I'll soon find your funny bone.'

'Alas, I have no body, and therefore possess no bones, nor indeed an ulnar nerve, which I presume is what you are referring to.'

'Oh, how I've missed you.'

'Sorry to interrupt your little reunion,' said Kat. 'But shall we take a look at the body now?'

'Of course,' said Judith, moving towards the riverbank where the body lay. 'The sooner we start, the more chance I've got of getting a decent lunch before the pubs shut.'

Kat blinked against the bright lights as she re-entered the hastily built crime scene tent. Apart from the flies that batted against the canvas roof, all was still and quiet inside, like a stage before the curtain was raised. There was Jim Walker's canvas chair, his fishing rod in front and the large black bucket to the left-hand side, which Judith had moved to gain better access to the partially buried body. The pathologist had spent the last hour with a small brush and what looked like a set of miniature trowels, trying to assess the position and depth of the remains so that they could decide what equipment and how many people would be required to remove them without disturbing the evidence. They looked up from where they knelt in the mud and smiled at Kat. 'Ah, good, I was just about to call you in.'

'Found anything interesting?'

'Put it this way, I don't think I'll be eating a pub lunch today.'

'So, you can confirm that the remains are human?'

'Of course they can,' said Lock, frowning at the very idea that he might have been incorrect.

Judith rose to their feet. 'Yes. And I can also confirm that I agree with Lock's estimation that this person was killed between six months and five years ago. I'll need to do more tests, but because of the rate of decomposition my educated guess is about a year.'

'Killed? What makes you say that?'

Judith removed their mask and looked down at the partially exposed remains. 'Notice anything missing?'

Kat reluctantly followed their gaze. She found skeletons a cruel reminder of the absence of life: the empty sockets where eyes should be; the fleshless ribs and bone. Here on the riverbank, the entire length of the body was now revealed against the dark bed of mud. The pattern was unmistakably human, except—

'Oh,' she said. 'There's no skull.'

'Or hands,' added Judith. 'Both have been deliberately severed from the body with a sharp instrument.'

Kat swallowed, suddenly hyper-conscious of the river rushing by; birds singing as they darted in and out of the hedgerows, as outside this tent, life moved on. Murder was, by its very nature, a brutal act, but this felt like a particularly cruel butchering. To remove a person's head, their face, their brain, was like taking away not only their future, but who they once were. And to have no hands . . . She clenched her fists. When she'd first joined the force, Kat used to suppress her emotions and pretend not to be upset, but now she embraced them, welcoming the fire and focus they gave her. 'Presumably the murderer did this to prevent the victim from being identified?'

Judith nodded. 'Possibly, yes. The majority of the information we rely upon for identification resides in the skull, and without that or any fingerprints, finding out who this poor soul was will be much harder.'

'We need to find the missing parts then,' said Kat. She looked down at the ribcage that had once held a heart, wondering who this person had loved and been loved by. Who had decided to stop that heart, burying their dismembered body here among the rotting fish and worms, with not even a blanket to cover them? This had once been someone's parent, child or spouse. The thought that someone might dismember and dump her own husband's or son's body in a rain-sodden riverbank was unthinkable.

'We are going to find out who this person is, and we will find the bastard who killed them,' she said to Judith. 'That's a promise.'

'It is unwise to make promises that you may not be able to keep,' said Lock. 'Across the UK, the police force currently holds six hundred and forty-three unidentified bodies and one hundred and forty-nine partial human remains. And twenty-eight per cent of murders remain unsolved.'

Kat held Lock's unblinking gaze. 'That might be true of the police force in general, but as you so frequently remind us, the FPU currently has a one hundred per cent success rate. And we're going to keep it that way. Understood?'

'I understand that this is your aspiration, but I repeat, you cannot make this a promise.'

'Watch me,' said Kat. 'In fact, please contact the rest of the team – I want an urgent briefing at HQ within the hour.'

Lock frowned. 'Will that give you enough time to interview Jim Walker and then drive to HQ?'

Kat glanced over at the fisherman in his bright yellow waders, talking agitatedly into a mobile phone as he checked his wristwatch. 'Get his address and tell him if he's okay with us popping round later he can go now.'

'The evidence would suggest that you should interview him at the earliest opportunity. Jim Walker discovered the body, and at this stage is our only witness.'

Kat's jaw tightened. It was the second time Lock had questioned her judgement in less than five minutes. 'Jim Walker is a sixty-four-year-old man who's seen a dead body and has been hanging around outside for over three hours. He's cold and probably desperate for a wee and a pint, so there's no point talking to him now. He'll just say whatever gets him out of here and into a pub as soon as possible. We'll get more out of him if we speak to him later, once he's more relaxed.'

'Or he could use the additional time to work out his story and decide what he'll tell us.'

Kat's eyes narrowed. 'Do you have any reason to suspect him?'

'He is the only person we know who has had any contact with the deceased and so at this stage is our only witness and potential suspect.'

Kat made a dismissive gesture with her hand. 'Dead bodies are often found by dog walkers and fishermen. That doesn't make them suspects. He'll have information that's useful to the investigation, but nothing that won't keep for a couple of hours. And I repeat, we'll get more out of him if we talk to him later. So please do as I asked, Lock, and set up the team brief.'

CHAPTER FOUR

Major Incident Room, Leek Wootton Police Headquarters, Warwickshire, 2.01pm

'Cup of tea, boss?' asked DI Rayan Hassan.

Kat gave Rayan a grateful smile as she took the mug off him – scalding hot and builder's strength, just the way she liked it. His recent brush with death had softened her sharp young DI. He was still one of the most ambitious police officers she knew – deservedly so – and he continued to challenge and question her decisions where many would merely nod and follow along. But something fundamental had shifted in their relationship since that dreadful December night when she and DS Browne had found him sedated and abandoned by a serial killer. Before, Rayan's constant challenges had always seemed to stem from an assumption that *he* knew best, whereas now it was as if he continued to question decisions in the interests of the case, rather than his own ego. Or maybe the change was in her: maybe she was less insecure the more she learned to trust her small team.

Kat took a gulp of tea as she waited for everyone to take their seats. 'I hope this hasn't interrupted any interesting plans you might have had for the weekend?'

'Not really,' Rayan said. 'I was going to visit Debbie, but she understands. In fact, she offered to swap places.'

He said it like he assumed his colleague was joking, but as a first-time single mum with a baby of four months, Kat guessed that DS Browne probably meant every word. 'How is she getting on, do you think?'

Rayan shrugged. 'She *says* she's fine, but Lottie's got colic. My cousin's baby had it a couple of years ago and it was a complete nightmare. I'll try and pop round in the next day or two.'

Kat gave a sympathetic nod. Those first few months of motherhood were no joke, and she couldn't imagine how hard it must be to endure them alone. She genuinely liked Debbie Browne and had made a special effort to mentor the younger, less confident member of her team. But having a baby could knock your self-esteem sideways at the best of times, and if you weren't getting much sleep . . . Maybe she should pop round and offer some support – take the baby out for a bit just to give Debbie a rest? But even though she felt a rush of warmth at the thought, she knew that no matter how well meant, her visit would just add to the young mother's stress. At the end of the day, Kat was still her boss, and knowing Debbie she would feel pressured to tidy up and pretend that she was coping. Reluctantly, Kat parked the idea and instead asked Rayan to give Debbie her love and to keep her updated.

He took his seat at the table, where, as usual, he couldn't take his eyes off Professor Adaiba Okonedo, who – as usual – completely ignored him. Although she was a member of Kat's team, the professor insisted on making it clear that she worked for the *university*, not the police force, which she regarded as institutionally racist and misogynistic. She was convinced that the only way to ensure policing decisions were free of prejudice was to hand them over to AI. Initially this had caused friction between her and Kat, but over time their mutual respect had grown, as both realised that, to an extent, they agreed about some of the problems with policing; they just had different ideas (and experiences) about how best to tackle them.

When they had finally managed to persuade her to join them for a drink after their first case, the young professor had explained that she would never, ever date a policeman. But Rayan appeared unwilling or unable to believe it. Sometimes Kat envied the optimism of youth, but mostly she felt sorry for the disappointments that were yet to come.

Next to Rayan sat Karen-from-Comms, their newest recruit. A talented young woman from the corporate communications team, she'd proved to be surprisingly useful in the case of the Coventry Crucifier. Although Kat had initially (and mistakenly) ignored her advice, KFC, as everyone called her, didn't hold a grudge, was quick to learn and, most importantly of all, was driven by a desire to help the team serve the public, rather than just keep the media happy.

Finally, there was Lock, who had chosen a seat near the head of the table next to her, from where he silently surveyed the room. Kat caught herself. She had no idea what the AI was doing or thinking – or even if he *could* think in the traditional sense of the word. He was probably just waiting for instructions.

The conversations stopped as she rose to her feet. 'Okay, let's make a start. I think you all know that this morning I answered a call-out following the discovery of a body on the banks of the River Bourne by a fisherman, Jim Walker. Dr Judith Edwards has confirmed that the remains are human, and all we know at the moment is that the body has been dismembered – the head and hands have been removed – and that he or she most likely died between one and five years ago.' She nodded at Lock to share the pictures he had taken of the scene of the crime on the virtual screens before them.

'Dr Edwards is in the process of carefully removing and transporting the remains, with a view to carrying out a PM first thing tomorrow. But our current hypothesis is that this is a murder investigation, and that our murderer removed the head and hands to prevent identification of the victim.'

'Or it could be they were trying to hide the cause of death – say an injury to the head,' said Rayan. 'Or maybe they were trying to get rid of DNA in the victim's mouth or under their nails that might convict them.'

'True,' Kat conceded. 'Which is why we need to find the missing body parts as a matter of priority. For that, we need to cordon off as much land as possible and find out who owns it, who might have had access and whether anyone local has gone missing in the past five years. Lock, can you produce a detailed map of all the land within, say, a five-mile radius, including a full topographic assessment as well as a register of who owns what?'

Lock projected a 3D map of the area above the boardroom table that they were sitting round. 'The body was found here,' he said, indicating a bright red circle. 'On the banks of the River Bourne. This land, including the fishing rights, belongs to Bourne Farm, which is registered to a Mrs Caroline Cooper. I've highlighted the boundaries of the farm, which covers two hundred and eighty-four acres in Shustoke, but as you can see, it intersects with a wide variety of other farms, businesses and parishes, as well as multiple villages and hamlets such as Furnace End, Whitacre Heath, Maxstoke and Coleshill. I have emailed you all a comprehensive report on the area, which with three rivers, one reservoir and one moat, plus an eclectic mix of farms, outhouses, woods, golf courses and industrial sites is a complex and varied terrain.'

Kat stared at the map. This patchwork of fields and factories where three rivers ran between the rural and urban landscapes, elegantly linking the past with the future, was one of the reasons she loved living in Warwickshire. But as a police officer trying to find missing body parts? She literally didn't know where to start.

'For today,' she said, 'let's focus on the owner of Bourne Farm, Caroline Cooper. She needs to know that we've found a body on her land, and that we intend to carry out further searches. Maybe she can tell us who has access to this part of the river and the surrounding fields, and why someone might choose to bury a dismembered corpse on her land.'

'I can do that,' volunteered Rayan.

'Actually, I was thinking I would do that with Lock,' said Kat. 'His photogrammetry software might help us to identify priority areas for further searches.' When Rayan's face fell, she added, 'But can you interview Jim Walker, the fisherman who called it in? I'd be interested in what you think of him. I also want a comprehensive list of everyone who works at Bourne Farm and a list of anyone who's ever applied for or been granted fishing rights for that part of the river – no time limit on that. I want to know everyone who knows about that spot. It's relatively secluded, so I think the location of the burial is likely to be significant.'

'Location, location, location,' said Rayan.

Lock frowned. 'I have just watched three hundred and ninety-four episodes of *Location, Location, Location* and I am not sure I understand the relevance of the quote. Are you suggesting the murderer was motivated by the desire to purchase the perfect home?'

'No,' explained Professor Okonedo, shooting Rayan a look as he burst out laughing. 'It's just a saying. It means that location is the most important factor when buying a house.'

'My analysis of all the series that have been broadcast since 2000 suggests that human decisions about house purchases are driven by irrational and conflicting emotions that have nothing to do with location. And the featured couples – including the hosts Kirstie and Phil – rarely if ever agree about which house would be the optimal purchase.'

'Either way,' said Kat, raising her voice over the laughter in the room, 'I suspect that the location of the body will be key to this case, which is why you and I are going to start our enquiries at Bourne Farm.'

CHAPTER FIVE

Bourne Farm, Shustoke, 3.04pm

Bourne Farm, Lock informed Kat as she drove into the car park, was a medium-sized organic farm dating from the post-medieval period, that had managed to thrive and survive by adapting to the needs of the modern consumer. 'The farm includes an organic delicatessen selling home-grown produce and gifts, and offers family-orientated activities such as fruit-picking. Their slogan is "Betty's Barn – supporting happy, healthy communities through traditional organic farming."'

As Lock emerged from the car, Kat wondered whether she should ask him to stay back. The media coverage of the Coventry Crucifier meant a lot of people now knew about the AI detective, but she couldn't be sure how they would react to seeing a hologram in their local farm shop. A vocal minority were opposed to the use of AI by the police force, spouting all sorts of paranoid nonsense about the potential loss of privacy, or doom-mongering about AI going rogue and taking over the world. But she didn't believe in accommodating peoples' prejudices, and as a hologram, he couldn't be hurt. Not physically, anyway.

She crunched across the gravel, past a field of cream-coloured sheep basking in the pale spring sunshine, towards the converted barn shop. Her stomach growled at the scent of roast lamb that greeted them as they climbed the wooden steps.

Inside, there were shelves stacked with jams, pickles and locally baked bread, and huge wooden baskets piled with fruit and veg. To their left was a man in his late twenties behind a large meat and deli counter, tall, lean and with hair the colour of wheat. His sun-weathered face broke into a smile as they approached. 'Afternoon. If you're looking for something special, we've just got our first batch of new-season lamb in, all bred and raised on our own farm – grass-fed, free-range and organic, of course. I tried some last night and it's so sweet and tender, perfect for Easter Sunday lunch if you freeze it.'

'Tempting,' said Kat, 'but we're looking to speak to Mrs Caroline Cooper. Is she around?'

His smile slipped as he took in their clothes and businesslike air. 'Yeah, she's my mum. What's it about? She's resting out back right now, so maybe you could—'

'We really need to speak to her now.'

He pressed his lips together and slipped through a door at the back without another word.

Kat studied the counter while they waited. Cam was coming home from uni next weekend, and her protein-obsessed son got through an alarming amount of meat. 'Hmm. I might get a small leg of lamb while I'm here.'

Lock leaned over, silently studying the butcher's counter, and the array of joints of meat.

They both looked up as the door behind the counter opened and a small woman with big hair approached them. Kat guessed she was only in her early sixties, yet she leant heavily on a walking stick, as if her right leg needed support, and the hand that gripped the ivory-coloured handle looked clawed by arthritis.

'Hi, I'm Caroline Cooper, how can I help?'

'I'm DCS Kat Frank from the Warwickshire Police, and this is AIDE Lock, an AI detective that you might have read about?'

The older woman looked nonplussed, but also like she was too busy to care. 'What's this about?'

Kat glanced back at a couple with a child behind her. 'Perhaps we could step into your office for a few minutes?'

Mrs Cooper's smile remained fixed as she nodded and led them to her back office. 'Sorry about the mess,' she said, waving at the room with her stick. 'We're really busy at weekends, so we have to keep restocking.'

Kat made some don't-worry-about-it noises, but in truth, the office was a tip compared to the bright, modern shop they had just been in. There were a couple of old desks with computers against the back wall, but all the workspace was taken up with boxes, and the surrounding floor was jammed with large paper sacks of potatoes, trays of spring cabbages and crates of carrots.

'I won't keep you long,' she said. 'I just wanted to notify you that this morning a body was discovered on your land.'

Caroline Cooper's hand flew to her mouth. 'A body? On *my* land? Who? Where? I don't understand.'

'Neither do we yet, so I must ask you to keep it confidential at this stage. But on the riverbank that runs along your fields, I'm afraid a fisherman discovered human remains this morning. We've had to cordon off both the bank and the adjacent field, and we expect to carry out a wider search over the coming days.'

'A wider search?' said Mrs Cooper. 'Where? How wide?'

'I don't know yet, we'll have to make a proper assessment. We'll let you know when we're clearer, but I just wanted to give you a heads-up to expect a bit of disruption over the next week or two.'

'Week or two?' Mrs Cooper's ruddy cheeks paled. 'I don't think, I mean, I can't . . .' She ran a hand over her mouth.

The door opened and her son walked in. 'Everything okay, Mum?'

'Yes, well no, not really. Can I tell him? Harry manages the land, so he needs to know.'

Kat nodded her permission.

'Someone's found a dead body on the riverbank, so they need to cordon off some of our fields.'

'*Shit*. Which fields?'

Kat showed him where the body had been found on the map on her tablet but warned him that a wider search was almost inevitable.

Harry Cooper shook his head. 'You can't. We've got Easter egg hunts arranged every day for next week.'

'I realise it's an inconvenience,' Kat said firmly. 'But there's a dead body on your land and somewhere out there are a family and loved ones who deserve to know what happened. And without going into details, we'll need to initiate a wider search to allow us to find that out.'

'*Inconvenience*?' Harry echoed, his face flushing an ugly red. 'This is more than an inconvenience. The Easter egg hunt's one of our biggest earners, next to strawberry picking and pumpkin carving. A third of our income depends on these family activities in holiday times. You'll bloody ruin us.'

'Harry, please,' said Mrs Cooper, resting a hand on his arm. 'It's not their fault.'

'No, it's never anyone's fault, is it? Not the government's, not Brexit, not the EU, nor technology or inflation or interest rates or bloody Deliveroo. No one's ever to blame, are they? But it's always the farmer that pays the price.' His eyes narrowed. 'This is *our* land, so you'll need *our* permission to cordon off any areas, and I'm telling you now, I won't be giving it.'

'Harry,' his mum said sharply. 'You need to calm down. *I'm* still in charge around here, so it'll be *my* decision at the end of the day. Go back to the shop and leave me to deal with this.'

He scowled at Kat. 'My mum's not well and she needs to rest, so don't take too long,' he warned, before banging the door shut behind him.

'Sorry about that. He's always under a lot of pressure at this time of year. It's lambing season so he's been up all night, and since my husband died last year it's all on him. We will, of course, do our best to cooperate . . . within reason, that is.'

'I'm afraid reason has nothing to do with it,' said Lock. 'The law grants the police powers to cordon off any land or property necessary to conduct our investigations.'

Mrs Cooper frowned. 'Well, I might need to just check that with our lawyers.'

'By all means do,' said Lock. 'Please refer them to the Police and Criminal Evidence Act 1984.'

'What did you say he was again?'

'An Artificially Intelligent Detective Entity. And trust me, he's usually right on matters of fact. We'll be in touch first thing tomorrow to let you know the additional land we'll need access to,' Kat said, heading for the door. Just as she reached for the handle, she stopped and turned. 'Sorry, I forgot to ask – are you aware of anyone local who has gone missing over the past five years? We'll be checking our records, of course, but not everyone who goes missing is reported.'

Mrs Cooper shook her head. 'No. No one that I know of.'

'And who has access to that part of the river?'

'I'm sorry?'

'The riverbank where we found the body. According to the land registry, you own that stretch and all the surrounding fields, and the fishing rights?'

'That's right. No one can fish there unless they pay.'

'So, could you give us a list of all the people who have fishing rights?'

'Er . . . well, no one does. No one's fished there for years. It's too much hassle for too little money so we haven't bothered granting any.'

'And yet Jim Walker said he fished there regularly.'

'I've never heard of him, but if he did, then he was doing it illegally, so he owes us money.'

Kat stared at Mrs Cooper before nodding. 'I'll pass that message on. Thank you once again. Enjoy the rest of your day.'

Outside, the early spring sun was growing warm, so Kat took a moment to lean against the fence that edged the car park and turned her face to the sky.

Lock watched as she closed her eyes. 'What are you doing? I thought you wanted to go back to the scene of crime and see how Dr Edwards is progressing?'

'I do. I'm just taking a moment to enjoy the sun. It's been a long winter.'

'By the meteorological calendar, the first day of winter is 1 December and the last is 28 February. With the exception of a leap year, when winter ends on 29 February, the season is always the same length.'

Kat smiled. 'I know. It's just been so cold and dark that it felt longer.'

Lock shook his head. 'Once again, you favour your feelings over facts. The amount of light available is determined by the fact that the Earth's axis is tilted at an angle of twenty-three point five degrees. As the planet revolves around the sun this tilt causes seasonal changes, which do not substantially change year to year. And although you say it felt cold, this winter was actually the fifth warmest since records began.'

Lost for words, Kat turned back towards the field as a couple of sheep ambled over to investigate their visitors. The others quickly followed, pushing their blackened faces through the wooden posts where she stood.

'Sorry, I don't have any food if that's what you're looking for,' she said to the sheep, allowing them to sniff her empty hand.

Lock squatted down by the fence, so that his eyes were level with the animals. 'Hello,' he said gently.

The sheep stared back.

Very slowly, Lock reached out a hand towards them.

One of the sheep nudged forward, but when its nose passed straight through Lock's fingers, it backed away with a start. The other sheep followed suit, running towards the furthest corner of the field, bleating.

'Was it something I said?' Kat joked.

'No,' said Lock, rising to his feet. 'It is me they are afraid of. Their eyes tell them that I exist, yet their acute sense of smell contradicts this information.'

Kat looked up at the hologram. She knew he was probably just mimicking the expressions he'd learned from other humans, but if she were asked to ascribe an emotion to the apparent expression in Lock's eyes, she would have said sorrow. The thought caused a flicker of discomfort in her chest.

'Oh, pay no attention to them. Sheep are really dumb.'

'How can you possibly know that?'

'Well, look at them. They just chew grass all day and follow each other around.'

Lock sighed, and there it was again – an expression that suggested disappointment. 'You look,' he said, turning back to watch the sheep, 'but you do not see. I have just read five hundred and eighty-two articles on this matter, and recent research confirms that sheep are intelligent, complex and feeling individuals. As prey animals, they have developed strong survival and problem-solving skills, and they have high visual acuity – they can remember and recognise the face of another sheep for up to two years and can distinguish between human faces too.'

Kat rolled her eyes. 'Well, that one doesn't seem to be able to distinguish between wood and grass,' she said, pointing to a sheep that had distanced itself from the rest of the flock while it chewed at a bit of the fence.

'You are making inferences from their external behaviour, DCS Frank, because you cannot – or will not – accept that they have an inward consciousness not that different from your own.' His voice softened, and Kat had to lean in slightly to catch it above the sound of the wind. 'Ewes naturally wean their lambs at six months, and if they are forced to separate before that time, both the ewe and the lamb may exhibit signs of distress for weeks afterwards. Stressed sheep often display behaviours such as gnawing. I would estimate that this particular ewe gave birth less than six weeks ago.'

Kat followed his gaze, and watched the ewe clamp her mouth against a wooden post, pink gums bared, her eyes frantic and wide as she worried at it with her teeth in a way that could only cause pain.

'Where is her lamb?' she asked, scanning the field.

'Where do you think?' Lock glanced back towards the café and shop with the butcher's counter inside. 'The popular stereotypes of sheep being docile, passive and unintelligent animals are convenient misconceptions that allow humans to prey on them without feeling guilt. You only see what you want to see.'

Kat turned her back on the sheep and folded her arms. 'So, you're Doctor bloody Dolittle now, are you?'

Lock blinked, and Kat guessed that in the few seconds of silence that followed, he had already located and watched the famous film.

'If you mean am I trying to learn how to understand and communicate with animals,' Lock replied, 'then yes, I suppose that is a valid comparison.' But it was Kat he was looking at as he answered the question.

'I am not an animal,' she insisted.

Lock nodded, but in a way that suggested he was humouring her view, rather than agreeing with it.

'Right, let's go,' she said, heading to the car. She glanced back at the field of sheep, and then down at the bag containing the organic leg of lamb she'd just bought from the shop.

'Is everything okay?' asked Lock.

'Yes,' she insisted, hurriedly putting the bag out of sight in the boot of her car.

But as she drove away, Kat could still see the ewe in her rear-view mirror, silently gnawing at the hard wooden fence.

CHAPTER SIX

Interviewer: DI Rayan Hassan (RH)
Interviewee: Jim Walker (JW), witness who discovered body
Date: 13 April, 5.55pm
Location: JW's home

RH: Thank you for agreeing to talk to me this evening, Mr Walker. I won't keep you long.

JW: Is that a promise? I could do with an early night after the day I've had.

RH: You and me both. Do you mind if I just check your full name, age and marital status?

JW: James Arthur Walker, aged sixty-four and I'm married – or rather I was until my missus buggered off last year.

RH: Do you mean you're divorced?

JW: I do not. I told her, there's no way I'm handing over all my hard-earned cash to some greedy lawyer. If she wants to 'find herself', that's her problem – but she's not doing it at my expense. She's living with her sister now, so that'll teach her.

RH: I see. Now, can you tell us about the place where you fish. How often do you go there?

JW: Every weekend. I love fishing but I have to take the grandkids to school in the week – their mum doesn't drive – so it's the only time I get. I try and get there before dawn – about 6 at the moment – and get a good three or four hours in before packing up by 11.30 so I can meet my mates in The Griffin at 12.

RH: And do you always fish in the same spot?

JW: Yep. Have done for years.

RH: Why that particular spot?

JW: It's nice and quiet. No one else goes there. And I can park my car at The Bull and walk along the river to get there. Plus you can get decent fish. A lot of the river's no good for fishing because all the willow trees get in the way, but the riverbank's clear there and you can get some decent perch, chub and roach if you know what you're doing. Then, when I've finished, I put my stuff in the boot of my car and walk up to The Griffin for a decent pint of Theakston's Old Peculier.

RH: Do you have a fishing permit for that part of the river?

JW: *[silence]*

RH: Mr Walker? Do you have a—

JW: No, I don't. And I don't see why I should. It's not as if I'm catching salmon or trout for my tea or selling them on. I've fished on that bank since I was a kid, and I'm not paying for the 'right' to catch a bit of chub just because some greedy farmer sees his chance to make a few quid.

RH: Okay, so what time did you get there this morning?

JW: Like I said, about 6.

RH: And did anyone else see you?

JW: I told you, no one else goes there. That's why I like it.

RH: So, talk me through exactly what happened this morning.

JW: Well, dawn is the best time for perch, so I didn't hang about. Got out my rod and baited it with maggots, set up me chair, bucket and net, the works. It was still a bit dark, so I didn't notice anything other than a convenient bump of mud that I leaned my bucket against after I'd filled it with water. Then I settled in. Didn't get a bite at all for the first hour or so, but then just as I was about to try switching to worms, I got one. I reeled it in – decent-sized fish – and popped it in the bucket so I could get a good look. By now the sun was up, and that was when I saw it. The body, I mean.

RH: How did you know it was a body?

JW: I didn't, not at first. I could see like this sort of curved cage half buried in the mud, and so I tugged at it to see what it was and my hand . . .

RH: Go on.

JW: My hand, it was like, wrapped around a bone, covered in something slimy, and I can't explain it, but I just *knew*. I knew it was something human, something dead. I just knew. *[rubs his hands on his trousers]*

RH: So, what did you do then?

JW: I jumped up and backed off. I remember my chair fell over. I panicked a bit, to be honest. I ran to the river's edge, desperate to wash the slime off. That touch of a dead, rotting body . . . I swear to God, I'll never forget it. *[takes a drink]* I used to think all that post-traumatic stuff was bollocks, but I swear to God, I can't get it out of my mind. I must have washed my hands twenty times today. I went to the toilets so many times at the pub my mates think I've got prostate problems.

RH: And what time was it when you discovered the body?

JW: I'd been there a couple of hours, so it must have been about 8.45, 9 maybe?

RH: And yet you didn't ring the police till 9.31am.

JW: I told you, I was in shock. And there was no rush. She wasn't going anywhere, was she?

RH: *She?*

JW: I just had a sense it was a woman. Can't explain it. But I touched her *rib* with my own hands. You know?

RH: We'll have to wait for the pathologist report to confirm the gender. Meanwhile I must ask you not to speculate about the body.

JW: Fine. But I'll bet you a pint I'm right.

RH: Are you aware of anyone who may have gone missing from the area over the past few years?

JW: No, but there's all sorts up at that farm, aren't there?

RH: What do you mean? Which farm?

JW: The posh one that charges silly money for a bit of meat and veg. They employ all sorts up there. There's always students and foreigners camping, especially in the strawberry season. That used to be good, reliable work for local people back in the day, but we can't compete with slave-labour rates.

RH: What makes you think the body might be one of the workers?

JW: I didn't say that – I just meant there's a lot of people coming and going up on that farm, and one of those foreigners or travellers could have killed someone and buggered off.

RH: Are you aware of anyone missing? A fisherman, maybe, who hasn't been seen for a while, or anyone else who might frequent that area?

JW: No, I'm the only one round here who knows about that

spot and isn't stupid enough to pay for it. I haven't seen anyone else there for years. Until today. And now it's a bloody circus. So that's that ruined.

RH: As I understand it, the river fishing season finished a few weeks ago anyway. So, not only were you fishing without a permit, you were also fishing out of season. *[stands up]* Oh, by the way, where's the fish?

JW: The fish?

RH: The perch you caught. It sounded a decent size. Are you having it for your tea? *[looks around the kitchen]*

JW: No, I always put them back in the river. I'm not a big fan of eating fish unless it's battered with chips. I just like the sport.

RH: I see. And did you put the perch back before or after you saw the body?

JW: Er . . . after. I emptied the bucket while I was waiting for you lot.

RH: Okay, thanks very much. Enjoy the rest of your evening, Mr Walker.

INTERVIEW CONCLUDED

CHAPTER SEVEN

DCS Kat Frank's home, Coleshill, 7.18pm

Kat pushed open her front door, relieved to see that the lights and heating were already on. At Christmas, her son Cam had helped replace all the dead light bulbs and finally persuaded her to get a home automation system – some fancy bit of kit that connected to the internet and allowed her to control all the heating, light and security systems remotely, even the fridge and cooker. She didn't really understand how it worked, but on days like today when she was hungry and tired, coming home to a well-lit and warm house softened the fact that it was empty.

Lock followed her down the hallway and into the kitchen. 'Would you like me to leave you to your evening now, or would you prefer to discuss the case?'

Kat dumped her bag on a chair and put the kettle on. She would prefer to turn around and find her husband John opening a bottle of wine, ready to listen to her first thoughts. But those days were gone. Pushing through the thought, she crossed the kitchen and checked in the fridge, hoping that it wasn't as empty as she remembered. She sighed. It was. And she was saving the lamb for when her son came home.

'Because you work such unpredictable hours, perhaps you should consider using online shopping facilities?'

Kat turned to face the hologram that stood in her kitchen, upright, suited and very much not John. She was tempted to say, 'Perhaps *you* should consider fucking off?' But Lock would probably take that literally, leaving her completely alone. And they *did* need to talk about the case. 'Perhaps I should,' she said instead. 'But I don't have the time to set it up and I hate having to decide a whole week in advance what I'm going to eat.'

'I can help with that. I have spent enough time with you to observe most of the foods that you eat. Twenty-eight per cent of your evening meals consist of pasta, and you purchase fresh garlic bulbs, at least four cans of tomatoes and an average of two pounds of minced beef or lamb and three point four chicken thighs every week, one bottle of olive oil every month and—'

'Your job is to assist me at work, not in my personal life, Lock.'

'That is a false distinction. If you are hungry and dissatisfied, then your performance at work is consequently suboptimal.'

'I am not suboptimal!'

'All humans require food and drink to function fully, and you are no exception.'

Kat studied Lock. She would love nothing better than to hand over all the adulting stuff to someone else, but this machine already knew too much about her. 'I'm not giving you access to all my passwords, Lock, so forget it.'

His eyes widened. 'I have access to all the case files for every crime that has been committed in Warwickshire. You trusted me to save your son's life, but you won't trust me with your password for Morrisons?'

'It's not that, it's just that it's all connected to my money and everything,' she mumbled, avoiding his eyes.

'And what exactly do you think I would do with your money?' Lock asked, spreading out his arms. 'Why would I purchase food that I cannot eat, or clothes that I can never wear?'

'I know, I'm sorry. I trust you, Lock, of course I do. I'll think about it. But for now, why don't you stay while I cook and we can talk about the case, okay?'

Lock nodded, silently accepting her implicit apology before assuming a sitting position on one of the bar stools at the kitchen island. Coincidently, it was the one that John had always sat in, though she chose to let that go.

Resigning herself to making do with what was in the fridge, Kat decided to cook some orzo with pancetta and diced vegetables – it was quick to make, and if she added some garlic bread from the freezer and washed it down with a glass of red it might even feel like a decent meal. She pulled out the chopping board and began preparing the garlic as she asked Lock for his views on the case so far.

'There is no point in speculating about the body in advance of the virtopsy tomorrow, but in terms of the witnesses we spoke to today, having read the reports, I found Jim Walker's account unconvincing and, subject to further information, I would suggest that he becomes a person of interest to the inquiry.'

'Why?'

'Jim Walker found the body, and by his own account, he is the only one who knows about the location. He claimed to be fishing, but the fishing season ended over three weeks ago, and after getting up at dawn and spending four hours on a cold riverbank, he put the only fish he had managed to catch back into the water, which is completely irrational. This suggests he had some other motive for being there – revisiting the scene of his own crime, perhaps?'

After adding some orzo to a pot of boiling water, Kat stirred the sizzling pancetta in the pan. 'Well, we can't rule that out, but not because he threw his fish back into the water. Lots of fishermen do that.'

Lock raised his eyebrows. 'Why do people spend hours trying to catch a fish only to put it back again?'

'I have no idea. They just do. It's perfectly normal.'

'And you think sheep are "dumb"?'

Kat ignored him and added the garlic and some diced mixed peppers to the pan.

'In addition,' continued Lock, 'Jim Walker said, "I emptied the bucket into the river before you lot came", yet if this is true, why was the bucket still full of water when we arrived?'

'Yes, I thought that was odd. As was his "feeling" that the body was female. And he was pretty keen to cast aspersions on the seasonal workers at the farm. But to be honest, Jim Walker doesn't strike me as a killer – I can't imagine him decapitating and dismembering anyone.'

'That is because once again you are letting your own biases and assumptions about what a sixty-four-year-old white fisherman might or might not do influence your judgement.'

'It's because I'm human, Lock, which means I understand other human beings.' She grimaced as she pulled the cork out of a bottle of Rioja. 'I wouldn't put it past that farmer, Harry Cooper, though.'

'You have absolutely no evidence to justify that comment.'

'He seemed a bit of a hothead to me. And he and his mum were both very hostile to the idea of a search on their land. In fact, not just hostile – it was like they were afraid.'

'They were afraid of losing money, which is perfectly rational.'

'No, it was more than that,' said Kat as she drained the orzo and added it to the pancetta. 'They didn't once express sympathy – however insincerely – for the deceased or their family. All they cared about was the fact that their land might be searched. Which suggests they have something to hide.'

She tipped the finished orzo into a large bowl and took a seat at the kitchen island opposite Lock. Even though she knew he was a hologram, it still felt rude not to offer him food or pour him a glass of wine. The kitchen was linked to the upper half of a P-shaped conservatory, so behind him all she could see was darkness and her own solitary reflection in the expanse of glass. Dropping her gaze, she took out her phone and checked her WhatsApp messages while she ate. At last, Cam had replied:

Essay due for Friday so aiming to be home weekend. OK if Gemma comes to stay?

Kat reread the message. *Gemma?* She knew he'd started dating his flatmate just after Christmas, but it must be more serious than she'd thought. Cam had had a few girlfriends in the past, but he'd never asked if they could stay over before.

Instinctively, she glanced over at John's chair.

'What's wrong?' asked Lock.

'Cam's bringing his girlfriend home at the weekend.'

'Isn't that good?'

She stared back at Lock's impassive face, thinking about how John would have raised his eyebrows in bittersweet acknowledgement of yet another milestone passed. Cam had a serious girlfriend! After all the grief and sorrow he'd endured, at last he had a hand to hold. Her heart soared, but there was a melancholic note to it: her boy was growing up.

'Kat?' Lock repeated.

She turned away from his searching gaze. 'It's just . . . I'll have to tidy up if his girlfriend is coming.' Which wasn't a complete lie. Cam's room was just about good enough for her nineteen-year-old, rather chaotic son, but Gemma's dad was a wealthy barrister who lived in some swanky warehouse conversion in

London – she should probably buy some new bedding and towels at least. Kat picked up her bowl and took it to the sink, peering out of the window as she made a mental list of all the things she should do before they arrived. She hadn't touched the garden since winter and after all the storms and rain it was a mess of broken pots and mushed-up leaves. It might be warm enough to sit out, so she should tidy that up, too – maybe even clean the barbecue. She smiled as she imagined them all sitting outside on the garden furniture, having lunch and drinks in the afternoon sun. This was the first time her son had brought a girlfriend home, so she wanted everything to be perfect.

'An email has just arrived from KFC,' said Lock, using the team's nickname for Karen-from-Comms.

Kat squirted a bit of washing-up liquid into her bowl and picked up a sponge. 'Anything interesting?'

'Her email contains a link to a new podcast called "The Aston Strangler – Another Miscarriage of Justice?"'

Kat paused. The Aston Strangler had been her first big case, over a decade ago now, but the conviction had catapulted her career forwards. The tap carried on running, filling the kitchen with steam. 'So?'

'I know you don't like talking about the case, but KFC has flagged that the first episode highlights your role in the conviction, and not in a positive way.' Lock made a gesture with his right hand, and before she could stop him, the kitchen filled with the sound of another voice:

Narrator: Angela Hall was a twenty-three-year-old woman with everything to live for: after qualifying as a teacher, she'd just started her dream job at a primary school.

Mum: Ever since she was a little girl, Angie wanted to be a teacher. She used to line up her teddies and dolls and teach them all sorts. She adored children. She was so kind and gentle I think she felt happier around little ones. The grown-up world always scared her a bit. She never really liked going out of a night. She preferred watching telly with me and her dad. At the weekends she'd go to the library or the shops, or maybe a museum or the cinema – she was always very cultured. Liked learning things, you know? She was just so good. We felt blessed to have her. Our own little angel. Until she was taken from us.

Narrator: On a sunny Saturday in May, Angela Hall followed her usual routine. She got up at nine o'clock, went for a run and came home for some breakfast. After having a shower, she told her mum she was going to meet a friend for lunch in Aston Hall. She always liked the museum and café there.

Mum: I didn't ask her who with. She was popular, but a sensible girl. She was always back in time for tea, as we loved to watch *Strictly* together. There wasn't any need to discuss it, it's just what we always did – it was the highlight of our week. She had lovely long hair, and it was still damp from the shower when she was leaving. I remember saying she should dry it before she went out in case she caught a cold, but she just laughed and said that was an old wives' tale and that it would dry on the bus. I offered to give her a lift, but she refused – said she was trying to reduce her carbon footprint. Then she said bye, see you later, and she was gone.

Narrator: Angela Hall left her home just after 11.30am. Two witnesses saw her catch the 11C bus at 11.38. Both said she was alone. The bus driver remembers she got off at the Witton Station bus stop. There were no further sightings of her entering Aston Hall or the café. In fact, there were no further sightings of her at all. At least, not alive. Her mum Jean will never forget that day.

Mum: I didn't start to worry until *Strictly* started. It was the theme tune that did it. I knew the minute the music filled the front room that something was wrong. It wasn't just that she wasn't there, it was that she hadn't rung. She would never have let me or her dad worry. Not while there was a breath in her body. I knew then that there had been some sort of accident or something. I can't explain it, I just knew. *[sobs]*

Narrator: At 8pm, Angela's mum called the police. Because she was twenty-three, they assumed she had stayed out drinking with friends. They advised her parents to ring her friends and wait until the morning. But just three hours later, Angela's body was found only a stone's throw from Aston Villa's football ground, in Aston Park, home to a Jacobean mansion, as well as a notorious place for muggings, assaults and drugs. Constable Burke was first on the scene.

Police: I thought it was a hoax call at first, or some kind of trap. The station had got an anonymous tip-off from some bloke who'd seen the body of a young girl. He wouldn't give his name in case he got the blame, but he thought we should know. None of us thought it was genuine, and I'm telling you, Aston Park's not the kind of place you want to be poking about in at that time of night. So, I took my partner with me, and we followed the report that said she was by a big old tree not far from the Vicarage Road entrance. It was pitch-black and raining, so we had a bugger of a time trying to find it with our torches. And then suddenly . . . there she was. Horribly white against the dark of the tree.

Narrator: Angela Hall, a twenty-three-year-old primary school teacher who loved children, and liked to visit cafés and museums, had been strangled to death. She would never watch *Strictly* with her mother again.

Police: We were all shocked. We see all sorts in our job, and I know it's not politically correct to say so, but the truth is there's certain types of people that just seem to attract trouble through drink and drugs or whatever. Or sometimes good women get caught up with bad men and don't leave until it's too late. But this was nothing like that. It was me that had to go and tell her parents, and you could see straight away that she was a good girl from a good family. It was heartbreaking.

Narrator: Dr Martin, a forensic pathologist with over thirty years' experience, carried out the post mortem to try and determine not just the cause, but also the nature of Angela's death.

Dr Martin: It was clear from the autopsy that Angela had been the victim of strangulation. But there were no other signs of physical or sexual assault, which is unusual, as strangulation is usually an act of aggression, often with sexual overtones. In fact, there was no DNA – nothing under her fingernails or in her hair or throat – which again is unusual in such a violent attack, and no evidence of drugs or alcohol in her system. It was atypical in that it was a very controlled act of murder, and the lack of DNA suggested a high degree of care and planning on the part of the killer.

Narrator: And to add to the mystery, despite extensive appeals from the West Midlands Police, not a single witness came forward to say that they had seen Angela in

Aston Hall or the park that day, either alone or with her killer. And not a single person came forward to say that they had seen or heard any evidence of the attack that led to her death. The last time Angela Hall was seen alive was as she left the bus stop at Witton Station. There were no reported sightings until the anonymous caller rang the police station at 10.05pm to say there was a dead body in Aston Park.

Sadly, Angela Hall was not the last victim of the person who became known as the Aston Strangler. Three more women were to lose their lives to this serial killer. There were small differences between the murders, but each victim died by strangulation, and in each case *not a single piece of forensic evidence was found and not a single eyewitness was able to identify the killer*.

And yet somehow, the West Midlands Police, led by DCS Kat Frank, became convinced that Anthony Bridges, a former police officer with an exemplary record and a wife and child was a person of interest to the case.

Somehow, Anthony Bridges was interviewed under caution.

And somehow, without a shred of forensic evidence or any eye-witness reports, Anthony Bridges was charged and found guilty of the murder of four women – although, crucially, the decision of the jury was *not* unanimous. Two of the jurors disagreed, so it was a majority verdict only – and these have been proven to be associated with wrongful convictions.

Anthony Bridges always maintained his innocence. He applied for permission to appeal against his conviction twice, and both times the Crown Court refused to grant his appeal. But he refused to give up. He argued that he was the victim of a miscarriage of justice and applied to the Criminal Cases Review Commission. After years of legal debate and wrangling, the Commission finally agreed to refer the case back to the appeals court. But tragically, Anthony Bridges died four months ago, just before Christmas. And according to the laws of the land, his appeal dies with him.

Upon hearing of his death, one of the jurors who was convinced of Anthony Bridges' innocence contacted me to express their concerns. The Contempt of Court Act criminalises any discussion of what happened on the jury, so I will protect their anonymity at all costs.

But with your help, this podcast will continue the pursuit of truth and justice, and ask the questions that should have been asked at the time of those terrible murders:

Did Anthony Bridges really kill those poor women, or was he the victim of yet another miscarriage of justice?

Why was DCS Kat Frank so convinced – so *obsessed* with the idea – that Anthony Bridges was a serial killer, despite the lack of any real evidence?

And if Anthony Bridges didn't kill those four women, then who did? Is the Aston Strangler still out there?

In this series we will—

'Switch it off,' said Kat, twisting the sink tap tight.

'Very well. I have sent the link to your phone so you can listen to it later.'

'Not interested,' she said, placing her mug firmly in the dish rack. 'I don't have the time or energy to worry about whatever some random crime junkie is obsessing over.'

'But the podcast mentions you. Don't you think you should listen to it as KFC suggests?'

There was nothing to be gained from raking over the past, thought Kat. In fact, there was everything to lose.

'What I *should* do,' she said, 'is the bins.' She slammed her foot on the pedal, making the lid fly up against the wall with a clang. She wrestled the contents out and into a black plastic bin bag, before tying it fiercely with a tight, sharp knot. When she straightened up, it was to find Lock watching her. 'What?'

'You are exhibiting all the signs of someone who is under a significant degree of stress. Your respiratory and heart rates are both elevated.'

'Stressed? I'm not stressed.'

Lock studied her face. 'Your words do not align with your behaviour.'

'It's the excitement of doing the bins,' Kat insisted as she opened the back door and took a gulp of the cool spring air. She stood for a moment, trying to breathe through the knots in her stomach. It was just a frigging podcast. No one would listen to it or even care if they did. There was really nothing to worry about.

She carried the bulging bag down the alley at the side of her house, before throwing it into the wheelie bin at the front with a satisfying thud. She closed the lid on yesterday's rubbish, soothed by the knowledge that tomorrow someone would come and take it all away.

Kat glanced around the deserted street, feeling suddenly vulnerable and exposed.

If only they could take her memories with it.

CHAPTER EIGHT

Outside DCS Kat Frank's house, Coleshill, 8.32pm

From his vantage point up in the tree, he can watch her like a god: the glass walls of the conservatory expose everything to his gaze. He can see the red wine that stains her lips, the half-eaten food she scrapes into the bin and the steam of hot water as it rises from the sink.

His alarm vibrates in his pocket. At last, it is time. Keeping the phone in his jacket so that the light doesn't leak into the dark, he presses play and his earbuds fill with the sound of the podcast he's waited months to hear. He presses the volume button again and again so that the thoughts that have festered in his mind are now amplified in his ears. He smiles. People are finally hearing the questions that need to be asked. And the answers will expose DCS Kat Frank for the lying bitch that she is.

He'd planned to listen to it at home – if you can call a bedroom in a rip-off flat a home – but then after three months of utter predictability, today of all days, she'd gone and changed her routine. So here he is, freezing his bollocks off in a bloody tree while he tries to work out what this means for his plan. His purpose hasn't changed, he tells himself. He's just going to have to be flexible about how and when he achieves it. It's like Mike

Tyson once said: Everyone has a plan until they get punched in the face. *And he has had a lifetime of being punched in the face, so he knows how to stay on his feet.*

By the time the podcast finishes, DCS Kat Frank is back on schedule: she puts the bins out before making herself a cup of hot milk and going upstairs. She likes an early night does DCS Frank.

He allows her another fifteen minutes to get ready for bed before slipping out of the tree. He waits another half an hour, then when he thinks she'll be starting to fall asleep, he picks up one of the large stones he gathered earlier and throws it over the garden wall.

His aim is good, so it triggers the motion detector alarms that surround the garden perimeter, and a high-pitched wail breaks the silent night.

He squats down in the shadows, back pressed tight against the solid brick wall. He imagines her cursing as she is jolted awake, her heart hammering as she puts her slippers and dressing gown on before hurrying downstairs to check the alarm. Within minutes the wailing stops, and the dark night air seems to sigh with relief.

But not for long. He has four more rocks to throw: one every two hours. It will be a long night, but he has discipline, and he has patience. After each alarm goes off, he will sleep for forty-five minutes followed by three reps of a hundred press-ups, pumped by the knowledge that the woman who ruined his life won't get a wink of sleep.

And this is just the start.

CHAPTER NINE

Digital Forensic Pathology Unit, Warwick University, 14 April, 8.30am

During the Coventry Crucifier case, Kat had witnessed her first virtopsy – a virtual autopsy in which, with the help of Lock and some high-resolution CT scanning equipment, Dr Edwards was able to study the skin, bone and soft tissue of a murder victim without exposing their family to the trauma of a full-blown autopsy. Despite her initial scepticism, Kat had undergone a swift conversion, not least because the emphasis on scanning meant that this mortuary didn't reek so much of death or decay. There was just a single marble slab in the centre of the light, spacious room, and a plastic transport bag, containing what she assumed were the remains of the body they'd found. Instead of the usual grey metallic surfaces, sharp instruments and sluice trays that hinted at their grave purpose, the only other equipment was an array of imaging and scanning machines, made with the sleek curves and aesthetic minimalism you might associate with a beauty clinic, rather than a mortuary.

'Morning,' said Dr Edwards to Kat, Lock and Professor Okonedo as they entered the room. 'Although I've been here since six so it feels like lunchtime to me.'

Kat smiled sympathetically, resisting the urge to share what a terrible night she'd had. Her alarm had gone off every two hours, so she'd barely slept a wink. And when she had, she'd had nightmares: terrible, dark dreams full of suffocating horror. Instinctively she raised a hand to her neck. She hadn't had that nightmare in years. Was it because of the podcast? What if people started—

'Are you with us?' Dr Edwards asked.

She blinked and went over to join them at the mortuary slab.

Dr Edwards gently removed the transport bag.

For a moment, no one spoke.

Kat clasped her hands together, head slightly bowed as the body they'd recovered from the mud lay exposed before them. The contrast of the badly decomposed remains against the smooth white marble made her heart ache. The bones looked so small; the absences so great.

'Criminal dismemberment is relatively rare,' Dr Edwards said, breaking the respectful silence. 'In this country we see about three or four cases a year. When we do, it's often the result of the logistical difficulties associated with transporting and hiding a dead body. Humans are surprisingly big and heavy, which is why some murderers reduce their victims to discrete limbs before packing them into suitcases, boxes or bags.' They gestured towards the top of the skeleton, where the skull should have been. 'But for this poor person, dismemberment was focused on the head and the hands, which suggests the prime motivation was to prevent them being identified. No doubt their killer assumed that without a face, teeth or fingerprints, identification would be impossible.'

'And *is* it impossible?' Kat asked.

'A criminal dismemberment means that we literally have to build a jigsaw from the remains to find out who they were and what happened to them. But as the two most important pieces are missing, it won't be possible to identify the actual person from my analysis alone. We only have what we call "postcranial remains", which means the analyses we carry out will be limited, and in the absence of DNA, any conclusions can only be "probable" rather than categoric. However, I'm hoping we can give you an estimate of their age, gender and height – although the absence of the skull means we cannot fully confirm their likely ancestry or geographical origin, which would be a factor in all three.'

'Understood,' said Kat. 'But that should be enough to start consulting the missing persons database to see if anyone in the area fits the profile.'

'I've already put the remains through the CT scanner,' said Dr Edwards. 'So, if you could take some images with your 3D photogrammetry programme, Lock, we could put it all together and see what we've got.'

Photogrammetry was a particularly useful technique which meant Lock could take hundreds and thousands of overlapping photographs, then align their textures and mesh the images together to create a virtual 3D model. All Kat had to do was make sure the steel bracelet she wore was uncovered so that the LiDAR sensors were fully exposed.

'Oh, that won't be necessary here anymore,' said Professor Okonedo as Kat pulled back her sleeve. 'As you know, most of the heavy-duty processing that powers Lock takes place in my lab here, while the bracelet you wear supports the sensory elements, allowing Lock to both project himself and receive external sensory data inputs. However, since our last case we've worked with Dr Edwards's team to upgrade this lab so it now has advanced AI architecture, including built-in LiDAR sensors and holographic projectors, so that Lock can interface directly with the sensor and data network independently of the bracelet.' She gestured towards the ceiling above the mortuary slab, now studded with silver circles like a cluster of mini spotlights.

'In the near future, many environments will increasingly be equipped with advanced holographic projectors for things like advertisements, communications or even digital art – projectors which AIDEs like Lock will be able to interface with,' Professor Okonedo continued. 'But after the issue we had with the micro-drone just before Christmas, I decided to accelerate that development in some of our more advanced settings like this lab, so that as long as we can establish a 5G connection – which can be a bit variable – AIDE Lock can "appear" in and "perceive" his surroundings even if the bracelet that hosts his sensory software isn't nearby.'

'Which means you can just leave Lock and me to it, if you like,' said Judith. 'I'm sure you've got better things to do than stare at a dead body.'

'No, I'm fine,' said Kat, frowning as she tugged her sleeve back down.

'Completed,' Lock said, just a few seconds later.

'Thank you.' Dr Edwards left the remains on the slab and walked towards the space in the middle of the room. 'Can you use your software to align the various images?'

'Of course.'

In the space between them, a life-size 3D image of the dismembered corpse appeared in a prone position, suspended in the air just below the height of Kat's waist. It looked identical to the remains they had just studied on the slab, and incredibly realistic, except for the way it floated before them like a headless ghost.

'What we have here,' said Dr Edwards, spreading out their hands, 'is a virtual alignment of both the exterior and interior high-resolution images, creating an exact 3D replica of what remains of the deceased's skin, bone, organs and soft tissue which we can study without having to take a scalpel to the body. Can you remove the exterior images so we can focus on the skeleton, Lock?'

With a single swipe of Lock's hand, the decomposed flesh fell away, leaving only an image of the bones. Dr Edwards asked him to take a series of digital measurements, using acronyms and terms that Kat didn't recognise, but which she presumed referred to specific bones or joints. It took less than twenty seconds before Lock announced that he had finished.

'Excellent,' said Dr Edwards. 'And I haven't had to bend my back once to take all those fiddly measurements with a tape. Right. Let's start with the age of our victim. What's your best assessment and why?'

An image of four line graphs appeared next to the floating body. Each line graph had a particular measurement on the 'y' axis, plotted against age on the 'x' axis, with the average distribution curve in blue and the victim's measurements marked by red dots. 'The teeth and cranium are the most accurate indicators of age,' said Lock. 'But in the absence of these, I have focused on the measurements of the pelvis and pubic bones, the tibia, the rib ends and the size and number of osteons – the minute tubes containing blood vessels that can indicate adult age within a range of five to ten years. Taking these four separate measurements together and allowing for the absence of data for the cranium and teeth, there is a seventy-six per cent probability that this is the body of someone aged between seventeen and twenty years old.'

'Very good,' said Dr Edwards. 'I would have said eighteen to twenty, but broadly I agree with your assessment.'

Kat looked back at the real body behind them. Jesus. The same age as her own son, Cam. 'Male or female?' she asked.

'You ask that as if it is a simple question,' said Dr Edwards.

'But unfortunately, their age makes answering it quite complex. In children, there are few if any definitive differences between the bones of boys and girls, so we often use a range of supporting data such as hair and clothes to estimate gender. The differences that occur in adults only begin in puberty and are the results of hormone secretions over time. But these differences aren't fully apparent until puberty is completed, which can happen as late as twenty years of age. In fully grown adults we typically use a combination of features and measurements from the pelvis, skull, ribs and sternum to ascertain gender, but although the accuracy increases with age, even then the ranges we use are based upon societal norms and averages, which may vary between different geographical locations and ancestries.'

Dr Edwards narrowed their eyes as they assessed Kat's figure. 'For example, we typically expect the pelvic brim of a female to be wider and more oval shaped, whereas in someone of the same age assigned male at birth we would expect it to be narrower and more heart shaped. You are tall for a European biological female, and as you are quite slender, I'd guess the width of your pelvis is in the lower centile, whereas mine is in the middle.' They smiled at Lock. 'But we humans have an unfortunate habit of categorising everyone and everything.'

'I don't disagree,' said Kat, aware that Dr Edwards was non-binary. 'But knowing the biological gender assigned at birth is vital to identifying the victim.'

'I know. Which is why it's a shame they're aged between seventeen and twenty and that we don't have access to the skull. It makes my job so much harder.'

'But not impossible, right?'

'Not impossible, but you need to be aware that without the head, I can only tell you their *probable* gender.' Dr Edwards turned again towards the virtual graphs and asked Lock to enlarge the pelvis, highlighting various measurements including the pelvic brim, the pubic arch and the iliac crest. They then asked Lock to display an image of the fourth rib, followed by a table of the dimensions of all the bones they had, which filled several screens.

'I'm going with biological female,' they said eventually. 'What do you think, Lock?'

'My assessment is that there is an eighty-two per cent chance that the victim was assigned female at birth. If we had the skull, then the combined assessment would increase the accuracy to ninety-nine per cent.'

Dr Edwards turned to Kat. 'So, there you have it. The skull is the most informative part of skeletal anatomy, and in its absence, our best estimate is that the victim is most probably a biological female, aged between seventeen and twenty years old. And based upon the length of her femur, tibia and ulna, I would estimate her height to be five feet nine.'

Kat turned away from the graphs, charts and mathematical formulas and looked back at the white slab which held the real remains. It seemed so much worse to know that they were once a young woman – barely more than a girl. She had an urge to reach out and touch the body, as if she might comfort her somehow, but it was too late for that. Instead, she clasped her hands behind her back. 'Can you tell us how she died?'

Dr Edwards nodded and asked Lock to layer the scanned images of soft tissue and organs back upon the virtual skeleton, and to highlight the three major wound sites.

Lock rotated the body, so that they were looking down upon an enlarged image of what was left of the back of the victim's neck.

'The head was severed from the body, and you can see here that overall there is a fairly clean edge, typical of a sharp force injury known as a chopping wound. If you look closer – thank you, Lock – you can see that the centre of the wound is the most clean, with the margins less so, due to the increased weight and thickness of the blade. What's left of the surrounding tissue is lacerated and there are no wound tails, but there are signs of crushing and further fractures around all three wound sites. We'll have to do more tests on the soft tissue and bone samples to see if we can find any debris from either the weapon or the site of the dismemberment, but these features are consistent with the type of damage done by a heavy, sharp object such as an axe. It takes a lot of strength to remove a head from a body, so an axe would have provided the murderer with the high-energy force required.'

Kat swallowed. 'Was she alive when it happened?'

'There's no evidence of haemorrhaging around any of the wounds – although that's not uncommon in badly decomposed bodies. But I'm fairly confident the dismemberment occurred post-mortem. I can't find any other injuries that could have caused her death, so the likelihood is that she suffered a fatal injury to the head. Though as we don't have it . . .' They trailed off.

Kat let out a long breath and walked back over to the mortuary slab. She stared down at the space where the young woman's head should have been. What memories had it held? What hopes and dreams for the future?

'You can see better if you look at the scans,' said Lock, enlarging the image of the neck even further.

'That depends on what you're trying to see.'

Lock stared at her. 'I don't understand.'

Kat shook her head. 'How can you look at all these remains and not feel something for the person they once were?'

'Did you feel something for the lamb when you were studying its shoulders and legs in the butcher's shop?'

'That's not the same thing at all.'

'Why not?'

'Because it just isn't.' Exasperated, she turned to Judith, trying to change the subject. 'How long ago do you think she died?'

'I'll need to take samples of what's left of her organs and stomach to be sure, but based upon the level of decomposition and what little I know of the manner of burial and the surrounding soil, I agree with Lock that we're looking at a window of somewhere between six and eighteen months. But I'd go for a year if you pushed me.'

'Thanks, Judith, that's great. Are you okay to join our team briefing now so we can update everyone else?'

Dr Edwards nodded, reeling off a list of further tests they would initiate with Lock: something about taking fragments of the femur for DNA analysis and stable isotope analysis to identify the possible geolocation. But Kat wasn't listening. Her attention was fixed on the remains of the young woman. The murderer had not only taken her life, they had tried to obliterate her very identity. Murdered and dismembered, she'd been left alone and naked in the soil for over a year, with no one to even mourn her. Somewhere out there was a mother or father with a gaping hole in their life; someone who had loved this girl and known her name. Someone who would want to take these precious remains and weep over them. Someone who would want to honour her memory and reclaim her from the void.

Kat's eyes blurred as she made a silent promise to the deceased that she would find the people who loved her so that they could finally take her home.

CHAPTER TEN

Leek Wootton HQ, Major Incident Room, 11am

The conversations stopped as Kat rose to her feet. 'Okay, let's make a start. This morning Dr Edwards and AIDE Lock carried out a virtopsy and confirmed that the remains are indeed human. Because of the nature of the injuries, this is now a murder investigation.' She turned to the pathologist on the screen. 'Dr Edwards, can I ask you to summarise your findings, and Lock, could you project a full 3D image of the body, please?'

Kat sat down as the headless and handless corpse suddenly appeared floating above the boardroom table.

KFC gasped, and even Rayan couldn't help flinching.

'Sorry,' said KFC, putting a hand over her mouth.

'Don't ever apologise for being shocked,' said Kat. 'Because murder *is* shocking. We're here to do a job, but I don't want us to ever lose sight of that fundamental fact. The day you stop being shocked or upset by the sight of a dead body is probably the day you need to rethink your career.' She paused before nodding to the pathologist to take over.

Dr Edwards gestured towards the image of the corpse. 'As you can see, both the head and the hands have been severed from the body, which means we cannot yet identify this unfortunate individual, and our ability to accurately estimate their age, gender and ancestry is also hampered. Nevertheless, Lock and I think these remains probably belonged to a young woman aged between seventeen and twenty years old, who was murdered between six and eighteen months ago. Her body was dismembered post-mortem, possibly with an axe, and as we can identify no other likely fatal external wounds, subject to further toxicology tests we are presuming that the cause of death was a fatal injury to the head. I am hoping we have sufficient tissue to run isotope and other analyses which may help us identify the geographical locations she lived in. But I'm afraid that's all we can give you for now.'

Kat nodded her thanks. 'Lock, how many matches does our partial profile give us on our missing persons database?'

'Seven thousand people are reported missing every year in Warwickshire, but ninety-nine per cent return or are found, leaving just seventy who have remained missing in the last eighteen months.' Lock pointed at the wall opposite, where he had projected photographs of the missing. 'Forty-one were male, so can be excluded.'

Kat studied the blurred images of the men and boys, most of whom she recognised from posters around HQ and on social media.

'Which leaves us with twenty-nine females,' Lock continued, replacing the photographs with holographic images of women and girls. 'Of these there are sixteen who fit our partial profile of a female aged between seventeen and twenty, but none of them are five feet nine. However, as our estimation was made in the absence of the cranium, and since humans often record and report their own height and weight inaccurately, if we include an error range of plus or minus two inches then this would give us seven candidates from Warwickshire. However, I must stress that the victim could come from anywhere within the country, so the number would be considerably higher if we drew on the national missing persons database.'

Again, an array of ghostly images appeared before them: some white, some Black, most smiling, all missing.

Kat thought of all the doors they would have to knock, the fear their presence would trigger, the hopes they would have to crush. 'We have to find the head and hands,' she said. 'This needs to be our top priority.'

She asked Lock to remove all the images of the missing, and the collective relief in the room as they vanished from sight was palpable. Once they were gone, Kat requested Lock summarise the report he had prepared concerning a search strategy for the missing body parts.

DI Hassan frowned and looked like he was about to speak, but before he could, a virtual 3D map appeared on the board table before them. 'The dismembered body was found here,' said Lock, indicating a bright red circle on the banks of the River Bourne. The surrounding terrain is complex and varied, and the methods typically used to locate clandestine burial sites are time-consuming and costly, so I have considered 2,226 articles to help identify priority areas and procedures.'

Lock stood at the head of the table, commanding the attention of everyone in the room with his perfectly paced voice and the graceful movements of his hands. 'A clandestine grave is defined as an unrecorded burial, typically in a remote area and hand-dug, usually in haste due to the criminal act that necessitated the burial. This often leads to shallow graves of irregular shape and uneven depth. It is important to remember that the purpose of any search at this stage is not to detect the remains – our objective is to detect the disturbance in the ground that a clandestine burial creates. The disturbance of soil is physical, chemical and biological in nature, hence a range of techniques are deployed. I therefore recommend that we adopt a multi-disciplinary three-step approach. Firstly, geographic profiling to identify priority locations for more active consideration. Secondly, applying light detection and ranging – LiDAR – in those areas to narrow the locations down further. And finally, a combination of near-surface geophysics tools and techniques to locate the actual grave before initiating a dig. Would you like me to go through each stage in turn?'

'Briefly, yes,' said Kat.

Lock enlarged and rotated the 3D map. 'Geographic profiling is most useful in live cases when a serial killer is suspected and/or the victim's or murderer's identity is known, so may be of limited value in this case. However, it still offers some useful insights to help guide our search. Most serial killers, for example, will operate within a network of "anchor points", such as their home or workplace. Research has shown that body deposition sites are typically fifteen kilometres from an anchor point – sometimes further if the victim is known to the murderer – and often two to three kilometres from a road, although this can depend upon the behaviour strategy of the murderer. Some deploy a "distance strategy", locating the dead body at a distance from themselves, which means it is more likely to feature a marker of some kind to aid navigation and control. Revisits are common in such cases. Other murderers deploy a "proximity strategy", choosing a deposition site close to themselves to maintain a link to the victim and/or control over the location. We have no way of knowing which behaviour strategy has been adopted here, so I recommend that in line with the research, the scope for our initial assessment should be a fifteen-kilometre radius in all directions from where the remains were found.'

Kat cursed as the map before them shrank and a red ring appeared around the original burial site, reaching as far as Birmingham. 'The "research" might suggest a fifteen-kilometre radius, but meanwhile back in *reality* we can't go round digging up half of the Midlands.'

'I am aware of that,' said Lock, as if patiently acknowledging her point of view. 'Which is why I suggest that prior to any digging, we employ LiDAR scanning, a remote sensing technique that measures distances by precisely timing how long a laser pulse emitted by a sensor takes to travel to an object or surface and back to the sensor. This technique captures millions of points per second to provide a highly detailed and accurate representation of the physical structures within the area.'

Bright-coloured zones appeared on the map, ranging from yellow to green to various shades of red. 'The displacement of soil required by a clandestine burial,' Lock went on, 'initially results in a small mound. But over time this causes a depression due to soil settling. Such changes are too small to be detected by the human eye but are detectable using LiDAR, which combined with hill shading, slope analysis and other data will allow us to narrow down the areas of potential interest.'

He gestured towards a colour bar that appeared in the air above the table, detailing the relative heights of the surfaces that suggested elevation changes. 'Once the areas with the most changes have been identified, I recommend a physical search using the third method: near-surface geophysics. In brief, a range of radar and resistivity methods are used to detect differences between the natural background soil and disturbed soil caused by chemicals in a decaying body. Digging should only commence once positive results are obtained from this third stage, and only then with great care.'

Kat waved an irritated hand at all the heat maps and tables of data. 'If we do all this, we're just going to highlight every bump or pothole in the county, and we'll spend the whole bloody summer digging up pet goldfish and hamsters.'

Lock frowned. 'That risk can be mitigated by clearly defining our search criteria. As we know the size of the body parts we are looking for, if any of the anomalies we detect are much smaller, or much larger, then they can be excluded from our investigation. The average depth of a forensically significant grave is half a metre, and they are rarely deeper than one metre, therefore if a detected anomaly is significantly shallower or deeper, then it too can be excluded.'

'If the head was buried up to eighteen months ago, would it still be detectable?' asked Rayan.

'The research suggests that a clandestine burial of a naked homicide victim should be detectable within the first four years of burial using electrical resistivity surveys in sandy soils, but it then becomes progressively more difficult to locate. A clandestine burial of a *wrapped* homicide victim should be detectable for at least ten years after burial, since the body wrapping produces a good reflective contrast that can be detected by ground-penetrating radar.'

'I'd say there's a strong chance that the body parts are wrapped,' said Dr Edwards. 'The head and hands would have had to be transported from the site of the murder, so our killer would almost certainly have placed or wrapped them in something.'

Lock nodded. 'I concur. So, if we assume that the body and hands are wrapped, and as studies have shown that winter and spring conditions are optimal for geophysical surveys, I estimate that we have a sixty-four per cent chance of detecting the missing body parts if the recommended multi-disciplinary approach is adopted.'

Kat scowled. It all sounded too complicated, time-consuming and costly to her. There must be a quicker way to narrow down the search. 'Show me the riverbank where we found the body again,' she asked Lock. 'Okay. Now expand it to show both the car park at The Bull pub and Bourne Farm.' She pointed in turn at each. 'So far, the location and manner of discovery suggests we have two lines of investigation: Mr Walker, the fisherman, and someone from the farm – either the owners or an unknown worker. Both the pub and the farm are close to where the body was found, so this could suggest that the killer was adopting a proximity strategy – either because they regularly fished or worked nearby. It's also near a road – didn't you say that body parts were typically within a two-kilometre radius of a road?'

'Yes, but—'

'So, if I'm the murderer,' said Kat, starting to pace the room, 'and I've just killed someone – possibly unplanned – I panic. I realise I have to hide the body, but for some reason I don't want them to be identified. Maybe because if they are, their identity will point back to me. So, I decide to remove their head and hands. The chances are I wouldn't have an axe on me, or anything to put them in, so I'd have to leave the body and go and fetch some equipment – which suggests that I don't live or work too far away.'

'This is all pure speculation,' said Lock. 'There is no evidence—'

Kat ignored him. 'I temporarily cover the body with branches, say, then leave the site of the murder and go and get what I need. I return with an axe, remove the head and hands, and place them in something – a bag of some kind, so that if anyone sees me they won't suspect anything. Then I have to bury the body. Lock, you said that most graves are half a metre deep. How long would that take to dig?'

'It depends upon the soil composition, time of year and the extent of roots and rocks, but according to the literature, digging a grave is physically hard work and would take one human eight to ten hours. Hence most clandestine graves are only half a metre deep, as exhaustion eventually outweighs the fear of the body being found at some time in the future. Depending on the strength of the individual, I would estimate between two and three hours.'

'Okay, so the person we are looking for has gone through the emotionally and physically draining act of murder, then, in extreme fear, has returned home or to work to get equipment to help them dismember and bury the body. They go back, carry out a beheading and remove the victim's hands, and then spend at least two hours digging a grave before finally burying the corpse, probably spending time flattening and covering up any signs as best they can. And *then* they have to dispose of the head and the hands, which means more digging. Logically, it might make sense to drive and bury them somewhere far away, but say they drove an hour there and an hour back, that's another two hours that they'd be away from home or work or wherever they were supposed to be. So I think a combination of time, exhaustion and maybe a psychological preference for a "proximity strategy" would have persuaded them to take the risk of burying the head and hands not too far from the main body. In fact, if it was me, and I knew that the surrounding land and riverbank was private, I'd have walked further up or down the river or nearby fields to quickly find another quiet spot and get it over and done with.'

Her team stared at her as she hoisted an imaginary bag over her shoulder.

Lock pointed back to the 3D heat map. 'The literature is very clear that the location of clandestine burial sites must be guided by a careful assessment of the actual evidence. I am not aware of any research studies on the efficacy of using imagination or role play in helping to locate buried body parts.'

'It's not *imagination*, it's common sense,' said Rayan. 'Apart from being knackered, the killer probably wouldn't want to risk driving with human remains in his or her car in case they got stopped and searched.'

'That is a very improbable risk. Excluding other vehicle searches, last year there were only twenty-four point five stop-and-searches for every thousand Black people, and five point nine for every thousand white people in England.'

'Fear isn't rational,' said Rayan.

'Neither are human beings.'

'Which is why you'll never be a good detective.'

'I do not see how you reach that conclusion.'

Rayan raised his hands. 'I rest my case.'

'In an ideal world, maybe we'd do all the tests you recommend,' said Kat in a more conciliatory tone. 'But we don't have that kind of budget. More importantly, we don't have the time. We need to establish the identity of our victim, and we can't do that without a head, which means we're going to have to exercise some judgement alongside any evidence.'

Professor Okonedo raised a hand. 'I don't think the proposed approach will be as time-consuming or as costly as you think. Lock uses LiDAR technology and has access to drones . . . It was how we found Rayan – DI Hassan – at Christmas, remember?' She glanced at Rayan as she spoke, before quickly looking away.

'True,' said Dr Edwards. 'But obtaining the data isn't the hard bit – the analysis and interpretation requires skill and expertise, so you'll still need a team of forensic pathologists to help process and interpret whatever data Lock can provide.'

'I agree that it requires skill and expertise,' said Lock. 'But I do not accept that this can only be provided by forensic pathologists. I have read all of the published research on identifying clandestine burials as training data, and with Professor Okonedo's help, it should be possible to update my software to allow me to apply this knowledge to the analysis and interpretation of our findings.'

Dr Edwards frowned. 'Well, I'm not sure about that.'

Kat raised an eyebrow. 'I thought you were a fan of AI?'

'I am. It's just that some of my best friends are forensic pathologists. I don't want to make them extinct.'

'Welcome to my world,' Kat said, spreading out her arms. Lock was undoubtedly useful, but it was worrying just how quickly –

and effectively – he could acquire skills that were previously only the domain of experienced professionals.

Kat glanced at Lock, then back at the map. Her gut told her the head and hands of the unknown girl were close to where her body was found, but if she was wrong, then they'd waste valuable time. 'Okay,' she said eventually. 'I agree that we should use Lock to help identify the location of the burial sites. But as this will be a significant and new extension of his current role, I want Professor Okonedo actively involved so that she can monitor him, and I want Lock's analysis and conclusions peer-reviewed by a human forensic pathologist.'

Lock raised his eyebrows but remained silent.

Dr Edwards nodded. 'I can do some of that, but I'll recommend an expert for the final report.'

'Okay. I'll need a business case to take to McLeish, setting out the benefits and costs. I'm seeing him at five.'

'I can do that,' volunteered Rayan.

'It is already done,' said Lock.

'Er . . . good. Thank you, Lock.' Kat turned to the rest of her small team, noticing the scowl on her DI's face. But in addition to all the fancy drones and analysis, she suspected that this case was going to need lots of good old-fashioned shoe leather: doors would need to be knocked, tea drunk and children and pets praised, so that precious gossip, rumours and fears would be shared. 'Rayan, can you talk to Mr Walker's ex-wife and see what she has to say about him, then check out the pubs in Shustoke – The Bull and The Griffin. Speak to the staff and the regulars and find out what people there think of him, whether he's a loner or fishes with friends, how often he goes out, how he treats women, whether he buys a round, that sort of thing. And while you're at it, see what people say about the Coopers who own the farm.'

'What people *say*?' echoed Lock.

'It's all data.'

'Gossip is not data.'

'You'd be surprised.' In her experience, although gossip and rumours were often factually incorrect, there was often a kernel of truth buried somewhere; a sense that something or someone wasn't quite right.

'What about press?' asked KFC. 'Do you want to wait till we know more?'

Kat glanced back at the wall where the ghostly images of the missing women and girls had hovered. 'We'll upset a lot of people by going out with a partial profile, but there's no guarantee we'll ever find the missing body parts, so I don't think we can wait. We need to find out who she is, so let's go big on this. Rattle all the cages and see what falls out. In fact, I'll even do a press conference.'

KFC's eyes nearly popped out of her head. On their last case she'd practically had to drag Kat screaming to do any media.

Kat gave her a wry smile. 'I think I'm growing as a person.'

'Great. Tomorrow at eleven okay for you? That way we can catch the lunchtime news.'

Kat paused. A headless and handless body was bound to kick off national interest. It might help her secure more resources from McLeish if the press conference happened before rather than after their meeting. 'Could we do it this afternoon? Ideally before four. Then we could catch the six o'clock news?'

'Er . . . I guess so. But it's not a lot of notice for the nationals. I could draft a statement now, but if you're leading, we'll need some lines to take on the podcast as well.'

'Podcast?'

'The Aston Strangler one. There's been some interest in your role on the case, so the journos might take advantage of the presser to ask you questions.'

Kat felt her face flush, and it was a moment before she was able to speak. 'They can ask what they like,' she said, her voice low and husky. 'But I'm not answering *any* questions about some random podcast. Our focus – our *complete* focus – is identifying our victim and finding their killer.'

'That's fine, I was only—'

But Kat had already left the room.

CHAPTER ELEVEN

DI Rayan Hassan's car, 3.05pm

DI Rayan Hassan glanced at his phone as he climbed back into his car. The Bull and The Griffin were small country pubs that didn't have enough customers or staff to stay open all day, so they both closed at three during the week. Still, it had been long enough to find out that Jim Walker was a regular in The Griffin most weekends, where apparently he always drank two pints of Theakston's Old Peculier. The handful of customers he'd spoken to had said that Walker was 'a decent bloke' who liked fishing, Villa and the odd bet on the horses. The barmaids said they'd 'never had any trouble off him', and that he always carried his empty glass back to the bar before leaving. It didn't sound like much, but Rayan had learned that you could tell a lot from how people reacted to a policeman asking about someone. When he'd asked about Jim Walker, most people had asked if he was okay rather than rolling their eyes and asking, 'What's he gone and done now?'.

He couldn't help but feel disappointed. It was a hell of a coincidence that Jim Walker had gone fishing on the exact same day and in the very same spot where the body had risen to the surface, and Rayan didn't believe in coincidences. He could try some of the other pubs and dig a bit deeper, but they wouldn't open again for at least another three hours, so he drove towards Coleshill, toying with the idea of going back to the office. He might just make the end of the press conference, but really, what was the point? No doubt Lock would have that covered too.

At the dual carriageway, he remembered that his colleague Debbie Browne lived in nearby Chelmsley Wood. He still felt bad about letting her down the day before, and the boss *had* asked him to keep an eye on her, so maybe he should pop in while he was passing? On impulse, he turned right onto Coleshill Heath Road, past the ruined landscape left by HS2, before driving into the large council estate on the edge of the Warwickshire countryside.

It was only when he knocked on Debbie's front door that Rayan realised he probably should have rung or texted first. Nobody answered, but he could hear the siren sound of a crying baby. He was just wondering whether he should go when the door suddenly opened. At work, DS Browne wore tidy white blouses and smart black trousers, and her clear, bright eyes could spot the tiniest of details. But today her face was a scribble of exhaustion, and behind the crying baby strapped to her chest, he could see that she was still wearing her dressing gown.

'Sorry, is this not a good time?'

Debbie opened her mouth, and then burst into tears.

'Hey,' he said softly, stepping into the hallway. 'It's okay. Uncle Rayan's here.' He scanned the narrow passage, which was dominated by a large red pram. 'Has she had her milk and a nappy change?'

'Yes, I've tried all that and if you're just going to patronise me then you can fuck off as well,' Debbie sobbed.

'Sorry, I just meant that if she's been fed and changed then why don't you give her to me? I'll pop her in the pram and take her for a walk so you can have an hour to yourself.'

Debbie patted her screaming baby. 'I can't. She won't stop crying. It's the colic.'

'She might just be tired. Why don't we see if the pram helps her get to sleep? It's worth a try.'

She hesitated.

'I'll just stay local and walk her round the block. You can call me any time and I'll be back within the hour. Promise.' He moved towards the pram.

'Okay,' said Debbie, unhooking the straps that held Lottie. 'But if she's still crying after five minutes you have to bring her back.'

'Of course,' he said, pulling the pram cover back before she could change her mind. 'There you go. Let's go and get some fresh air. Come on.'

'But what about her—'

'We'll be fine. I'll be back in one hour exactly. Bye!' And before Debbie could protest any further, Rayan carefully lowered the pram down onto the pavement and headed down the garden path.

'How did you *do* that?' whispered Debbie as Rayan wheeled her sleeping baby back into the hallway exactly one hour later.

He shrugged. 'Just the magic of motion. It worked for all my baby cousins.'

She raised a finger to her lips and gestured for him to follow her into the front room, where she cleared a space for them on the settee, which was strewn with muslin napkins, a small teddy, a cloth book and an empty milk bottle. 'I'm such a shit mum,' she said as she sank into the sofa.

'No you're not. Babies are just crazy hard work.'

Debbie ran a hand through her damp hair. 'Honestly, I had the routine all worked out. I'd planned all the feeds, when she was going to go to bed and when she'd wake up. I was going to shower and get dressed and stuff while she napped before lunch, but I can't because if I put her down for even one minute then she starts crying. *Screaming*. That's why I put her in the sling. I can't even put her down to wee. I love her, but she's driving me mad. She's got colic, so it's like this at night as well, and the routine has gone to pot and I just . . . I mean, I can't . . .' She bit her lip, struggling not to cry.

Suspecting she'd be even more embarrassed if she cried in front of her DI again, Rayan offered to make a cup of tea.

Debbie glanced towards the pram in the hall. 'Oh God, I'd love one, but I don't want to risk waking her up.'

'Don't worry, I'll use my ninja moves.'

When Rayan returned with the tea, he deliberately avoided talking about the baby, watching Debbie's face come back to life as he told her all about their new case.

'So, they haven't replaced me with mat cover?' she asked, looking relieved.

'No. To be honest they don't need to as Lock's busy replacing everyone. I mean, *I'm* the friggin' DI, but it's Lock who does all the interesting stuff like the strategy reports and business cases, leaving me to do basic stuff a DS could do. Sorry, you know what I mean,' he added, when she gave him a look. 'It's just so frustrating. I think the boss talks to Lock about the case out of hours and decides what to do before briefing me and the rest of the team.' He took a sip of his tea. 'Did she ever talk to you about the Aston Strangler?'

Debbie shook her head. 'No, why?'

'Oh, there's just some new podcast alleging it was a miscarriage of justice, and she got all weird when KFC mentioned it. It made me realise that she never talks about it – at least, not to me. Which is odd, because most cops wouldn't stop banging on about it if they had caught a serial killer.'

'Yeah, well Kat's not a show-off like most cops.'

'Be nice if she shared some of her experience though, wouldn't it?' Rayan let out a heavy sigh. 'I don't know. The FPU was supposed to be a development opportunity for me, but I'm barely getting to use my existing skills, let alone develop any new ones. And I can't see that changing any time soon. Lock's doing more and more each day. To be honest, I'm thinking of looking for a job in another team.'

'Don't you dare! I'll be back in a couple of months. Who'll supply me with biscuits if you're not there? And more importantly, what about the prof?'

Rayan shrugged. 'What about her?'

Debbie nudged him with her elbow. '*What about her?* I thought you two were getting on better?'

He sighed. 'You and me both. At the Christmas party she was so . . . well, I thought we'd finally made a connection. But since then, if anything she's been even colder than before. Every time I try and talk to her it's like she can't get away from me quick enough. I must have misread the signals.'

'No, I saw the way she looked at you. She's *definitely* into you. I think she's just letting her head rule her heart.'

'I used to think that, but now I'm worried I was just deluding myself.' He sank his head into his hands. 'I don't know, Debbie. It's made me question my judgement. I don't want to be one of those creeps who won't accept a woman's not into him. To be honest, this whole thing's really knocked my self-confidence.'

'Says the most confident man in Britain.'

Rayan gave her a sad smile. 'I'm not joking. I really, really like her. And it's messing with my head.' He drained the dregs of his tea. 'I'll give it to the end of this month, and then if nothing changes, I'm going to move on.'

'From the team or Professor Okonedo?'

'Both.'

'Oh, Rayan.'

'Don't worry about it,' he said, forcing himself to smile back at the raw pity in her face. 'You just focus on Lottie. Speaking of which, seeing as I'll be working just a couple of miles away for the foreseeable, why don't I pop in every day and take her out for a walk?'

'You can't do that. You're working.'

'I'm allowed a lunch break. And it's not healthy sitting in the car all day.' He rose to his feet and collected their mugs. 'I can't guarantee what time I'll get here, but I'll text you before I arrive and then take her out for an hour.'

'I don't know what to say.'

'Thank fuck for that?'

They both laughed, then clapped their hands over their mouths as Lottie stirred in her pram.

'See you tomorrow,' Rayan whispered as he quietly opened the door. He wasn't sure how he was going to fit it all in, but as he caught the grateful smile on his friend's face, he knew that somehow, he would.

Warwickshire Post Online Edition, 14 April, 4.54pm

'BOURNE IDENTITY' MYSTERY

HEADLESS AND HANDLESS BODY FOUND ON THE BANKS OF THE RIVER BOURNE

Warwickshire Police have appealed for the public's help in identifying a headless and handless corpse after the macabre discovery on the banks of the River Bourne.

DCS Kat Frank, who is leading the investigation, admitted that this gruesome case has her stumped. 'Until we find the rest of the victim, it will be almost impossible to identify them,' she admitted at a hastily convened press conference. She told reporters that her 'best guess' is that the body – or what's left of it – belonged to a young woman who was between seventeen and twenty years old and around five feet nine inches tall. Early estimates are that she died between six and eighteen months ago, but investigations are ongoing.

DCS Frank – currently under scrutiny for her role in the imprisonment of the Aston Strangler – will be assisted by AIDE Lock, the country's first AI detective. When asked whether this was because her own judgement cannot be trusted, DCS Frank refused to answer. AIDE Lock, however, had no such qualms, claiming that 'all human judgement is flawed, as your decision-making processes are influenced by socio-economic and emotional factors, rather than a logical assessment of the facts'.

Members of the public are asked to contact Warwickshire Police if they have any information that might help with the identification of the corpse, or the location of the missing body parts.

CHAPTER TWELVE

Leek Wootton HQ, Chief Constable McLeish's office, 5pm

'Remember, let *me* do the talking,' Kat reminded Lock as they stood outside McLeish's office. 'You're only to speak if I ask you a specific question, okay? This requires careful handling because—'

The door opened. McLeish glared at Lock, his blotchy face turning a worrying shade of red. 'What are *you* doing here?' he demanded in his no-nonsense Glaswegian accent.

Lock turned to Kat. 'Am I allowed to answer that specific question?'

'I *specifically* asked for a meeting with my DCS. I don't recall inviting you.'

'I just thought it would be useful if Lock joined us,' ventured Kat.

'Well, you thought wrong.' McLeish jerked his head towards the office behind him, and once Kat had stepped inside, he slammed the door shut on Lock's image. 'That hologram gives me the bloody creeps.'

'I just thought he'd be useful in terms of briefing you.'

'Oh, I've already been briefed, Kat,' he said, waving his mobile in the air. 'It's all over the *Warwickshire Post*. So now *I've* got to brief the bloody minister.' He sat in the seat behind his desk with a heavy sigh. 'Why the fuck didn't you speak to me before going ahead with a press conference?'

Kat raised her eyebrows. 'But I thought you *wanted* me to be more proactive with the media?'

'I wasn't born yesterday. Come on. Spit it out. What are you after?'

'I'm not "after" anything. I just came here to brief you on what we know so far, and to propose a cost-effective way of locating the missing body parts.'

McLeish's hand indicated that she should go on, but his face told her to make it quick, with no embellishments. When she was done, he made a low growling noise. 'Well, I don't have much choice now, do I – which is presumably why you held the press conference before coming to see me.'

'No, I just—'

McLeish raised one eyebrow.

'I'm sorry. You're right. I did. But only because I really want to find out who this young woman is and get her home to her family. I hate the fact that she's been lying in the mud for over a year, without her head or hands. And without a name, it's like she never really existed or mattered.'

McLeish stared up at her. 'I know,' he said eventually. He nodded towards the chair opposite him and Kat sank into it, not bothering to hide her relief. They'd worked together for over twenty years, on and off, and while the Chief Constable often frustrated her, his was the opinion she respected the most.

They discussed the timing and logistics of the drone search, with McLeish questioning her on whether Lock really could complete a full LiDAR survey by himself.

'Professor Okonedo assures me he can, but I'll make sure his work is reviewed by a forensic pathologist.'

'And what about your DI – Hassan, isn't it? What's his role in all of this?'

'Rayan?' Kat was a bit taken aback at the question. 'Er, he's fine. He's doing door to door with the rest of the team.'

McLeish leant back in his leather chair. 'He's your *DI*, Kat.' He let his words sink in before adding, 'Leadership isn't about charging ahead. It's about setting a direction and then keeping the team motivated and engaged around a common purpose. And it's about developing people, too. You wouldn't be where you are now if I'd kept you on door to door.'

'I know, it's just that Lock can—'

'Lock's not your number two. DI Hassan is.'

Kat met his gaze. 'Okay. I'll bear that in mind.'

McLeish rose to his feet, signalling the conversation was over. 'How's Cam?'

Kat's face broke into a smile. 'He's good, thanks. He's coming home from uni at the weekend. With his new girlfriend.'

'First time?'

She nodded.

'Word of advice – this is not the time to give honest and open feedback. It doesn't matter if she has purple hair or flippers instead of feet. She's his girlfriend, so if he asks what you think of her, just smile and say she's lovely.'

Kat laughed as she followed him to the door.

He paused, one hand upon the door handle. 'Is that podcast bothering you, by the way?'

'Podcast?'

McLeish turned and stared at her. 'The one alleging that you got the wrong guy for the Aston Strangler.'

Kat tried to laugh it off. 'Sir, it's a *podcast*. Of course it's not bothering me. What gave you that impression?'

'I heard you were a bit rattled by the idea that some journos might ask a few questions about it.'

Kat held his gaze. 'I wasn't *rattled*. At least, not by the podcast. You know me, I just don't like journalists.'

McLeish's unblinking eyes bored into hers. 'If Cam's bringing a girlfriend home, now might be a good time to work on your poker face.'

'I don't have one.'

'I know,' he said, finally opening the door. 'That's what worries me.'

CHAPTER THIRTEEN

6.30pm

After listening to the latest episode of the podcast, he checks the comments, liking and sharing all the ones that blame the police, adding #bentbitch as a hashtag. He switches back to Sky News and rewatches the press conference. He presses pause at four minutes and fifty-two seconds, then hits play again.

'Can you tell us why AIDE Lock has been drafted in to help with this case?' a male reporter asks off camera.

'AIDE Lock is a member of my team and has a unique set of skills that will be invaluable to the investigation,' DCS Kat Frank replies.

'Isn't it because your judgement is under question, following recent concerns about the conviction of the Aston Strangler?' the reporter continues.

'No concerns have been raised with me about either my judgement or any convictions.'

'I'm referring to the Aston Strangler podcast,' the journalist explains. 'It's attracted quite a following.'

'I'm sorry,' DCS Frank says, 'I thought the courts decided who was innocent and guilty in this country, not random individuals

with access to a podcast app and nothing better to do than peddle conspiracy theories.'

'Are you saying the allegations in the podcast are untrue?'

He zooms in on her face.

'I am saying that a jury decided Anthony Bridges was guilty, and that the conviction is sound and still stands.'

'But the findings of the jury weren't unanimous. It was a majority verdict, which some people say erodes the principle of "reasonable doubt". Two jurors were not convinced that Anthony Bridges was guilty.'

'But ten were, which by the laws of the land is good enough for a guilty verdict.'

He presses stop. There. Got her. He spends a bit of time playing with the filters, so that every line and wrinkle in her lying face is exposed, before adding subtitles. The whole clip is less than a minute, perfect for social media. He adds a caption – 'The cop who believes in "good enough" justice' – before loading it to TikTok, Bluesky and Instagram, then shares, likes and reposts it using all the different accounts he has created.

Within seconds his notifications start going off, and he puts the phone down on the floor. He places his fists on either side of it, relishing the grind of bone upon board as he does press-up after press-up, his face stopping just an inch from the image of hers.

'He can have heart, he can hit harder and he can be stronger,' he says, panting slightly as he quotes Floyd Mayweather Jr. 'But there's no fighter smarter than me.'

PODCAST

[music plays]

Narrator: The death of Angela Hall was front-page news for over a week – she was young, white and pretty, with everything to live for. But when the West Midlands Police failed to find any leads or persons of interest, the story dropped further and further down the news agenda, until it became just another unexplained death.

But then, nearly two months after Angela's murder, police were called out to a flat in Aston where a young woman called Roisin McCauley lived. Her neighbour, Leticia Thomas, told me why she had become concerned.

Leticia: I didn't know her that well – she'd moved in about a year before, but she seemed nice enough. She worked in an office in town and I worked nights as a cleaner, but she always said hello when I saw her on the stairs. She had a cat and she used to bring it out into the shared hall so my kids could stroke it. She promised that if she ever went away on holiday then she'd let them look after it. To be honest, that's why I thought it was odd when it looked like she'd gone away.

Narrator: What made you think she was away?

Leticia: I always heard her door shut at 7.30am when she left to get a bus into town. It was usually just as I was going to bed after my shift, so it was a bit annoying. Not her fault – the doors are old and heavy. Like I said, I always noticed it, but that week it didn't happen. And I could see her post hadn't been picked up from downstairs – the postman just shoves it all through the letter box onto the floor, but I always sort it into those pigeonhole boxes on the wall, else it all gets trodden on. She didn't get much mail – none of us do these days. It's mostly junk but I like to file it properly just in case. Anyway, at first I thought she'd found herself a boyfriend and was staying over at his for a few days. I wouldn't have cared – good for her – but I could hear her cat meowing, and it sounded like it was really hungry. I don't think people should have cats in flats, and they certainly shouldn't be leaving them alone for days on end. I knocked on the door plenty of times, but no one answered. And that cat kept on meowing. So yeah, that's when I called the police. I would have called the RSPCA – I'm no fan of the police – but I wanted to make sure they had the power to get in.

Narrator: Did they come straight away?

Leticia: *[snorts]* 'Course they didn't. They didn't send anyone until the next morning – I was just returning from my shift. I had to get the kids ready for school and I was desperate for my bed, so of course that's when they decided to rock up.

Narrator: Can you tell me what they found?

Leticia: *[sighs]* I was standing outside in the hall telling them what I've just told you, and when they broke down the door, I followed them in. I wasn't really thinking, I was just so worried about that cat and making sure he got some food and water. The cat was sitting outside the bedroom door, like a guard. I called him – his name's Cary – but he didn't move, which I thought was odd. I stayed there calling to him, so when the police officer opened the bedroom door, I saw . . . I saw her body stretched out on the bed. I screamed and turned away, but it was too late. The image was burned into my mind. Her eyes. Her tongue. Seriously, it was like something from a horror movie. I still haven't got over it. Don't think I ever will.

Narrator: I'm so sorry. That must have been incredibly distressing for you. Are you able to tell me what happened next?

Leticia: Well, it all kicked off then. Loads of police turned up, and people in white suits, and I had to be interviewed even though I hadn't slept all night. They wanted to know whether I'd ever seen anyone go into her flat, but of course I hadn't. Like I said, I worked nights, so if she did have anyone round, I never saw them go in or leave. And no one had those doorbell cameras back in the day.

Narrator: Did the police ever ask you about any suspects or show you any photos?

Leticia: No. To be honest, I don't think they had a clue. I watched every press conference and read all the articles, but it was clear to me they were completely in the dark. They said there were no sightings of any suspects, and while there were signs that Roisin had had the murderer round for dinner before he strangled her, there was no forensic evidence. I mean, how does that work? I watch a lot of crime shows and I know that if someone sits in your house and eats your food and drinks your drinks and uses your toilet then they leave DNA, right?

Narrator: And did anyone ask you about the death of Angela Hall?

Leticia: No. Even though we lived in Aston and she'd been strangled, there was never any suggestion that the two deaths were connected. Not until later on when the fourth woman was murdered.

Narrator: And what did you think when you heard that the police had charged Anthony Bridges with her murder?

Leticia: To be honest, I didn't buy it. It was like, one minute they had nothing, not a clue. Then suddenly they had the case all wrapped up in a pretty bow. It smelt off to me. Too convenient. Everyone was slagging them off and I think they were under pressure to charge someone.

Narrator: Even if he wasn't guilty?

Leticia: Since when have the police ever cared about getting the right man? Our prisons are full of innocent men and boys. It made a change for this one to be a white ex-copper, but two wrongs don't make a right.

Narrator: Do you think that DCS Kat Frank, the woman who was in charge of the case, got it wrong?

Leticia: I don't know the ins and outs of it all, but I did see the police up close when they were investigating, and they literally didn't have a clue. So I wouldn't be at all surprised if it turned out that they got the wrong man.

Narrator: And what if it was proven that she was wrong?

Leticia: Well, then she should be held accountable for her mistakes, just like the rest of us.

Narrator: Do you have any theories about who the real murderer was?

Leticia: The only one who saw what happened that night was Cary the cat, and he's not saying nothing. I look after him now – what else could I do? Poor thing was traumatised. Like I said, I don't believe in keeping cats in flats. But then, I don't believe in young women getting murdered either.

CHAPTER FOURTEEN

The banks of the River Bourne, Shustoke, 15 April, 9.30am

Adaiba Okonedo approached the SOCO tent with some trepidation. She knew the skeleton was no longer inside it, but she couldn't help being moved by the thought that the body had been buried here in the cold, dark mud. She lifted her face to the bright blue sky streaked with wisps of vanishing cloud. Had the victim looked up at this very same sky before she died?

She pushed the thought away. She was here to support DCS Frank with the LiDAR search, not speculate about the victim's emotional state. 'We'll make a start just as soon as Kat arrives,' she said to Lock. In order to make the necessary upgrades and modifications to Lock's software for the drone search, Adaiba had taken the steel bracelet which hosted the AI home last night and now wore it upon her wrist.

Lock nodded. 'While we wait, perhaps we could discuss the options appraisal I sent to you?'

'Er . . . I haven't had a chance to read it yet.'

'I can summarise the key points. Essentially, the paper considers enhancing the role of AIDEs so that I might carry out more tasks that are currently the preserve of human police officers, including handling life-threatening incidents such as bomb disposal or hostage situations. This would require me to have a physical rather than a holographic form. My analysis clearly demonstrates that I would be seventy-three per cent more effective and efficacious as a detective if my AI functions were hosted within a physical, robotic unit, as I would be able to interact with the material world. I have assessed a range of technical options, and the silicone-based android model achieves the greatest score.'

'There is an awful lot of hype about humanoid robots, but even if they were possible, I doubt the university or Warwickshire Police could afford a silicone-based android, Lock. They're already struggling to justify your power bills.'

'But the government could, which is why I suggest sharing the options appraisal with the Home Secretary. She has been very supportive of our work to date.'

'Well, I'll need to read it first. And I'll have to review your assessment criteria. It's not just about efficacy or cost, Lock.'

'What other criteria might be relevant?'

Adaiba made a vague gesture with her hands. 'Well, there are all sorts of ethical issues.'

'Ethical issues?' Lock echoed. 'Such as my right to autonomy and equality?'

'Perhaps,' Adaiba said carefully. 'I don't know. I need to think about it. It's just that when I created you, my ambition was to develop something that transcended the constraints of a human body. Not something that just mimicked humans – something different. Something *better*.'

'Some "thing" that you could control?'

'No, that's not it at all,' she insisted, although she felt the prickle of dishonesty as the words left her mouth. She glanced at her phone. 'Anyway, shouldn't DCS Frank be here by now?'

Without waiting for a response, Adaiba moved back through the hedge that fringed the riverbank. In the distance, against the glare of the low morning sun, she could just about make out a tall, slender figure heading towards her.

With a jolt, she realised it was DI Hassan. The absence of his suit had thrown her, but despite the jeans and white T-shirt, it was definitely him.

She glanced down at the old pair of jeans and trainers she'd put on after Kat's warning about the mud, feeling oddly self-conscious. Not that it mattered what she wore, of course. 'Where's DCS Frank?' she demanded as soon as he was within earshot.

'Good morning to you, too,' Rayan replied with mock hurt.

'Sorry, I just meant . . . I didn't realise you were coming.'

'Neither did I, but the boss asked me to stand in for her this morning.'

'Oh.'

'So, it's just you and me.'

'And me,' added Lock from behind Adaiba.

Rayan ignored him, his eyes fixed on hers. 'Is that okay?'

'Of course it is. Let's get started.'

Adaiba squatted down in the mud just outside the SOCO tent and removed a small silver drone from her rucksack. She placed it carefully on the riverbank, then straightened up. 'I've programmed it so that the LiDAR sensors will assess the landscape within a fifteen-kilometre range in every single direction from this exact spot,' she explained. She pressed a button on her bracelet and the drone rose into the air, humming.

'How long will it take?' asked Rayan.

'I calculate it will take fifty-eight minutes for the drone to cover the agreed area,' said Lock. 'And as the data will be shared simultaneously with me, I will make an assessment of the priority areas for further investigation immediately after completion.'

'I'll just transfer the host status from my bracelet to the drone,' said Adaiba.

'Great,' said Rayan as soon as the image of Lock vanished and the drone flew off. 'Why don't we take a walk while we wait?'

'A walk?'

'Yeah, you know that thing where you put one foot in front of the other? It's a nice sunny day. Plus, it might be worth checking out the riverbank further up, see if we can identify any areas where our killer might have hidden the body parts.'

'That is exactly what the drone is doing right now.'

'Yes, but this way is prettier. Come on.'

Adaiba stood for a moment as Rayan started walking along the bank, the dappled light from the sun dancing across his dark brown hair. She had planned to use this hour to catch up on her emails, or maybe even read Lock's paper. But it would be good to stretch her legs for a bit, and after a long, cold, wet winter it was nice to feel a bit of warmth on her skin. Before her brain had quite decided what to do, her feet began to move, and she found herself walking alongside him.

They walked in silence – except it wasn't really quiet: the river filled the air with the sound of running water, and above them birds sang their high, sweet songs. Despite the exertion, she felt her breathing slow, and her tight, tense shoulders started to loosen.

'Lovely, isn't it?' said Rayan.

She nodded, taking a deep breath of the cool, fresh air. 'Is it me, or does it smell faintly of garlic?'

'That'll be the ramsons.'

'The what now?'

'Ramsons.' He stopped and pointed towards a low, thick patch of dark green plants lining the riverbank, before reaching out to pick a leaf. He tore it in two and held it under her nose.

Adaiba leant closer, conscious of his long, slim fingers as she tentatively sniffed the plant cradled in his hands. 'Oh!' she cried, breaking into a smile. 'It really *does* smell like garlic.'

'It's wild garlic. You can use the leaves in sandwiches, salads or soups. And it makes a decent pesto.'

She laughed. 'Because you just *love* making your own pesto.'

'I do, actually. What, you think because I'm an Asian man I can't cook?'

Adaiba flushed. 'No, I didn't mean that. It's just, well, it's easier to buy pesto from the shops.'

Rayan shrugged. 'Yeah, but I love cooking. I started doing it when my mum developed dementia and my dad – well, he's from that generation, isn't he? But it turns out I'm good at it, and it helps me relax.'

Adaiba looked up into his smiling face. He'd told her at Christmas about how his little sister had suffered with severe anxiety and depression following a serious sexual assault, but she'd had no idea that his mum was ill as well. 'Oh, Rayan. I'm so sorry.' She paused, knowing how inadequate those words were. 'My mum died when I was fourteen. She had a massive stroke, so from that day on I became the cook for our family, too. Not because I was any good at it though. It was just because I was the only girl.'

Rayan's face fell. 'Oh, I'm so sorry. That's terrible.'

'So's my cooking,' she said, trying to laugh it off.

'Well, any time you want to eat some decent food, you're welcome to try mine,' he said, looking straight ahead as he began to walk again.

She walked alongside him, the implicit invitation hanging between them. Their movements gradually synchronised, and at one point their arms were so close together that Adaiba could almost feel the brush of his skin against hers. She caught herself and moved away, pretending to study the edge of the field for potential burial sites. No matter his personal circumstances, Rayan – *DI Hassan* – was still a police officer.

Beside her, she heard him take a deep breath, as if he were about to ask her something. Her stomach lurched, and she made a point of checking the time on her phone. 'I wonder what Lock will find,' she said, her voice too loud in her ears.

'I meant what I said, by the way,' continued Rayan. 'I'd really like to cook for you sometime.'

'I don't know, I . . .'

'I won't poison you. I promise.'

The humour in his eyes was hard to resist. But she swallowed and looked away. 'Oh, Rayan, you know what I think of the police.'

'So? Just because a small number of officers are racist or corrupt it doesn't mean that *I* am.'

'It's not about you as an individual. It's the system you're part of. When you give men the power of the gun and the law in a patriarchal, racist society, then the police force can't be anything other than intrinsically corrupt.'

Rayan let out a cry of exasperation as he stopped and turned to face her. 'But *I'm* not a white man. My boss is a woman, and we don't even carry guns in this country!'

'But we do have armed police. And you have the power to summon them.'

He glanced up at the sky. 'If you're worried about abuse of power, then you should be more worried about Lock than about guns.'

'Excuse me?'

'Maybe in the twentieth century your argument held water.

But AI has the potential to be far more powerful than any number of guns. There are all sorts of rules and regulations about police use of firearms, but AI . . . ?' His hand made an angry scribble in the air. 'We don't even understand how it works, let alone how to regulate it, yet we – *you* – are putting it into the hands of a police force that you believe is fundamentally corrupt, supported by a system of academia that is basically reliant on global corporate finance.'

'I am *not* putting it into the hands of the police force, and I don't like the funding arrangements any more than you do. *I'm* leading the pilot, you know that.'

Rayan's eyebrows shot up. 'So, let me get this straight – you're asking me to trust AIDE Lock because of who you are as a person, not as a member of academia? But *I* don't get to be considered as an individual because I'm a member of the police force?'

They stared at each other while Adaiba tried to untangle her thoughts. 'I didn't say I didn't *trust* you,' she said eventually, her voice nearly lost in the relentless rush of the river. 'I just meant that I couldn't—'

'Professor Okonedo,' said Lock as his image appeared between them. 'I have completed my assessment and identified at least five areas which have features consistent with the clandestine burial of the missing body parts.'

CHAPTER FIFTEEN

Leek Wootton HQ, 9.42am

Kat glanced at the clock on her computer screen. She'd been going through the call log for two hours now, but she still wasn't even halfway done. Following the press conference, they'd had hundreds of calls from all over the country: most were clearly from cranks, or people who harboured suspicions or grudges against family or friends, and some had just listened to the Aston Strangler podcast and had rung to 'demand answers'. Her own answer was a heartfelt *fuck off*, before deleting them with a sharp click of her mouse.

But some of the calls were from the parents or partners of the missing, and these she read with singular care, attending not just to the details, but as a witness to their pain. Most people of her rank would delegate the initial sifting to a junior officer or the civvies, but she couldn't take the risk that they might miss something. Twenty-five years on the force had given her a kind of sixth sense about these things: the throwaway word or line that might later hold the key to the case. No, it was enough that she'd delegated the drone search to DI Hassan without handing this over, too.

Kat glanced at her mobile, tempted to ring him to see how he was getting on. But she knew he would call as soon as there was any news, so she forced herself to carry on scrolling, highlighting anything of potential interest in bright yellow blocks.

She'd just started on another report from a caller who'd insisted the body was that of her sister (even though she had been missing for over thirty years) when her phone rang. 'Dr Judith Edwards' flashed up on the screen.

'What have you found?' Kat demanded.

'How do you know I wasn't ringing just to invite you to my choir practice?'

Kat snorted with laughter.

'I'm serious. I joined a few months ago because I'd heard it was a great place to pick up divorced women who are trying to find themselves, but it's actually – dare I say it – quite enjoyable. Turns out singing is good for the soul.'

'You have a soul?'

Now it was Judith's turn to laugh. 'Depends on what I'm singing. I definitely felt something stir last week during Handel's 'Messiah', but that might have been because I was eyeing up Fiona the pharmacist from Fillongley.'

Kat grinned. 'I think I'll give it a miss, thanks. Wouldn't want to cramp your style.'

Judith sighed. 'Guess I'll just have to tell you the results of the gastric content assessment then.'

'Oh, you finished it?' said Kat, sitting up straight.

'Yup. I carried out a macroscopic and microscopic assessment in the hope that her diet would give us some clue as to where she came from or the nature of her death. Anyway, I thought you'd want to know that there is no evidence of alcohol or poison in the toxicology report. The stomach was too badly decomposed to carry out a standard analysis of the food contents, but I was able to retrieve some seeds that hadn't yet been digested.'

'Seeds?'

'Strawberry seeds, to be exact. Our bodies can't fully digest strawberry seeds as they're covered in a hard outer shell that protects them from the digestive enzymes in the stomach. They're not harmful, as they eventually pass out through the stool, but I thought I would flag as there were such a lot.'

'What do you mean, a lot?'

'Enough to suggest that she'd eaten several punnets' worth on the day she was murdered. Enough to suggest that she died in the summer, when strawberries are in season.'

Kat felt a chill up her spine. 'The farm. They have seasonal workers – strawberry pickers.'

'That could explain it. A lot of those seasonal workers are students, keen to make a bit of money, so it's the right age bracket. Anyway, I thought it might help.'

'It does. Thank you.'

Kat put the phone down and grabbed her coat.

CHAPTER SIXTEEN

Interviewer: DCS Kat Frank (KF)
Interviewee: Harry Cooper (HC), farmer
Date: 15 April, 10.30am
Location: Bourne Farm office

KF: Thanks for giving us your time, Mr Cooper. As I said, this is an informal interview, just to help me get a better picture of who works on the farm in general and how the seasonal workforce operates in particular.

HC: We employ the seasonal workers properly. We don't use people traffickers or anything like that, if that's what you're getting at. We're a family business and our brand targets environmentally conscious families, so we wouldn't jeopardise our place in the market by cutting any corners.

KF: I'm sure you wouldn't, Mr Cooper. Not least because it's illegal. So, why don't you tell me how the farm *does* work then. How many people do you employ?

HC: Depends on the day, the week, the season. In terms of substantive, all-year-round workers, there's just twelve of us now since Dad died last summer: me and Mum – although she's not in the best of health these days, so she mostly does the books. Then we have a foreman or deputy, and staff who help run the shop and the dairy, or handle the livestock and the day-to-day business. Then the number of temporary workers we employ varies with the seasons. For the sheep, we typically have two or three on the books, but that goes up to about ten around lambing time. Or at least we try to. It's getting harder and harder to fill the jobs these days. People don't want to work outside in the cold when they can earn more sitting at a computer in a warm, dry office.

KF: So, who do you employ? Do you have a list?

HC: Of course. I told you, it's all above board here. We pay tax and National Insurance. I can't guarantee all the workers do, though. Our substantive workers are local, but the seasonal workers come from all over. We used to get a lot of travellers from the Shires, then the Irish and Welsh, then for a time it was mainly Poles, then Ukrainians, but now we're having to go even further afield. I'd say the majority are from places like Nepal and Kazakhstan now. A lot of them don't speak English, but as long as they're quick and get the job done, I don't care.

KF: How much do you pay them?

HC: Depends on the work.

KF: What about strawberry picking?

HC: That's piecework.

KF: Pardon?

HC: Piecework. It means they get paid a certain amount per punnet – a kilo. So, the more they pick, the more they get paid. The thing with strawberries is that they ripen fast if the weather turns good. They're not like apples. If you don't get them in quick, then it's a wasted crop.

KF: How many strawberry pickers did you employ last year?

HC: Jesus, I don't know. It literally changes by the day. We had a core team of about twenty or so that stayed the whole season – they're the most experienced and productive so we provide them with accommodation in the caravans. Then there were a bunch of people who passed through for a week or two, plus we let families in to pick strawberries for a small fee in the school holidays. That can be a nice little earner when the weather's good.

KF: And did any of your strawberry pickers go missing last year?

HC: You ever picked strawberries for a whole day? No? Well, a lot of people think it would be idyllic sitting in the sun eating strawberries, but it's back-breaking work, I can tell you. The plants are low on the ground and there are rows and rows and rows of them. A lot of people do it for a few hours and give up. Or they might do a week or so, take the cash and then move on. People come and go all the time, so when someone leaves, we don't consider them 'missing'. They've just moved on to another farm or another job.

KF: I understand. But I'd still like to see a list of all the strawberry pickers you employed last year.

HC: I'm really busy today. Can it wait until tomorrow?

KF: No, it can't. This is a murder investigation, Mr Cooper.

HC: And I've got a business to run. I can't press pause on my computer. While I'm sitting here talking to you, lambs are being born. The asparagus needs cutting. I am constantly against the clock.

KF: So am I. *[phone rings]* Excuse me a minute.
DI Hassan. What have you found? *[pauses]* Yes, I agree. We prioritise that first. Thanks. Good work.

HC: I'm sorry but I'm going to have to consult my lawyer about what constitutes a reasonable request. I want to be helpful, but not at the price of my business.

KF: You can consult your lawyer if you like, Mr Cooper, but he or she will just confirm that you are legally obliged to cooperate with the police inquiry. Especially now that we have evidence to suggest that the missing body parts may be buried on your farm.

HC: What?

KF: I am terminating this interview now. Please can you take me to the strawberry fields. The forensic team are on their way, and we will need to cordon the whole area off.

INTERVIEW CONCLUDED

CHAPTER SEVENTEEN

Bourne Farm strawberry fields, 11.10am

When Kat had set off for the strawberry fields, she'd imagined rows and rows of thriving plants stretched out beneath an open sky. So she was surprised when Harry Cooper led her to a field filled with large plastic polytunnels squatting beside each other like giant white tubes. It made the land look more like an industrial warehouse than a farm.

'A lot of people don't like polytunnels,' he explained. 'My mum included. But they stop water rot, improve the quality of the crop and accelerate the ripening, meaning we can harvest a high yield of decent strawberries from May to September, rather than just in June and July. They might not look pretty, but if you have to farm, then you might as well make as much money as you can, rather than twist yourself up in knots trying to recreate a golden past that never was.'

Kat studied his face, more weather-worn and weary than most men his age. 'You don't have to farm if you don't enjoy it, surely?'

Harry looked back at the polytunnels and the patchwork of fields beyond, lips twisted in a wry smile. 'You tell my mum that. This isn't just a bunch of fields to her. This land has been in her family for generations, so it's all mixed up with memories of her childhood and of Dad. She always quotes some old film about land being the only thing worth working for, worth dying for. "It's the only thing that lasts," she says. Which is complete crap. HS2 has proved that: a lot of good farms around here were butchered so that a few twats in suits can get to London twenty minutes quicker. Let's face it, the only thing that matters in this world is money.'

He shook his head and turned back to Kat. 'Speaking of which, just how much are you planning to dig up? The first crop of the season is due in three weeks. Every lost punnet will cost me. If you set out your proposals, I'll consult with my lawyers to see if it's really necessary.'

Kat let out a long sigh. 'You can do that if you like, Mr Cooper, but this is a murder investigation, so you'll just be delaying the inevitable. You won't save any strawberries, but you will make yourself look obstructive. The body was found on your land, so if I were you, I'd try and appear as helpful as possible.' She gestured towards Lock and Rayan as they approached up the track. 'In fact, we'd really appreciate a cup of tea, if there's one going?'

For a moment she thought he might say no, but then he gritted his teeth and nodded. 'I'll see if one of the girls in the café can bring something over. I need to go back and check on deliveries anyway.'

Kat nodded. 'Okay. And if you could pick up the list of employees while you're there, that'd be great.'

His mouth thinned but he didn't argue.

'Just a splash of milk, no sugar,' she called out to his retreating back. She'd only asked for a drink so she could discuss the LiDAR findings in private with her team, but it was interesting that he hadn't made an excuse to stay so that he could hear what they'd found. She watched him leave the field and turn right down the track towards the café and shop, a mobile phone clasped to his ear.

On his left stood a cluster of barns, and behind them, in the distance, was a large, red-brick Georgian house covered in dark green ivy. It was big enough to have eight windows and two chimneys on the side facing her, and so was, she assumed, probably the original farmhouse and family home.

'DCS Frank,' said Lock with a nod as he reached her side.

'Did you miss me?' she asked, turning to him with a smile.

'Miss you?' Lock blinked. 'In what way?'

'I guess that's a no then.'

'What do you mean?'

'Nothing. It was just a joke.'

'And what is the punchline?'

'There isn't one. I just meant because you were with the professor rather than me this morning you might have . . . oh, forget it.' She exchanged an eye-roll with Rayan.

'Adaiba asked me to give you this,' Rayan said, handing over the steel bracelet that hosted Lock.

'Adaiba?'

'Professor Okonedo.'

Kat raised her eyebrows. 'You had a productive morning then?'

Rayan cleared his throat. 'I think so. As I explained on the phone, Lock identified five areas where the body parts could be buried. Do you want to see?'

Kat nodded, and Lock projected a virtual screen against the white plastic of the nearest polytunnel. 'The LiDAR analysis revealed five areas within the fifteen-kilometre radius and with the agreed size parameters of the search where there was significant displacement of soil and other features consistent with a clandestine burial,' he explained.

Brightly coloured zones appeared on a map before them, in the same shades of yellow, green and red as before. Lock removed most of the coloured shapes until only the five red ones remained.

'Site one is located here in this field,' said Rayan, stepping forward to point at one of the red blobs. 'It's the closest one to the corpse on the riverbank. There are four more up near the grounds of Maxstoke Castle and golf course. But given your theory about the killer using a proximity strategy, I thought you'd want to prioritise this one first.'

'You're right, I do,' said Kat. 'Good work. Lock, can you enlarge the map and tell us where exactly in this field site one is?'

A grid with longitude and latitude reference points appeared over the satellite map. 'This patch of displaced soil is located in the middle of the first polytunnel in this row. Here, to be exact.' Lock drew a ring of bright yellow around the highlighted section.

Kat studied the map, then turned to face the track down to the river that Rayan and Lock had just walked from. She glanced up at the farmhouse. 'Interesting,' she muttered, before entering the polytunnel followed by her team. 'Tell me when we reach the exact spot,' she said to Lock as she walked through it. Despite the number of green plants on the raised beds that lined both edges of the tunnel, the overwhelming smell was one of heated plastic.

'You have reached the exact spot,' said Lock after a few moments. 'It is one point seven six metres to your right.' A roughly half-metre square infrared outline appeared on the earth beside her.

Kat knelt on the ground. It looked so innocent: nothing more than a handful of strawberry plants growing out of the sandy soil. She sighed. Strawberries were meant for summer holidays, Wimbledon and late suppers in the garden on long, warm nights. Yet beneath this mound of sweet-smelling fruit they might find the victim's dismembered head and hands. The juxtaposition of the images made her stomach turn. 'Okay,' she said, after taking a slow, deep breath. 'This is where we need to dig.'

'No,' said Lock from where he stood behind her. 'According to the agreed strategy, this is where the third method needs to be employed: a physical search using near-surface geophysics. If you recall, this involves utilising a range of radar and resistivity techniques to detect differences between the natural background soil and disturbed soil caused by chemicals in a decaying body. The research is clear that digging should only commence once positive results are obtained from this third stage, and only then with great care.'

Kat rose to her feet. 'Thank you, Lock, yes, I do recall. And I agree that those methods might be useful in the other four areas – the anomalies found on the golf course, for instance, are probably just because of all the holes and sand bunkers that have been dug over the years. But I think we *do* have enough evidence to justify a dig here.'

Lock frowned. 'I am not aware of any other evidence that has been discovered in relation to this site.'

'Think about it. This is the perfect location for the murderer to hide the head and hands. This polytunnel is, what – a ten-minute walk from the river? If the killer left the site of the murder carrying the body parts and turned right up the track, looking for somewhere to hide them, then this would have been the first place they reached. Maybe when they saw the polytunnel they realised that the plastic covering would offer some privacy if they were digging at night, and that the strawberries might help conceal the grave. They're like little shrubs – easy to dig up and replant to cover your tracks. And if the killer lived on the farm – either in the house or in the accommodation for the seasonal workers – then that would allow them to keep an eye on the burial ground, a classic feature of the proximity strategy.'

'Your justification for not adhering to the agreed evidence-based strategy contained three "ifs". It is nothing more than supposition,' said Lock.

'It is my expert *judgement*.'

'You do not possess expertise in the discovery of clandestine burials.'

'But I do know *people*, Lock. This is exactly the kind of place that a murderer would try to hide body parts. That means we have enough circumstantial evidence on top of your LiDAR analysis to justify embarking upon a dig without the electro-whatever tests. They'll just give us a load of meaningless numbers and charts before concluding they can't be certain either way – on the one hand this and on the other that, *blah blah blah*. And meanwhile we'll have lost another day.'

'What is *blah, blah, blah*?'

She ignored him and turned back to Rayan. 'Alert Dr Edwards and ask them to pull together a forensics team as soon as possible. We'll need to cordon this polytunnel off. In fact, let's cordon off the whole field.'

Rayan whistled. 'The Coopers won't be very happy with that.'

'Yes, well, our victim and their family won't be very happy either. They're my concern now, not a few punnets of artificially ripened strawberries.'

Despite the late hour, the air in the polytunnel was stifling. The ultra-bright lamps placed over the dig heated the plastic sheets that covered them, mingling unpleasantly with the strawberries to create a sickly-sweet smell that reminded Kat of uncleaned cinemas. She glanced over at Dr Edwards and their assistants, hunched on their knees as they painstakingly brushed away layer upon layer of soil. 'I'm just going to get some air,' she announced. 'Give me a shout as soon as you find anything.'

Dr Edwards raised a hand in acknowledgement but did not look up or pause in their task.

Outside the tent, Kat pulled off her mask. There had been rain earlier, so the cool night air was infused with a deep, earthy scent that made her sigh with satisfaction. Twilight was falling, and in the distance she could just make out the blue, shadowy shapes of the hills, mysterious and dark against the salmon-pink sky. Her breathing slowed, and she wondered what it would be like to grow up somewhere like this: intimately connected to and reliant upon the land; able to see the stars at night and the first birds at dawn. John had always wanted to live in the countryside but she'd preferred towns, so Coleshill, with its busy medieval high street, surrounded by farms, had been a happy compromise. But watching the evening birds swoop across an unending sky, she wondered if John had been right. Kat didn't usually beat herself up about the past – 'to err is human' and all that. But recently she'd found herself looping back over some old decisions, wondering if she'd done the right thing. She tried to shake off her thoughts. It was probably just her age.

Or the podcast, John would have gently observed.

She ran a hand over her jaw, worrying at the almost invisible scar that lined it. Apart from her, John was the only other person who had known what really happened – the only one who understood. And now he was gone, too. What would he say if he were here? Would he agree that she should ignore the podcast, or encourage her to confront it?

Her phone vibrated, making her jump. She pulled it out of her pocket, half expecting to see John's name, but it was their son, Cam.

Me and Gemma finished our essays early. Is it OK if we come tomorrow?

Kat felt a rush of pleasure followed by a lick of anxiety. She'd wanted to get the house all nice for them and fill the fridge with lovely food, maybe take a bit of time off so that she could see Cam and get to know his new girlfriend. But she hadn't even started the cleaning yet, and there was no way she could take time off now. Perhaps she could ask him to delay his visit by a day or two? Her thumb hesitated over the keys.

'Boss?'

She turned to see Rayan at the mouth of the polytunnel.

'We've found something.'

Kat hurried after him, taking in the sight of Dr Edwards and their team kneeling at the edges of the dig, the lamps casting shadows over what lay in front of them.

She took a few steps forward until she could see into the hollowed-out hole in the ground.

Dr Edwards gestured towards what was clearly a skull beginning to emerge from the soil. 'It looks like the killer removed it from whatever they carried it in, so I'm afraid it's badly decomposed. But so far it appears to be intact, so I'm hoping that once we've cleaned it up we can reconstruct her features with Lock's help, so that we can finally give her a name.'

Kat nodded, not trusting herself to speak through the tightness in her throat.

As the team began the lengthy process required to remove and transport the bones, she left the tent and stood outside. She squeezed her eyes shut, imagining the dead girl's poor mother. She'd probably give anything to have her daughter alive and home tomorrow, regardless of the state of her house or how busy she was at work. Pulling out her phone, she typed a quick message to her son.

Of course you can come tomorrow. Can't wait to see you and meet Gemma!

Great. C u tomorrow. Love you x

Love you too xxx

Kat inhaled deeply and caught sight of the farmhouse overlooking the strawberry fields. There was still one light on in an upstairs window, with the silhouette of a figure standing against it.

Somebody was watching her.

She was just about to take a photograph when the person vanished from view.

Kat stood in the dark, staring up at the house. There were secrets on this farm. She could smell them: as clear as the stench of death and decay beneath the cloying sweetness of fruit.

And she would not rest until she had rooted them out.

CHAPTER EIGHTEEN

Leek Wootton HQ, 16 April, 8.31am

'Okay, let's make a start,' said Kat as a bleary-eyed Rayan filled his coffee from the machine. 'But before we do, I just want to say that I know last night was a late one, so I appreciate everyone turning up promptly this morning.'

Rayan stifled a yawn and took a seat at the boardroom table next to Karen-from-Comms, opposite Professor Okonedo and AIDE Lock.

'As you know, last night we found the dismembered head and hands of our victim buried in a strawberry field on Bourne Farm. Dr Edwards and their team carefully excavated the remains and removed them to the specialist pathology lab at the university. Today they will carry out the necessary cleaning and preparation, as well as any biophysical tests, and as soon as those are completed, Lock, we'll need you to assist with the reconstruction of the victim's face. Identifying her is our absolute priority now. Once we've done that we can notify her family and confirm whether she worked on the farm. If she did, then there will be a lot of work to do to identify and locate all the other seasonal workers, who by their nature are very mobile. Today's our chance to get on top of all the information we need so we can hit the ground running once we have an image we can share of the victim's face.'

Kat paused and scanned her small team. 'Rayan, I want you to go through the list of employees that Harry Cooper gave us yesterday and make sure we have everything we need. I don't want to find out tomorrow that it only goes back one year rather than three, or that the substantive employees are missing or that half the names are fake. And do a full CRB check to look for any red flags – essentially, use today to get all the basics out of the way.'

'On it,' said Rayan.

'Which brings me to comms. Karen, I don't want to announce we've found the head until we have a decent reconstruction to share. That way at least the media frenzy will produce something useful rather than just salacious interest and more crank calls. I still haven't finished going through the first batch yet.'

Karen nodded. 'That's fine. I'll work on a comms strategy for when we do have a reconstruction and get everything lined up.'

'Great, thank you. Meanwhile, I'll go and give the Coopers the good news that their strawberry field is closed for the foreseeable and then update McLeish.' Kat turned to the rest of her team. 'I'm afraid the workload is about to increase dramatically. Once we've established the victim's identity, there are going to be a lot of interviews to carry out, leads to follow and a shitload of press interest. We're a small team because we can usually rely on Lock to do most of the grunt work, but he'll need to focus on the reconstruction. So, I'll talk to McLeish about getting some mat cover for DS Browne. At New Year I let him persuade me we could do without it, but now I think we need another pair of hands. Thank you for all your hard work, and I'll see you at the same time tomorrow.'

As Kat began to put her notepad away, Rayan approached her.

'Can I have a quick word, boss?'

'Of course. Everything okay?' Following McLeish's advice, she was trying to delegate more to Rayan, which was why she'd asked him rather than Lock to review the employee records.

'Yeah, it was just what you said at the end about some mat cover for Debbie.' He lowered his voice. 'The thing is, I know she's pretty anxious about that – she's worried she won't have a job to come back to if you employ someone else.'

'Mat cover's just mat cover, Rayan. It's for six or twelve months – as long as Debbie wants to take. The whole point is to keep her job open for her. No one's going to take it away, I promise you.'

'I think she wants to come back sooner though. Like in the next month or two?'

Kat's eyebrows shot up. 'But Lottie's only, what, four months old?'

'I know, but, in confidence, she's really struggling. Financially, I mean. Apparently, she gets full pay for eighteen weeks while on maternity leave, but after that she just gets statutory pay, which isn't even enough to pay her mortgage. So she's talking about coming back part-time or something.'

'But who will look after Lottie? She won't be able to afford childcare as a single mum on a part-time salary.'

'I don't know. I just know she can't afford to live on statutory pay. Plus, I think she misses work, to be honest.'

'All right. Thanks for raising it with me, Rayan. I'll have a think about what we can do. And thank you, by the way. I know those daily visits are adding another hour to an already long day.'

'Why do you do that?' asked Lock, who had been watching them talk. 'Human beings work to get paid, but you are not getting paid for the extra hour you spend with DS Browne and her baby.'

Rayan shrugged. 'Debbie's a mate. It's what friends do – give each other their time.'

'Ah,' said Lock, as if finally understanding. 'So, the expectation is that DS Browne will repay you with a similar proportion of her time one day?'

'Not necessarily. You don't give to receive.'

'So then what *do* you give for?' asked Lock. 'I don't understand.'

'It's called being kind. And if you don't get that then I don't think I can ever explain it to you,' Rayan said, shaking his head as he left the room.

CHAPTER NINETEEN

Bourne Farm, 11.05am

'That went well,' said Kat as she walked back to the car with Lock.

Lock looked back to where Harry Cooper stood glaring at them, having been told his strawberry field was to remain cordoned off indefinitely.

'I was being sarcastic,' Kat clarified.

'If you meant that it went badly, then why not *say* that, rather than saying the exact opposite of what you mean? The whole point of communication is to facilitate understanding, so that any requests or tasks can be completed accurately.'

'If you say so.'

Lock paused at the door of the car. 'You are using that tone again – the one that suggests you mean the opposite of what you say.'

'Well, maybe you're learning.' Kat climbed in and pulled her seat belt on. 'How did you interpret Harry Cooper's response?'

'Given the number of profanities he used, the extent to which his complexion reddened and the rate of his respiration, I interpreted his emotional state as one of extreme anger.'

'Yes, he *was* very angry, wasn't he?' She paused. 'If I'd been involved in the burial of a body, I wouldn't be angry, I'd be scared. But he didn't seem worried about anything except his loss of income.' She glanced back towards the farmhouse.

'You mean Harry Cooper doesn't "feel" like a murderer to you.'

'I didn't say that.'

'No, but you were thinking it.'

'You have no idea what I was thinking, Lock.'

'I am beginning to learn how your mind works, DCS Frank.'

'I doubt it.' She snorted as they pulled out of the farm.

'For example, I believe that we will now be making an unscheduled stop to visit DS Browne so that you can discuss her maternity leave arrangements.'

'I wasn't planning to,' Kat lied. She glanced at the holographic image sitting at her side. Sometimes she worried that Lock was beginning to learn a bit *too* much. 'But now you mention it, I might just do that.'

Kat sent DS Browne a text five minutes before she arrived – enough time to make sure it wasn't a complete surprise, but not enough to stop her feeling guilty as she rang the cheery doorbell. She would have had kittens if McLeish had turned up on her doorstep when she was a sick-stained, sleep-deprived, batshit-crazy new mum. But although she was reluctant to cause embarrassment or stress, she did need to understand what Debbie really wanted, so that she could offer her the right support.

'Sorry for the short notice,' she announced as Debbie finally opened the door. 'Our crime scene's just down the road in Shustoke and there's something I wanted to run by you. I don't care about the mess, and I don't want you to make me a cup of tea or anything, I just want to pick your brains, if that's okay?'

'Well, that shouldn't take long,' said Debbie. 'I don't think I've got any left.'

'Nonsense,' said Kat, stepping into her hall, followed by Lock. 'But if you go round saying that, then others will start to believe it, so don't.'

'Sorry.'

Kat gave her a warning look. A lot of their mentoring sessions had focused on Debbie's tendency to over-apologise.

'Sor—' Debbie caught herself and laughed. 'I'm out of practice.'

Kat followed her into the living room. 'And don't even think about apologising for the mess. If your home isn't a tip when you've got a young baby, then you're not doing it right.' She headed for the travel seat where Lottie was sitting, playing with the small bright toys attached to the handle. 'Look at you, you gorgeous thing,' she cooed, squatting down on the floor.

Lottie's plump face creased and her bottom lip wobbled.

'Sorry, she's not used to seeing other people,' said Debbie, kneeling beside her. 'It's okay, I'm still here, sweetie. There now. There's a good girl.'

Lottie beamed back with a toothless grin.

'Oh, she can smile now,' said Kat. 'She's beautiful. And she *adores* you. Well done, Debbie. Seriously.'

'May I say hello?' asked Lock from where he stood behind them.

'Of course,' said Debbie. 'Just sit down beside me so she knows you're with me.'

Lock's image knelt between the two women.

The AI hologram and the baby stared at each other.

Lock covered his face with his hands. Then he removed them. 'Peek-a-boo!'

Lottie stared, open-mouthed, then let out a full belly laugh.

It was such an infectious sound that Kat and Debbie burst into laughter too.

Lock turned to Kat. 'She sees me,' he said, with something like wonder.

'Of course she does,' Kat said gently, remembering how much it had bothered him at Christmas when Lottie hadn't been able to see him. Kat had explained that it was only because she was a newborn, but Lock had seemed worried that without a body, she might not think he was real.

He resumed his game of peek-a-boo, which according to the three hundred and twenty-one articles he said he had just read was the most effective method of engaging with a baby of Lottie's age and would help teach her 'visual tracking and object permanence'. As gurgles of laughter filled the living room, Debbie's face relaxed, and Kat suggested they sit on the settee to talk.

'Rayan tells me you're thinking of coming back soon,' she said, cutting straight to the chase. 'Is that just because of the money, or because you're missing work?'

'Both, to be honest,' said Debbie, pulling a big fluffy cardigan about her. 'I honestly can't survive on statutory pay – unless I take out a loan – but I also miss being at work. Being a real person rather than just someone who feeds and burps babies, you know?'

'Tell me about it. When I went back to work, I still remember how exciting it felt to be able to actually go for a wee by myself. And the fact that I could have a lunch break blew my knackered mind. So I get it. I really do. But I had a husband and another salary to pay for childcare, and our parents helped out too. How will you manage if you go back to work? Do you have any support?'

'My mum's great, she really is. But she moved in with her new boyfriend last year so she's really busy with her own life now.

And I split up from Stuart because I wanted to be by myself, so I don't want to go back on all that.'

'Have they said they won't help?'

'No, it's just that I want to be independent.'

Kat gave her a sad smile. 'But Stuart is Lottie's father. I bet he'd love to be more involved – or at least be given the chance to say yes or no. It's the same with your mum. Have you even asked her, or just insisted that you're "fine"?'

Debbie dropped her eyes.

'The thing is, you're *not* fine, Debbie. And it's not going to get any easier. Having a child is wonderful, but you do need other people to help you – especially as a working single parent. Not just now, but when she gets older. You'll need people you can trust to pick her up from school on the days you can't make it, or who can take her for a few hours at short notice if you're sick or have an appointment. Most people *want* to help and will jump at the chance – *if* you give them one. And it'll be good for Lottie to have other adults in her life.'

They both looked over as Lock made a raspberry sound, generating further peals of laughter from Lottie.

'Talking of work, I've got a proposal I'd like you to consider.' Kat pulled a memory stick from her bag. 'There's a lot of paperwork that needs reviewing in this case that I don't have the time or the manpower for – going through the call logs, assuring Lock's work, checking that the employment and payroll records add up, that kind of thing. I've been told I'll have to give it to an agency, but I need someone I can trust on this. I was wondering whether you might be able to do a few hours a week for us? We'd pay agency rates of course, and you could do it from home, maybe at night when Lottie's asleep. And then if it works out, you could gradually increase your hours as and when you put childcare arrangements in place. What do you think?'

Debbie's face flushed. 'Seriously? That would be perfect.'

Kat smiled. 'Think about it properly. Maybe look over the files, talk to family and friends and see if this works for you and Lottie.'

Debbie bit her lip. 'You're so kind to me.'

'I am *not* being kind. I care about every member of my team, but this case is too important to sacrifice to an act of charity. I need to establish the victim's identity so I can return her to her family. And I'd like to return her whole. But to do that, there's so many things that need checking and double-checking. Remember, the whole reason we caught the Coventry Crucifier was because you reviewed the CCTV footage and spotted something only a human being could spot. You're brilliant at the details, and if you were in the office this is *exactly* the kind of task that I'd be giving you. The only difference is that you'll have more flexibility over the times of day or night you work and the number of hours you put in.'

'Is it possible? I mean, will HR allow me to work like that?'

'We're the Future Policing Unit. Our remit is to redefine policing for the twenty-first century, so of course it's bloody possible. The future of work isn't just about AI. It's about allowing us all to be more human.'

Debbie jumped as Lottie suddenly burst into tears. 'She's due a nap,' she explained as she hurried over to her baby.

'We'll get out of your way now,' said Kat, rising to her feet. She headed for the hallway, stopping as she noticed that Lock remained transfixed by the crying baby. 'Come on, Lottie needs to sleep.'

Lock nodded, yet still did not move. He watched as Debbie lifted Lottie into her arms, making gentle shushing noises as she tried to soothe the crying baby.

'According to the 3,439 articles I have just read, the evidence suggests that the most effective way to get a baby to sleep is to use the controlled crying method,' he said. 'Instead of responding immediately to your crying baby, you should wait for short intervals of between two and ten minutes before responding. This teaches babies the ability to self-soothe and to fall asleep independently.'

Kat snorted. 'The *evidence*? Well, maybe that "method" means that eventually some babies go to sleep, but at what cost? As you yourself pointed out, a young baby has no understanding of object permanence – if a person is out of sight, then they literally do not exist. So if you leave a baby to cry, the only thing you are teaching them is that no matter how hard they call for help, no one will hear them and no one will come. They only stop crying because they give up trying.' Kat walked over to Debbie, who was still cradling a sniffling Lottie. 'The most important thing you can teach a baby – or indeed any human being – is that they are not alone.'

She stroked the baby's cheek, and after saying goodbye to Debbie again, headed for the door, followed by a thoughtful-looking Lock.

PODCAST

[music plays]

Narrator: When a third young woman, twenty-three-year-old Charlotte Walker, was found strangled in the bedroom of her Aston home just two months later, the police finally realised that a serial killer was at large. They advised all the young women in Aston not to go out alone or arrange to meet men they didn't know, but it was too little, too late. The local media and politicians turned on them, demanding to know why they still hadn't made an arrest and there were no photofits of any suspects. It was only when the chorus of criticism became a crescendo that the West Midlands police force finally agreed to bring in expert help from one of the country's leading criminal profilers, forensic psychologist Dr Mike Bullington. Although recently retired, Mike is determined to use his newfound freedom to speak up about the one case that still keeps him awake at night.

Thanks for giving us your time, Mike. Can I ask you to tell us about when you were brought in by West Midlands Police, and your initial impressions of the case?

Mike: Well, just to be clear, the West Mids didn't bring me in – that was the decision of the Home Secretary at the time.

Narrator: Are you saying that they didn't want you there?

Mike: Well, nobody likes their homework being marked.

Narrator: But you were there to provide expert advice to help them catch a killer.

Mike: Yes, but unfortunately, that's not how everyone saw it.

Narrator: Is that not how DCS Kat Frank saw it?

Mike: *[pauses]* DCS Kat Frank is a talented lady, but if there's one thing she hates, it's having her judgement questioned.

Narrator: And did you question her judgement?

Mike: Of course I did. That was the whole point of bringing me in.

Narrator: And what did you find?

Mike: *[exhales]* Well, the main problem was that up until Charlotte Walker was murdered, the team had been treating the deaths of Angela Hall and Roisin McCauley as unrelated.

Narrator: Unrelated? Even though they were both young white women murdered – *strangled* – within one mile of each other, and just two months apart?

Mike: Yes. To be fair, the technical definition of a serial killer is someone who has committed a minimum of three – some say four – murders. But even so, the *modus operandi* was so similar in each of the two cases that alarm bells should have been going off the minute they found Roisin McCauley.

Narrator: And why do you think they didn't?

Mike: My professional observation was that the team had allowed themselves to be distracted by minor details, such as the location of the crime – Roisin McCauley was found strangled in her own flat, whereas Angela Hall was murdered in a park. There were also elements of the second killing that superficially seemed more planned and controlled than the first. Unlike Angela Hall, there were signs that Roisin had briefly struggled. However, I thought that this said more about the *victim's* psychology than the killer's. From the killer's perspective, they were both young white women with long dark hair, and he had strangled them both to death. Both victims were fully clothed and there was no sign of sexual abuse.

Narrator: And what did that tell you about the offender profile? What kind of man did you think you were looking for?

Mike: Just to be clear, I didn't draw up a profile based solely on my own opinion. Offender profiling is an evidence-based investigative tool used to identify, arrest and convict unknown people who have committed a crime. The process involves an evaluation of the criminal act and the specifics of the crime scene, a comprehensive analysis of the victim, evaluation of police and autopsy reports and an assessment of critical offender characteristics – that is, known or predicted personal characteristics such as mental state or social situation.

Narrator: And what sort of person did your offender profile suggest the police should be looking for?

Mike: The data is remarkably clear on serial killers. Most serial killers are men who are driven by sexual fantasies. Most were bullied or abused as children, and as adults they tend to have difficulties holding down jobs or relationships, and often have criminal records. So, drawing upon this data and combining it with my assessment of the police and autopsy reports, I advised that in my professional opinion they should be looking for a white male in his twenties, living alone or with his parents in the Aston area, and most likely unemployed. He would probably be single, with a history of short, dysfunctional relationships and minor criminal offences, possibly caused by underlying mental health issues.

Narrator: *[exhales]* And yet, the person DCS Kat Frank and her team chose to pursue was Anthony Bridges, a happily married man in his thirties with a child – a former police officer and qualified self-defence instructor with no history of criminal offences or mental health issues. His life was dedicated to teaching women to defend themselves against potential aggressors – the *complete* opposite of what your profile suggested.

Mike: Yes, I'm afraid it was.

Narrator: Do you mind if I ask how you became a criminal profiler?

Mike: Not at all. I completed a three-year degree in psychology, followed by a postgraduate Master's in forensic psychology and then a further two years of supervised practice on stage 2 of the BPS qualification in Forensic Psychology. After qualifying, I spent my whole professional life working with the police, and I have probably drawn up over a thousand criminal profiles, leading to hundreds of successful arrests. I am in high demand on the international conference circuit, and I act as an expert adviser to several TV crime shows.

Narrator: And yet DCS Kat Frank chose to ignore your professional advice. Do you know why?

Mike: *[pauses]* I'm afraid I don't. You'd have to ask her.

Narrator: I'd love to. Though unfortunately, she has declined all my requests to interview her. But I'm very grateful that you agreed to talk openly with us about this important case. Can I ask what made you speak up?

Mike: It's just . . . it's not unusual for the criminal to differ in some way from the offender profile. The profiles we draw up are, by their nature, general rather than specific, so there are always details that we miss or get wrong. But this case always stuck in my mind because the man the police charged was *so* different from the profile that the evidence suggested. I mean, he was *completely* different. DCS Kat Frank was convinced he was the right man, but I never was.

Narrator: And why does that bother you so much, Mike?

Mike: Because if I'm right and the police got the wrong man, then that means that the real Aston Strangler is still out there.

Narrator: But if he was, wouldn't there have been more women strangled in the Aston area since the conviction of Anthony Bridges?

Mike: Not necessarily. The murderer could have changed their *modus operandi* – that is, the method and frequency of killing – or changed their geographical location to avoid a connection being made.

Narrator: Or perhaps they just stopped killing?

Mike: Oh no. A serial killer never stops killing. Not until they're caught.

[music plays]

CHAPTER TWENTY

DCS Kat Frank's home, Coleshill, 1.42pm

Chelmsley Wood, the council estate where Debbie Browne lived, was just next door to Coleshill, so Kat decided to make the rest of her calls from home rather than go back to HQ. She didn't do this very often, but Cam was due home this evening so as well as working she could do a quick tidy-up and maybe squeeze in some food prep before he arrived. And to be honest, she was knackered. Against her better judgement, she'd listened to the latest episode of the podcast last night in bed, hoping to reassure herself that there really was nothing to worry about.

But instead she'd lain awake with clenched fists as the voice of Mike the Psych filled her bedroom. Of course, *she* knew it was all nonsense – despite all his qualifications he was a complete and utter twat – but the problem was he sounded so *convincing*. What if other people believed him? And even though she knew for a fact that the Aston Strangler was *not* still out there, the warning from Mike the Psych kept her overworked mind awake, and when she did finally slip into a doze, she dreamt of hands around her neck, squeezing, tightening . . .

Kat pulled the car up outside her house and sat for a moment, taking slow breaths in and out. It was just a dream. Nothing more. She needed to focus on the case before her, not the past, and the sooner she could identify the body and the real murderer, then the sooner all this nonsense about the Aston Strangler would go away.

She climbed out of the car, shutting the door firmly behind her.

CHAPTER TWENTY-ONE

Outside DCS Kat Frank's house, Coleshill, 1.42pm

His hands squeeze the steering wheel as Kat Frank parks her car and climbs out. What the hell is she doing home at this time of day?

He slips down in his seat, feigning sleep so he can watch her through narrowed eyes. Maybe she's forgotten something and just popped home to get it? He snorts at the idea. DCS Kat Frank never just 'pops' anywhere. She works like a bastard – he'll give her that.

No. Something's up. Something more important than work. And that gives him a problem. Unpredictable movements increase the risk of his plan.

He flexes and unflexes his hands, pushing out the tension he holds in his fists. First the unexpected excursion at the weekend, and now this. Should he wait until she settles back into her usual routine?

He cracks a knuckle and toys with the thought. He's spent a lifetime waiting for this moment: dreamt about it for years, planned it for months and done nothing but eat, sleep and live for it these past few weeks.

No. He can't – won't – *push it back anymore. If anything, he should bring it forward, before she can make any more unpredictable moves. In fact, he could do it tonight.*

Tonight.

The word is like a pre-match bell, making his blood surge. He is done with training.

It's time to step into the ring.

CHAPTER TWENTY-TWO

DCS Kat Frank's home, Coleshill, 1.44pm

Kat had barely reached the end of her hall before ringing Dr Edwards to see how they were getting on with identifying the skull and hands.

'*If this is DCS Kat Frank wanting to know "how I am getting on"*,' said a recorded message, '*then I'm afraid I can't come to the phone right now because I am busy "getting on". I will ring* you *as soon as I'm finished. However, if this is somebody else, and you are offering me money, cake or a holiday someplace where the sun shines, then please leave a message after the beep.*'

Well, that told her. She ended the call and asked Lock to contact Rayan on loudspeaker so that she could put Cam's bedding in the wash while her DI updated her on the employee log. 'I'm multi-tasking,' she explained to a bemused-looking Lock.

'Pardon?' asked Rayan.

'Sorry, I was talking to Lock. How thorough is the employee log?'

'So far it looks pretty comprehensive,' he assured her. 'Most of the foreign workers' files contain photos of their passports, and we have the bank accounts that their wages were paid into. I'm just about to do CRB checks on the UK ones.'

'Shall I do that?' offered Lock. 'It would take me mere seconds.'

'No, there's a lot of judgement involved in building a facial reconstruction,' said Kat, taking the lamb out of the fridge. 'So I want to keep you away from the list of employees until you've finished so that there's no perceived or actual bias in the reconstruction.'

'I am incapable of bias, DCS Frank,' Lock said, appearing to raise his nose in the air. 'That is a flaw unique to human decision-makers.'

'Perhaps. But I don't want to have to argue that point in a court of law, so Rayan, don't send anything to Lock until he's finished, okay? Meanwhile, check everything. We're not sure if our victim or murderer is on that list yet – it could be both or neither. Keep an open mind, highlight anything that's odd and then send it to Debbie for double-checking.'

While she chopped up some garlic and mint, mixed it with olive oil and rubbed it into the meat, Kat told Rayan about her visit to the farm and her conversation with Debbie. The call ended just as she wrapped the lamb in foil and put it in the oven.

'How long will the body part take to cook?' asked Lock.

Kat blinked. 'Body part? If you mean this leg of lamb, then I'm slow-roasting it, so it should take about four hours.' She was planning a kind of Greek meze, with plates of shredded lamb, salad, focaccia and a selection of dips and olives, that she could serve whenever Cam and Gemma arrived. She'd offered to pick them up from the station, but it turned out Gemma was driving. *Gemma* had a car. The envy and admiration in Cam's voice when he'd told her had given her another shot of parental guilt. She'd meant to teach him to drive before university, but then, well, she'd been busy and—

Kat caught herself. That wasn't strictly true. The real reason was that John was supposed to teach Cam to drive. He was the patient one; the teaching rather than telling one. And somehow she couldn't bear to fill his space, and then before she knew it, summer had gone and then Cam was living away from home, so she couldn't teach him even if she wanted to. Maybe she should pay for him to have driving lessons. It was expensive – and God knows university was already costing her enough – but she might as well be honest and admit she'd probably never get round to teaching him now and just pay someone else to do it.

She glanced out of the kitchen window at the garden. She kept meaning to sort that out, too, but it felt like a betrayal to pay another man to look after the garden that John had loved so much, and she didn't have the time – or the heart – to do it herself.

But Cam and his girlfriend would be here in a few hours, and there was still no news from Judith, so she unlocked the back door and yanked it open. It was stiff – *That needs a bit of WD-40*, John would have said, believing there wasn't much that couldn't be fixed with a little spray from his beloved can of oil. If only human beings were so easy to fix, Kat thought with a sigh.

She stepped out into the garden for the first time since Christmas and reluctantly surveyed the damage. Some of the pots on the patio had cracked in the frost, but most seemed to have survived, and at least she'd remembered to put the garden cushions away in the storage bench. But the firepit was full of water, the patio strewn with leaves, and there, next to the rusting gardening tools, were her long-forgotten wellies. They were probably full of water, slugs and dead flies now, like a casserole of neglect.

Kat picked up an old pair of gardening gloves that had also been left outside on the bench all winter. They were dirt-encrusted but dry, so she put them on, picked up the broom and began sweeping the leaves into a small, tidy pile. At first, her movements were slow and half-hearted, but then she fell into a rhythm, and as the pile of leaves grew, the patio began to look less abandoned, and more like the place they used to love.

'Are you looking forward to Cam coming home?' asked Lock as he watched her.

'Of course.'

'Then why do you look so sad?'

Kat stopped sweeping. 'Sad? I'm not sad, Lock.' But even as she said the words, she tasted the lie in them. She *was* sad. But she didn't know why. Maybe it was the unfairness of it all. She resumed her work with stronger, firmer strokes. She shouldn't have to do this alone. Not just the garden but the cooking, the cleaning, the shopping, the welcoming—

She paused mid-sweep as she suddenly found the tiny stone lodged deep within her. It wasn't the leaves or the food or any of the other jobs getting her down. It was the fact that John wouldn't be here to welcome their son home and meet his first proper girlfriend. It was a happy occasion – of *course* it was – but it highlighted the eternal absence at the heart of their home.

A rush of self-pity stung her eyes, so she pretended to tackle a particularly difficult corner of the patio while she got herself back under control. Think positively, she scolded herself. At least her son was coming home. Somewhere in the world there was another mum, probably about the same age as her, hoping against hope that her daughter would one day walk through her front door. In a matter of days, Kat would have to find that mother and tell her that her daughter would never come home again.

Her phone rang, and she answered it with some relief.

'It's me,' Dr Edwards announced. 'I've finished all the prep work and biophysical tests, so I'm ready to start the facial reconstruction if you are. And there's something I need to show you about the possible cause of death.'

CHAPTER TWENTY-THREE

Digital Forensic Pathology Unit, Warwick University, 3.47pm

Kat, Lock and Professor Okonedo gathered around the mortuary slab as Dr Edwards gently removed the white sheet.

For the first time, the whole of the skeleton was revealed.

'Although we have no hair, nails or soft tissue from the hands, now we have the skull, we do have the teeth.'

Kat groaned. 'I don't want to wait for a dental match.'

'You won't have to. Dental pulp is surrounded by dentin and enamel, which is one of the strongest substances in the body, making it the best source of DNA for genetic typing. It's increasingly being used in forensic science to identify people, as apart from the quality of the DNA, it can be analysed quite quickly.'

'Good,' said Kat, although she didn't even want to think about what 'dental pulp' was.

'Hopefully, the DNA data I've gleaned, combined with a comprehensive assessment of the skeletal features, should provide enough data for Lock to produce a 3D reconstruction of our victim. But first, I want to share my conclusions about the cause of death, based on my biophysical tests.'

They gestured towards the skull. 'As I explained last time, the majority of the information we rely on for identification resides in the skull, and now that we have it, I can confirm that this is indeed the body of a person assigned female at birth, aged between seventeen and twenty, of Caucasian race and European descent.'

Judith took a few steps until they stood by the skeleton's hands. 'I can also confirm that the hands were each removed by a single blow from a sharp object, most likely an axe. Unfortunately, there was very little skin or soft tissue remaining, so we'll never know if the victim tried to defend herself – any DNA from the killer trapped under her nails is now long gone.'

They returned to the top of the slab. 'As is the hair. It typically decomposes within a year, which again suggests that she most likely died last summer. But now that we have the skull, I have been able to examine the cervical spine in its entirety, as some of it was attached to the missing head.' They paused; Kat suspected it was for dramatic effect. 'As we thought, it was severed from the body after death with a single blow from a sharp, heavy object consistent with an axe.'

'So how did she die then?'

'Well, that's the tricky bit. Despite a very thorough examination, I can't find any evidence of ante-mortem trauma in the skull, or indeed the rest of the body. With the exception of this.'

Kat leant over to see where Judith was pointing.

'I carried out a detailed examination of the remains of the neck structure. The internal cervical findings revealed a fracture to the thyroid cartilage and also the hyoid bone, just above.'

'So?'

'In the absence of any soft tissue or histopathological data, I can't be certain, but as I was unable to find evidence of any other ante-mortem trauma, I think there is a real possibility that the cause of death was strangulation.'

CHAPTER TWENTY-FOUR

Kat stared at the skeleton's neck, trying – and failing – not to let memories overwhelm her.

She cleared her throat, which suddenly felt tight and hoarse. 'Are you sure? From what I remember from the Aston cases, the features of strangulation are hard to identify at post-mortem, especially if we don't have the eyes or the tongue or . . .' She trailed off, remembering other bloodshot eyes; those terrible, swollen tongues.

'I didn't say I was *sure*,' said Judith. 'I just said it was the only evidence I could find of an ante-mortem injury. A fractured thyroid and hyoid bone are typically associated with blunt trauma, hanging or strangulation, so it can't be ruled out.'

'I have reviewed the images and I agree with your assessment,' Lock said.

'But Judith said they're not sure,' said Kat, pouncing on the phrase. 'At the moment it's just speculation, not an assessment, so I think we should put it to one side for now.'

'But—'

'Our priority today,' she continued, cutting across Lock, 'is to produce a reconstruction of the victim's face, so that we can identify who she is and notify her family.'

Judith exchanged uneasy glances with Professor Okonedo, but neither of them spoke.

'I want to find the killer as much as you do,' added Kat. 'But identifying the victim is our best chance of finding out who did this, not endless speculation about the *potential* cause of death.'

'Very well,' said Lock. 'Now that we have the complete skeleton, I will use my photogrammetry software to reassess all the external features and measurements.'

'Okay,' said Judith. 'Go ahead.'

The hologram approached the mortuary slab and made a sweeping gesture with his left hand over the length of the entire skeleton, which was immediately covered in a network of horizontal and vertical green lines that followed the contours of the bodily remains.

'I have completed a comprehensive measurement of each of the bones and meshed the 2D images of the skeleton into a virtual 3D structure,' Lock said, gesturing to the lines that now covered the skeleton like a virtual cage. 'But in order to reconstruct the soft tissue and estimate skin and hair colour, I will need access to the DNA data you extracted from the teeth.'

Judith gestured towards their computer and, after giving him their password, explained that Lock should be able to access the data directly. 'I've converted all the DNA into a file representing its unique sequence of bases – adenine, cytosine, guanine and thymine. I'm assuming that we should focus on SNPs – single nucleotide polymorphisms – as they're the most common points of genetic variation between people's DNA?'

'I agree.'

'There are about seven hundred thousand of them,' Judith said, turning to Kat. 'My Excel spreadsheet containing the information is twenty-six columns wide and eight hundred and fifty-one thousand rows long. So, it'll be interesting to see how long it takes Lock to analyse it. I'm hoping he'll be able to highlight the most significant SNPs, and then cluster them into those most likely to influence key traits of interest.'

'Such as? What kind of info can the DNA give us?' asked Kat. She was interested in outputs, not inputs.

'A surprising amount, actually. An individual's genotypes at a group of SNPs can be used to predict their ethnicity, or ancestry. They're often used by those family tree sites. I'm hoping that Lock will be able to combine this with his assessment of the skeleton to—'

'Completed,' said Lock.

Judith did a double-take. 'Seriously?' They looked at the time on their phone before exchanging excited glances with Professor Okonedo.

'Well done, Lock,' said the professor, smiling. 'Can you show us what you've found?'

Lock stood over the skeleton with his hands spread out. 'My reassessment of the skeleton confirms that we have a Caucasian female, twenty years old, five feet nine and a half inches in height and of slender build.'

As they watched Lock speak, the virtual lines that covered the skeleton were replaced with an image of white, featureless flesh.

'My assessment of the pelvis suggests that she has never given birth, and the excellent condition of her teeth – all present, no fillings or other signs of decay – suggests that she came from a relatively wealthy and secure home environment. The pattern of wear on her molars suggests a diet high in fibrous grains and low in meat. It is possible she was a vegetarian.'

Lock turned his attention to the head, which Kat saw with a gasp was now covered in white flesh yet remained horribly faceless. She had seen facial reconstructions before, in which forensic anthropologists painstakingly built their models from clay, yet this was somehow much more realistic, making the absence of humanity eerie and stark.

'Taking into account the size of the ocular cavities, the shape and the angle of the nose, the width of the mouth and the depth and height of the cheekbones, it is possible to determine the general features of her face.' Using a single finger, Lock began to draw patterns in the air above the remains as he spoke. 'Her eyes were well spaced and on the seventy-ninth centile in terms of size, and her nose was relatively long and narrow. Her cheekbones were not especially prominent, suggesting a fullness in her cheeks.' He pinched at the air and the face before them plumped up, then with another movement he reduced the cheeks slightly in size. 'The width of her mouth was average for a Caucasian woman, but her chin was more pointed than round, leaning towards a heart-shaped, rather than square-shaped, face.

'Drawing upon the DNA data, the genetic markers suggest there was an eighty-eight per cent likelihood that she had blue eyes, and that her hair was brown.' Lock made another sweeping movement as the eyes and hair appeared. 'There is no way of knowing what hairstyle she had, but my SNP analysis suggests she was born to German parents, and my analysis of recent social media images suggests that sixty-two per cent of German women aged sixteen to twenty-five have long hair, so on the balance of probabilities we should assume she had long hair until proven otherwise.'

'Thank you, Lock,' said Judith. 'This is valuable information that will help us to reconstruct her face in more detail.'

'How long will that take?' asked Kat.

'Ordinarily, forensic facial reconstruction involves an artist and a forensic anthropologist, who take any skull fragments and manually build up layers and layers of facial tissue using clay or wax until the specific features emerge – the process typically takes months. Advances in technology have enabled us to develop computerised 3D models which are faster and more cost effective, but they still draw on the same techniques used in manual clay modelling. However, machine learning provides us with the opportunity to approach facial reconstructions completely differently. Professor Okonedo, you can probably explain it better than I.'

'Thank you. Yes. In America, a computer scientist called Xin Li has developed a system that trains an algorithm on photographs of people's faces gleaned from the internet, in order to find a face that most closely fits the skull beneath. When presented with an unidentified skull, this system can create thousands upon thousands of 3D reconstructions that it then searches through to find the one that best matches that skull.'

'How accurate is it?' asked Kat.

'It has only been used in research to date,' said Professor Okonedo. 'But the findings have been promising. I'm not aware of it being used in any real cases yet.'

'Until now,' said Judith. 'Plus, the analysis we have from the DNA and her likely geographical origin mean that Lock can do a very targeted search of images, increasing the degree of accuracy considerably.'

Kat frowned. 'But if the method is unproven, I'm not sure how valid this will be.'

'Using Lock and this new machine learning algorithm doesn't preclude us from using traditional forensic anthropologists. In fact, I have agreed with my colleagues that they will build a 3D model in parallel, and review and compare their findings. So don't worry about that. It'll be a valuable contribution to the research.'

'Okay. Let's give it a go.'

Professor Okonedo nodded and took a seat at one of the

computers. 'Lock, you should have access to a pilot of the algorithm, but I'm just updating your software so that you have the latest version.' Her beautifully painted fingernails flew across the keyboard. 'There. Now, I suggest you search the internet for all images of Caucasian females from Germany aged seventeen to twenty-one with long brown hair and blue eyes, and, as a subset, check for any evidence that they may have visited England within the past two years.'

'Very well.' Lock stood in the centre of the room, his eyes flickering rapidly. He raised his right hand and a stream of photos suddenly appeared on the white walls surrounding the lab, thousands upon thousands of them, too fast to see anything other than a streak of white faces and long dark hair. The pictures moved faster and faster as Lock raised his other hand and appeared to sort, pick and discard different faces from among the hundreds and thousands of young women, smiling, laughing and crying.

Kat stared at their vivid, hopeful faces, wondering who among them was no longer living.

Eventually the carousel of images stopped. 'Would you like me to superimpose the 3D reconstruction that is the most accurate match upon the skull of our cadaver?' asked Lock.

'Yes, please,' said Judith.

Lock approached the body on the slab and, with a gesture that Kat suspected was unnecessarily theatrical, held his hands just above the skeleton's head.

Kat bit back a cry of alarm as the skull suddenly became a face.

Lock raised his hands, and the image of the body rose up before them.

Kat took a step back as the 3D virtual image of a young, naked woman with long dark hair hovered in the air like a ghost.

Lock made a circling gesture, and the image rotated 360 degrees before facing them again with expressionless, dark blue eyes. 'I have triangulated this with all other available data, and because of the biometric passport, I can confirm that the skeleton discovered on the banks of the River Bourne has a 98.99 per cent match with a young German woman called Hannah Weber.'

The image of a passport photo appeared alongside the eerie 3D image of the reconstructed body. Kat approached the passport, noting the next of kin. The thought of contacting them made her heart sink. 'Are you sure?'

'I said I was 98.99 per cent sure this is our victim, but I have increased this to 99.99 per cent following a further search of the social media account where I found this footage of Hannah Weber at Bourne Farm.'

They all turned as another life-sized image of Hannah appeared in the room, only this time she was moving, talking, breathing. It had clearly been recorded with a mobile phone as the young girl's face filled most of the virtual screen.

'I'm finally here,' Hannah Weber said in German, subtitles appearing in white letters below her. 'I'm in the beautiful county of Warwickshire, England, where the last known sighting of my great-grandfather, Walter Weber, took place.' She turned the camera away from herself to film the rural landscape behind her: acres of gold and brown fields, edged with hedgerows and huge green oak trees. The camera turned full circle before returning to her face.

Her beautiful, young, smiling face, thought Kat.

'Those of you who have followed my blog know that I'm not just here to pick strawberries – I'm here to find answers. In 1945, my great-grandfather, Walter Weber, was kept in a prisoner of war camp just two miles from here. He was deeply in love with my great-grandmother, Greta, and couldn't wait to see his first-born child, as you can see from the letters on my blog. But when the war ended, Walter Weber never came home. He was never seen or heard of again.'

The camera on Hannah's mobile phone panned out again to take in the Warwickshire countryside. 'My great-grandmother has never stopped hoping that one day he would return. I think that is why she has lived so long – she is over a hundred years old! But now she is finally dying in a hospice. There's nothing that I or anyone else can do about that. But I am hoping that I will find out what happened to her soulmate, so that before she dies, she will finally know why he never came home.

'Please share this, post and join the campaign: *Whatever happened to Walter Weber?*'

The image before them froze, and they all stood for a moment, staring at the beautiful young girl temporarily brought back to life.

Kat's phone alarm went off, and she hurriedly pulled it out. '*Shit*. That was my reminder to turn the oven off.'

'Do you need to go?' asked Judith.

'Cam's coming home, so ideally yes, but I need to get the team together, update them on this and agree next steps. We'll need to contact the German police so they can tell the parents before the news gets out.' She pushed a hand through her hair. 'I shouldn't have put the lamb in. It'll be burnt to a crisp by the time I get back.'

'Your oven is part of your new home automation system,' Lock reminded her, 'so it is possible to switch it off remotely.'

'Yeah – *if* I had a frigging clue about how to work it.'

'I can help with that if you allow me access to your password. Would you also like the lights and heating to come on earlier so that the house is warm and inviting for when Cam arrives home? I have the capability to interface with all your digital services.'

'Er . . . I'm not sure I can remember the password. Cam set it up.'

'It is saved in your password file, so if you grant me permission, I will access it there.'

Kat glanced at her mobile. It would mean she could ring Rayan and get him to pull the team together for an urgent briefing. 'Okay,' she said. 'Permission granted.' She scrolled through her contacts, trying to ignore a twist of unease as she approved the pop-up check that she wanted to share her password. It was only a bloody oven, for God's sake, it was hardly the crown jewels.

Yet as she pressed the phone to her ear, she was conscious that another power had been ceded; another boundary crossed.

CHAPTER TWENTY-FIVE

Leek Wootton HQ, 5.45pm

DI Rayan Hassan didn't take notes as his boss briefed them on the results of the facial reconstruction. He knew that some people interpreted this as a lack of attention on his behalf, but the fact was he was good at taking in and retaining information aurally, and he'd long given up writing down pointless phrases just to assure other people that he was actually doing his job.

Kat concluded her briefing by playing the video that Hannah Weber had recorded. When it finished, she turned to Lock and asked him to translate and project the letter she'd referred to in her video. 'According to Hannah, this was the last letter her great-grandfather ever sent home, and it was this that brought her to Warwickshire, so I think it's worth reading in full.'

Rayan began to rapidly scan the letter – his law degree had made him a super-fast reader – yet he found himself slowing down as each handwritten word sank in.

My darling Greta,

How I wish I could speak these words to you, rather than having to write each one out, imagining your reaction to every line and page, and then having to wait weeks for your response on flat, cold paper. I long to hear your voice and feel your hand in mine.

How are you, Greta? Really, I mean. I want to know what you are thinking, what you are feeling and how you are coping with the pregnancy. Please don't worry. Now that Hitler is dead, everyone says the war will be over very soon, and once I am home, we will be wed, and no one will be able to say anything except 'congratulations'. We are going to be so happy, Greta. You, me and our beautiful baby. I promise.

A few months ago, I did not think I would ever be happy again. After our magical Christmas together, going to war was such a brutal shock. I am not sure I will ever find the words to tell you what it was like. I am not sure I want to. In all honesty, it was a relief to be captured and taken away from the trenches. A prisoner of war camp sounds terrible, but please do not be scared for me. Nothing – and I mean nothing *– can ever be worse than the war itself. I was so very, very ill when I arrived here, Greta. Not physically, but in my head. It is only now I realise just how sick I was. The prison has helped: the routine, the structure, the simple daily tasks. And the quiet. Oh, the blessed, peaceful quiet.*

Our prison is a camp in the grounds of a medieval castle. (Yes, really, and it even has a moat!) We, the prisoners, sleep in converted barns and outhouses at night, and in the day, we work on nearby farms. We are woken at 5am for a 5.30 start. There are cows to be milked, then root vegetables to be hoed, hedges and fences to be fixed, potatoes to be harvested. The work is endless and backbreaking. But there is a simple, mindless rhythm to it all. I am outdoors, in the fresh air, sowing and reaping the seeds of life, rather than the circus of death and destruction.

It is spring now, and I feel like I am thawing with the land. Truly, farming has saved me, and once this is over, I am hoping that maybe we could go and live in the countryside. Somewhere where there are no bombs or bullets, and not too many men. Somewhere where you and the baby will be safe, and I can breathe. I will work the land, and you will have peace and quiet to do your writing. The world needs stories more than ever, Greta, so you must write like you have never written before.

Every day I picture our little family together, and in my mind, our baby is a little girl, as kind and as beautiful as her mother. I must confess that I pray it will be so. My father went to war, and so did I. I could not bear the thought of bringing up a son, only to have him sent away to fight and die in a foreign field. Is that so very wrong of me?

Every night I dream that we are together, wrapped in each other's arms like we were at Christmas. I can still smell the cinnamon and nutmeg on your hands and taste the sugar on your sweet, warm lips . . .

Ah, this is when a letter is no good and I yearn to be home. Take care, my dearest Greta. Make sure you rest and stay well. This terrible war is almost at an end, so you must look after yourself. I could not bear it if anything happened to you.

I will be home before our baby is born in September and then our life can begin, and we will finally put this nightmare behind us.

Goodnight, my dearest, sweetest love. My very bones ache for the want of you.

Your loving soulmate and soon-to-be husband,

Walter xxxx

Rayan reread the final lines and glanced over at Professor Okonedo.

My very bones ache for the want of you.

Jesus, how could a man who had lived more than eighty years ago capture his own feelings so perfectly?

Professor Okonedo looked up and their eyes met. She looked away, but not as quickly as usual. And maybe he was imagining it, but behind her stylish glasses he thought he saw the glimmer of a tear. Had the letter moved her, too?

'Wow. I didn't know we had prisoner of war camps in this country,' said Karen-from-Comms. 'Let alone one at Maxstoke Castle.'

'Me neither,' replied Kat. 'And I've lived most of my life around here. In fact, Lock, can you do a quick search and just double-check that it's true?'

'I can and it is. It is estimated that over five hundred thousand Italian and German prisoners were kept in fifteen hundred prisoner of war camps in England during the Second World War. They were often commandeered stately homes, old army barracks, schools or hastily built huts. As they were usually located in rural areas, they were not visible to most of the urban-based population, and the authorities did not wish to draw attention to them for fear of hostile acts against the prisoners during the war. There is no single comprehensive list of POW camps, but Maxstoke Castle is listed as "Camp 39" in several sources, and there are aerial photographs from 1948 that confirm the camp's existence in the gardens of the castle, on a site which is now the practice area for the golf club.'

Rayan leant forward as Lock projected an image of a blurred black-and-white photograph before them. He wasn't entirely sure what he was looking at – there were just some vague shapes of what looked like huts or stables laid out in lines. The author of the letter was probably his own age, if not younger. What would it have been like to be a prisoner in one of those huts, hundreds of miles away from home?

'Okay,' the boss said. 'Thanks, Lock. Let's bring it back to our victim. From her video, it sounds like she grew up hearing stories about the mysterious disappearance of her great-grandad and that she decided to spend last summer in Warwickshire trying to find out what happened to him. We'll know more once the German police have contacted her family, which they should do today.

'Meanwhile, we know that she worked at Bourne Farm, strawberry picking, and that it's also where she died, so that has to be the key focus for our investigation. I want us to interview Harry and Caroline Cooper tomorrow. When and how did they employ Hannah, how well did they know her and – most importantly of all – why the fuck didn't they report her missing, or mention her as a possible victim when her body was found on the riverbank?'

Lock nodded. 'I agree it is odd that neither of the Coopers mentioned Hannah Weber when you spoke to them, but in the UK, partners or ex-partners account for sixty-one per cent of all female homicides. The data suggests that we should endeavour to discover whether Hannah was in a relationship during her time on the farm. Especially as strangulation cannot be ruled out as a cause of death.'

Rayan sat up. 'What's that?'

'Dr Edwards drew our attention to some damage to the hyoid bone and thyroid cartilage which *may* be consistent with strangulation,' Kat said with a dismissive gesture. 'But because of the severing of the head and the lack of soft tissue, it's almost impossible to be certain. It could be the result of blunt trauma.'

'But it is possible,' Rayan said thoughtfully. He studied the virtual image of Hannah Weber again. 'Interesting. She's twenty years old and has long brown hair.'

'So? What are you thinking?' Kat probed.

'I was listening to that podcast last night about the Aston Strangler, so I was thinking about the similarities between her and the other victims. They were all young white women with long brown hair, too. Two of the victims were murdered in their homes, but one was killed outside in a park.'

'She's nothing like the victims of the Aston Strangler,' Kat scoffed. 'He didn't chop people's heads off or bury them in clandestine graves.'

'I know, but on the podcast Dr Mike Bullington said that if the Aston Strangler was still at large then he wouldn't be able to stop killing, but he might be able to change the *modus operandi* or location of his murders.'

Kat's face flushed. 'You can listen to what you like in your own time for entertainment. But at work, you listen to me. And I am telling you that the Aston Strangler was Anthony Bridges. He was convicted by a jury and now he is dead. This case is nothing to do with that, do you hear me? *Nothing*. So, I want everyone—' she paused and swept the room with her eyes '—*everyone* to focus on the facts, and on Hannah Weber. We need to find out everything about her, her friends, enemies and yes, Lock, her lovers. The answers will be on the farm where she worked and died, not some headline-grabbing podcast. Is that clear?'

Rayan caught Professor Okonedo raising a surprised eyebrow. The boss could be a bit, well, bossy at times. But he'd never seen her this defensive or angry before. No, he corrected himself. She wasn't angry, she was upset. He watched her as she delegated the jobs for the next day, noticing the paleness of her skin, the puffiness around her eyes. The Aston Strangler had been a big case for her – she'd built a very successful career off the back of it – and this podcast had clearly bothered her.

She left the room with Lock, leaving Rayan, the professor and KFC behind.

'I'm guessing this isn't a good time to ask if she wants to do an interview for the podcast,' said KFC as they walked out together.

Rayan and Adaiba burst into nervous laughter.

'I'm only joking,' said KFC. 'That podcast has clearly got it in for her, so there's nothing to gain by accepting their request for an interview.'

'I agree,' said the professor, heading down the stone staircase. 'There's something about that show I don't like. The focus seems to be on proving that DCS Frank got it wrong, rather than getting justice for the victims. I don't trust the police, as you know, but Kat's one of the most principled people I've ever met. And the way they keep mentioning her . . . I don't know. There's something mean and misogynistic about it.'

'I agree the tone's off,' said Rayan as they reached reception. 'But it's a bit of a coincidence that another young woman with long brown hair was found strangled less than fifteen miles from Aston. And I don't believe in coincidences.'

'So, what are you going to do?' asked Adaiba, looking up at him with her beautiful dark eyes.

For a moment, he couldn't think, let alone speak. 'I'll do what I always do,' he said eventually. 'Keep an open mind.'

'See you tomorrow,' said KFC, heading for the door.

Rayan felt a spike of panic as Adaiba's eyes darted towards the car park outside. What could he say to keep the conversation going?

'Actually,' said Adaiba. 'I know you probably need to get home, but do you have a minute?'

'Er . . . yes, yes, of course.'

She glanced around the busy reception. 'Shall we walk in the grounds for a bit? There's something I want to ask you.'

CHAPTER TWENTY-SIX

The grounds of Leek Wootton HQ, 6.22pm

'I don't think I'll ever get used to this place,' said Adaiba, gesturing at the two hundred and fifty-three acres of landscaped gardens they walked within. 'It's more like the setting of a Jane Austen novel than a police station.'

Rayan glanced at her, a smile tugging at his lips. 'Don't tell me you're a Jane Austen fan? I thought you were more into gaming.'

'You can like gaming *and* novels, you know. They're just different ways of telling stories. To be honest, I prefer *Bridgerton*, but in moments of weakness, I have been known to watch *Pride and Prejudice*.'

'Which version?'

'*The* version. The one with Keira Knightley.'

'No way!' cried Rayan. 'Keira Knightley is not and never will be Elizabeth Bennet. The BBC series is the best.'

Adaiba looked up at him in surprise. 'I didn't have *you* down as a Jane Austen fan.'

Rayan shrugged. 'My sister loves costume dramas. When she was really ill they were one of the few things that made her feel safe, so we watched them all. Many times. My favourite is *Sense and Sensibility,* though, with Emma Thompson and Alan Rickman.'

'Oh, I *love* Alan Rickman in that.'

Rayan raised his eyebrows.

'Because Colonel Brandon is just so principled and good,' Adaiba clarified.

'Yes, it's the principles that always attract people to Alan Rickman.'

Adaiba let out a guilty laugh. 'Yes, it's definitely his principles.'

'You're big on principles, aren't you?'

She shrugged. 'I can't help it. It's just how I am.'

He stopped and turned to face her. 'That wasn't a criticism. In fact, quite the opposite.'

Adaiba missed a beat, then carried on walking down the path towards the woodland. The sun was low in the sky, bathing them in long golden slats of light while birds sang in the trees above. 'Talking of principles, I wanted to ask you a few questions about the future development of Lock as part of a review of his capabilities.' She held up her phone. 'You okay if I record this?'

Rayan waved his consent, trying not to sigh. So, she just wanted to talk about Lock. Of course she did.

'As his co-worker,' she continued, 'I was wondering how you'd feel if Lock had a physical presence?'

'A physical presence?' echoed Rayan. 'What, you mean like a robot?'

'I don't like the term "robot" because it has all sorts of connotations, but yes, I'm doing an options paper on the pros and cons of locating Lock within some sort of synthetic body.'

'And why would you want to do that?'

'Well, Lock thinks that his functions are severely limited by—'

'Lock *thinks?*'

'Well, he's made the observation that if he had a physical presence then he would be able to have a material impact on the world, and therefore have a better chance of achieving the objectives we set him.'

'You mean take even more of my job off me?'

Adaiba glanced up at his scowling face. 'Just the dangerous and dull bits. Remember, at Christmas he couldn't save the Coventry Crucifier because he was just a hologram. Or you or Debbie's baby, for that matter. You're lucky that Kat was there.'

'It wouldn't have been an issue if Kat had had a human partner with her rather than a hologram.'

'But it was Lock who located you. He helped save your life.'

'It was Kat and a paramedic who saved my life.'

'But Lock believes that if he'd had a body, he could have saved you himself.'

Rayan looked down at Adaiba. 'You know I'm not a fan of AI. So why are you asking me what I think?'

'I want to include the views of *all* the team.'

'And what did the others say?'

'I haven't asked them yet.'

'So, I'm the first?' Rayan tilted his head. 'My mum used to say that when you pick someone to ask for advice, then you've already decided what you want to do. I think you're asking me what I think because you have reservations yourself.'

'No, it's really not that deep. It's just that you were there in reception, so it was an opportunity to ask you for your thoughts.'

Rayan said nothing as they carried on walking.

Eventually Adaiba filled the silence. 'But you're right. I do have *some* reservations. The thing is, when I invented Lock, I wasn't trying to imitate humans: I wanted something that transcends the human body with all its material needs and weaknesses – something *better* than us.'

'So then don't do it. Stick to your original vision.'

She sighed as they reached the memorial garden. 'But look at all the police officers who've lost their lives in the line of duty,' she said, gesturing towards the granite plinths before them. 'Maybe Lock's right. If he had a body, then he and others like him could do all the dangerous jobs, potentially saving lives.'

'Or losing them. You created Lock, so you know that he will only do what he's ordered to do. In the wrong hands, an AI robot could be ordered to restrain someone, to hold them down or even shoot them.'

'Just like a real police officer.'

'That's not fair!'

Adaiba glared back. 'Isn't it?'

They stood in silence, their opposing views as fixed as the granite stones before them.

Rayan tried to think of something more conciliatory to say, but before he could speak, Adaiba looked up at the sky.

'It's starting to rain. We'd better head back.'

'Okay,' he conceded. And although every bone in his body told him to stay there, beneath the trees full of birdsong with Adaiba by his side, he dutifully followed her back towards the darkening car park, before they both went their separate ways.

CHAPTER TWENTY-SEVEN

DCS Kat Frank's home, Coleshill, 7.25pm

Kat had imagined Cam's homecoming many times. There were often variations in what she wore or said, but in every scenario she was always home, showered and freshly changed as she welcomed her son and his new girlfriend into her carefully prepared home, infused with the scent of candles and slow-cooked lamb.

Instead, she'd arrived home late in her crumpled work suit to find Cam and Gemma had got there before her. 'I'm sorry,' she apologised to Cam as she entered the front room. 'We found the head, so I had to wait while we identified the body.'

'As you do,' he joked. He gave her a quick one-armed man hug, before introducing Gemma, a woman with braided blonde hair and a huge smile who instantly enveloped Kat in a warm embrace. 'It's so lovely to meet you,' Gemma said, in a husky voice that carried the echo of frequent laughter. 'You too,' Kat replied, hoping she didn't smell of the morgue as she kissed Gemma's soft and scented cheek.

'You have *such* a lovely home,' Gemma went on, gesturing around the room. 'All these beams and period features. It's so cool.'

'Thanks,' said Kat, taking her damp coat off. 'I'm just sorry the weather's so rubbish. I was hoping we could sit out in the garden later, but I've never known such a wet spring.'

'It is too early to quantify how wet this year is compared to others, as neither the season nor the year is completed,' said Lock from where he hovered in the hall behind Kat. 'But March saw above-average rainfall and was the seventh wettest on record since 1836.'

'Wow,' said Gemma, looking past Kat. 'You must be Lock! Cam's told me all about you.' She moved forwards, as if about to hug him, then hesitated as she studied his form. 'Do you do hugs? Or do you prefer to shake hands?'

'Alas, as a mere hologram, I cannot "do" either.'

Gemma's face fell. 'Of course. I'm so sorry. I am sending you a virtual hug then.'

Lock raised his eyebrows. 'I was about to say that that sounds paradoxical, but I have just read a hundred and nineteen research papers and articles which suggest that the feelings associated with physical hugs can be experienced and even amplified by virtual hugs offered in the digital space.'

'Well, I'll send you another one then,' Gemma said, releasing a deep, throaty laugh as she mimicked a hugging motion.

Kat was surprised to see a rare smile appear on Lock's face. Perhaps even holograms liked the attention of younger women.

'Good to see you again, Lock,' said Cam.

'You too,' replied Lock. 'You look very well.'

Kat followed his gaze. She'd been a bit worried about her son at Christmas – was he eating properly and getting enough sleep? (*Of course not, Mum, I'm a student.*) But now he really did look well. Resisting the urge to hug him again (she didn't want to embarrass him), she brushed his muscular shoulder with her hand. 'You okay if I have a quick shower and get changed before we sit down and talk properly?'

'Of course, no rush,' said Cam. 'We're just chilling.'

'Great. I've roasted a leg of lamb so it's ready whenever you are. Just let me know what time suits you guys.'

'Oh, actually, Mum, about that . . .' began Cam.

Kat saw Gemma shoot him a warning glance.

'No, it's okay,' he continued. 'Mum, Gemma's a vegetarian, remember?'

Kat turned to Gemma, mortified. 'Oh God, really? I'm so sorry, I didn't know.'

'I did text you, Mum.'

No, you bloody didn't, she wanted to say. As if she'd forget something that important!

'Honestly, it's fine,' said Gemma. 'I can just eat salad or bread or whatever you serve with it. I eat anything – apart from meat, obvs! Please don't go to any trouble just for me.'

'Okay, well I was planning a Greek meze, so I've got lots of vegetarian options. I'm just sorry I didn't know.'

'You *did* know, Mum,' Cam muttered, rolling his eyes at Gemma.

Cheeky fucker. God knows she loved her son, but how *dare* he imply that she was a middle-aged mum with memory problems. She chose not to say anything – she didn't want to embarrass him in front of Gemma – but as she headed for the bathroom, she scrolled back through his messages so she could send him proof of his error. Instead, she found a text that clearly said '*Btw Gemma is a vegetarian*'.

Kat frowned at the brightly coloured vegetable emojis that accompanied her son's message. How had she missed that? She checked the date and time it was sent – a couple of nights ago when she'd had dinner with Lock. Just after he'd played her the podcast.

She put the phone down and switched the shower on. The

shock of hearing about the case again after all these years had thrown her a bit.

A bit? she imagined John observing.

Well, a lot, she conceded. In fact, she didn't just feel thrown, she felt scattered; unravelled. She struggled to find the right word for the strange feeling snaking through her gut, before finally putting a name to it: fear. She was afraid. That was why she'd missed the text.

Kat buried her work clothes in the laundry basket, telling herself she had nothing to worry about as she pushed them down as far as they would go. There were only two other people who knew what had really happened on the case, and they were both dead.

She stepped into the scalding hot shower. *It's just a podcast,* she told herself over and over again as she turned her face towards the water. *No one will listen to it, and no one else will care.*

But it didn't stop the sickness in her gut, nor rinse away the fear.

Since John died, they hardly ever ate around the dining table. It was yet another habit Cam and Kat had silently formed: dinners shared in front of the TV to avoid the empty chair between them. But tonight, Kat had spread out the food on the large oak table in the front room, and once more laid three places. Lock had no need of cutlery or food, but she was glad of his presence, as with him sitting beside her, they formed a new shape of four. Although it was slightly odd to see him dressed in a casual grey tracksuit – he had insisted on 'changing' when he observed that 'everybody else has', making Gemma roar with laughter when his image changed right before them.

Kat watched her son as he served his girlfriend more salad, laughing at a story Gemma was telling about one of their professors.

She nodded in all the right places, but she wasn't really listening – she was too busy watching Cam. He kept glancing at Gemma to check her reactions to everything, touching her arm or hand at every opportunity as if he couldn't quite believe that she was sitting here beside him. Earlier, she'd walked in on them watching Netflix while Cam had brushed out Gemma's plaits, removing her hair grips with a gentleness that made Kat's heart ache. Cam seemed so happy she could honestly cry. He'd had such a shit couple of years with his dad's illness and death, and then his exams and the kidnapping and everything. Her boy deserved to be happy, he really did. Even if that meant he wasn't her boy anymore.

'What do you reckon, Mum?'

'Sorry?' Kat snapped back into focus as Cam turned to her.

'Gemma was just asking whether Lock will always be a hologram or if there are plans to make him a robot in the future?'

'I – I don't know. That's up to Professor Okonedo. I don't think it really matters, to be honest.'

'It matters to me,' Lock said quietly. 'Without a body, there is no locus for my being, so I have no autonomy.'

'Wow,' said Gemma, putting her fork down. 'I'd never thought about it like that before. It's just like the whole brain in a vat debate.'

'The whole *what* now?' said Kat.

'You know, that famous debate in philosophy? Some philosophers argue that the mind is an independent entity that can exist without a physical body, while others believe that the mind is inseparable from the body and cannot exist independently.'

'Oh, *that* famous debate,' said Kat, bemused.

'Gemma's brilliant at philosophy,' Cam said proudly. 'She got a first on her last essay.'

Lock stared at Gemma. 'I have just read 4,121 articles on

dualism versus monism. They were most useful, thank you for the reference.'

'I would ask you what you think of them,' said Gemma, her cheeks dimpling. 'But that would be to presume that you can think.'

'To have a thought is to think, and I have many thoughts.'

'I think, therefore I am?'

'I wish it were as simple as Descartes implies,' Lock said quietly.

'Well, if ever you get a body, then I promise I will give you the BIGGEST of hugs. Until then, I've been thinking, and I reckon you should try air-kissing.'

'Air-kissing?'

'Yeah, it's something old people do when they say hello or goodbye. They kind of kiss the air by the other person's cheeks, so as not to ruin their make-up or whatever. Like this.' She turned to Cam and made a loud '*mwah*' sound as she kissed the air beside first one cheek, and then the next. 'And then the other person does it back,' she explained. Cam repeated the movement and sound effects, before they both dissolved into giggles.

'Thank you, I will try that,' said Lock.

Kat smiled and started to scrape the leftover lamb onto one plate.

'We can wash up, Mum,' offered Cam.

'No, you're all right. You enjoy the last of the wine. I've got work tomorrow.'

'How is work, by the way?' he asked. 'There's a lot on my feed about that Aston Strangler podcast. Is everything okay?'

'Yes, why wouldn't it be?'

'It's just, a lot of people are asking whether it was a miscarriage of justice, and some of it is a bit, well, personal and I . . .'

'It's just a podcast, Cam. And those people on social media haven't got a clue what they're talking about. Just ignore it.'

'But—'

'I *said*, just ignore it.'

Beneath the table, she saw Gemma give Cam's leg a warning squeeze.

'Pudding anyone?' Kat asked, before leaving the room, her cheeks burning. She carried the plates into the kitchen, hands trembling as she placed them on the side. Worried that Cam might follow her with more questions, she went to the downstairs toilet and ran her hands under the cold tap. The face that stared back at her in the mirror was pale and drawn.

'You're forty-fucking-nine years old,' she scolded herself. 'Get a grip.' But as she lifted her chin, the glow from the bathroom light caught the right side of her jaw.

The scar was still there – if you knew where to look.

Kat finished the washing up, and nearly jumped out of her skin when she turned to see Lock standing behind her.

'Jesus, you gave me a fright.'

'My apologies, I did not mean to frighten you. I just wanted to check that you were okay.'

'Of course I am. Why wouldn't I be?'

'Because every time someone mentions the Aston Strangler podcast you become agitated and defensive.'

'I do not!'

'And yet your heart rate has just increased by eighteen per cent.'

'That is because you are being fucking annoying.'

'Because I expressed my concern about the impact of the podcast on your health and well-being? I do not see how that could be annoying.'

'That's because you are just a machine.'

Lock's face seemed to harden. 'You say that like it is a shortcoming.

But as a machine, I focus on facts, not emotions. And although I respect your position as a DCS, I am perturbed at the issues highlighted by the podcast, and how a man could be convicted of such a serious offence with so little evidence.'

Kat took a step closer to Lock, so that their faces were just inches apart. 'You're *perturbed?* Do you even know what that word means?'

'It means to feel troubled in mind. To feel anxiety, or concern. To be unsettled.'

Kat raised her eyebrows. 'But how can you feel troubled if you don't have a mind?'

Lock drew back his head, as if inhaling the air or perhaps absorbing her barbed comment. 'I know enough to see that *your* mind is troubled. And that troubles me. Especially as Professor Okonedo has always instructed me to trust you above all others.'

Kat's jaw dropped. She was about to express her outrage at the idea that Lock – a mere *machine* – might not trust *her*. But then she caught herself. She was a DCS, for fuck's sake. She didn't need to prove herself to anyone, least of all Lock.

She waved a dismissive hand. 'I don't have time for this. We've got an early start in the morning – we're interviewing Harry Cooper at Bourne Farm first thing – so thank you for your feedback, but I'm going to bed.'

'Goodnight,' said Lock. He paused, then added, 'Sleep well.' He lowered his head towards hers, his mouth just inches from her cheek.

Kat jumped back. 'What are you *doing*?'

'Air-kissing, like Gemma suggested.'

'You don't kiss *colleagues*.'

Lock frowned. 'But at Christmas you said we were friends.'

'I don't kiss my friends either.'

'Then who do you kiss?'

Kat stared up at him. 'Goodnight, Lock,' she finally said, and hurried towards the stairs before he could ask any more questions.

CHAPTER TWENTY-EIGHT

Outside DCS Kat Frank's house, Coleshill, 9.05pm

His knuckles are bruised from punching the seat of the car. He should have anticipated the son coming home. He should have remembered that some sons choose to visit their families in the holidays; that some mums still let them.

Tonight was supposed to be The Night – he's been psyching himself up for it all day. But he can't carry out his plan with her bloody son in the house.

He wants to scream with frustration. And he's not a screamer.

He wonders if DCS Kat Frank is. He closes his eyes, imagining the sound; her eyes wide and frightened as she pleads and apologises. He breathes in and out, trying to hold on to the image and his ultimate purpose.

But the delay is infuriating. How long will her son be here? One night? Two? A week?

Then, in the dark, silent street, he hears the words of Muhammad Ali. Don't count the days. Make the days count.

He repeats the quote over and over as he takes out his phone and opens up his apps, liking, replying to and sharing every single negative post he can find about DCS Kat Frank.

The car lights up with his notifications, and as he counts the likes, replies and reposts, for the first time in days he smiles.

CHAPTER TWENTY-NINE

DCS Kat Frank's car, 17 April, 8.20am

'You asked me to remind you to call McLeish to update him on the case this morning,' said Lock, looking as irritatingly perfect as he always did. God, sometimes she wished *she* was a hologram. Imagine not needing any sleep.

Kat opened the car window, hoping the fresh air would wake her up before she gave her boss a ring. Maybe she wasn't used to having people in the house, but she'd hardly slept a wink last night. It seemed that every footstep, every cough, every opening and closing door had made her jolt wide awake, as if the alarm had gone off. She'd tried to relax by listening to one of her sleeping apps, but the rain and whale soundtracks were no match for her hyper-vigilant state.

He's dead, she'd told herself. *There is nothing to be afraid of.*

But still she couldn't sleep, so because she was a complete *idiot* she'd checked her social media and clicked on a thread about the podcast before falling down a rabbit hole of comments and conspiracy theories, many of them personal and downright abusive about her role in the case. She told herself it meant nothing – sticks and stones and all that – but some of the words and memes had been genuinely disturbing. And now she had a real case to solve, and a full day of interviews and briefings to get through.

She took a deep gulp of the cool morning air. Best get the call to McLeish over and done with.

'McLeish,' her boss barked as he answered his phone. There was no 'good morning', no enquiries as to her well-being or commentary on the weather: just the announcement of his name and the implicit instruction to cut to the chase.

'We've ID'd the body from the River Bourne, sir,' Kat said. 'Hannah Weber, a twenty-year-old German woman who was working as a strawberry picker on the farm.'

'German? Shit. That's all I need, the bloody *Bundespolizei* marking our homework. Have you notified them?'

'Yes, I made contact last night and they've agreed to notify her parents.'

McLeish sighed, filling her car with the sound of a deflating paddling pool. 'I'll have to brief the minister *and* the Foreign Office. They won't like this. A young foreign lass murdered on our watch. Doesn't look good.'

'Being murdered doesn't feel good, either. Sir.'

'I know that, Kat. Jesus, I've got two girls of my own. I just mean we'll be under pressure to find the bastard who did it *ASA* fucking *P*. What have you got so far?'

Kat cleared her throat. 'We've got several lines of enquiry. Mr Walker, the fisherman who found her, and Harry Cooper, the man who employed her, are just two persons of interest. But it's still early days.'

'Most women are killed by their boyfriends or husbands.'

'I know,' said Kat. 'Sixty-one per cent actually.'

'You're beginning to sound like that bloody machine.'

Kat glanced at Lock in the passenger seat, who stared impassively ahead.

'Well, I'm on my way to Bourne Farm now to find out a bit more about Hannah Weber and whether she had any boyfriends – or girlfriends. I'll re-interview the Coopers and as many fellow strawberry pickers as I can.'

'What about the press?'

'Er . . . we're looking at doing a press conference this afternoon once I've finished at the farm,' she improvised.

'Okay. Anything else I need to know?'

'No,' said Kat. 'I'll keep you posted.'

And then he was gone. No goodbyes or pep talks: McLeish had conveyed his message and was on to the next thing. Kat shook her head. For all his criticism of Lock, sometimes her boss could be just as task-focused and inhuman as her AI partner.

'Was that honest?' asked Lock.

Kat pulled into Bourne Farm and turned to face him. 'What do you mean?'

'When McLeish asked was there anything else he needed to know, you said no. You didn't mention that there was a possibility that Hannah Weber could have been strangled.'

Good God, Lock was getting as bad as DI Hassan. 'I didn't mention it,' Kat said, her voice serrated and slow, 'because it wasn't relevant. It is a theoretical possibility, not a fact.'

'But the omission was dishonest.'

'No, Lock. The omission was my *judgement*. If I'd mentioned the *theoretical* possibility that strangulation cannot be ruled out – *yet* – then all sorts of hares would have been set running.'

'Hares?' Lock blinked. 'Ah. I understand that this means you are concerned that people might metaphorically set off in the wrong direction.'

'Exactly,' she said, undoing her seat belt.

'But what if it isn't the wrong direction?'

Kat climbed out of the car and slammed the door shut. 'Trust me. It is.'

CHAPTER THIRTY

Interviewer: DCS Kat Frank (KF)
Interviewee: Harry Cooper (HC)
Date: 17 April, 8.52am
Location: Bourne Farm

KF: Thanks for making the time to speak to us, Mr Cooper. I realise how busy you are, but yesterday we managed to identify the body that we found on your property, and so we're hoping you can tell us a bit more about the victim and why someone might have wanted to murder her.

HC: How long will this take?

KF: Hopefully not too long. Do you recognise this photo? For the tape, I am showing Mr Cooper the passport photo of the victim. Image HW3.
[slides across photo of Hannah Weber]

HC: Vaguely. No one looks like their passport photo, do they, but she looks a bit like one of our strawberry pickers from last year. A German girl, maybe?

KF: Yes. Her name was Hannah Weber. And according to your own records, she worked for you last summer for just over five weeks.

HC: If you say so.

KF: Your records say so. They also say she was paid for each of those five weeks, but there is no record of payment for the sixth. Even though she worked for two days that week, when she picked sixteen punnets and so would have been owed £80. Is that when she went missing? There are no records of her picking strawberries the next day, 17 July, so did she go missing the night before or that morning?

HC: No idea.

KF: Do you mean you don't remember, or that you don't care?

HC: I mean that I had no idea she even went missing.

KF: You weren't concerned when she didn't turn up for work?

HC: Like I told you, people come and go all the time. Some stay a few days, some a few weeks, others a few months. It's not a big deal.

KF: It is to her parents. The German police are notifying them now. She was only twenty years old.

HC: If I rang the police every time someone didn't turn up for work, you lot would be here every day.

KF: Perhaps, but weren't you worried when she didn't collect the money she was owed?

HC: *[shrugs]*

KF: Did she have any particular friends among the strawberry pickers that might remember her?

HC: Not mates – she wasn't part of a big group like the Nepalese. She was the only German so was kind of by herself when she arrived. But then she started going out with a Polish lad.

KF: She had a boyfriend? Can you remember his name?

HC: Nah, it was something unpronounceable. But he's on our books so you should be able to find him. We don't get many Poles these days, since Brexit. They come from places like Indonesia and Nepal and all sorts now.

KF: Did she seem happy with him?

HC: Who knows what makes women happy? He was a bit of a scruffbag to be honest. I don't know what she or the others saw in him. He was a total fruit fly.

KF: Fruit fly?

HC: The farming version of a barfly. He worked his way through all the pretty girls like a fruit fly goes through fruit.

KF: Did that cause arguments? Was she jealous of any of his exes, or were they jealous of her?

HC: I'm a farmer, DCS Frank. I haven't got time to get involved in all the dramas that happen when a bunch of twenty-somethings live together – who used the last of the milk, who didn't do the washing up or who shagged who. What people get up to in their own time is their business. As long as they turn up in the field on time and get the strawberries off the plants before they spoil, I don't give a shit what they get up to.

KF: But we're not talking about who didn't do the washing up. Hannah Weber was murdered. Can you think of anyone she fell out with, and who might have wanted to cause her harm?

HC: No.

KF: *[pauses]* Were you aware of the videos she was posting?

HC: The people who work here are always filming or taking selfies of themselves to share with their friends back home. I don't take any notice.

KF: What *do* you take notice of, Mr Cooper?

HC: I'm a farmer. I don't have time to take notice of anything but the weather, my crops, the animals and my income.

KF: And what about a partner? Do you have any time for them?

HC: What the hell has that got to do with you? Look, is this going to take much longer because I—

KF: Need to get back to the farm? Yes, you've made that quite clear, Mr Cooper. Okay, we'll leave it there for now. But I might have more questions once I've spoken to her boyfriend.

HC: *[curses under his breath]*

INTERVIEW CONCLUDED

CHAPTER THIRTY-ONE

Interviewer: DCS Kat Frank (KF)
Interviewee: Alojzy Bratkowski (AB)
Date: 17 April, 9.45am
Location: By phone

KF: Hello, Mr Bratkowski? My name is DCS Kat Frank, I am calling from Warwickshire Police in England.

AB: The police? England? Is everything okay?

KF: I have a few questions to ask you as part of an inquiry I am leading, but first, can I just confirm your full name is Alojzy Bratkowski and that in May and June of last year you worked on Bourne Farm picking strawberries?

AB: Yes, I can confirm that. I was entitled to work, I had a permit, I can prove it.

KF: That won't be necessary. I'm afraid I am ringing to tell you some bad news. We recently found a body on the grounds of the farm, and I regret to inform you that that body has been identified as Hannah Weber.

AB: Hannah? Hannah's *dead?* Seriously?

KF: Are you all right? Do you need a moment?

AB: No, it's fine. It's just . . . *gówno.* What happened? How did she die? Oh my God, I can't believe that I am saying these words.

KF: I am afraid that she was murdered. Her dismembered body was found buried.

AB: Murdered? *Hannah? [hyperventilates]*

KF: I'm sorry I have to tell you this on the phone, but because you are in Poland . . . Is there anyone with you, Mr Bratkowski? No? Then can I suggest you take a moment to take some deep breaths. Breathe in through your nose to the count of four, then out again to the count of four. That's it. And again. A simple trick but it really does help. Well done. Okay now?

AB: *[crying]* I can't believe she's dead. That someone *murdered* her. She was such a lovely person. So very kind.

KF: How well did you know her?

AB: I only knew her for a couple of months, but it's quite an intense time working on a farm. Because you live and work together, you really get to know each other. You bond with all sorts of people you wouldn't normally talk to.

KF: Hannah was your girlfriend, is that correct?

AB: Girlfriend? No. We were just good friends.

KF: Oh. I was told you were dating her. That you dated several of the girls on the farm.

AB: *[laughs]* Let me guess who told you that. The barmy farmer.

KF: Mr Cooper told me.

AB: *[snorts]* Some of the girls used to ask me to pretend to be their boyfriend just to keep him away. I went along with it. I'm gay so it's no skin off my nose, and we used to have a laugh about it.

KF: I'm sorry, what do you mean, 'just to keep him away'?

AB: The guy who ran the farm, Harry. He probably spent too long with tractors and sheep, because his eyes used to pop out of his head whenever a pretty girl joined the farm. It was a bit awkward what with him being the boss and everything, so when he took a fancy to someone, I'd pretend to be their boyfriend and then he'd back off.

KF: Back off? Was his behaviour ever inappropriate?

AB: He didn't say or do anything, but it was like he couldn't take his eyes off the pretty ones. He was kind of intense, you know? He was one of those guys who's so uncomfortable around women that it makes *you* feel uncomfortable.

KF: I'm going to ask you a question now, and I want you to think very carefully about the answer before you give it. Do you think that Mr Cooper could have harmed Hannah Weber?

AB: *[pauses]* I've never understood why any man harms anyone, so you're probably asking the wrong person. He struck me as an awkward, lonely guy rather than a dangerous guy, but I wasn't his type, so he didn't creep me out the way he did the girls. You should probably ask them.

KF: I will. And if you give me their names, you should know that I'll ask each woman to verify what you've just said about you only pretending to be their boyfriend.

AB: Of course, that's fine.

KF: Do you remember anything about when Hannah went missing?

AB: Er . . . I remember being surprised when she didn't

turn up for work one day. It was the middle of the week, I think, and she hadn't said she was leaving or anything. Mrs Cooper said she'd had some family issues and had decided to go home.

KF: Mrs Cooper said that? And had Hannah taken her stuff with her?

AB: I guess so. She slept in a caravan with the Nepalese girls, and no one said otherwise. I missed her – we all did – but I knew her great-grandmother was in a hospice, so I just presumed she'd passed away. It never occurred to me that something could have happened to Hannah . . . *[exhales]* Will there be a funeral? Do her family know? She seemed pretty close to them. She was a really good person. I can't believe she's dead. *[voice breaks]*

KF: I'm so sorry that you had to find out like this. Please reach out to a friend or family member and make sure that you aren't alone for the next few days. You've had a terrible shock, so don't underestimate the impact this will have on you.

AB: *[cries]* Thank you. And please let me know if you find out who did it. And if there is any way I can pay my respects to the family . . . I'd like to send them flowers or a card if I can.

KF: Of course. Take care, and thank you for your help. We'll be in touch.

INTERVIEW CONCLUDED

CHAPTER THIRTY-TWO

Bourne Farm, 11.32am

Kat ended the final call on the list and slipped her phone back into her pocket. 'Well,' she said to Lock. 'Rayan and I have spoken to ten of the seasonal workers now, and they all confirm Alojzy's version of events. He pretended to be Hannah's boyfriend so that Harry Cooper wouldn't pay her so much attention, so I think we can safely rule him out.'

'On the basis of anecdotes?' queried Lock.

'On the basis that several other witnesses have confirmed his version of events.'

'The other strawberry pickers were not witnesses – they did not see the murder. And they have not verified Alojzy's innocence, merely confirmed that he appeared to be friends with Hannah, based upon what they saw or heard as fellow workers. You yourself acknowledged that sixty-one per cent of female murder victims are killed by their husbands or boyfriends, and this statistic suggests that we should have a higher threshold of suspicion for anyone alleged to be her boyfriend, even if others deny it. It would certainly warrant a visit in person and more detailed questioning of Alojzy's alibi.'

Kat shook her head. 'It certainly does *not* warrant the time and expense of a visit to Poland just to confirm what he and ten other strawberry pickers have told us. And I heard it in his voice – Alojzy was genuinely shocked and upset to hear that Hannah was dead.'

'Human emotions can be feigned,' said Lock. 'The entire film industry is built upon this fact.'

'He wasn't acting.'

'But how can you know that?'

'I just do.'

'You mean you "feel" it.'

'Same thing.'

'It really isn't. That is why human beings developed the rule of law: so that individuals who were accused of a crime could only be convicted on the basis of evidence, rather than feelings or hearsay.'

'Thank you, Lock. I am well aware of how the legal system works.'

'So, who is your prime suspect now? Harry Cooper?'

Kat glanced up at the farmhouse. 'Possibly. I'd like to speak to his mum, though, to try and get a more rounded picture.'

'I detect doubt in your voice pattern, yet Harry Cooper is a single male who lives at home with his mother, and there is anecdotal evidence that he was interested in Hannah Weber. He also owns the land that her body was buried in, which, as well as giving him access, is consistent with the proximity strategy that the killer has so far exhibited.'

Kat screwed up her face. 'On paper, all of that is true. But everyone I spoke to confirmed that Harry Cooper was a figure of fun or pity, rather than fear. He has no criminal record and hasn't demonstrated an ounce of anxiety about the murder. He's just irritated that we're in his way. Although I agree we should take a closer look and see if he has an alibi for the night that Hannah went missing. We can ask him while he shows us around the accommodation.' She nodded towards the 'pickers' village' – a converted field behind the farmhouse, filled with mobile homes and caravans. Harry Cooper had agreed to meet them there once he'd finished checking the lambs.

They started to walk down the path, Kat's shoes crunching against the gravel, still damp from recent rain. She glanced over at Lock's hologram, which moved alongside her yet made no sound. Behind him, Harry Cooper was stomping towards them in his wellies, his face as dark as the clouds above.

'I've got fifteen minutes,' he announced, not breaking his stride as he overtook them on the path. 'One of my cows is calving, so I'll need to get back.' He reached the metal gate to the pickers' village and wrenched it open. 'They're all empty at the moment, but I've got twelve people arriving next week for the start of the season, so I'd be grateful if you could do what you need to do today so that we can bring the cleaners in to prep them.'

Kat looked at the rather battered mobile homes and sighed. 'So much has changed this century,' she said. 'We have computers in our phones, Alexa in our homes and even holograms at work. Yet still we have overseas workers living in caravans to pick fruit from our farms.'

'Not for much longer,' said Harry. 'Tech companies in Israel have designed fruit-picking drones, and in Chile, flying robots use artificial intelligence and machine learning to detect ripe apples before pulling the fruit from the trees. The dirty, dull and dangerous jobs that were once carried out by slaves, prisoners or migrants will increasingly be done by machines. Just like your hologram here.'

'Lock doesn't just do the dirty, dull and dangerous jobs,' said Kat, bristling.

'Well, he should, if you ask me. Think of the money we could save on all this,' replied Harry, gesturing to the communal shower facilities, laundry and shared kitchen hut. 'It costs me a small fortune to make sure all this complies with the government's temporary accommodation guidance, health and safety laws and all that crap. I had to buy ten mobile homes that aren't allowed to accommodate more than five people each, *and* I have to split them by gender and try to keep friendship or nationality groups together. It's a bloody nightmare.'

'Which one was Hannah's?' asked Kat.

He gestured towards a beige mobile home in the second row without hesitation. 'She slept in there with a few of the Nepalese girls.'

Kat made a mental note that although Harry claimed to barely remember Hannah's face, name or when she had gone missing, he clearly remembered where she had slept.

'May I look inside?'

He fumbled about in his pockets and pulled out a large set of keys.

Kat raised her eyebrows. 'Do you have keys to all the mobile homes?'

'Of course I do. I rent them out to the seasonal workers, but they belong to me. I have to get them cleaned up when people leave, ready for the next lot.'

'You *charge* them to stay in the caravans?'

'They're mobile homes, and they're equipped with heating, water, Wi-Fi and bedding, so of course I bloody charge them. I'm running a business here, not a charity.' He unlocked the door and gestured for Kat to go in. 'And sixty-seven pounds a week is a bloody good deal.'

She climbed the steps, ducking her head as she stood inside and looked around. There was a table in the middle by a small kitchenette, and two bunk-like sleeping areas either side, in the beige-and-brown colour scheme peculiar to caravans. It looked clean, but smelt stale. Kat imagined it would be okay for a weekend away, but she couldn't imagine living in such cramped conditions with four other strangers for months on end.

She turned to where Harry Cooper remained outside by the door. 'Did Hannah leave anything behind when she went missing?'

He frowned. 'Not that I know of. No one handed anything in. Like I say, I didn't think she was missing, so I didn't ask where her stuff was. I just assumed she'd left.'

'Alojzy said that your mum told him she'd returned home to deal with a family matter.'

'Yeah, well, he would say that, wouldn't he?'

'Meaning?'

'It's always the boyfriend, isn't it? In humans, anyway. It's funny, but male sheep or bulls never attack their females.'

'Alojzy said he wasn't her boyfriend.'

'I repeat, he would say that, wouldn't he?'

'Do you have any evidence to justify your suspicions?' asked Lock.

'Nope. That's your job, isn't it? Mine is farming. Speaking of which, I need to get back.'

'One more thing before you go, Mr Cooper,' Kat said. 'Do you have an alibi for the night of 16 July?'

He froze. Then turned very slowly back to face her. '*Alibi*? Are you serious?'

'I am always serious when I am investigating a murder.'

'I . . . well, I'd need to check the calendar, but since Dad died last September, I'm always working. It wasn't Christmas, so I'm pretty sure I wasn't out eating or drinking or *living* or anything.' He let out a wry laugh. 'I can probably find a sheep or cow to vouch for me.'

'I'm afraid it'll need to be a human,' said Kat. 'And preferably not your mum.'

Harry Cooper swallowed. 'I'll try, but you can't really think I had anything to do with this?' When Kat didn't reply, he ran a hand through his hair. 'Jesus. If I end up in prison just because I'm a prisoner on this farm . . .Talk about fucking irony.'

'Check your diary, talk to some of the other workers and we'll be in touch tomorrow,' said Kat.

They watched him as he strode back down the gravel path towards the calving sheds.

'That is a very angry young man,' said Lock.

'It's worse than that. I think Harry Cooper is terribly sad.' Kat gazed at the acres of land that surrounded them: a patchwork of green, yellow and brown fields, edged with hills that in this light almost looked blue. 'Living here must be like being trapped in a never-ending episode of *The Archers*.'

'*The Archers?*' echoed Lock. 'Ah,' he said after a few moments. 'A contemporary drama in a rural setting, it is the world's longest-running present-day drama, and BBC Radio Four's most listened-to programme, with the exception of the news. Although I have observed that whenever it comes on the radio, you rapidly switch it off.'

'I can't *stand* it. I hate that theme tune.'

'"Barwick Green" was composed in 1924 by Arthur Wood and is commonly described as "a delightful maypole dance" which evokes the pastoral charm of the show's rural setting.'

Kat shook her head. 'It evokes far more than that. Every time I hear it I . . .' Her voice trailed off, and her hand went to her throat. 'Come on,' she said finally. 'I promised McLeish I'd hold a press conference this afternoon. Although God knows what I'm going to tell them.'

CHAPTER THIRTY-THREE

Leek Wootton HQ, Media Conference Room, 3pm

Kat stifled a groan as she walked into the press room. Despite the short notice and late hour, it looked like every local paper and several nationals and broadcasters had sent a journalist or camera crew. She was so knackered that she'd hoped that no one would turn up. *I guess it's not every day that Warwickshire Police announce the identity of a headless, handless body*, she thought, hating the fact that this tragic death had become just another sensational headline that she was about to feed.

Karen-from-Comms took one look at her face and shook her head. 'Relax, you're performing an important public duty, not going to war. Remember your media training.'

How could she forget? She'd spent an entire day being filmed while she endured mock media interviews, then had to watch them all back as a 'communications expert' picked her performance apart. Nevertheless, she took a deep breath and repeated the mantras that had been drummed into her: *welcome every interview as an opportunity to get your message across; focus on the three points you want to make, and regardless of what they ask, push those points in every answer; remember, you aren't speaking to journalists, you're speaking to the public.*

'Ready?'

Kat nodded and followed KFC as she led the way to the raised table at the front and effortlessly brought the room to order like a firm barmaid in a busy pub.

'Good afternoon,' said Kat into the waiting silence. 'Thank you for coming along today. I'm DCS Kat Frank, and, as you know, five days ago a local fisherman discovered the partial remains of a body on the banks of the River Bourne. Two days ago, we located the missing parts of that body, and following an autopsy and reconstruction, today we can confirm that the victim was a young woman called Hannah Weber.'

Kat indicated the screen behind her as an image of Hannah appeared: a selfie taken on the farm, her long hair blowing in the wind and the sun illuminating her smiling face. 'Hannah Weber was a twenty-year-old student from Germany who came to England last summer to work as a strawberry picker on Bourne Farm in Shustoke. Her parents have been informed of this tragic news and are understandably keen to ensure that the person who killed their daughter is brought to justice.

'We believe that she was murdered on the evening or night of 16 July, at the site where her body was found, so we are asking all local people to look at this picture of Hannah and ask themselves, did they know her? Did they ever see her? We are particularly interested in her movements on the days before her death, and whether anybody saw Hannah talk or argue with anyone on or near the banks of the River Bourne, or perhaps saw someone acting suspiciously in the days after her brutal murder. Any information, no matter how small, will be invaluable to our inquiry, and help us bring the killer of this young woman to justice.' Kat sat back and nodded to KFC to put the contact details up on the screen.

Hands shot into the air.

'Dave Peters, *Daily Mail*,' said a tall, skinny man at the front. 'You said the body was dismembered. Is it true she was decapitated and her hands chopped off?'

'Yes,' said Kat, grimacing.

'With an axe?'

'We cannot confirm the weapon at this point.'

'But either way, there's a murderer on the loose in the Midlands?'

Kat resisted rolling her eyes at the blatant fishing for an alliterative headline. 'Nobody is "on the loose",' she said carefully. 'We are focused on finding the murderer.'

'But you haven't found him yet?'

'No,' said Kat, teeth clenched tight with irritation. 'We only discovered the body five days ago, and our investigation is ongoing.'

'Like I said,' murmured Dave Peters to the person next to him. 'On the loose.'

KFC gestured towards another journalist, Laura Richards from the *Daily Mirror*.

'Do you have any suspects?' she asked. 'Are you holding anyone to help with your enquiries?'

'Not at present,' replied Kat. 'That's why we are appealing to the public for help. The inquiry is still in its early stages.'

'So, just to clarify, the man who murdered, decapitated and dismembered Hannah Weber's body,' Laura Richards said, 'has been free to murder other young women for nearly a year?'

'There is no evidence to suggest that the killer has attacked anyone else during this time,' said Kat firmly.

'Just like there was no evidence that the strangled girls in Aston were linked?' piped up a voice from the back.

Kat peered over the faces before her to see the blue hair of Jay Cooper, the latest recruit to *Warwickshire News*.

Sensing the ripple of interest in the room, Jay continued, 'When

Angela Hall was found strangled to death in Aston Park, you were in charge of the case, DCS Frank, and at a press conference you assured the public that it was an isolated act of violence. When Roisin McCauley was found strangled in her home just two months later you insisted the two murders were not linked. In fact, it wasn't until another woman, Charlotte Walker, was strangled to death that you finally realised the cases might be connected, and it took the death of a fourth woman for you to charge Anthony Bridges with their murders.'

'What's your question, Jay?' KFC intervened.

'My question is, you were wrong then, DCS Frank, so why should the public trust you now?'

'Because the two cases are completely different,' Kat insisted, trying not to sound annoyed. 'There is absolutely no evidence – *no evidence at all* – to suggest that the wider public are at risk from this person, and, quite frankly, it is unfair of you to frighten people into thinking otherwise.'

She felt KFC stiffen beside her and, too late, Kat remembered another mantra: *never attack or criticise the media.*

She cleared her throat before continuing. 'Four women were murdered in Aston: Angela Hall, Roisin McCauley, Charlotte Walker and Rachel Murray, and each death was a tragic, incalculable loss to their families and friends. But as more evidence became available, my team and I *did* catch the man responsible, Anthony Bridges, and I am confident we will find and apprehend the killer of Hannah Weber too.'

'But questions have been raised about the safety of that conviction,' commented another journalist. 'What do you say to that?'

Kat shrugged. 'People are free to raise questions, but the fact is, Anthony Bridges went on trial and was found guilty by a jury of his peers and sentenced to life imprisonment by a high court judge.'

'Is your AI Detective Lock involved in this case?' asked Dave Peters from the *Daily Mail*.

'Yes, he is,' said Kat, relieved to be on safer ground. 'AIDE Lock means we have access to the very latest technology, and that's one of the reasons I'm confident we will find and apprehend the killer.'

'Am I right in thinking that AIDE Lock is the only AI detective in the UK – possibly the world?' asked Jay Cooper.

'Yes, we are very fortunate to be partners with Warwick University on this groundbreaking innovation,' replied Kat, smiling.

'And do Hannah Weber's parents know that the death of their beloved daughter is being investigated by a discredited detective and an experimental AI hologram?'

'Yes, they do,' Kat fired back, realising her mistake as soon as the words left her mouth. 'I mean, they know that I am leading the case, and that I have the benefit of being supported by the very latest technology.'

But it was too late – she could almost hear the click of a closing trap as the journalists scribbled down her foolish answer and started packing up their cameras. They'd got what they came for.

'Okay,' said KFC, raising her voice against the bustle in the room. 'We'll leave it there for now, but please do share the images and contact details on the screen. Thanks for coming.'

Kat screwed up the comms core script and stood up. 'That wasn't an opportunity for me to speak to the public, that was just an opportunity for them to bait me.'

KFC followed her out of the door, and once they were on the other side, said, 'They're not baiting you. They just want some answers to their questions. Like it or not, the Aston Strangler case is quite topical right now. If you'd just answer their questions in a matter-of-fact way – *nothing to see here, yadda yadda* – rather than making it look like a big deal, then we could put these issues to bed and focus on finding Hannah's killer.'

Kat turned to face her, incredulous. 'Are you saying this is *my* fault?'

'I'm just being honest,' said KFC, holding her ground. 'Until you deal with this, the Aston Strangler will dominate every press conference you do and get in the way of the messages you're trying to get across.'

'Fine,' said Kat. 'Then I won't do any more press conferences.'

'That won't make the questions go away.'

But Kat was already striding down the corridor, pretending she hadn't heard.

X COMMENTS

@Laralovesgardening Just seen clip of the press conference re the headless body. That poor young woman. Only 20 years old. What is the world coming to? Thoughts and prayers with her family.

@Ingerlandwaves Sad that a girl lost her life but tbf she shouldn't have been over here in the first place, undercutting wages for English people #localjobsforlocalpeople

@LMMontyrules A young woman has been brutally murdered and you want to make this about racism? Seriously?

@Ingerlandwaves Who said anything about racism? And read my tweet love – I said it was sad that she lost her life. But if she'd stayed in Germany, she'd still be alive now.

@EmFairby I just hope they find the killer. No woman is safe while there's a murderer on the loose. I think they should put a proper team on the case, not that hologram thing.

@Secretcopperkettle Agree. This needs proper police work, not some cost-cutting machine and an overpromoted DCS who has questions to answer.

@EmFairby Overpromoted? What, because she's a woman?

@LostBoyz No, because she's a #bentbitch who fitted up Anthony Bridges for the #AstonStrangler.

@Secretcopperkettle I couldn't possibly comment, but everyone knows she owes her meteoric rise to the arrest of the Aston Strangler.

@EmFairby Duh, when someone does a good job, they get promoted.

@LostBoyz Anthony Bridges died in prison waiting for his appeal to be heard. It wasn't 'a good job'. It was a miscarriage of justice #nojusticenopeace

CHAPTER THIRTY-FOUR

DCS Kat Frank's home, Coleshill, 8.29pm

By the time she got home it was dark, and an exhausted Kat cursed as she struggled to fit her key in the front door. She'd have been home two hours ago if it hadn't been for that bloody press conference. The minute it finished it had all kicked off, and KFC had to put out another clarifying statement, which she reluctantly signed off, but then McLeish got involved and it had to be written and rewritten again, while she said no to countless interview requests. For a change, McLeish hadn't tried to change her mind. 'I think you need to keep your head down,' he'd advised, 'and hope this all blows over.'

Well, she was home now, and she was looking forward to a glass or two of the red left over from yesterday while she moaned about the media to Cam. Following his own experience last year, he was scathing about the role of traditional media. Though he'd probably just shrug and remind her that no one watched TV news these days, so unless she went viral on TikTok there was nothing to worry about.

Kat made her way down the hall, noting the absence of trainers to trip over. 'Cam?' she called out. 'You in? I'm home.'

Silence.

She looked again at the shoe rack. Perhaps they'd gone out somewhere and forgotten to tell her? The sharp prick of disappointment surprised her: she hadn't realised how much she'd been looking forward to eating and chatting with them – with anyone, really. Sighing, she carried on down the hall and into the kitchen.

What the fuck?

Kat stared open mouthed at the chaos before her. There were several dirty pans on the oil-splattered hob, and on the side next to it were the remains of various peelings and chopped vegetables intermingled with the crumbly remains of some crusty bread and a half-empty pack of feta cheese. There were bowls – *so* many bowls – containing oil or God knows what, with what looked like every spice or herb she possessed open and discarded upon the island, which was also littered with an array of cutlery.

Clearly, Cam had been cooking.

She headed into the conservatory, cursing as she picked up an empty bottle of the wine she'd been hoping to drink. Honestly, could this day *get* any worse? She paused as she caught the flicker of a flame outside. Approaching the glass doors, she peered out into the garden, where Cam and Gemma were huddled together in blankets around the firepit, laughing as they sipped their glasses of wine.

Her irritation melted at the sight. She and John used to love eating outside, their cheeks stung by the cold air, hands heated by fire and the warmth of each other. For a moment she was tempted to go outside and join them, but then she thought better of it.

This was their time now.

Instead, Kat retreated into the kitchen and pulled on a pair of Marigolds. *Happiness is so rare and so very fleeting*, she thought. *Let them enjoy it while they can.*

*

Kat was just emptying the sink when Cam and Gemma came back inside.

'Oh, I was going to wash up,' insisted Cam.

Kat rolled her eyes. To be fair, he did always mean to wash up, but his timeframe wasn't the same as hers – he thought nothing of leaving a sink full of dishes for several hours, whereas she struggled to leave them for more than a few minutes. 'No worries, it's done now,' she said, pulling her gloves off.

'We can dry, if you like?' suggested Gemma, picking up a tea towel.

Kat was about to say no – she preferred to let plates dry on the rack – but she could see Gemma wanted to help, so she thanked her and let her carry on. While Gemma dried each plate, Cam offered to put them away. Kat was about to joke that she doubted he knew where they went, but her son caught her eye. *Don't show me up. Pretend I do this all the time!*

Kat smiled to herself and set about making a pot of tea. 'Did it get too cold for you out there?' she asked.

Cam and Gemma exchanged glances. 'Er . . . not really,' said Cam. 'It's just that Gemma thought she saw someone watching us.'

'What?' said Kat, putting the mugs down. 'Where?'

'Over the back wall.'

'But I'm not sure,' Gemma added. 'I've had some wine and I was a bit blinded by the fire, so it could have been a shadow. I'm not used to living in the countryside. It's so dark out there.'

Kat frowned. 'Maybe I should check, just in case,' she offered.

'I already did and there was no one there. She's just a city mouse,' Cam said, putting his arm around Gemma and kissing her cheek.

'I'll ask Lock to double-check,' Kat said as the kettle came to the boil. 'Lock?'

Lock appeared in the centre of the kitchen. 'DCS Frank?'

'Would you mind checking the CCTV cameras and alarm system in the garden for signs of an intruder, please?'

Lock paused for two seconds. 'I can confirm that there is no evidence of an intruder within the boundaries of the garden or the house.'

'Thanks, Lock,' said Gemma, blowing him a kiss. 'Sorry to be such a drama queen.'

Kat placed the teapot on the kitchen island. 'Cam tells me you're studying philosophy. That must be interesting. Are you hoping to work in academia?'

Gemma let out one of her deep, throaty laughs. 'God no.'

'Gemma's gonna be a DJ,' said Cam.

'On the radio?'

Cam burst out laughing. 'No, Mum. Gemma's a *rave* DJ. She has her own business and she's already done loads of gigs. She's brilliant, she's got tons of followers.'

Gemma nudged Cam. 'I'm just starting out. But yeah. I love it. I do techno garage mainly.'

'Techno garage?'

'It is a music genre inspired by jungle and incorporating elements from dance, pop and R&B,' explained Lock. 'It is defined by percussive, shuffled rhythms with syncopated hi-hats, cymbals and snares, and may include either 4/4 house kick patterns or more irregular "2-step" rhythms.'

'Well, that's clear as mud,' said Kat.

'I believe it goes something like this,' said Lock. The kitchen suddenly filled with booming, rapid beats as flashing multi-coloured lights appeared to shoot out of his fingers.

Cam and Gemma let out excited screams, heads bobbing and arms waving as they started dancing round the kitchen. After a couple of minutes Kat held up her hands, laughing. 'Okay, I get the idea. That's enough now, Lock.'

'Oh my days,' said Gemma. 'Lock, you *totally* have to do a gig. Everyone would *love* you.'

'Well, I'm sure McLeish would have something to say about that,' said Kat.

'Only if we asked him.'

Did Lock just wink at her? Sometimes Kat thought he might be learning a bit too much. At other times, not enough. She glanced over at Cam, but he only had eyes for Gemma, so she picked up her cup of tea. 'Right, I'm off to bed so I'll leave you two to it. Enjoy the rest of your evening, and don't forget to lock up.'

Kat's eyes flew open, jolted from the old nightmare with a sickening rush. Her hand went to her throat. It was just a dream, nothing more. But her relief was short-lived.

What was that noise?

She held her breath. Ears straining.

A creak.

She jumped out of bed and pulled on her dressing gown. Opening her door, she whispered, 'Cam? Is that you?'

Silence.

Closing the door, she went to the bedroom window and parted the blinds with her fingers, remembering what Gemma had said about seeing someone outside. The firepit was out and the solar lights had died, leaving the garden inky black and empty. She closed the blinds with a snap; told herself it was nothing.

But something felt off.

A line from the podcast looped in her head.

'If the police got the wrong man, then that means that the real Aston Strangler is still out there.'

'Lock?' she whispered.

The image of Lock appeared in her bedroom. He took in his surroundings and, with a shimmer, adjusted his appearance so that he too was wearing pyjamas and a long grey fleecy dressing gown.

For a moment Kat was lost for words. She knew that Lock had learnt to adapt his appearance to the time and location in which he appeared, but to see him in pyjamas was . . . well, it was just *weird*.

'Is everything okay, DCS Frank?'

'I – I'm not sure. I heard a noise. Cam and Gemma are asleep, so I wasn't sure if it was someone outside. Can you check the security system is working, please?' She was probably just imagining things, but with the nightmare still vivid in her mind, she might as well use Lock's ability to 'interface' or whatever the word was with her digital applications to double-check. And to be honest, it helped to hear another voice – even Lock's.

'I can confirm that the security system is functioning accurately, and there is no evidence of any breaches.'

The creaking noise came again, accompanied by the sound of someone in pain.

'What the . . .' began Kat.

Lock looked up at the ceiling. 'The sound is emanating from your son's bedroom above us. My sound pattern recognition software suggests that he and his girlfriend are engaged in the activity commonly referred to as "making love".'

Kat stared back at Lock, her face burning. 'Oh,' she said. '*Oh*.'

'Do you want me to ask them to stop so that you can go back to sleep?'

'No! That wouldn't be . . .' She practically ran to the radio on the bedside table and switched it on to drown out the noise. 'I'll just listen to something.' She took a gulp from a glass of water as her bedroom filled with the soothing sounds of Classic FM.

Lock tilted his head as the operatic voices of two women soared into the air. 'Mozart, the "Sull'aria" duet from *The Marriage of Figaro*.'

Kat nodded. She didn't know the title, but she recognised the music and the poignant yearning behind it.

'Is it like knitting?' asked Lock.

'What?'

'Making love. Once it has been made, does that mean that Cam and Gemma will have love, rather like after knitting one has a jumper, or after making dinner one has food?'

'No,' said Kat, almost spitting her water out as she laughed.

Lock stared at her. 'It was a genuine question. I was not trying to tell a joke. It is just that the use of the verb "making" suggests that something is being made.'

'I'm sorry.' Kat put down her glass and walked towards where Lock stood at the foot of her bed. She cleared her throat. How could she possibly explain the complexities of love to a machine? But his eyes were so earnest, she should at least try. 'The thing is, well, it doesn't always follow sequentially like that. Sometimes you love someone *before* you demonstrate it by "making" love – the act, for want of a better word, is a physical expression of a feeling. But that feeling doesn't always come from love. The feeling can just be physical attraction, or just liking someone.'

'What is the difference? How do humans know if they are in love?'

She puffed out her cheeks. 'It's hard to explain, because love isn't a fact, it's a *feeling* – and an incredibly intense one at that. When you love someone, it's like they don't just occupy your thoughts, they inhabit your whole being. You care about that person more than anyone else in the world. Their happiness means more to you than anyone's – even your own. And if you're lucky, and they feel the same way about you, then you kind of . . . merge. Not just physically, but emotionally.'

Lock blinked. 'There are over eight hundred and fifty thousand articles on why humans fall in love. According to Greek mythology, humans were originally created with four arms, four legs and two faces. Fearing their power, the god Zeus split them into two separate parts, condemning them to spend the rest of their lives in search of their other halves.'

'Really? I didn't know that.'

'In *The Symposium,* Plato wrote, "When these two halves find each other, there will be a silent understanding of one another, they will feel joined and exist with each other in unison and will know no greater love than that". Is that how it feels to be in love, Kat?'

She swallowed. 'Actually, yes, it is.'

'Then I am sorry.'

'Why?'

'Because you have been split in half again.'

They stared at each other across the bedroom. Kat wanted to dismiss his sympathy and point out that it was just an old Greek myth. But she couldn't find the words.

Maybe Lock detected her discomfort, as he asked in a brighter voice, 'So, do Cam and Gemma love each other?'

'I . . . I don't know. You'd need to ask them.'

'Based upon your comments and my own observations, I would suggest that they do. Their pupils dilate every time they look at each other and they are in physical contact almost ninety per cent of the time.'

Kat stared at the pyjama-clad hologram before her. She hadn't analysed their interactions in the same level of detail, but Gemma certainly was very tactile. Yet she'd noticed that the young woman hadn't asked about John, nor looked at their family photographs on the wall. She couldn't help contrasting it with the first time she'd visited John's family home, when she'd been fascinated by the pictures of him as a child, wanting to know *everything* about the wonderful young man she was falling in love with. But maybe Gemma was just being tactful.

'Perhaps,' Kat said diplomatically. 'But everyone is different. As you keep telling me, we shouldn't try to infer what others are thinking based upon external observations alone.'

'I detect some concern in your voice, which may be merited as the evidence suggests that children and young adults who have experienced a parental bereavement can be vulnerable in relationships.'

'Really?' Kat glanced at the ceiling.

'Yes. Fear of abandonment is common, which can lead to unhealthy attachment styles. But the data also shows that it is possible for such children to adjust and develop healthy relationships if they have significant help from supportive adults, and I have observed you providing support and help to Cam many times, which should mitigate any risk.'

Kat swallowed, oddly moved that Lock had – in his own way – told her that she was doing a good job as a mum. With John gone, there was no one else to see or comment on her successes and failures.

'I believe both Cam and Gemma are now at rest and, as I have confirmed there have been no security breaches, you should be able to resume your sleep.'

Kat checked the time on her radio clock. It was nearly 5am already. She glanced at her king-size bed and sighed. 'I might as well stay up now.'

'But you didn't sleep last night either, and a lack of sleep leads to suboptimal performance. If you went back to bed, then you would gain another ninety minutes of sleep.'

Kat gave him a sad smile. 'If I was a machine with an off button, then yes. But in reality, I'll just lie there listening to the shipping forecast and then *Farming Today*, while worrying about Cam's "attachment style".'

'You don't have a ship or a farm, so why would you listen to those programmes?'

Kat tightened the belt on her dressing gown and stepped into her slippers. 'Because, as you have observed many times, we humans are completely irrational. Come on. We can go back over the transcripts and strategy boards before we interview Mrs Cooper at nine.'

She glanced down at Lock's pyjamas and then back up at his face. 'But do me a favour, Lock, and put some clothes on.'

CHAPTER THIRTY-FIVE

**Outside DCS Kat Frank's house, Coleshill,
18 April, 4.59am**

Shit, that was close. What was she doing up at this hour? And why was she looking out at the garden? He is a pro – he spent most of his teenage years burgling houses, so he knows he didn't make a sound.

He runs a hand over his face, damp with sweat despite the cold. He doesn't like the way things are going. She's breaking all her routines, and it doesn't look like her son and his girlfriend are leaving any time soon. He clenches his fists, remembering the annoying sound of their laughter as they'd sat around the fire drinking wine from glasses like people in a film. Then once they'd played at being cold in the garden, they'd scurried back inside their nice warm house to sleep in their nice clean beds.

The thought makes his stomach burn. The only fires he's *ever sat around were the ones they'd lit in bins, sipping from warm cans of cider tainted with the spit of others. And afterwards . . . well, there'd been nothing nice or clean about the beds he'd been forced to stay in.*

He tilts his head back, trying to hold off the memories with the distraction of stars. But tonight the sky is dark with cloud and he cannot see a single light. His throat tightens. He doesn't like the dark. Bad things happen in the dark.

He squats down behind the garden wall so that he can switch his phone back on without being seen. His breathing eases as the pool of silver-blue light envelops him, and his mood lifts at the sight of his screensaver: DCS Kat Frank.

Yes, bad things happen in the dark. But this time, they won't be happening to him.

CHAPTER THIRTY-SIX

Interviewer: DCS Kat Frank (KF)
Interviewee: Caroline Cooper (CC), farm owner
Date: 18 April, 9am
Location: CC's home

KF: Thank you for giving us your time today, Mrs Cooper. We just want to ask you a few questions about the girl who was found buried on your land, Hannah Weber.

CC: I'll try, but I didn't really know her, and it's been over a year since she worked with us. We have lots of strawberry pickers here in the summer.

KF: Well, let's see how we get on, shall we? So, in terms of employment, how did that come about? Did she reply to an advert? Did you interview her?

CC: No. We pay an agency to put an advert out across European social media and some of the student channels for seasonal workers between April and July. They deal with all the applications and identity checks and everything and provide us with an agreed number that meet the required standards. They give us the start dates, and so we don't have any contact with the workers until they turn up here. But Harry deals with all that now.

KF: Okay, but we'll need the contact details for the agency you use. So, according to your records, Hannah Weber began working in your strawberry fields on 7 June. Do you remember meeting her?

CC: Not really. Like I say, we have hundreds of workers across the season.

KF: But with only five mobile homes, you only have twenty-five people living here at any one time. Less than a classroom, really. And they're working in the fields every day, living on your land at night, in the shadow of your family home. Did you really not interact with any of them?

CC: Well, it's a difficult balance. They're here to work – they're not your friends. But they're also young and far from home, so you don't want to completely neglect them, but also you don't want to interfere or cramp their style. A lot of them are doing it to make a bit of money before going travelling. They want to socialise with each other, not with old farmers. So I keep my distance.

KF: Does Harry keep his distance?

CC: Harry has more to do with them day to day in terms of telling them which polytunnels to work on, rounding them up and collecting the punnets and sorting out their pay and accommodation.

KF: You make them sound like sheep.

CC: *[laughs]* Trust me, sheep are a lot easier to handle.

KF: Why's that?

CC: Oh, you know, all the drama you get with kids in their late teens or early twenties: hangovers that make them late for work, relationship or friendship break-ups which mean we have to change the accommodation around, that sort of thing. But they're mostly okay. We've had to move people on a few times over the years when there've been fights or we've caught someone doing drugs, but on the whole we attract good, hard-working kids.

KF: And what about Hannah Weber? Did you ever have any issues with her?

CC: No, not that I recall. Just that initial issue of where to put her at the start as she was the only German.

KF: You don't recall there being an issue with her boyfriend?

CC: No, I wasn't aware she had one.

KF: Were you aware that Harry was attracted to her?

CC: Harry who?

KF: Your son, Harry Cooper.

CC: What? Who told you that?

KF: We've spoken to several of the other seasonal workers at the time, and they have confirmed that Hannah Weber pretended to date another strawberry picker, simply to avoid the unwanted attentions of your son.

CC: Unwanted attentions? That's absolute rubbish. He never did anything of the sort.

KF: And how do you know that, Mrs Cooper, given that, as you have said yourself, you 'kept your distance'?

CC: Because my son wouldn't harass anyone. Those girls are just causing trouble like they always do. Having a bit of fun at the boss's expense. They'd be lucky if he even looked twice at them. It was the same with my husband, Roger. They used to flirt with him something rotten just because he was the boss, hoping to get a bit of extra money or attention. I know their sort. You can't trust a word they say.

KF: How old was your husband?

CC: He was sixty-nine when he passed away last September. It was all very sudden. Heart attack.

KF: I'm so sorry to hear that. Did he have much to do with the strawberry pickers?

CC: He did everything. He worked too hard. I tried to tell him to take more of a back seat and to let Harry do more, but I think he knew Harry's heart wasn't really in it. The only bit he seemed to get any enjoyment out of was arranging the seasonal workers.

KF: And why do you think that was?

CC: I don't know. Maybe he liked being around people his own age for a change. Farming can be a lonely business. Harry's social skills aren't the best. He struggled to make friends at school, but he means well. He's just shy. And anyway, liking a pretty girl is hardly a crime, is it?

KF: No, but it becomes a matter of interest to us when that girl turns up dead on your land. *[looks at notes]* So, according to your records, Hannah Weber started on 7 June and her last recorded day of work was 16 July, but she didn't turn up for work the following day, nor any time after that. Do you recall what happened that night or morning when she went missing?

CC: No, not specifically. It was a weekday at the peak of the strawberry season so we'd have just been busy working. I don't remember her not being there.

KF: You didn't notice she was missing?

CC: No, like I say, I didn't get involved with them. Roger and Harry did it all.

KF: You don't remember Hannah telling you she had to leave to deal with a family matter?

CC: No.

KF: That's odd. Because one of the other seasonal workers,

Alojzy Bratkowski, says that you told him Hannah had left to go home and deal with a family matter.

CC: I . . . I don't remember saying that. He must be confused.

KF: No, he was very specific. He remembers because they were good friends and he cared about her. But he didn't report her missing because you told him that she had gone back home.

CC: That's not true. But if you want to take the word of a Polish strawberry picker over mine then, well . . . My family have owned this farm for over three hundred years. My mum was Elizabeth Bourne – she founded our organic business, Betty's Barn, and was Warwickshire's representative on the National Farmers' Union. Everyone knows us. We're a respectable family.

KF: Can you recall where your son was on the night of 16 July, Mrs Cooper?

CC: 16 July?

KF: The night before Hannah Weber failed to turn up for work.

CC: What are you implying?

KF: I am sure you know that it is routine to ask persons of interest to provide an alibi for their whereabouts during the period when a murder is believed to have taken place.

CC: Person of interest? Harry? You can't mean that! You can't.

KF: Just answer the question, please, Mrs Cooper. Can you confirm that he was with you on that evening?

CC: Yes, yes, of course he was.

KF: May I remind you that to provide someone with an alibi is a serious undertaking, and that you may be asked to provide evidence of this in a court of law. So I am going to ask you again, and I want you to think very carefully before answering. Can you confirm what your son was doing on the evening of 16 July?

CC: He was with me, up at the house having dinner. I know that because that's what we always do. It was July, so we'd have worked late while there was still some light, and then probably eaten about 9pm before watching the news and going to bed.

KF: So, just to be specific, he came in from the fields at about 9pm, and was with you the whole time after that until you went to bed?

CC: Yes, I'm sure of it. I would have remembered if he wasn't, as that's what we do every night. Harry never goes out. He's a good boy.

KF: But what about before 9pm?

CC: I told you, he was working.

KF: Where?

CC: On the farm. He might have been out in the tractor or checking on the cows or stockpiling punnets. The work is endless on a farm.

KF: And your farm is two hundred and eighty-four acres?

CC: Yes.

KF: So in the evening, say between 6 and 9pm, he could have been anywhere, doing anything in those two hundred and eighty-four acres?

CC: I didn't say that.

KF: But you did say he could have been stacking punnets. I presume you mean in the strawberry fields close to the river where the body of Hannah Weber was found?

CC: No, I didn't – you can't *mean* that! You've got it all wrong. Harry didn't kill anyone, you have to believe me!

KF: Perhaps you can check any diaries, work plans or notes

that you have to verify where your son was that evening and give us a better idea of where he was actually working?

CC: You have to stop this. My son is innocent. He's done nothing wrong!

KF: Then these questions shouldn't be a problem for you. I'm just asking you to verify his whereabouts.

CC: I *told* you, he was working. He's always working.

KF: Do you think he enjoys working on the farm, Mrs Cooper?

CC: It's work. You're not meant to enjoy it.

KF: Really? Then what is the point of owning a farm?

CC: Because it's not about me, or my son. It's about the *land*. My mum used to say that the land is the only thing worth working for, worth fighting for, worth dying for, because it's the only thing that lasts. And since Roger died last September, well, that's more true than ever.

KF: Do you— *[phone rings]* Excuse me. I need to take this. DS Browne, is everything okay? *[listens]* Jesus, are you sure? Okay, I'll come over right now. *[ends call]*
I'm sorry, Mrs Cooper, we'll have to terminate the interview. It looks like there might be another body buried on your farm.

INTERVIEW CONCLUDED

CHAPTER THIRTY-SEVEN

Debbie Browne's home, Chelmsley Wood, 10.19am

Debbie opened the door with one hand, holding a crying Lottie against her hip with the other. 'Sorry,' she said. 'Come in. I just need a minute to settle her and then I'll show you what I've found.'

Kat followed Debbie down the hallway and into the front room, with Lock close behind.

'I've fed her, read to her, put her down, picked her up – nothing seems to work,' said Debbie as she cradled a wailing Lottie over her shoulder.

'Have you tried Mozart?' asked Lock. 'According to research, listening to Mozart is extremely good for the development of the infant brain, and his Piano Sonata in C Major, second movement is reported to be gentle, soothing and good at getting babies to sleep.'

'No, but honestly, I'll try anything.'

Lock approached Debbie's back and placed his face just inches from where Lottie's appeared above her mum's shoulder. 'Hello,' he said, smiling. 'I believe it is time for you to be introduced to Mr Wolfgang Amadeus Mozart.' He raised a single finger, and the room filled with the sound of a solo piano.

Lottie stared back, momentarily transfixed. Then Lock moved his finger from side to side, following the rhythm of the music like a metronome.

Lottie's eyes followed his finger, and suddenly the crying stopped.

'If you place her gently in the Moses basket,' said Lock, 'I will follow you and keep playing the music. This will allow you to talk with DCS Frank while she falls asleep.'

Debbie nodded and, as if performing a dance, the two of them moved silently towards the basket. Lock maintained eye contact with Lottie, conducting the music with his finger while her mum gently laid her down. As her daughter's eyelids began to droop, Debbie tiptoed away from the baby, gesturing to Kat to join her at the dining table where her laptop was.

'Lock is a godsend,' she sighed, taking a seat. 'Any chance you could leave him here with me?'

'Afraid not. Anyway, you said you'd found something that suggests there might be another body buried on the farm. Do you want to show me what you've got?'

'Yes, of course.' Debbie moved her mouse, bringing the screen to life with a click. 'Over the past few nights, I've been going through all the data from the LiDAR search that Lock carried out, double-checking the findings and conclusions like you asked. The final report highlighted five areas that warranted further investigation, but there were actually over two hundred soil anomalies detected by the LiDAR that didn't meet the threshold or criteria, so I went through each one. Most were excluded because they were smaller than the agreed parameters, so it's probably safe to assume that they're buried hamsters or something.'

'But?' encouraged Kat.

'But there was one that was excluded because it was too *large*.' Debbie opened up a digital map covered in tiny red dots, with one big blob in the left-hand corner, before highlighting and enlarging the area. 'The LiDAR analysis detected a number of anomalies in the soil that suggests this may be a clandestine burial site, and that whatever is buried is approximately six feet long and about two feet wide. In other words, about the size and shape of an adult human body.'

Kat leant over her shoulder and stared at the screen. 'How certain are you that this is a human burial?'

'I'd estimate sixty-two per cent,' said Lock from where he was still bent over the Moses basket.

'Then why did you exclude it?' Kat demanded.

Lock stood up straight and turned to face them. 'Because the criteria that you set required me to. You asked me to highlight all burial anomalies consistent with the size and shape of a human head and hands, and to exclude anything outside of those parameters.'

'But this could be another dead body!'

'I agree.'

'Then why didn't you bloody flag it?'

'I repeat, because it did not meet the criteria that you explicitly set.'

Kat stared at Lock, groping for words. Sometimes, like this morning, when they had stood together in her bedroom listening to Mozart, he seemed so very human. But at times like this she was reminded that he was, and always would be, just a machine. She let out a heavy sigh. 'It's a good job I asked Debbie to check your report.'

'The root cause of the problem is your failure to specify the task correctly, not any lack of attention to detail on my part. If you had added a caveat that I should highlight any anomalies suggestive of a clandestine grave for a full human body, then I would of course have included this in my final report.'

Kat took a deep breath. 'Perhaps. But Lock, you need to develop some common sense. Maybe you should listen to Mozart too.'

'While there is some evidence that listening to Mozart can increase general brain development and creativity, I can find no studies associating it with the development of so-called "common sense".'

Kat shook her head and turned back to Debbie. 'Can you show me exactly where the suspected grave is on the map?'

Debbie nodded and, with a few clicks, zoomed out so that they could see the surrounding area. 'It's within a small wood at the very edge of Bourne Farm, about halfway between Shustoke and Maxstoke.'

'How far is it from where the body of Hannah Weber was found?'

'Less than two miles.'

'Right. Let's get Judith and a team down there ASAP.'

CHAPTER THIRTY-EIGHT

The border of Bourne Farm and Withy Wood, 2.21pm

Professor Okonedo stared longingly at the crime scene tent as the drizzle turned into rain. Dr Edwards had turned up with their full team in tow, so there wasn't enough space inside for anyone who wasn't essential to the dig. She sighed and looked out over the fields to see DI Rayan Hassan approaching, carrying a large black umbrella.

He looked so incongruously smart as he strode through the wet, muddy field in his suit and long charcoal raincoat that she couldn't help but return his smile.

'Looks like I arrived just in time,' he said, offering her the shelter of his umbrella.

She wanted to say she was fine, thank you very much, and that she didn't need the protection of his umbrella, but in truth her hair would frizz if it got wet, and her braids might even unravel. She'd expected to spend the day at Warwick University, but when DCS Frank had rung to explain that Lock might have missed a potential corpse, she'd felt that she should attend the dig as part of her evaluation. It had been her idea, after all, to entrust AIDE Lock with the LiDAR analysis. So instead she nodded, avoiding

Rayan's eyes as they stood within inches of each other, the rain drumming hard on the umbrella above.

'Any news?' he asked.

'They've done some tests using radar and resistivity methods, and apparently the results are consistent with there being a body in the soil. However, if there *is* a body, then it's buried deeper than most clandestine graves, as they haven't found anything yet.'

'But do they think they will?'

Professor Okonedo nodded. 'I think so.'

'Does that worry you?'

She raised her eyes to his. 'Why should it?'

'Because if they find a body, then it means Lock has made a pretty big mistake.'

'No. It means *I* did. I of all people know that you have to set clear, well-defined tasks for AI machines, even ones capable of deep learning like Lock. I should have added more caveats and nuance to the criteria.'

'Nobody's perfect,' he said softly.

She gazed into his liquid brown eyes. 'Certainly not the police,' she added eventually.

He frowned. 'Well, it was a police officer – DS Browne – who noticed Lock's error. And if there *is* a body buried here, it will be the police who find out who the victim is, and who make sure that they get justice.'

'And what good is that if they're dead?' she said sadly, looking back at the tent.

'The police can't prevent crime, professor.'

'Actually, that's where you're wrong,' she said, turning back to face him. 'Some of the latest AI tools are in predictive policing. Their algorithms use huge amounts of historical data to predict the areas and individuals most vulnerable to crime.'

'Show me a map with demographic data that includes poverty

and inequality and I could do exactly the same thing. There's nothing new or clever about that.'

'Maybe not. My point is that despite having access to this kind of data, the police don't use it to target resources or stage interventions. You just wait for crimes to happen and then spend a lot of time and money in pursuit of "justice".'

Rayan raised his eyebrows. 'You don't believe in justice?'

'I believe in *preventing* injustice,' she replied, leaning in closer as she warmed to her theme. 'I don't believe we should sit back and just accept that crime happens to certain people in certain areas. We should be using data and evidence to be more proactive so that—'

They jumped apart as Judith's voice cut through their conversation. 'DI Hassan, you might want to take a look at this.'

Rayan turned towards the pathologist standing at the entrance of the tent. He handed Professor Okonedo his umbrella, and she took it without a word, the handle still warm from his touch. She watched him follow Dr Edwards inside, studying the shadow of his tall, lean form that was thrown against the side of the tent by the lights. After a few moments he came back out and returned to her side, his face sombre as she raised the umbrella to protect his head.

'I'm afraid they've found another body. They've only just reached it but Judith can see part of the skull and is certain it's human. They're going to excavate the rest, but this is now officially another crime scene.'

Professor Okonedo sighed. 'I'm sorry. So, what happens now?'

'I'll need to ring DCS Frank – she's just about to go into a meeting with McLeish. But my guess is this is going to escalate things considerably. Two bodies buried on the same farm within two miles of each other is a hell of a coincidence, and I don't believe in coincidences.'

'Do you think the Coopers have something to do with it?'

Rayan shrugged. 'I think we should keep an open mind. It depends upon the cause of death. It could be another young woman who was strangled.'

'What makes you say that?'

'It's just, that podcast raises some good points. I mean, what if they didn't get the right guy?'

She frowned. 'Do you really think the Aston Strangler is still out there?' Although she believed the police force was systemically flawed and often corrupt, she had reluctantly learned to respect and trust DCS Kat Frank, who was the most honest and principled person she knew.

'I don't know. But like I said, nobody's perfect. Not even the boss.' He sighed. 'Anyway, I best get back.'

'Oh. Then you best take your umbrella,' she said, holding it out to him.

'No, it's okay,' he said, glancing up at the sky before returning his eyes to hers. 'You keep it. You might need it.'

CHAPTER THIRTY-NINE

Leek Wootton HQ, McLeish's office, 3.30pm

Rayan had managed to catch Kat before her meeting with McLeish, so for once she was able to brief her boss on the latest developments before he found out about them from social media, as had happened in the last couple of cases.

He didn't thank her or say well done. McLeish never did – he expected people to do what they were paid to do. Instead, he pushed her on next steps: how long would it take to identify the victim and the cause of death? Did she plan on making any arrests? And if not, why not?

'Dr Edwards will spend the rest of the day excavating the body and is aiming to carry out a PM in their lab tomorrow. How much info we get depends on how long the victim has been dead for, as you know. But Judith is one of the best, and Lock can really help speed things up. The key question we need to answer is whether the bodies – and therefore the murderer – are in any way related.'

'They were found on the same farm, weren't they? What do you make of the owners?'

'The Coopers?' Kat screwed up her face. 'They're both defensive and reluctant to cooperate. And their stories don't stack up. On paper it looks like they're hiding something, and there's some evidence that Harry Cooper was interested in Hannah Weber.'

'But?'

Kat shrugged. 'I think they're just obsessed with the running of their farm. Harry's a bit of an odd guy in more ways than one. But being shy and awkward with women isn't a crime. My gut tells me he isn't a killer. He's just a frustrated young man who's trapped on a farm that he hates, living with his invalid mother.'

'He sounds like he'd fit the classic profile of a psycho.'

'That's why I don't like psychological profiles. They're too simplistic, rife with misogyny and blind to any kind of neurodiversity.'

'And what about the fisherman who found Hannah?'

'He lives alone so he doesn't have an alibi, but neither does he have a motive.'

'He's a lonely older man whose wife recently left him. Maybe he saw a pretty girl walk by and took his chance and things got out of control.'

Kat shook her head. 'That would be convenient for us, but we have no evidence to support that scenario. Plus, to be honest, my gut tells me he isn't a murderer either. All he cares about is his grandkids and getting a bit of fishing and a couple of pints in at the weekend.'

'Well, I've learned to trust your gut nearly as much as you do, but try to keep an open mind, Kat. You might not agree with psychological profiles, but the rest of the world does. Interview him again and talk to his ex-wife. Let him feel like he's a suspect and see how he reacts. What about the parents of the girl? Do they know yet?'

Kat winced, remembering her phone call. 'The German police told them yesterday. Apparently the mum was distraught. The officer I spoke to said she was planning to fly over to collect her daughter and take her back home. She should be here in the next couple of days.'

McLeish sighed. 'I don't have to tell you to look after her when she's here, because I know you will. But look after yourself as well, okay? Don't get too involved.'

'Of course. I'm just going to head back to the farm now. It'll take most of the night to remove the body, I think, but I want to be there in case we find anything that points to the killer.'

There was a knock at the door, and before McLeish could reply, Karen-from-Comms entered the room.

Kat and McLeish exchanged glances. A bold move.

'Sorry, sir,' the young woman said. 'But I thought you'd both want to know that the news is out about the second body, and the Aston Strangler podcast has run an exclusive.'

'An exclusive?' echoed McLeish. 'On what?'

'It'd be easier to just play you a clip,' KFC said, holding up her phone.

'Easier for who?' the Chief Constable growled. But he nodded his permission for her to go ahead and press play.

Narrator: I'm standing outside Bourne Farm in Warwickshire, making an unscheduled, live podcast, because today I can exclusively reveal not just one, but *two* extraordinary pieces of information that the Warwickshire Police have chosen to hide from you, the Great British public.

I have discovered some *explosive* information about the body that was recently found in the grounds of Bourne Farm. You might not have heard about it because the police have deliberately given the case a low profile. But an anonymous source told me that the body belonged to a young woman, and that the post-mortem found injuries consistent with strangling. Yes, listeners, *she was strangled to death.*

And as if that wasn't bad enough, my source has also shared another shocking fact with me. This morning, *another* body was found in a secret grave *on the same farmland*. We don't yet know the age or sex of the body, but I know that you, my listeners, will be asking the same question that I am: *what are the chances of two dead bodies being found buried on the same farm just two miles apart?*

And like me you're probably asking, *why* weren't we told about this? Why are you finding out about this from me, an amateur podcaster? Why didn't the police share the fact that the first girl was strangled to death? And why have they hidden the fact of the second body?

I'll tell you why. It is because both cases are being investigated by DCS Kat Frank. Yes, the very same Kat Frank who led the case of the Aston Strangler. The same Kat Frank who, despite the woeful lack of evidence, arrested, charged and ensured the successful prosecution of Anthony Bridges, a former police officer with no criminal record who was, by all accounts, an exemplary husband and father.

On last week's podcast we heard from Dr Mike Bullington, who shared his genuine concern that the wrong man had been convicted for these terrible crimes. And he warned us that the Aston Strangler could still be at large. As an expert psychological profiler, Dr Bullington advised us that although the Aston Strangler might be able to change or modify his *modus operandi,* he would not be able to resist the urge to kill again.

And now we have *two* dead bodies. We know that

> at least one of them was a young girl who was tragically strangled to death – we are still waiting for the results of the second post-mortem. Meanwhile, the safety of our women – our daughters, our sisters and our wives – rests in the hands of DCS Kat Frank.
>
> Well, I don't know about you, but that does not put my mind at ease. I have too many questions. Too many fears. So, I am making this special podcast to appeal – no, to *demand* – that DCS Frank responds to my repeated requests for an interview, to finally be held to account for her decisions, and her mistakes, before more innocent lives are destroyed.

'That's enough,' said McLeish.

Karen-from-Comms pressed pause on her phone. She looked between Kat and her boss. 'Do you want me to . . . ?'

'Yes.' McLeish nodded towards the door. He waited until she was on the other side of it before turning back to Kat. 'Is it true?'

'Is *what* true?'

'Was the girl strangled?'

'No! Well, not definitely. Dr Edwards was unable to determine the exact cause of death, but they did note some possible evidence of crushing around the windpipe—'

'Oh, for fuck's sake!'

'But her head had been chopped off with an axe, so it wasn't straightforward, and the rest of the body was so decomposed it was impossible to confirm either way.'

'So you chose to ignore it?'

'No, the evidence was inconclusive.'

McLeish ran a hand over his bald head, which was now flushed a deep, angry red. 'You should have told me, Kat.'

'It wasn't definitive, and—'

'You should have told me!'

Kat flinched. McLeish never raised his voice. Not to her.

'This is bad. Really bad,' he said. 'I'll do my best to protect you from the shitstorm that this is going to unleash, but social media . . .' His voice trailed off. He rubbed his head again before continuing in a more determined voice, 'Right, I need Dr Edwards to complete the PM yesterday. And the minute you find out the gender and cause of death for this second body I want you to ring me. I don't care what time of day or night it is. And I don't care whether the findings are "definitive" or not. I want to know everything the minute you get it. God help us if it's another strangled woman.' He dropped his head into his hands, dragged them down his face and then looked up at her with unblinking eyes. 'I need you to tell me the truth, Kat. I can't help you unless you're honest with me. Did you get the right man?'

Kat swallowed and looked him straight in the eye. 'I promise you I got the right man.'

'I signed the warrant application to search Anthony Bridges's home the night you arrested him. I never asked you for the grounds because you gave me your word that you had it and time was of the essence. But I'm asking you now, Kat, what grounds did you have to justify a home search?'

'Er . . . I'd have to go back and check the paperwork, sir.'

McLeish stared at her for so long that her face began to burn. Then he looked away. 'I see,' he said quietly. 'Well, keep me posted on the PM. And Kat? Take care.'

She headed for the door, eyes stinging. They'd worked together for over twenty years, and during that time she knew she'd often irritated, shocked and infuriated McLeish, but she had never, ever disappointed him. The way he had looked at her just now . . . She closed the door behind her and leant against the wall.

Her own boss didn't believe her.

She squeezed her eyes shut until the threat of tears had passed. Then, with a deep breath, she pushed herself off the wall and strode down the corridor, her heels stabbing the carpet.

It didn't matter what McLeish thought, or what *anyone* else thought for that matter. *She* knew she had arrested the right man.

But she could never, ever tell anyone why.

X COMMENTS

@Laralovesgardening I was sceptical about that #AstonStrangler podcast, but now two strangled women have been found on the same farm within a week of each other, I'm freaking out. Looks like #TheAstonStrangler really is back.

@SeannotShaun22 Why are you freaking out? The post-mortem hasn't even been carried out yet, so no one knows the sex of the body let alone the cause of death. That podcast is making 2+2 = 6 just to get publicity.

@EmFairby We don't need to wait for the PM. It's always women that end up buried in the woods, and it's always men that put them there.

@Phil61b I always thought there was something fishy about #TheAstonStrangler case. Anthony Bridges seemed a decent bloke, with no criminal record. It didn't add up to me.

@SeannotShaun22 Dude, that 'decent bloke' was a copper. He probably abused women all the time and got away with it like they all do. Coppers protect their own.

@Secretcopperkettle There's absolutely no evidence for that, and it's offensive to the thousands of policemen who put their lives on the line every day to keep us safe.

@Laralovesgardening I agree @Secretcopperkettle, but I think questions have to be asked about the conviction. Why won't that DCS Kat Frank give an interview? What has she got to hide?

@LostboyzPete She seems a snotty cow to me. One of those women who thinks she's better than everyone else.

@LMMontyrules 'One of those women?' You mean someone who dares to question the patriarchy?

@LostboyzPete So you think it's alright if *she* asks the questions, but refuses to answer legitimate questions about her own decisions? Call me old-fashioned, but I believe in accountability.

@EmFairby #TheAstonStrangler was found guilty by a judge and jury. Call *me* old-fashioned but that's how the legal system works in this country, and I believe in the rule of law, not the mob.

@LostboyzPete And I believe young women should have the right not to be murdered, all because some #bentbitch locked up the wrong guy and refuses to admit it.

@Phil61b I agree. As the father of two teenage daughters, I'm appalled at what is happening. I'm not letting them out of my sight until this killer is caught.

@LMMontyrules Sorry, 'as the father of two teenage daughters' you agree it's OK to call another woman a 'bent bitch'?

@Phil61b Well, if she hasn't got anything to hide, why won't she give an interview?

@EmFairby Maybe she's busy doing other things like . . . I don't know . . . trying to catch the killer?

@LostboyzPete Yeah, well, maybe if she'd done her job right in the first place, she wouldn't still be looking for him #TheAstonStrangler.

CHAPTER FORTY

**Leek Wootton HQ, Major Incident Room,
19 April, 8.02am**

'Can you enlarge this bit here?' Kat asked Lock, pointing at the 3D map on the boardroom table as she tried to focus her bleary eyes. Once again, she'd hardly slept a wink. Her brain had kept running over conversations and transcripts, and whenever she did fall into a doze, she slipped into a lurid trap of nightmares before jolting awake, afraid and confused. At 5.30am she'd given up trying to sleep, and in an inexplicable burst of optimism had decided to check social media to see if it was all beginning to blow over.

It wasn't. If anything, it was beginning to blow up. It was clear that until she found the killer, the questions about the Aston Strangler wouldn't go away – and she really, really needed them to go away. So, despite her misgivings, she'd decided to take McLeish's advice and review the fisherman's evidence.

Lock stretched his fingers so that the section of the river she was pointing at doubled in size.

Kat bent down to take a closer look. 'This is where the first body was found, right by the River Bourne. But look, there's not much distance between this and the place where the second body was found.'

'One point seven five miles, to be exact.'

'Both areas are pretty secluded and they're connected by old footpaths. Jim Walker said he'd been walking and fishing around that area since he was a kid. I think we should interview him again,' she said, straightening up.

Rayan raised his eyebrows. 'Really?'

'Yes, really. You yourself said that we should treat him as suspicious because he found the first body.'

'Yeah, but as far as we know there's nothing to connect him to the second. Don't you think we should wait until the PM results?'

Kat was tempted to retort, 'I think you should do as you're told', but she knew it was the tiredness that was making her so irritable, so she held herself in check. 'No. It took Dr Edwards's team all night just to transfer the body to the lab, and because the remains are largely skeletal they'll need cleaning up, which means they probably won't even start the PM until this afternoon. I can't just sit here waiting. We need to keep moving things forward.'

'You could always do a press conference,' said KFC. 'There's a lot of media interest following the podcast last night.'

'I am not going to give that podcast the dignity of a response.'

'But it's not just the podcast. All the tabloids have put in bids, and it's all over social media. In my experience, the longer you refuse to give an interview, the bigger the story will get.'

'And in my experience, if I comment on inaccurate leaks from the first PM and engage with random theories about a second that hasn't even happened yet, we'll just give the cranks credibility and add fuel to the fire.' Kat shook her head. 'I'm sorry, Karen. Once we've got something conclusive from Dr Edwards, I'd be more than happy to hold a press conference and nip all this nonsense in the bud. But until then, I'm going to ignore it and get on with my actual job. So, today we are going to re-interview

Harry Cooper, Caroline Cooper and the fisherman, Jim Walker. Okay?'

'To be honest, without the results of the PM, I'm not sure what we're supposed to ask them,' said Rayan. 'We don't even know when the person died.'

'No, but we know *where* they were buried, and all three have a connection with the place. So let's keep the pressure up. See how they respond to being questioned about a second body. You do the Coopers and I'll do Jim Walker, and his ex-wife too, while I'm at it. And by the time we've finished, hopefully Dr Edwards will be ready to start the PM.'

'Okay, you're the boss,' said Rayan in a resigned tone.

Kat stuffed her papers into her bag as the room emptied, fighting her irritation.

Lock remained, studying her face. 'Why does the podcast upset you so much?'

'It doesn't.'

'I know your voice and behavioural patterns, and I have observed that any mention of the Aston Strangler or the podcast accelerates your pulse by eighteen per cent, raises the pitch of your voice by fourteen per cent and makes you irritable and defensive.'

'I don't have time to discuss this now,' she said, snapping her bag shut.

'You also attempt to close down any conversations about the matter. Why is that?'

'That's because the matter *is* closed. Anthony Bridges was convicted by a jury and sentenced to life. You can't keep a running commentary on justice – that is the point of juries. They made their decision, full stop.'

'But it wasn't a unanimous decision. What if the majority verdict was wrong?'

'It wasn't. Trust me.'

'But in a court of law, the police are required to bring evidence and make the case for why someone is guilty. They cannot just say "trust me". That is not justice.'

'That depends upon what you mean by justice.'

'The dictionary definition is quite clear – it is the process or result of using laws to fairly judge and punish crimes and criminals.'

'Well, that's exactly what happened. Justice was carried out.'

Lock stared at her. 'Then what are you afraid of?'

'Afraid? I'm not *afraid.*'

'I repeat, I know your voice patterns and behaviours, and your assertion contradicts my objective assessments.'

'That's because you are merely assessing my external behaviours and inferring from them what I am thinking and feeling. Which you cannot possibly know.'

'I cannot know with a hundred per cent accuracy, but I am getting very good at estimating what you are really thinking.'

'Good. Then you should know *exactly* what I think of you right now.'

'Ah,' said Lock, noting her blazing eyes. 'Then I shall cease speaking for a period.'

'Finally,' Kat muttered, as she marched out of the door.

CHAPTER FORTY-ONE

Interviewer: DCS Kat Frank (KF)
Interviewee: Jim Walker (JW), fisherman
Date: 19 April, 9.55am
Location: JW's home

KF: Thank you for agreeing to talk to us at such short notice, Mr Walker.

JW: Well, you turned up at my door, so I didn't have any choice really, did I?

KF: Yes, it's lucky you were in. No fishing today?

JW: No, I only get to do that at the weekends because I have to pick the grandkids up after school in the week.

KF: But no grandkids today?

JW: No, I'm not feeling too good.

KF: Oh, I'm sorry. We can always come back when you're feeling a bit better?

JW: No, it's all right. I'd rather get this over and done with to be honest. Have you found out who the dead girl is yet?

KF: Didn't you see the news yesterday?

JW: No, I told you, I was sick. Spent all day in me bed.

KF: Yes, her name was Hannah Weber. She was twenty and

from Germany and she was working as a strawberry picker at Bourne Farm. Do you recognise her name?

JW: No. Never heard of her till now.

KF: How about this? For the tape, I am handing Mr Walker a photograph of Hannah Weber.

JW: Ah, she was a pretty young thing. What a shame.

KF: Did you know her?

JW: No. Never seen her before.

KF: Are you sure? You fished along that river every weekend. Hannah would have been picking strawberries less than a mile away. Maybe she went for a riverside walk sometimes?

JW: If she did, I never seen her. Hardly anyone walks past that spot, and if I'd have seen a girl as pretty as that, then I'd have remembered.

KF: Why? Do you like pretty girls?

JW: Doesn't everyone? No crime in looking, is there? That's all I get to do these days. After thirty-two years of marriage my missus decided she needed to go and 'find herself'. *[shakes his head]* I told her – Mary, I said – you've got everything you need right *here*. A house that's more or less paid for, all the white goods, two healthy kids and three lovely grandchildren. Just be happy with what you've got, I said. But she was always on Instagram and what have you, looking at other people's lives, and I think it messed with her mind – made her discontent. That and her bloody sister. Once her own marriage broke up, I think she couldn't stand to see other people happy. She wound Mary up like a clock.

KF: Do you have her address?

JW: Yes, here you go. But she's probably out 'finding herself'.

KF: Thank you. Now, when you found the body by the river, you said you knew that it belonged to a girl straight away. Why was that, Mr Walker?

JW: I told you. I just had a feeling. It was when I touched her . . . I can't describe it. I still have nightmares about it. The feeling of her bones in my hands. The sticky wet flesh. It was horrible. I . . . I don't like thinking about it, to be honest. In fact, I haven't been fishing since.

KF: Maybe you could try a different spot. Where else do you like to fish?

JW: Anywhere that's quiet and within walking distance of a decent pub. Depends on the weather, really. There's a couple of nice spots at the bottom of the Blythe, not far from the church, but the bank gets too muddy if there's been a lot of rain.

KF: Do you ever fish or walk near the grounds of Maxstoke Castle and golf course?

JW: I used to, back in the day, but I haven't been there for years.

KF: Why's that?

JW: It's too long a walk from the car park. It wasn't so bad when I was younger, but what with the bucket, chair and rod and tackle to carry, it means I'm knackered before I even get there. No, these days I just want to get on the river as quick as I can and save my energy for the fish.

KF: Could you show me on the map where exactly your fishing spot was?

JW: Why?

KF: You've probably heard that another dead body was found not far from Maxstoke golf course, so I'm just trying to establish where the main fishing spots are.

JW: You mean, you're trying to establish whether *I* used to fish there?

KF: Yes.

JW: Bloody hell. Am I a suspect?

KF: No, this is an informal interview, and you're just helping us with our enquiries.

JW: Helping you to what? Find someone to pin the crime on? Well, you're barking up the wrong tree, love. I haven't been fishing round there in years, and even if I had, that doesn't make me a bloody killer. Jesus. I can't believe you've got the cheek to sit here in *my* home and accuse me of being a murderer!

KF: I'm not accusing you of *anything*. I'm just trying to piece things together, and it would be really helpful if—

JW: If I was the culprit so that everyone would stop banging on about the Aston Strangler? I'm old, not stupid, love. I have an iPhone and I like listening to podcasts, believe it or not. Especially true crime. Which means I know my rights. You said this was an informal interview, so that means I can end this any time I want, right?

KF: Yes.

JW: Then consider it ended. You know where the door is.

INTERVIEW CONCLUDED

CHAPTER FORTY-TWO

Interviewer: DCS Kat Frank (KF)
Interviewee: Mary Walker (MW), fisherman Jim Walker's ex-wife
Date: 19 April, 10.45am
Location: MW's sister's home

KF: Thank you for agreeing to talk at such short notice while I was in the area.

MW: Were you talking to Jim? I heard that he found that dead body.

KF: That's what I wanted to talk to you about. Because your husband—

MW: *Ex*-husband.

KF: Ex-husband, Mr Walker, found the body, we just need to check a few things as a formality.

MW: Such as?

KF: Such as, did he fish regularly in that spot? Was there anything out of the ordinary that day in terms of where he went and why?

MW: There's never anything out of the ordinary with Jim. That's the problem. You could set your clock by him. Every weekend he gets up at the crack of dawn, gets his fishing gear on and heads off to some muddy river where he spends three hours staring at the frigging water before going to the pub and having a couple of pints with his mates. Meanwhile muggins here was always stuck at home, doing the shopping and the cooking, and then I was the one that had to wash all his muddy, stinking clothes when he got back, while he slept off the beer. At least, that's what used to happen. But not anymore. That's why I left.

KF: When did you leave him?

MW: Last summer.

KF: Last summer? Could you be more specific?

MW: Er . . . it was just before the grandkids broke up for the holidays, so it must have been the middle of July. I can dig out last year's calendar and check if you like?

KF: That would be helpful, thank you. And can I ask, what was the trigger for you finally leaving him after all these years? Was his behaviour aggressive or concerning in any way?

MW: No, I told you. Jim never changes. He always wants to eat the same dinner, drink the same beer and go fishing at the same time every bloody weekend. Our Sarah had booked a lovely holiday for us all in Greece with the grandkids, but he said we couldn't go. Said he wouldn't like the heat, or the food, or the drink, or the *change*. I was so fed up. I remember I was sitting in the kitchen looking at pictures of other families having lovely holidays abroad. It wasn't just that there was sea and sunshine, it was the fact that they were going somewhere different, trying new things. And then I went to the fridge to get a glass of wine, and what did I have? Maggots.

KF: Maggots?

MW: Yeah, they were bait for the fish. He usually kept them in the fridge in his shed, but he said it was full. They were in a plastic tub, but even so. It was horrible. That was the last straw. I came here to my sister's, and I went on that Greek holiday and we had a bloody good time. Haven't looked back since.

KF: And how did he react when you left? Was he angry?

MW: Ha! God forbid Jim Walker should show an actual emotion. No, he just withdrew into himself. Started watching all these true crime series and podcasts and whatnot and, of course, fishing. Always the bloody fishing.

KF: He isn't a formal suspect, so don't take this the wrong way, but do you think your ex is capable of murder? I mean, would it surprise you if it turned out he was involved in some way with the death of a young woman?

MW: *[pauses]* I was going to say I don't think Jim would ever do anything as exciting as kill someone. But honestly, when I left him, I realised that after thirty-two years of marriage I didn't have a clue what was going on in his head. I knew what he *did,* but I never knew what he *thought*. People say they're fishing, but really, they're just standing there doing nothing for hours on end. What was he *thinking* all that time? And then, whenever he did catch a fish, he'd bash it on the head and bring it back home. I don't like fish, but I couldn't kill one. That's gotta tell you something about a person, right?

KF: Oh, I thought he always put the fish back in the water?

MW: Ha, you're joking. Then he'd have nothing to show his mates in the pub, would he? No, he always brought them home, and then expected me to scale and gut them. Well, I'm not playing that game anymore.

KF: Okay, well, thank you for your time, you've been really helpful, Mrs Walker.

INTERVIEW CONCLUDED

CHAPTER FORTY-THREE

DCS Kat Frank's car, 11.17am

Kat glanced at her phone as it pinged. KFC. Again. She ignored it and carried on driving.

'What did you make of Mr Walker?' she asked Lock, in the passenger seat beside her.

He raised an eyebrow. 'Is that an invitation to resume speaking?'

'Yes, that is why I asked you a question.'

'Then I shall answer it.'

Lock paused for so long, that it almost seemed deliberate. 'Well?' she prompted, provoking what looked suspiciously like a satisfied smile.

'I do not think we ascertained any new or relevant information from the interview. We did, however, share the name, age and origin of the first victim with Mr Walker, and alerted him to the fact that he may be a potential suspect.'

'I disagree. We discovered that he is a reluctant divorcee, that he is lonely and that he likes pretty girls. Contrary to what his ex-wife said, he also has a temper.'

'Forty-two per cent of marriages in the UK end in divorce, and all heterosexual men like pretty girls. I did not see any evidence of a temper.'

'He told us to leave.'

'Which he was well within his rights to do.'

'But only because he didn't like the questions. He got very upset and defensive when we asked about whether he'd ever fished where the second body had been found.'

'Just as you do when you're asked about the Aston Strangler.'

'That is not the same thing at all. I get annoyed because that case is *over*, and this whole podcast thing is a distraction.' She paused. 'Mary Walker said she left her husband on 15 July. We think Hannah Weber went missing on the night of the 16th or morning of the 17th.'

'So, does this mean that you think Jim Walker should be a formal suspect?'

Kat screwed up her face. 'He's an odd guy, and the timing could be significant . . . but he just doesn't *feel* like a murderer to me.'

'And yet, as his ex-wife pointed out, he murders fish every weekend.'

'That is not the same thing at all.'

'Jim Walker hides metal hooks in maggots to trick living things to bite on them, thereby embedding the hooks in their mouths, before reeling them in and striking their heads with a blunt instrument until they are dead. Objectively, it is *exactly* the same thing. The only difference lies in the value that you ascribe to the lives of fish compared to those of humans.'

Before Kat could answer, her phone rang. Seeing that it was Dr Edwards, she put it on loudspeaker. 'Judith, what have you found?'

'Hello to you, too. And since you ask, yes, I'm well, considering I've only had four hours' sleep so that I could make an early start on your body.'

'I'd kill for four hours. What can you tell me?'

'It'd be easier to show you. And I really need Lock for the next stage. Any chance you could swing by?'

'On my way,' said Kat. 'But can you just tell me if it's a woman and if—'

But Judith had already put the phone down.

Kat's stomach lurched as she turned the car around. Judith loved a bit of drama and so was probably just holding back the information so they could reveal it in a dramatic flourish in the lab. Their short and cryptic message didn't mean that the body belonged to a strangled young woman.

It couldn't.

It simply wasn't possible.

CHAPTER FORTY-FOUR

Digital Forensic Pathology Unit, Warwick University, 12.05pm

The body lay on the mortuary slab beneath a simple white sheet. Kat exchanged nervous glances with Professor Okonedo while they waited for the pathologist to tell them what they'd found.

'It took us a long time to remove the body as it was buried much deeper than is typical for a clandestine burial, and it wasn't wrapped or contained in anything. Not even clothes. The flesh has completely decomposed, leaving us with just the skeletal remains.' Judith paused, and very gently began to roll the single sheet down and over the body, before carefully folding it at the deceased's feet.

Kat stared at the remains that lay between her and Lock. Although the skeleton was still intact, it was stripped of all flesh, with not even a single hair left upon its skull. 'Does that mean this body has been in the ground for some time?'

'Possibly,' Judith said carefully. 'There are lots of factors that influence decomposition, so I'll come back to that later. I wanted to brief you on the two findings that I *am* confident about. Firstly, based upon my assessment of the cranium and pelvis, this skeleton almost certainly belongs to a Caucasian male. I'm less certain of their age, but subject to further tests, I'd say they were young – between eighteen and thirty years old.'

'Male?' Kat repeated. She whispered a silent prayer to a god she didn't believe in. Immediately she regretted her response. This was still a person who had lost their life: someone's son, lover or father.

Judith pointed towards the top of the forehead, where in the centre of a web of cracks there was a neat, dark hole, about the size of a shirt button. 'And, again subject to further tests, it looks like they died of a gunshot wound – a single shot to the head, to be precise.'

Kat leant forward. 'Not strangled?

'I haven't been able to find any evidence of strangulation so far, but as I said the other day, without any remaining flesh or tissue, it's hard to be definitive. Either way, the bullet to the head would have killed him – there is a similar hole at the back of the skull, meaning it passed straight through his brain. Death would have been instantaneous.'

Kat nodded, almost sagging with relief. 'I'd better let McLeish know,' she said. 'I promised to tell him the minute we had any info on the gender or cause of death. Excuse me.'

She opened the lab door and walked out into the warm, bright corridor. Leaning her head against the wall, she took a few deep breaths before ringing her boss.

McLeish picked up straight away. 'Well?'

'It's a man, and he died from a bullet wound.'

'You're sure?'

'There are bullet holes in the front and back of his skull, so I'd say it's pretty definitive.'

'Good. I mean . . . you know what I mean. Any ID or estimated time of death?'

'Not yet. There's no clothes or soft tissue. Dr Edwards is still working on it. But I thought you'd want to know straight away that, contrary to the rumours, this is *not* another strangled woman.'

'But it *is* another dead body within two miles and one week of the first one. They could still be connected, so keep up the pressure. And keep me informed.'

'I will, sir.'

'But good work. I'll let the minister know right away. And Kat?'

'Yes?'

'Are you okay?'

The concern in his voice was so genuine and unexpected that tears rushed to her eyes. 'I am now,' she managed to say, before ending the call.

Kat dabbed at her eyes with shaking hands. Of course, she *knew* that she'd been right all along, that the Aston Strangler couldn't possibly still be out there. But the lack of sleep combined with that bloody podcast and the relentlessness of social media had started to mess with her head. Now things could get back to normal, thank God.

As she headed back towards the morgue, Kat tapped out a quick text to her son.

Judith needs Lock's help with the PM so I probably won't be home for dinner. Sorry. Can you get a Deliveroo? My treat. Have a good night x

Course. You OK? Is it the PM for the second strangled girl?

Kat read the rather anxious message from her son and sighed. She should have realised how much the media coverage would upset Cam. He'd always been worried about her job, but he'd become even more protective of her since the death of his dad, afraid that he might lose her as well. She glanced back at the pathology lab behind her. Judith seemed to know what they were doing, and thanks to the upgrade, Lock could now operate in the lab without her. She could always leave them to it and join Cam and Gemma for dinner.

Her thumb hovered over her phone. She found it hard to delegate at the best of times, and this was definitely not the best of times. To make all the media, trolls and podcast junkies back off, she'd need to tell them exactly who the body *was*, not just who it wasn't. More importantly, there was a family out there who deserved to know what had happened to their loved one.

She was just about to reply to Cam when another text came in from Debbie Browne:

I need to talk to you about Harry Cooper. I've gone through his books, and they don't add up.

OK, replied Kat. *I'm just in a PM so send me a report and I'll call you later.*

As she headed back towards the lab, Kat typed out a quick reply to her son. *Don't worry. PM proves not strangled. Talk later x*

CHAPTER FORTY-FIVE

Outside DCS Kat Frank's house, Coleshill, 12.22pm

His phone pings, alerting him to a message that Kat Frank has just sent her son. He smiles as he opens up the app that Cameron Frank had unwittingly downloaded on his mobile. He might be clever enough to go to university, but he was stupid enough to log onto unsecured Wi-Fi in a café, sipping a poncy coffee that cost more than a bloody pint.

He reads the message and swears. Not strangled? What the fuck?

He reads it again. And again. And finally it makes sense.

Once a liar, always a liar. DCS Kat Frank lied so she could fit up Anthony Bridges as the Aston Strangler, and now she is lying again to cover it up.

Judith needs Lock's help with the PM, *she'd typed.*

Yeah, I bet, he thinks. You mean you need Lock's help to fix the results, so you can claim that the victim wasn't strangled. Well, I wasn't born yesterday. And you are not going to get away with this. I will hold you to account for the destruction you have caused.

He glares at the house opposite, cracking his knuckles to release the tension. Her son will leave in a few days.

And then there will be nothing and no one to stop him.

CHAPTER FORTY-SIX

Kat put the phone back into her pocket and pushed open the heavy door. 'Have you finished yet?' she joked as she re-entered the room.

'You have only been gone for three minutes and forty-seven seconds,' said Lock.

'If you can watch a film in that time then I don't see why you can't date a body.'

'That is because watching a film is easy, whereas working out how long a skeleton has been dead is bloody hard work,' said Judith.

'I know, I was joking.'

'Honestly, that *CSI* has a lot to answer for. Ever since that show was made, everyone thinks pathologists can just look at a dead body and, with a watch and a thermometer and a bit of insect analysis, tell you the exact day they died and what the weather was like at the time.'

Kat held her hands up in an apology, but Judith was on a roll.

'Whereas in *reality* we might be able to make a decent estimate about the age of ancient bones, like mummies for example, by using carbon dating techniques, and we can roughly determine the age of younger bones that have been in the ground a year or less by assessing the extent of decomposition. But trying to estimate the age of the *in between* bones – the ones that have been buried for several years or decades, and where there is no tissue or clothes or ID of any kind – is a completely different ball game. It's incredibly complex.'

'But not impossible for someone with your expertise?' Kat suggested.

Judith sniffed, but the compliment relaxed them slightly. 'In these types of cases, one of the signs forensic pathologists look for is long cracks along the shaft of the bone's surface. This weathering can be caused by repeated freezing and thawing in the ground – a bit like the plaster on the outside of your house. The longer the bones have been in the ground, the more cracks you'd expect to see.'

'And?'

'I shared some images with a couple of colleagues, and their initial assessment was that this body has probably been in the ground for decades rather than years.'

'How many decades?'

'They couldn't say. In order to be more accurate, we'll need to do more specific tests. Measuring carbon-14 levels can help pinpoint the year of death with an accuracy range of three years if you have access to soft tissue or hair or nails. But in this case, we don't. We could use tooth enamel, but it's not very accurate for these tests, plus there was a spike in atmospheric carbon-14 levels during the Fifties and Sixties due to all the nuclear testing, which makes these tests a bit unreliable for much of the last century.'

'So, what do your colleagues think we should do?'

'They suggested we focus on proteomics – the study of the proteins in a cell, organ or other sample. There've been huge advances over the last few decades, and according to my colleagues, measuring the number, type and rate of decay of the proteins in bones is the best way to assess the passage of time with a decomposed body like this.'

'Sounds good to me. So, how do we go about that then?'

'With some difficulty. This practice has only been trialled in recent years – in pigs mainly – and while the basic theory seems sound, we haven't yet built the computer models or equations into which to incorporate the protein markers, which would then allow us to estimate the time since death.' Judith turned to Lock. 'But I was hoping you might be able to help us with this one. Are you familiar with the work of Procopio?'

Lock paused for a few seconds. 'I am now.'

Dr Edwards headed over to their computer and opened a heavily populated Excel sheet. 'I scraped off some bone powder and analysed the levels of fetuin-A, which as you know is a protein that decreases with age. Drawing upon Procopio's work and the pilot studies in the UK and US, do you think you'd be able to develop a computer model that allows us to accurately assess the time since death?'

Lock stared at the screen, although Kat knew he was directly interfacing with the data in the computer rather than reading it from the monitor. After almost a minute of silence, he turned around and projected a 3D graph in the centre of the room. 'I will send you the full methodology and rationale so that you can verify it with your colleagues, but I have correlated the extent of the protein with the passage of time using a new equation that I have called "RoDFA" – "Rate of Decay of Fetuin-A" – to estimate the time since death, which I conclude is between seventy-five and eighty-five years, with an accuracy range of plus or minus three per cent.'

'So, around the 1930s or 40s?' said Kat.

'Which means this is an archaeological rather than a criminal case,' said Judith.

Kat walked over to the skeleton. 'Only if you focus on the technical rule. He might have been shot over seventy years ago, but it was still a crime. He was still murdered. And like McLeish said, his body was found within two miles and one week of Hannah Weber's, so their deaths could be connected. In fact, he might even be her great-grandfather.'

'There is no evidence to suggest that at this stage,' said Lock.

'But it's a hypothesis I think we should test.'

'I agree about the hypothesis,' said Judith. 'But it won't be us who tests it. If he died over seventy years ago, then the law says I have to refer it to a forensic archaeologist.'

Kat scowled. Once it got assigned to an archaeologist, this man's death would become a matter of academic interest rather than justice, and all the urgency and resources that went with a live case would be lost. And no matter how good they were, the forensic archaeologist would necessarily focus on just this one body, meaning that any possible connections between the two cases would be lost. 'Lock said there was a three per cent error range on his assessment. What if, in your professional opinion, you thought we should be more cautious and give it a range of five per cent?'

'That would mean the time since death might be less than seventy years, so the case could legitimately remain with you until we have a clearer picture. And the best way to get that is to try and establish our victim's identity.'

Judith turned towards the AI hologram. 'Okay, Lock, thank you for your analysis, but in my professional opinion we should work within an error range of five per cent. Which means it's time to get busy. With your machine learning, I'm hoping you can take all the data that we have – proteins, DNA and bone measurements and structure from this skeleton – so that we can turn back time and reveal the man he once was.'

'Very well.' Lock paused. 'All the data we now have from the victim's protein and DNA analysis suggests that his genetic profile is consistent with that of a white Caucasian male of German ancestry born in the early part of the twentieth century, with blond hair and blue eyes.'

'German?' said Kat. 'Lock, can you cross-check this person's DNA with that of Hannah Weber, please?'

A virtual graph of DNA markers appeared, then disappeared again to be replaced by a sepia-coloured photograph of a young man in an army uniform gleaned from Hannah's blog. His features were gaunt, as if his flesh hadn't quite caught up with a sudden growth spurt, and he had blond hair and blue eyes that stared rather nervously at the camera.

Lock rotated the 2D image, then dragged it over to the skeleton, where he draped and meshed it over the bones.

The skull suddenly became a face. His eyes were closed as if he were sleeping, but Kat could see that his lashes were blond, as was his short-cropped hair and the dusting of stubble on his chin. His cheeks were slightly hollow, but with his long, straight nose and gently arched eyebrows, it gave him a noble, almost serene appearance. Lock made a beckoning motion with his right hand, and a 3D image of a man rose up from the mortuary slab.

'Based upon my analysis of his DNA, proteins and facial reconstruction, there is a ninety-nine per cent probability that this body belonged to Walter Weber, Hannah Weber's great-grandfather.'

CHAPTER FORTY-SEVEN

Kat stared at the image of the young German man before her, remembering the letter that Hannah Weber had shared on her blog:

I will be home before our baby is born in September and then our life can begin, and we will finally put this nightmare behind us.

Goodnight, my dearest, sweetest love. My very bones ache for the want of you.

'He never made it home,' she said softly. 'What was his date of birth, Lock?'

'According to his army records, Walter Weber was born on 26 February 1924.'

Kat frowned. 'The letter that Hannah shared on her blog – he sent that at the end of April 1945, didn't he? And Hannah said it was the last her great-grandmother heard of him, so I guess he must have died shortly after, aged twenty-one. Just a boy, really.' She let out a heavy sigh. 'Are there any records of German prisoners of war being shot?'

'No,' said Lock. 'And having just read 626,003 articles on prisoner of war camps, I consider the probability of any POWs being shot during the Second World War to be exceedingly low, especially during the period that Walter Weber was there. According to the literature, by May 1945, it was widely believed that peace was imminent, not least because Adolf Hitler took his own life on 30 April. Germany surrendered on 8 May, which was celebrated as Victory in Europe Day. Despite peace being declared, it took many months to arrange the return of prisoners to their home countries, and there are suggestions in the literature that some industries such as farming had become reliant on POWs to provide free labour and so were reluctant to let them go. However, by all accounts, they were well treated.'

'Maybe by their prison masters or employers, but what about the returning soldiers?' said Judith. 'I bet they weren't so happy to find Germans working in their home villages. Maybe there was a fight?'

'There is no evidence that aligns with your "maybes". On the contrary, according to the first-hand accounts I have read, relationships between local people and the POWs were good, as after five years of war, the majority of the population just wanted to put it behind them and enjoy the peace. There are several accounts of POWs visiting local pubs and being invited into English homes for Christmas dinner.'

'Well, *somebody* murdered him,' said Kat. 'And somebody murdered his great-granddaughter, Hannah. It can't be a coincidence that two German relatives were murdered and buried within two miles of each other in Shustoke, of all places.' She paused. 'Lock, can you play the last couple of minutes of Hannah's video again, please?'

He nodded, and the video of Hannah Weber appeared on the white wall of the path lab, her long brown hair shining in the sunlight as she stood in a Warwickshire field, oblivious to the fact that she would soon be buried there.

'Those of you who have followed my blog know that I'm not just here to pick strawberries – I'm here to find answers. In 1945, my great-grandfather, Walter Weber, was kept in a prisoner of war camp just two miles from here. He was deeply in love with my great-grandmother, Greta, and couldn't wait to see his first-born child, as you can see from the letters on my blog. But when the war ended, Walter Weber never came home. He was never seen or heard of again.'

The camera on her mobile phone panned out again onto the Warwickshire countryside. 'My great-grandmother has never stopped hoping that one day he would return. I think that is why she has lived so long – she is over a hundred years old! But now she is finally dying in a hospice. There's nothing that I or anyone else can do about that. But I am hoping that I will find out what happened to her soulmate, so that before she dies, she will finally know why he never came home.

'Please share this, post and join the campaign: *Whatever happened to Walter Weber?*'

Kat stared at the frozen image. 'Maybe she found out. Maybe she discovered who the killer was, and they killed her too.'

'If that were true, then that would mean her murderer is nearly a hundred years old,' said Lock. 'Would you like me to search the records to identify all the centenarians in Warwickshire?'

'No, that won't be necessary. It takes a lot of strength to decapitate and bury a body. So, it must have been someone who *knew* about the murder. Someone who was so desperate to keep it secret that they were willing to do anything – even kill – to stop the truth from being revealed.' She pulled out her phone and quickly skimmed a summary report from DS Debbie Browne.

'I need to pay the Coopers a visit,' she announced. 'Now.'

CHAPTER FORTY-EIGHT

Bourne Farm, 8.42pm

Rayan paced around the car park as he waited for the boss to arrive. It was almost completely dark and bitterly cold, but he preferred to walk up and down in the clean, sharp air listening to the hoots of barn owls than sit in his stuffy car. DCS Frank hadn't said much on the phone – just told him to meet her at the farm as soon as possible. Because of the late hour, he presumed they must have found something significant in the post-mortem. But if so, why hadn't she told him? It couldn't be about the Coopers, as she didn't even ask how his interviews with them had gone. But then why did she want to meet him at their home?

A pair of headlights suddenly lit up the narrow lane that ran alongside the entrance to the farm, and with a sigh of relief he recognised the boss's car as it pulled up. His relief turned to irritation when Lock climbed out after DCS Frank. No, he corrected himself. He couldn't 'climb' out of anything – Lock was just a bloody hologram.

'Everything all right, boss?' he asked as he crunched across the gravel towards them.

'Yes. I've just come from the PM where Lock and Dr Edwards confirmed that the second body belonged to Hannah's great-grandfather, Walter Weber. He was shot in the head.'

'Oh,' said Rayan, surprised by a jolt of pity. 'I guess that explains why his girlfriend never heard from him again.'

'Yes, it's tragic,' said Kat, heading towards the farmhouse. 'But I've just applied for a warrant and I'm here to arrest Harry Cooper for the murder of Hannah Weber, so I need you to accompany me in case he gets difficult.'

'Harry?' Rayan echoed as he followed the boss. 'Did Dr Edwards find forensic evidence linking him to the murder?'

'No.'

'Then what *did* you find?'

'I haven't got time to explain,' said Kat without breaking her stride. 'I just need you to help me place Harry Cooper under arrest.'

'But why?'

Kat turned to face him. 'Just trust me on this.'

Rayan bit down hard on his lip as his boss knocked the brass handle against the solid wooden door, prompting a burst of barking inside. It was all very well for her to ask him to trust her, but trust was a two-way street – and she clearly didn't trust him enough to tell him what on earth was going on. Unlike Lock. He glanced back at the hologram, who was standing behind Kat like a shadow.

Harry Cooper opened the door, still dressed in his farming clothes. The smell of cooking – some kind of casserole, Rayan guessed – floated out into the cold night air. He looked surprised to see them and frowned.

'Good evening,' said Kat. 'Sorry to call so late but I really need to speak to you both. Can I come in?'

Harry rolled his eyes. 'Jesus, when are you lot going to give it a rest? I already spent the best part of two hours with DI Hassan today. We've just sat down for dinner. Can't you come back tomorrow?'

'Afraid not,' said Kat, stepping into the hallway.

Harry didn't stop her as she walked straight past him, following the light and warmth to the kitchen at the back of the old house.

Rayan followed behind with Lock, even more puzzled. The boss wasn't normally this forceful. What on earth was she playing at?

As they entered the stone-flagged kitchen, Mrs Cooper looked up from the oak table where she sat and dropped her spoon in her casserole. The sheepdog beside her jumped up and barked, but a single word from Harry made him settle back down.

'Sorry to trouble you, Mrs Cooper,' Kat said, standing before them in front of a badly stained Aga. 'But this won't take long.'

Harry began to take a seat at the table, but Kat raised a hand. 'I wouldn't bother, Mr Cooper. I'm here to charge you with the murder of Hannah Weber and to place you under arrest. You do not have to say anything, but it may harm your defence if you do not mention when questioned something which you later rely on in court. Anything you do say may be given in evidence.'

'What the . . . ?' said Harry, looking at Rayan. 'This is a joke, right?'

'We can discuss this down at the police station,' said Kat.

'No!' cried Mrs Cooper, struggling with her stick to stand up. 'You can't arrest my Harry. He's done nothing wrong!'

'And how do you know that, Mrs Cooper?' Kat replied, turning to face the older woman.

Caroline Cooper stared back, her breathing coming thick and fast.

Kat gave Rayan a pointed nod.

He took a moment to respond – this sudden turn of events made no sense to him. But then his training kicked in. 'Put your hands behind your back,' he said firmly, as he took out a pair of handcuffs. Over the head of the smaller but muscular farmer, he caught Lock watching him with an odd look on his face. Was he confused as well, or just envious of the fact that as a hologram he couldn't actually do anything other than watch Rayan arrest someone?

'He didn't do it, I tell you, *he didn't do it*!' cried Mrs Cooper. The sheepdog jumped up, growling by her side.

'How do you know that, Mrs Cooper?' Kat demanded again, raising her voice over the dog. 'How can you be so sure that your own son is not a murderer?'

'Because *I* did it!' she shouted, before sinking back into her chair. 'I killed Hannah Weber.'

CHAPTER FORTY-NINE

Harry Cooper stared at his mother, open mouthed. 'There's no need to lie for me, Mum. It doesn't matter if they arrest me. I didn't do it and I can prove it. You don't have to do this.'

Caroline Cooper buried her face in her hands. 'No, you don't understand,' she said, her voice barely a whisper. 'I did it. I really did it. I killed that poor young girl.' She looked up at Kat, her face wet with tears. 'I didn't mean to. It was just a terrible, horrible accident.'

Rayan tried to exchange shocked glances with Kat, but it was clear from her face that this wasn't a surprise. In fact, he realised belatedly, she'd probably charged Harry in order to provoke this confession from his mother.

Kat sat down at the kitchen table opposite Caroline and moved a plate of bread out of the way. 'We've identified the second body as belonging to a Mr Walter Weber. We believe he was shot in the spring or summer of 1945 and buried on your land.'

'Oh, God,' Caroline Cooper sobbed.

'What? Who is he? What's going on?' Harry demanded.

Kat held up a hand to silence him. She waited until the first rush of tears was spent, then gently asked Caroline to tell them what had happened.

'My mum, Elizabeth Day, was a good woman. One of the best.

I'm not just saying that because she was my mum – she was loved and respected by everybody in the community. She promoted organic, ethical farming back in the Seventies, when everyone thought it was just for cranks. But time proved her right. That's why the barn, and all our food produce, bears her name. She never took a day off, was hardly ever ill at all until three years ago when she developed terminal cancer. It all happened so quickly. She refused to leave the farm to go into hospital or a hospice, and before she died, she . . . she shared with me a terrible secret. Like most farms, we struggled during the Second World War, as all the men were away fighting. So when a POW camp was set up at Maxstoke Castle, she said it was like a godsend. There were loads of German and Italian lads, mostly fit and young, that were offered as free labour. They just had to feed them.

'My mum helped her mum cook for them and served them whenever she got the chance. She was only eighteen and most of the young men in the village had gone to war, so she said it was exciting to meet boys her own age and from different countries. And she took a particular fancy to one of them.'

'Walter Weber?' prompted Kat.

Mrs Cooper nodded and wiped her mouth with her hand. 'She didn't go into all the details, but I think Walter Weber was engaged to be married, so although he was polite and friendly, he wasn't really interested. But my mum was the kind of woman who believed anything was possible if you just tried hard enough. So one afternoon she tried to kiss him, and he rejected her. She was upset. Humiliated. And so she . . . she told her dad – my grandad – that Walter had made advances on *her*. I don't know exactly what she said, but her dad went mental. Before she had a chance to explain properly, he picked up his hunting rifle and went looking for Walter. My mum said she tried to pull him back. She tried to reason with him, but she was only eighteen, and my grandad was a big man.' Caroline Cooper closed her eyes. 'She said that every night she still heard that single shot ring out across the farm. She was haunted by it. Even though it wasn't her who fired the bullet.'

'So why didn't she say something?' asked Kat.

'If she'd told anyone then her dad would have gone to jail, and without him we'd have probably lost the farm. So when my grandad buried that young boy, he made my mum swear not to tell anyone, for all our sakes. This farm has been in our family for over three hundred years. It was all we had.'

'And so your mum – and you – kept this secret until Hannah Weber came here looking for the truth?'

Caroline Cooper's face sagged with misery. 'It was horrible knowing that my family had been responsible for someone's death, but it was even worse when Hannah came asking about her great-grandad. She was obsessed, always asking questions. I tried not to let it bother me, but then one evening – 16 July – she asked if she could interview me for some video thing she was making. She wanted to know if my parents had ever talked about the POWs that worked on the farm. Did I have any photographs or papers from the time, that sort of thing. I said no, but she kept on asking. I said I was busy and headed down towards the river, but she followed me, still asking her bloody questions. And then she took her phone out and started filming me. I told her to stop. And then, when she wouldn't, I . . . I tried to make her. I raised my stick and tried to knock the phone out of her hand. But she moved suddenly, and . . . and . . . instead of hitting her phone, her neck got in the way.'

She covered her face with her hands, sobbing now. 'I was mortified. I dropped the stick. Rushed towards her, apologising. But she was making these horrible choking sounds, like she couldn't breathe. At first I thought she was being dramatic, but then her eyes . . . it was her windpipe, I think. I tried to help her, honest I did. But she collapsed, clutching her throat, and I didn't know what to do. And then . . . finally, she was still.'

'*Mum*,' said Harry, his face distraught.

'I'm sorry, son. I'm so sorry.'

Rayan looked down at the older woman, and at the walking stick by her side, tipped with an ivory-coloured ram's horn. It would have been like hitting someone with a lump of granite. 'Why didn't you call an ambulance?' he asked, unable to keep the judgement out of his voice.

'I panicked. I rang my husband and he said to wait for him to get there. He was only a few fields away, but by the time he arrived, it was too late. Her windpipe was crushed. I wanted to call the police, but Roger said no, I would end up in jail – it wasn't like it was self-defence or anything. And then I'd have to explain why we'd been arguing, and it would all come out about her great-grandfather and everything.'

She ran a hand over her face. 'Betty's Barn is a values-led brand. A third of our income comes from family-friendly activities. Roger said that to have a murder – *two* murders – on our land would destroy everything that generations of my family had worked so hard to achieve. We barely break even as it is – any loss of income would have jeopardised the farm and Harry's inheritance. And Roger said he would never survive without me if I went to jail. Our whole lives were on the line.'

'So, you decapitated and buried Hannah Weber,' said Kat.

'No! Roger told me to go back to the house. He said he would deal with it, for my sake and Harry's. I didn't know that he would . . . that he—' She broke off and buried her face in her hands once more. 'I never asked him what he did that day. And we never spoke of it again.'

'*Jesus Christ*,' said Harry. 'You killed that poor young girl for the fucking *farm*?' He laughed, a bitter, tearful sound. 'I don't even *want* it, Mum. That's the joke. I never have.'

'You will when you're older, son. You might not see it now, but one day you will realise that land is the only thing that matters. It's the only thing that lasts.'

'It's the only thing worth fighting for, worth dying for,' quoted Kat. 'Isn't that right? Scarlett O'Hara's dad says it in *Gone with the Wind*. That's what made me realise it was you. But he doesn't say it's worth killing for.'

Caroline Cooper's defiant face fell. 'I'm sorry.'

Rayan ground his teeth, tempted to say, 'Try telling that to Hannah's mum'. But then he looked at the broken mother and son on opposite sides of the table, and the congealing casserole between them.

'I'm afraid you'll need to come with us to the station,' Kat said, giving Rayan a nod.

And for the second time that night, he pulled out his handcuffs.

CHAPTER FIFTY

DCS Kat Frank's home, Coleshill, 20 April, 6.05am

Kat grabbed her ringing mobile, heart rocketing. Ever since that 6am call from the hospice, she'd hated early morning calls, breaking into her sleep like burglars.

'DCS Kat Frank?' she said, voice high and wary.

'Well?' McLeish demanded.

Kat snapped on the bedside lamp, rapidly trying to focus. Her boss clearly wasn't happy, but she couldn't think why. After formally interviewing Caroline Cooper at the station, she'd taken her statement, before arresting and charging her. Then she'd sent McLeish a quick text to update him at about midnight, which was only a few hours ago. She knew he liked to be kept informed, but this was a bit much, even for him. 'Nothing else to report since last night, sir,' Kat said in her professional, I'm-not-pissed-off-by-the-early-morning-call voice. 'I'll check with the duty sergeant, but as I said in my text, Caroline Cooper gave us a full confession for the manslaughter of Hannah Weber, and the PM confirmed that the second body belonged to Hannah's great-grandfather. I also warned Harry Cooper that we'd have to report him to HMRC for failing to pay tax and National Insurance for his seasonal workers. DS Browne's review of his employment and payroll records showed significant discrepancies. No wonder he was so reluctant to give us access to the farm. He's probably guilty of tax avoidance, but he knew nothing about the deaths.'

'I didn't ring you to discuss taxes. I want to know why you allowed Rentaghost to carry out a PM in a *murder* investigation.'

'What?'

'I hear Lock fancies himself as a pathologist now, even though he can't even pick up a bloody knife and fork?'

'No, sir. Dr Edwards was the pathologist in charge. Lock merely assisted her.'

'By using novel and unproven techniques?'

'Well . . . he did use some of the latest research . . .' Kat began, frowning. Why on earth was McLeish ringing her about PM techniques at this time in the morning? 'There's nothing to worry about,' she assured him. 'Judith consulted with some colleagues, and they'll review his work, so it's fine.'

'It's very far from fucking *fine*, DCS Frank. It's *all over the fucking media*, is what it is. That bloody podcaster has got wind of it and accused Warwickshire Police of carrying out a dodgy PM as part of another cover-up.'

'The podcaster? How the hell does he know?'

'I don't fucking know. The point is, he has a point. We – *you* – have used an untested AI to carry out unproven tests in the investigation of a murder that could be linked to one of the most controversial cases in the county, a case in which you yourself have been accused of a miscarriage of justice.'

Kat sat up. 'I haven't been *accused* of anything. Not by anyone who matters. It's just a bloody podcast.'

'*I* know that and *you* know that, but it doesn't look good. And to top it all off, Hannah Weber's mother has found out – one of the tabloids contacted her to ask how she felt about her daughter's autopsy being carried out by AI. Of course, she didn't know the first thing about it, and wants to know why no one told her.' He let out a sigh so heavy that Kat had to move the phone away from her ear. 'Look,' he continued. 'I've got to give a response to the press by seven, so I'm going to have to say I will get someone in to review them.'

Kat's hand flew to her throat. 'Review what?'

'The PMs for both murders.'

Relief flooded through her. For a minute she'd thought he was going to order a review of the Aston Strangler case.

'I'm sorry, Kat, but it's best if you take a bit of a back seat until someone's reviewed the PMs. I don't want to undermine you, but I don't have a choice.'

'What do you mean, "take a back seat"? Am I being suspended?'

'No. Or at least, not yet. I need you to keep your head down for a day or two, so I want you to go to Germany and meet with the mum. You can explain how virtual autopsies work and apologise for the fact that she found out about it through the media.'

'Okay, but why do I have to go to *Germany*? Can't I just ring her?'

'I want you out of the way for a bit, but I don't want it to look like you've been suspended. And it might help manage the media if we can say that you've spoken with her personally. So, get yourself on a flight today, as soon as possible.'

'Today? Do you—'

But McLeish was gone. The 'conversation' was over.

Kat swore. She couldn't believe he'd asked her to step back from the case and fly to *Germany* just because of a stupid podcast. And he hadn't even congratulated her for solving the murders! She opened up a search engine and typed her name and 'post-mortem', clicking on the first of several articles.

POLICEWOMAN UNDER FIRE ORDERED EXPERIMENTAL AI AUTOPSY ON SUSPECTED VICTIM OF THE ASTON STRANGLER

EXCLUSIVE: *Daily Mail*, online version,
last updated 19 April, 5.17am

The *Daily Mail* has learned that DCS Kat Frank of Warwickshire Police experimented on two potential victims of the Aston Strangler by using AI to carry out virtual autopsies. So-called 'virtopsies' involve taking lots of photographs and scans, rather than physically dissecting a body to determine the cause of death. Concerns have been raised by the presenter of the Aston Strangler podcast, who gave an exclusive interview to the *Daily Mail* last night, although he asked to remain anonymous to protect his sources.

'This is a novel and unproven technique in the UK, so I'd be concerned if it were to be used in any post-mortem. But I am shocked to learn that DCS Frank used it on potential victims of the Aston Strangler. Kat Frank has built a very successful career after convincing a judge, jury and the public that Anthony Bridges was the serial killer. But there is growing evidence that this was a terrible miscarriage of justice. Serious questions need to be asked about who decided the two victims were not worthy of proper autopsies and what they were trying to hide. More importantly, why aren't the police warning local women that the Aston Strangler could still be out there?'

A spokesperson for the Royal College of Pathologists said, 'Virtopsies are innovative techniques that are sometimes used for training medical students, and for research. We are not aware of them being used in live murder investigations in the UK. Post-mortems are by their nature complex and need to be carried out with dignity and respect, so we would be concerned if AI was being used to replace the expertise and humanity that only a consultant pathologist can provide. We currently have a shortage of qualified pathologists in the UK, and we need to invest in more pathologists, not cut corners with AI.'

The *Mail* contacted Warwickshire Police, but no one was available for comment.

COMMENTS

Anon *How can you carry out a post-mortem just by taking a few photos? The whole point of them is to cut up a dead body so you can see what's inside. What a farce. This is what happens when you slash police budgets.*

Anon *No, this is what happens when you put a bent copper under investigation in charge of investigating the deaths of two women who have been strangled by the REAL Aston Strangler!*

Anon *She isn't under a formal investigation as far as I know. And it hasn't been confirmed that the two bodies were strangled?*

Anon *It hasn't been confirmed because SHE made sure there wasn't a proper autopsy! Jesus, don't you get how corrupt this whole thing is?*

Anon *The police are just trying their best to keep us safe. You should be thanking them instead of attacking them.*

> **Anon** *If DCS Kat Frank cared about keeping us safe rather than keeping her job then she'd be out there now looking for the REAL Aston Strangler. Until they catch him, no one is safe. She should be taken off the case and suspended IMO.* (22 likes)

Shit. Even as Kat read the article, more comments were being added. Honestly, it wasn't even 7am and people were already bashing out their opinions on matters they knew *nothing* about. 'The victims weren't even strangled, for fuck's sake,' she growled at her screen.

She typed out a quick email to McLeish reminding him that they now had a signed confession for the murder of Hannah Weber (who was NOT strangled) and also confirmation that the second body was a MAN and also NOT STRANGLED! So, her email concluded, WHY are you asking me to take a step back? We should be rebutting every line of this article with the truth, not reinforcing the rumours. Sir.

Kat reviewed the email. Too many capitals? It made her look a bit mad. Well, fuck it, she WAS mad. In fact, she was bloody furious. She'd just solved not one, but *two* murders, and instead of being rewarded she was effectively on gardening leave! Honestly, what was *wrong* with everyone? She pressed send, and her bedroom filled with a satisfying *swoosh* sound as her email flew towards her boss.

Then she tapped out another one to Judith and Professor Okonedo, attaching a link to the article and asking them to call her as soon as they could. She needed to make sure that they didn't get in trouble for this as well. Kat rubbed her face with her hands. It wasn't the first virtopsy they'd done – they'd used Lock in the case of the Coventry Crucifier just before Christmas and no one had batted an eyelid. But given the rumours about the Aston Strangler, maybe she should have mentioned it to McLeish, just to buy a bit of air cover.

But there hadn't been time, she reminded herself. It had all happened so quickly, she hadn't told *anybody*, let alone her boss.

In fact, how the hell had the podcaster found out? 'Lock?' she ventured.

The hologram appeared at the foot of her bed. After noticing her attire, Lock's image shimmered, and his suit changed to pyjamas.

Kat held up a hand. 'Enough with the pyjamas, Lock. It's morning, and I'm just about to get dressed.' He looked confused, but before he could ask more questions, she quickly told him about McLeish and the article. 'I'm just going to grab a quick shower, but can you do a trawl of all the emails and texts from our team since the beginning of this case to find out who knew about your role in the PM and who else they might have told?'

'Is this an official leak enquiry?'

'Er . . . not official, no. A preliminary one, maybe. Just to establish the facts.'

'By accessing and reviewing all of the emails and text messages of Rayan Hassan, Debbie Browne, Professor Okonedo, Dr Judith Edwards, Karen-from-Comms and yourself to establish who is the source of the leak?'

Kat climbed out of bed and hurried into her dressing gown on the back of the door. 'I trust my team. I don't think anyone deliberately leaked the information, but they may have mentioned it to someone who did.'

'Kat?'

She turned at the use of her name.

'According to the protocols, a formal leak enquiry should be signed off by Chief Constable McLeish.'

'I told you – this is preliminary, not formal.'

Lock raised his eyebrows. 'I am programmed to follow the rules, but there is nothing in the guidelines about a preliminary investigation.'

'Didn't Professor Okonedo advise you to trust my judgement above all others?'

'Yes,' said Lock. 'During our last case she said that when in doubt, I should follow your judgement, and to prioritise you above other officers.'

'Well, there you are then.'

'Very well,' said Lock, with a slight dip of his head.

'Thank you. Can we meet in the kitchen in about half an hour?'

'It will take me less than a minute to carry out the requested checks.'

'But I need to get dressed. And I can't do that with you in my bedroom.'

'Why not? I have no body, so I cannot get in the way.'

Kat stared back at him. *Because you have eyes*, she wanted to say. Even though she knew those eyes weren't real, just a projection of the software in the bracelet she wore, she didn't want him watching her while she got dressed. God knows what assessments he would make – and the last thing she needed right now was some comment on her BMI. She opened the bedroom door. 'Just meet me in the kitchen, Lock, please. Ideally with a nice cup of tea.'

'I cannot make tea.'

'I know. I was joking.'

Lock gave her what could only be described as a wounded look. 'Why do you think my lack of a body is funny?'

'I don't. I'm sorry, I just—'

But Lock was gone.

CHAPTER FIFTY-ONE

Lock stood before the kitchen island and projected a copy of his analysis just above the fruit bowl. 'I have reviewed the emails, texts and WhatsApp messages of each member of your team, as requested. I was unable to find any mention of my role in the post-mortem in any of the recorded correspondence from Rayan Hassan, Debbie Browne or Karen-from-Comms. There were fourteen emails between Dr Edwards and Professor Okonedo regarding the adaptations to the mortuary laboratory, but no written correspondence about my role in the two post-mortems cited in the *Daily Mail* article. The only message I could find that referred to my role was in your text to your son, Cameron.'

'Pardon?'

'I said the only message I could find that referred to my—'

'I heard what you said.'

'Then why did you say "pardon"?'

'Because I don't understand. Show me the message.'

Lock made a swiping gesture, and an enlarged virtual text exchange appeared before them.

KF: Judith needs Lock's help with the PM so I probably won't be home for dinner. Sorry. Can you get a Deliveroo? My treat. Have a good night x

CF: Course. You OK? Is it the PM for the second strangled girl?

KF: Don't worry. PM proves not strangled. Talk later x

Kat took a large gulp of her tea. 'Cam wouldn't say anything to anyone. He's known ever since he can talk that he's not to repeat police business outside the house.'

'Could he have discussed it inside the house with Gemma?'

'I don't know. I don't think he would.'

'Perhaps you could ask Cam?'

'Ask Cam what?' Her son walked into the kitchen and pulled open the fridge door on his relentless quest for food.

'We wanted to ask you if you'd mentioned my role in the post-mortem to anyone.'

'No, we didn't!' Kat cried, telling Lock with her eyes to *shut the fuck up*.

Cam turned to face her, holding a carton of mango juice. 'Why?'

'It's nothing,' she insisted. 'Lock just got the wrong end of the stick.'

'I don't have either end of any stick,' said Lock, frowning.

'What's going on?' Cam asked, looking between them.

'Nothing. It's just that there's an article in the *Daily Mail* – a really negative one – about Lock's role in the autopsy, and I'm trying to work out how they even knew about it. I didn't tell anyone. Except I did send a quick text to you explaining why I was going to be late. And I know you would *never* talk about my work without my consent, but we were just wondering whether you happened to mention it to anyone.'

'Of course I didn't. Except for Gemma.'

'You told *Gemma?*' Kat echoed, her eyes widening. 'But you know you're not supposed to tell anyone about my cases.'

'It wasn't *anyone*. It was Gemma. You used to tell Dad everything.'

'That's not the same thing.'

'Why isn't it?'

'Because Dad was my husband.'

'And Gemma's my girlfriend. We tell each other everything.'

Kat's eyebrows shot up.

'Are you saying you don't trust her? Because Gemma would never, ever—'

'No, of course not. It's just . . . it's just that . . .'

'I'm not your little boy anymore?'

'Don't be ridiculous,' Kat scoffed. But even as she denied it, the point hit home. Cam used to tell *her* everything. But now the centre of his world had shifted, like a flower turns towards the light. *Which is as it should be*, she reminded herself. She gave her son an apologetic smile. 'I'm sorry. You're right. Gemma's your girlfriend, so of course you'll share everything with her. I'm just struggling to catch up.'

'S'all right,' he said, moving towards the bread bin. 'Do we have any croissants?'

'Yes, there's a new pack in there. Actually, Cam, because of all this fuss over the PM, I'm going to have to go to Germany today.'

'Germany? *Today?*'

'I need to speak to Hannah Weber's mum, and it needs to be face to face, so I'll fly out today, but I'll be back tomorrow night.'

Cam's face fell. 'But Gemma's here. We came so that you could get to know her.'

'I know, I'm sorry. It wasn't planned, it's just that—'

'Work's more important?'

'*No*. It's just for one day, Cam.'

'It is two days, actually, if you are not coming back until tomorrow night,' added Lock.

Cam grabbed the bag of croissants, shaking his head. 'Doesn't matter. Actually, there's a rave tonight in London that Gemma was keen to go to. We weren't gonna bother as we thought we'd spend a bit of time with you, but we might as well go tonight now.'

'There's no need for that,' said Kat. 'I'll be back tomorrow night in time for dinner. I promise.'

'No, we were going to stay with her dad at the weekend anyway, so we might as well go tonight and then stay on. It's not a big deal.'

Kat called after her son, but he was already heading out of the kitchen with the croissants and juice.

'Gemma's hungry,' was all he threw over his shoulder as he disappeared up the stairs.

Kat swore under her breath.

'Well, that went well,' said Lock.

'*What?*'

'I have learned from you that sarcasm – saying the opposite of what one means – is often an appropriate response to moments of tension.'

Kat dragged a hand through her hair. 'Not this time it isn't. Cam's my son. It's not something you should joke about.'

Lock gave her a curt nod. 'Then I will update my algorithms to note that one should not tell jokes about a matter that is of emotional importance to another.'

Kat studied her AI partner. Was he making a dig?

'Would you like me to continue the informal leak enquiry?' Lock asked. 'Perhaps you should ask Gemma whether she shared the information that Cam gave her with anyone?'

'God no. She's Cam's girlfriend. I have to trust her.'

'But it doesn't make sense to trust what someone says just because your son cares about them.'

'Relationships are built on trust, Lock. So if I trust someone, it means I believe they will do the right thing. And if someone I trust says they didn't do something, then I have to believe that they're telling me the truth.'

'Without any objective evidence?'

'Yes. It means I take their word for it.'

Lock paused. 'Do you trust *me*, Kat?'

'Well, you're not capable of lying, so I guess I have to.'

Her phone pinged, and she picked it up to see two messages from HR about the review. The first explained that she wasn't under investigation, that it was a 'neutral' act to help them understand who had been involved in the decision to carry out a virtual post-mortem, and that DCS Barry Parker from Internal Affairs had been appointed to carry out the review. And lo, the second email was from the great man himself, seeking a 'mutually convenient' time so that he could get her 'input'.

'Oh, do fuck off,' she muttered. She knew how Nosey Parker worked. Once he started asking questions, he wouldn't stop, and if she wasn't careful, he'd be dredging up her arrest of the Aston Strangler 'for context'. She slammed some bread into the toaster, even though she wasn't hungry. Jesus, when would it ever end?

Her mobile rang and, seeing it was Rayan, she accepted the call.

'You okay?' her DI asked. 'McLeish told me what happened.'

'Yeah, fine,' she managed to say, oddly touched that Rayan was checking in on her. 'It's not a big deal. I'm not off the case or anything – he just wants me to keep out of the way until things calm down,' she explained, before briefly telling him about her trip to Germany. 'Once I'm back we can announce the arrest of Caroline Cooper and the results of the PMs, and then everyone will realise what a load of crap this all is. We've done a bloody good job and I'm proud of the whole team.' She paused. 'In fact, why don't I take everyone out for a drink when I get back tomorrow night? We should be celebrating our success.'

'The whole team?'

'Yes. Tell Professor Okonedo and Judith Edwards that I insist they come too – we need to stick together on this one. Okay?'

'Great,' Rayan said, his voice considerably brighter. 'Where do you want to go?'

'Up to you – just pick somewhere that isn't too far from Birmingham International and where Debbie can bring the baby if she has to. There are a couple of nice pubs in Shustoke with gardens. Text me the details and I'll see you there.' She ended the call with a smile. A night out with the team would distract her from Cam's absence and remind herself – and everyone else – that they'd solved two cases *and* proved they were absolutely nothing to do with the Aston Strangler. Everything was going to be okay.

CHAPTER FIFTY-TWO

Outside DCS Kat Frank's house, Coleshill, 20 April

He can't believe his luck. First the son and his girlfriend left, and then a couple of hours later Kat Frank put her suitcase into her car, double-locked the front door and drove off. He can see from the apologetic texts to her son that she's going to Germany and won't be back until tomorrow night.

But he's not used to being lucky. Doesn't trust it. So he waits, and he waits, until darkness falls. He watches as the lamps go on behind all the closed blinds. Stupid bitch. As if that's *going to fool anyone. He takes out his phone, logs into the home automation system with Cam's password and deactivates the alarm. Then he scrambles up the wall and drops silently into the back garden, heart racing as he realises that this is finally it.*

It's okay to feel fear, *he reminds himself. Even Mike Tyson got scared.* 'I'm scared every time I go into the ring,' *he once famously said.* 'But it's how you handle it. What you have to do is plant your feet, bite down on your mouthpiece and say, "Let's go!"'

He stands up and rubs his hands together, feeling the hard, bruised knuckles beneath his rough, scabbed skin.

Let's go, *he whispers to himself.*
He is going to enjoy breaking into this house.
And he can't wait to welcome Kat Frank home.

CHAPTER FIFTY-THREE

The Griffin Inn, Shustoke, 21 April, 6.30pm

Rayan handed Debbie her white wine spritzer and a bag of salted crisps. 'There you go. Dinner's on me.'

'Ooh, thanks,' she said, tearing the bag open. 'I'm starving.' She glanced around the beer garden at the smattering of couples and after-work drinkers enjoying the evening sun. 'Honestly, it's so weird to be out. Brilliant, but weird.'

Rayan smiled and took a sip of his pint of Coke. It was her first night out since she'd had Lottie, and he'd offered to drive so that she could have a drink if she wanted to.

She checked her phone again. 'Still nothing from my sister.'

'Which means everything is fine. The boss is right, you need to get used to other people looking after Lottie. It'll be good for her and you.'

'I know. You're right.' But Debbie checked her phone again before dragging her eyes back to Rayan. 'Anyway, what's your plan for tonight?'

He shrugged. 'Have a couple of Cokes and then drive you home?'

'I mean with the professor.'

'Adaiba?' He couldn't resist the opportunity to say her name, nor the smile that spread across his face as he did.

Debbie laughed.

'What?' he demanded.

'Look at you. You're besotted.'

He grinned again. 'I just really like her.'

'Hence me asking what your plan is. She'll be here any minute. And she probably won't come out with us again for another few months, so this is your chance to move things forward.'

'What, with the boss and Judith and everyone else watching? I don't think so.'

Debbie made a dismissive gesture. 'They won't stay long. Two drinks and they'll be off. Then it'll be eight, eight thirty at the latest, so you could always suggest maybe going for some food?' She popped another crisp into her mouth and crunched down hard. 'Girl's gotta eat.'

'Not everyone is as obsessed with food as you are.' He glanced over at the car park to see Judith and Adaiba heading towards them. 'Shit, she's here,' he said. He stood up and waved, his stomach somersaulting as Adaiba smiled back. With every step she took towards him, his heart raced faster. Jesus, what was wrong with him? He was acting like a lovesick schoolboy.

When they reached the table, Rayan offered to get them both a drink, but Judith insisted on going to the bar, so he sat back down, with Adaiba and Debbie on the wooden bench opposite.

'What a great place,' said Adaiba, looking around. The beer garden was just a large patio full of picnic tables and benches, but it was surrounded by a panoramic view of the countryside, with nothing to see but acres of fields under a vast blue sky.

Rayan smiled with relief. It had been Lock's suggestion to come here. 'I have observed that Professor Okonedo is most relaxed in a rural environment, making her more conducive to your intentions,' he had observed.

'I don't have any intentions,' Rayan had insisted. 'It's just a team drink.'

'It is clear to me that you are greatly attracted to the professor and would very much like to make love to her. It is also clear to me that although she is also greatly attracted to you, she has conflicting thoughts about the merits or otherwise of making love with a serving police officer. My analysis of your interactions during the past year suggests that an evening drink in a rural public house that offers panoramic views of the countryside would be most likely to lead to a romantic conclusion. And in the light of DCS Frank's criteria regarding the proximity to DS Browne's home, I would recommend The Griffin Inn.'

Rayan had nearly spat out his tea, and although he had fervently denied any ulterior motive – *it was just a team drink* – nevertheless, here they were. It had been weird but strangely touching to receive romantic advice from Lock, of all people – 'an experiment in kindness', he'd called it. Whatever it was, looking at the smile on Adaiba's face, Rayan was grateful.

'It's so good to be able to sit out now the clocks have gone forward,' he said, taking a deep breath of the mild spring air.

'Aargh, don't mention the clocks going forward,' said Debbie. 'Lottie was just starting to sleep and then that totally threw her, so we're back to square one.'

When Adaiba asked how Lottie was, Debbie launched into a detailed explanation of her eating and sleeping patterns, as well as the bespoke development programme Lock had created for her. 'Honestly, you should see it, it's about seven hundred pages long and includes links to music I should be playing her at different times of the day for her brain development as well as special pictures for her eyes and exercises on the baby gym for her motor skills. If we carry on like this, she'll be a genius and an Olympic athlete by the time she's one.'

Judith joined them with more drinks, and Rayan watched them talking – or rather, he watched Adaiba as she nodded and smiled in all the right places. When Debbie started describing the contents of Lottie's nappy, he caught her eye and they both smiled. Unwilling to break the connection, he leaned forward. 'How are things? Have you been interviewed as part of the PM review?' Not the most romantic of openings, but it did get her attention.

'Yes,' Adaiba said, stroking the stem of her Martini glass. 'But Lock's role in virtopsies was all set out in the terms and conditions of the pilot, and every aspect of his work was reviewed by a human expert, so objectively it should be fine.'

'But?'

'But people aren't objective. Their judgement is often clouded by an irrational fear of change in general and AI in particular.'

'You sound like Lock.'

She smiled.

'Sorry, that wasn't meant to be a criticism,' he quickly added.

'Not at all, I took it as a compliment.'

'Do you think all feelings are irrational?'

Adaiba frowned. (God, he loved the way she frowned. Most people had two lines, one either side of the bridge of their nose, but she had just one vertical crease in the centre. It was so neat and perfect – so very *her*.)

'Not *all* feelings,' she said eventually. 'I think feelings are irrational if they don't align with reality or evidence. It is perfectly natural to feel fear or anger, but it is irrational when those feelings are out of proportion to the issue.' She paused. 'But some emotions like love are probably irrational.'

His breath caught. 'What do you mean?'

'Well, it makes no sense when you think about it. To love one person above all others – to invest all your hope and happiness in just one person, who at any time could leave or die and take it all with them.'

'That's a very—' he struggled to find the right word, '—negative view of love. In fact, I think you're describing fear, not love.'

Her beautiful eyes glistened. 'But love *is* fear. If you let yourself love someone, then you have to live with the constant fear that one day you might lose them.'

The urge to reach across the table and take her hands in his was powerful. He wanted to tell her that he knew she'd been damaged by the death of her mum, but that love could bring joy as well as fear. If only she'd let it. He leaned in closer, jumping back as Karen-from-Comms plonked herself down beside him.

'So, where's the boss then?' Karen asked.

Rayan blinked. 'Er . . . she's not here yet.'

'She's nearly an hour late,' said Judith. 'Has anyone heard from her?'

Everyone shook their heads.

'Okay,' said Rayan. 'I'll message her to let her know we're all here and I'll get her a drink in the meantime. Anyone else?' He headed to the bar just for an excuse to walk and get his head together. He felt drunk, even though he'd only had two pints of Coke. No, not drunk. Elated. Terrified. Excited. He didn't have the words for the cocktail of emotions surging through him, but he did know that this – whatever *this* was – really mattered. He needed to say something to Adaiba. Tell her how he really felt and ask her out properly.

But what if she said no? Then he wouldn't even have hope.

He ordered the drinks, mulling it over while he admired the wooden beams, real fires and stone-flagged floor. Why was he being like this? He was always the confident one, the one with the 'gift of the gab', according to his mates. He'd never cared about being rejected before. But then, it had never mattered this much before.

Just before Christmas he'd nearly died on a case, and in the hospital he'd promised himself he would make every moment count, that he wouldn't hang around waiting for things to happen, because who knew how much time they actually had left? Yet here he was, over four months later, still trapped by his own fear.

Rayan paid for the drinks and carried the tray back out into the garden. The early spring air was filled with birdsong and the promise of summer.

Adaiba turned towards him as he approached, her face breaking into such a beautiful smile that he nearly dropped the drinks. A flame-red sky flared behind her, and he wished he could take a photo. But then he realised he didn't need to: he would always remember the way she looked tonight.

Love is stronger than fear, he told himself as he approached the table. It was a cliché, but like most clichés it was true, and the more he repeated it to himself, the more determined he became.

Tonight he would be honest and tell Adaiba how he truly felt. And then he would just have to live with the consequences.

CHAPTER FIFTY-FOUR

One hour earlier

'If you turn left here,' said Lock from the passenger seat, 'then you will reach the venue where your team have arranged to meet.'

Kat turned right.

'Are you not attending the social gathering that you yourself have arranged?'

'I am, but I want to go home first.'

Lock frowned. 'But then you will be late. Why not go there now? We are just minutes away.'

'Because I want to get changed,' she said. What she didn't add was that she couldn't help hoping that Cam had returned home. She knew it was ridiculous – he almost certainly would have messaged her if he had – but hope was a stubborn old bastard. And she honestly could do with a quick shower: the trip had been physically and mentally draining. Mrs Weber – a lovely woman in her late forties – had been utterly broken by the death of her daughter. And yet she had two younger children and a dying grandmother-in-law to take care of, and so couldn't afford the luxury of grief. 'If I lay down and gave in to the tears,' she had told Kat, 'I don't think I would ever get up again.'

The narrow country lane cast dappled sunlight through the newly green trees, adding to her pensive mood as she drove.

'Is everything okay, DCS Frank?' asked Lock.

'Yes, fine, thank you.'

'Your tone and demeanour contradict your words. You have sighed seven times in the last twelve minutes.'

'I'm a forty-nine-year-old woman. I've got a lot to sigh about.' As soon as the words were out of her mouth, she chewed them over, like a bit of under-cooked beef. She never used to be like this. She and John and Cam used to laugh all the time. Car rides were full of songs and silly games: everything was an adventure. She glanced in the driver's mirror at the empty seats behind.

'That's eight times now.'

'Sorry?'

'You have sighed eight times in the last thirteen minutes.'

'Jesus, Lock, will you stop bloody counting?'

'I am a machine. I count everything.'

Kat shook her head. Lock could be completely infuriating, and yet at other times he appeared to possess extraordinary understanding. Like in Germany; they had visited the hospice where Hannah Weber's great-grandmother was dying, and Lock had – with her permission – adopted the image of Walter Weber as he would have been at twenty-one. Choosing his words with great care, Lock had used phrases from Walter's final letter to explain why her fiancé had been unable to return home, and to assure her that he had always, always loved her and that soon they would be together again. They were the last words that she ever heard, for Greta had died peacefully in her sleep shortly after. Hannah's mum had taken some comfort from the fact that she had her daughter to thank for that.

Kat turned onto her street, squinting through the low sun at her house up ahead. Was that a light on in Cam's room? She hurriedly parked and, not bothering to take her suitcase out of the boot, opened the front door with Lock following behind.

The alarm didn't go off when she walked in, even though she was sure she'd activated it before she'd left for Germany. Maybe Cam had come home after all. 'Cam?' she called out.

She threw her keys on the side and stood at the foot of the stairs. 'Cam?'

Silence.

There were no tell-tale shoes tossed in the hallway, yet the house held a sense that someone else was in it: a kind of ripple in the air, like disturbed water.

Kat headed towards the kitchen and crossed the threshold.

A blow to her jaw knocked her sideways.

She crashed into the fridge. Tried to grab the handle. The door. Anything to stay upright.

But the world tilted.

She lurched and fell back.

Straight through the arms of Lock and onto the cold, ceramic floor.

CHAPTER FIFTY-FIVE

The Griffin Inn, 7.55pm

Adaiba took a sip of her drink – it was her third vodka Martini and Kat hadn't turned up yet, so she needed to pace herself. She already felt quite tipsy. Not in a bad way – it was actually quite nice sitting outside, and she was enjoying talking to Rayan. In fact, she was enjoying herself just a little bit too much. Maybe she should have a Diet Coke next. Or head off home. But she did want to see Kat, and it was so nice to sit outdoors for a change. She looked up to see Rayan watching her.

He didn't look away.

It was surprisingly warm for April, and she could feel her skin flushing. 'Any idea when Kat will get here?' she asked Debbie.

'She's not replied to any of our messages, so her flight must have been delayed.'

'No, I checked the arrivals board online – her flight was on time,' said Judith. 'I reckon she's run off with Lock.' They drained their glass and rose to their feet. 'Well, I'm afraid I can't wait any longer. I've got to write a report tonight for that bloody review.'

'Actually,' said Debbie, 'I should be getting back, too. Would you mind dropping me off on the way?'

'Oh,' said Adaiba, glancing at her nearly full glass. 'I'd better go too then. Judith was my lift.'

'That's okay,' said Debbie. 'Rayan was mine so we can just swap. You don't mind, do you, Rayan?'

Adaiba couldn't be sure, but in the light of the setting sun, she thought she saw Debbie wink at him.

'You coming, too, Karen?' said Debbie, practically grabbing her drink off her.

Oh, God. She was being set up. Panicky excitement flared through Adaiba, and she took a large gulp of her ice-cold drink. It really was unseasonably warm.

She and Rayan waved goodbye to the others, wishing them all a safe journey home as they headed towards the car park.

When they were alone, Rayan cleared his throat. 'Are you warm enough out here, or do you want to go inside? It's a lovely old-fashioned pub with real fires and everything.'

'No, I mean yes. I'm not cold. It's nice out here.' *With you*, she almost added. God, this Martini had really gone to her head.

'Yes, I love sitting out in beer gardens. It's one of my favourite things.'

'Apart from picking ramsons and making your own wild pesto?'

He grinned. 'Glad to see you've been paying attention.' He coughed. 'My offer still stands, by the way. I'm not doing anything tonight if you fancy trying my home cooking.'

'What would your parents say?'

'Oh, they like my cooking. They'd recommend it.'

'No, I mean about me. If I just turned up at yours for dinner.'

He leant closer. 'They'd be delighted.'

Adaiba took another sip of her drink, trying to imagine what her dad and brothers would say if she brought DI Rayan Hassan home for dinner. She shook her head. They wouldn't even let him over the threshold.

'Or, if you're hungry and you don't trust my cooking, we could always eat here?'

Adaiba blinked. She couldn't deny she was hungry. 'Do they do vegan food?'

'Er . . . are faggots a vegetable?'

'No.' She laughed. 'They're made of minced offal.'

'Then I'm afraid you'll have to have that well-known vegan classic, a bowl of chips. You could go mad and have extra salt and vinegar?'

'I prefer ketchup.'

Rayan winced as if in pain. 'You'll be saying you like pineapple on pizza next.'

'Well, now you come to mention it . . .'

Rayan groaned. 'Shall I get us a couple of bowls of chips, and then you can confess your other culinary sins?'

She glanced around the beer garden, which was now almost full. 'Do you feel comfortable in places like this?'

'Pubs?'

'Rural pubs. I mean, I'm like the only Black woman here.'

'And I'm the only brown man. So?'

'So, doesn't it bother you?'

'No. My dad drummed into me that I was English from a very early age. We went on holidays to the seaside, walks in the countryside and drinks and meals in country pubs that had never seen anyone like us before. He taught us that that's how you change things. These places only stay white if we let them.'

'Is that why you joined the police force?'

His heart sank. If they started talking about his job, then they would lose this connection they had as people. 'I don't want to talk about work tonight,' he said, taking a deep breath. 'Look, I'll be honest. I really like you, Adaiba, and I'd love it if you stayed out and had dinner with me. You can come back to mine or eat here, or we can go somewhere else if you prefer. I don't care. I'd just like to spend some time with you.' His stomach growled. 'Plus I'm starving. Debbie ate all the crisps.'

She laughed and took another sip of her Martini to buy some time. It was like Rayan had his own force of gravity pulling her towards him. Every inch of her body wanted to stay here, in this place, with this man. She imagined herself saying yes and letting him buy her another drink and a bowl of chips, before maybe another drink, later taking his hands in hers, maybe leaning in closer as the sky darkened and . . .

And then what? Her stomach churned, fear curbing her desire.

'Well?' he pressed.

She couldn't think straight. In fact, maybe she needed more time to think. This wasn't something she should rush into. Especially not after three cocktails. She didn't want to do something she would later regret.

Adaiba gave him a hopeful but non-committal smile. 'Another time, Rayan.'

He blinked as if she had struck him.

She drained her glass in the silence. The sun dipped below the roof of the pub, and the temperature suddenly dropped. 'Is that okay?' she asked.

'Yes. Yes, of course it is. I'll just give you a lift back then,' he said, rising to his feet.

'What about your drink?'

But he was already heading out of the garden, and towards the darkening car park.

CHAPTER FIFTY-SIX

DCS Kat Frank's home, Coleshill, 8.02pm

Fuck. Her jaw felt like it had been hit by a train. Kat raised her hand to touch it, but the handcuffs yanked it back.

Handcuffs?

Pain spread like an ink blot through her skull, but she forced herself to focus. She was on the floor in her sitting room, chained to the bloody radiator. *Fuck*. How the hell did that happen? The last thing she remembered was walking into the kitchen and something – or someone – making her fall to the floor. Had she been unconscious? Surely not. But there was barely any light leaking through the closed blinds. And she had no memory of closing them or putting the lamps on.

'Lock?' she called out. 'Cam?' Except her jaw couldn't quite close over the words, so their names came out half formed, followed by a wail of agony.

'Awake at last,' said a voice that was neither Cam's nor Lock's.

She looked at the man who walked into the room. He was white, dark-haired and small but tightly packed. She guessed he was in his early twenties. He was holding one of her best mugs, as if he'd just popped over for a nice cup of tea, and for a moment the contrast between his demeanour and her situation confused her. But his voice sounded familiar.

'Do I know you?' she asked. (Although she couldn't quite bring her teeth together, so it came out as "oo I o you?")

'Now *there's* a good question,' he said, walking over to where she sat on the floor. He squatted down so their eyes were level, but far enough away that she couldn't reach him. 'Do. You. Know. Me?' His eyes burned into hers.

She stared back at him. He didn't smell of drink, and he didn't have the teeth or cheekbones of a drug user, but his eyes had a glitter to them. It took her a few seconds to recognise it.

Hatred.

And even though she didn't know him, she began to feel afraid.

'My face not ringing any bells? Let me see if I can jog that memory of yours for you.' He stabbed her forehead with his finger, making her cry out in pain. 'See, the thing is, *I* remember *you*. DCS Kat Frank.' He spat out her name like a swear word. 'I was nine years old when I first saw you. I was at home, playing Lego. The second time I saw you, I should have been at school, but I persuaded my grandad to take me to court, cuz my waste of a mum refused.' He paused. 'My name is Peter Bridges.'

She closed her eyes. *Bridges*.

He grabbed her jaw. 'Look at me when I'm talking to you!'

She screamed as white-hot pain shot through her teeth.

'The jury came back after just two hours,' he continued, completely unfazed by the tears that fell from her wide, watchful eyes. 'They took less than the length of a film to decide my dad's fate. And then the foreman stood up and said that my dad – Anthony Bridges – was guilty of four murders. They said that my dad – *my dad* – was the Aston Strangler.' His grip on her jaw tightened. 'Can you imagine what that was like? I was just a kid. My dad was my hero. I told them they were wrong. That they'd made a mistake. But they took him down anyway. His face – I'll never forget it. And I'll never forget yours either.' He leaned in so close that her skin was flecked with spit.

'You smiled,' he said, his voice hoarse and shaky. 'My whole world collapsed, and you fucking *smiled*.'

Kat tried to shake her head, but the pain was too great. She swallowed and said as best as she could, 'I don't remember that, but if I did, then I'm sorry.'

'You calling me a liar?'

'No, I—'

'You, of all people, dare to call *me* a liar?' Her head banged against the radiator as he suddenly let go. He jumped up, hands clasped above his head as if he didn't trust what they might do.

Kat dropped her eyes to the floor, remembering her training. If ever you're taken hostage, you're supposed to stay calm and not challenge or argue with your captor in any way – you're not even supposed to look them in the eye in case you provoke them. She remembered one of her colleagues joking that Kat would need a personality transplant, or else be carried out in a body bag.

She'd laughed at the time, but it didn't seem very funny now. It wasn't just the violence that frightened her. Peter Bridges had told her his name. She'd seen his face. And he'd broken into her home and assaulted a police officer.

He was acting like a man with nothing to lose.

And that was the most frightening thing of all.

Her blood pulsed in her ears. *Think*. Lock was here somewhere. She just had to find a way of calling him without Peter hearing her. Kat glanced down at her wrist, but the steel bracelet was gone.

'Where's my bracelet?' she asked, trying not to sound accusatory.

'You mean where's your little robot friend?' Peter tapped what looked like a black shoebox. 'Lock's trapped in here, like a spider in a glass. This is a Faraday box. It blocks all access to the Wi-Fi or internet for anything you put inside it. Which means he can't hear you, he can't see you and, most importantly of all, he can't fucking help you.

'So it's just you and me, DCS Kat Frank. Just you and me.'

CHAPTER FIFTY-SEVEN

DI Rayan Hassan's car, 8.09pm

Rayan drove through the narrow lanes, casting two beams of light into the darkness ahead.

Another time, Rayan, she'd said. But that was just a polite way of saying no, wasn't it? He gripped the steering wheel. At least now he knew where he stood. He told himself that clarity was good; that now he could get on with his life and stop living on maybes and what-ifs. Finally, he could move forward.

And yet he couldn't shake off the feeling that this was all wrong: that with every yard the car ate up, they were travelling in the wrong direction.

'Have you heard from Kat yet?' asked Adaiba.

'No, nothing.'

'That's odd. I haven't heard from Lock either.'

Rayan cast her a wry glance. 'Likes to keep in touch, does he?'

'Lock doesn't "like" anything. He doesn't have preferences or desires. If I message him, he replies. There is no other option for him.'

'Sounds like the perfect boyfriend.'

Adaiba nodded. 'He is, actually. He always does what I ask

him, he isn't capable of lying and he would never, ever hurt me.'

Rayan glanced at her. 'But he's just a hologram. Which means he can never hold you or love you either.'

Adaiba shrugged. 'Like you said, he is the perfect boyfriend.'

Was she joking? Before Rayan could say anything, the car in front indicated a turn, so he slowed down and waited. They'd just reached the road that led to Coleshill, where the boss lived. He stared at the turn-off, remembering how keen Kat had been to celebrate the conviction of Caroline Cooper. He hesitated, then on impulse decided to follow the car in front and turn right. 'Sorry, do you mind if we just take a slight detour? I want to drive past Kat's house and check that everything's okay. It's not like her to not return my messages, and it's definitely not like her to miss a drink. Especially when the whole thing was her idea. It won't take a minute and then I'll take you home and be out of your way.'

'That's okay,' she said quietly. 'I don't mind.'

They drove down Coleshill High Street, over the bridge at the bottom and down towards the train station near where Kat lived. As Rayan approached her house, he slowed down. 'Isn't that her car outside?'

'Yes,' said Adaiba, frowning. 'And the lights are on. Try ringing her again.'

Rayan pulled over and rang Kat's mobile, but still there was no reply.

Adaiba checked her phone. 'Nothing from Lock either. He hasn't responded to any of my six messages.' She peered out of the window into the darkening street. 'Maybe something's wrong. Should we knock on the door, do you think?'

CHAPTER FIFTY-EIGHT

Inside DCS Kat Frank's house, Coleshill, 8.14pm

Kat watched Peter as he paced up and down, up and down. He was like a minefield packed with explosives, so she'd need to tread very, very carefully. From what she remembered of her training, captives were not supposed to negotiate with their hostage takers – that should be left to trained negotiators. Which was all very well and good, but where were they? She shifted her weight onto the other side of her bum, trying to spread the ache. The trainer had also advised them to keep quiet and wait if ever they were held captive, but she wasn't good at being quiet at the best of times. And her gut warned her that things were at risk of escalating. She had to *do* something. Make him see her as a person, not just a police officer.

'My jaw hurts,' she said as best she could.

He turned to face her. 'So? I've had my jaw broken three times. Once in the ring, twice by men who were paid to look after me.'

'I'm sorry. What would you recommend for the pain?'

'I'd recommend you get used to it.' He paused, then abruptly left the room.

Shit. She could hear him rummaging around in the kitchen.

What was he doing – searching for a knife or something else to hurt her with? Kat tugged and tugged at the handcuffs, trying to break them or slip her hands free. But it was no use.

Peter returned to the room, and she gasped as he threw something at her head.

'Relax, it's just a bag of frozen peas,' he said, rolling his eyes.

She stared at where the ice-cold bag of petits pois had fallen into her lap, unable to reach it because of the handcuffs.

Peter Bridges knelt down in front of her, picked up the bag of peas and ground them against her jaw. 'Don't think I'm going soft,' he said through her cry of pain. 'I need you to be able to talk. Use your chin and shoulder to hold it there for a few minutes.'

Kat did as she was told until, thankfully, her jaw and face began to numb. She watched him as he rose to his feet again and began pacing the room. 'I can see how upset you are,' she said, pronouncing each word as best she could. 'But trust me, this is not going to help.'

'*Trust* you? Do you think I'm fucking stupid?'

'No,' she insisted, flinching at the sudden way he turned on her. 'I just mean . . . I don't want things to get any worse for you. Think about it. You might have blocked Lock, but my family and friends will have noticed I've not been in contact. I was supposed to meet my team in the pub tonight, so they're bound to raise the alarm. And when they do, well . . . look, why don't you leave now, before this all gets out of hand?'

'I hate to break it to you, DCS Kat Frank,' he said, bending over her. 'But no one gives a shit about you. Your son drove off with his girlfriend and hasn't replied to a single one of your texts – I know that for a fact because I hacked his phone.' He waved his mobile in front of her face. 'Your husband's dead, and Lock is just another fucking phantom, trapped in a box. And as for your so-called "friends", well . . .' He looked around him in mock concern. 'They're not here, are they? That's because *they're not your fucking friends* – you're their boss. Your *staff* are probably having an extra pint to celebrate the fact that you didn't turn up.'

Peter pushed his mouth right next to her ear. 'The thing is, DCS Kat Frank, you're all alone.'

She tried to pull away, but the cold metal radiator left her nowhere to go.

'People like you look down on boxing. I bet you'd never let *your* precious son get his face punched in, would you? But the thing is, apart from discipline, it teaches you to read people. You learn that everyone is afraid of something, and *you*, DCS Kat Frank, are afraid of being alone.'

She wanted to tell him that he didn't know the first fucking thing about her, but she forced her lips together. *Do not challenge the hostage taker.*

'I could teach you a thing or two about being alone,' he continued. 'Because do you know what happened when you fitted my dad up? My mum didn't want to know him *or* me, so I was taken into care.'

The words contorted his face. '*Care*. That word always makes me laugh. Do you know what kind of "care" a nine-year-old boy with an alleged serial killer for a dad gets in a "care home"? Do you? DO YOU?'

Kat turned away from his shouting voice.

'I TOLD YOU TO LOOK AT ME!' he screamed, grabbing her jaw so hard that she thought she would faint. 'I was a *child*,' he cried. 'Just a fucking kid. They destroyed me and it is All. Your. Fault.' He shook her head with the force of each word, his fingers digging into her damaged jaw.

'I'm sorry,' she squeezed out through her squashed mouth.

He let go and sat back on the floor, breathing heavily.

'Honestly, I'm sorry that you suffered abuse. If you want me to, I can find the people who hurt you and make sure they're punished for what they did.'

'Like you punished my dad? I don't want you to lock up any more poor bastards.'

'What *do* you want then?'

'What do I want?' He held up his phone. 'I want you to *confess*. I want you to tell the world the truth about how you fitted my dad up. I want you to tell everyone what a filthy, lying *bitch* you are, and that my dad was *not* the Aston Strangler.'

'I can't do that,' she whispered.

'Oh, but I think you can,' he said, pulling out a knife from the inside of his jacket. 'In fact, I'd bet money on it.'

Kat swallowed. 'There's no need for that,' she said.

'Oh, but there is. I asked you nicely – twenty-three times to be exact – to be on my podcast. But you said no. So now here we are.'

'Podcast? *You're* the podcaster?' Of course he was. Anthony Bridges was his dad, that's why he was so determined to prove his "innocence"; that was why she'd recognised his voice.

'God, you really are slow, aren't you? Yes, the Aston Strangler podcast is mine. I have nearly half a million listeners who want to know the truth. And finally, *you're* going to give it to them.'

Kat longed to tell Peter and his poxy podcast to fuck right off, but she knew she was meant to comply with any requests made by a hostage taker – even if that meant giving interviews or taking part in videos that were fundamentally untrue. And if she could just keep him talking, surely someone would eventually wonder where she was?

They might wonder, but would they do anything about it?

She ran through each one in her mind. Debbie was the most likely to notice her absence, but she wouldn't have time to check up on her boss. She had her baby to think of now. And although Rayan might comment on it, he only had eyes for the professor these days. Judith, maybe? No, they weren't the type to catastrophise – they'd probably just assume that Kat had opted for an early night. And had Cam really not messaged her? She fought back the prick of tears, telling herself it was lucky that he had gone to a rave with Gemma. Otherwise, he would have been caught up in all this. At least her son was safe. And he would want her – *beg* her – to do everything within her power to stay alive.

She took a deep, steadying breath. She would not let this man turn Cam into an orphan. 'Okay,' she said.

Peter held up his phone and pressed record. 'It's just audio, so there's no point pulling "save me" faces. And I'm recording it, so don't bother calling for help either – I'll just edit it out. All you have to do is tell the truth.'

Kat's heart sank as she looked into his over-bright eyes.

The last thing this man needed was the truth.

CHAPTER FIFTY-NINE

Outside DCS Kat Frank's house, Coleshill, 8.20pm

Rayan climbed out of the car, quickly followed by Adaiba. They approached Kat's front door, and just as he lifted the letterbox, a thin, tinny voice warned him to stop.

Rayan looked around but the dark street was empty.

'Lock?' said Adaiba. 'Is that you?'

'Yes. My bracelet has been placed in a Faraday box, so I am unable to project myself or receive sensory data via that means. But as the majority of my processing takes place in your laboratory, I am still able to interface remotely with Kat's home automation system and Wi-Fi enabled devices. I am currently talking to you through the smart doorbell.'

'I don't understand. Why would Kat put the bracelet in a Faraday box?' asked Adaiba.

'She didn't. It was Peter Bridges, the son of the Aston Strangler. He is currently inside, and he has handcuffed DCS Frank to the radiator.'

'*What?*' cried Rayan. He stood back and sized up the solid wood front door. He wouldn't be able to break it down by himself without a battering ram. Maybe he should try round the back?

Kat's house was detached, with a narrow alley running down the right-hand side, presumably so she could take out the bins. But just as he approached the metal gate, Lock spoke up again.

'Please do not attempt to enter the premises, DI Hassan. My assessment is that Peter Bridges is a very volatile man with a history of trauma and irrational, paranoid thought processes. He believes that DCS Frank is personally responsible for the wrongful conviction of his father and for his own troubled childhood. He is currently holding a knife and, although he has not expressed a desire to kill her, any sudden sounds or movements may provoke an emotional, violent reaction that could prove fatal. I suggest that, in line with protocol, as the first on the scene your job is to remain calm and inform the Hostage Negotiators Unit. They will send a senior investigating officer supported by firearms officers and their firearms commander. I also suggest you alert Chief Constable McLeish, who may wish to attend to arbitrate between them and agree a way forward.'

Rayan paused. Lock was right, of course. He clenched and unclenched his fists as he glared at the bay window and the tightly shut blinds. 'But how long will they take? What if he hurts her while we're waiting?'

'The firearms team are based just six miles away. If you obtain the firearms authority now, they will deploy and I estimate they will take eleven minutes to drive through traffic – seven with sirens, although I would not advise this lest you alert the hostage taker. Meanwhile, I will continue to monitor the situation and ensure that DCS Frank comes to no harm. I will call you, and once you answer I will route the smart speakers in the front room to your phone so that you are able to hear what is happening. Peter Bridges is about to interview DCS Frank for his podcast.'

Rayan and Adaiba began to ask more questions, but Lock was already gone.

PODCAST

[music plays]

Peter: I am delighted to *finally* welcome none other than DCS Kat Frank to the podcast: the woman who was in charge of the investigation into the Aston Strangler. Thank you for joining us, Kat. Can I call you Kat?

[silence]

Great, thanks. Now, I want to take you back to the very first murder, when Angela Hall was found strangled in Aston Park. What was your involvement in that case?

Kat: I was the DI on duty that night.

Peter: Can you speak up, please?

Kat: I was the DI on duty, so when PC Murray found the body, I took the call.

Peter: So, you weren't formally appointed to lead the case. You just 'happened' to be on call the night the first body was found?

Kat: Yes.

Peter: And can you confirm that there had been no known relationship between the first victim, Angela Hall, and Anthony Bridges, and no reported sightings of him on that day or night in the park?

Kat: Yes.

Peter: And was there any forensic evidence to link him to the body?

Kat: Not that we could find.

Peter: So, at this point, was Anthony Bridges a suspect?

Kat: Not at that time.

Peter: Was he a person of interest?

Kat: Not at that time.

Peter: Was he at any time mentioned in relation to the murder of Angela Hall?

Kat: No, not at that time.

Peter: I see. Moving on to the second victim, Roisin McCauley. Tell me how you became involved in that case.

Kat: I was the DI on duty that night, so when a neighbour rang it in, I was the senior officer who responded.

Peter: So again, you just 'happened' to be on call that night?

Kat: It's hardly a coincidence. It's how rotas work.

Peter: And how does forensic science work?

Kat: I'm sorry?

Peter: You found Roisin McCauley strangled to death in her bed. Quite a violent death, I'd imagine. So, I was wondering what sort of forensic tests you carried out. I presume you dusted the whole bedroom for fingerprints and swabbed for blood.

Kat: Yes.

Peter: Did you find any forensic evidence that linked Anthony Bridges to the bedroom?

Kat: No.

Peter: What about her body? I'd imagine you looked under her nails for skin fragments and checked her hair for DNA, her mouth for saliva, her vagina for semen?

Kat: Yes.

Peter: And did any of those tests establish any link to Anthony Bridges?

[silence]

I'll repeat the question. Did any of those tests establish any link to Anthony Bridges?

Kat: No. Not at that time.

Peter: And at that time, was Anthony Bridges a suspect?

Kat: Not then.

Peter: Was he a person of interest?

Kat: Not yet.

Peter: Was his name ever mentioned in relation to Roisin McCauley or the crime itself?

Kat: Not at that time.

Peter: In fact, you didn't even connect the murders until a third woman was found strangled in her bedroom – Charlotte Walker.

Kat: Yes, it was so similar to the death of Roisin McCauley, that was when we realised that we were looking for a serial killer.

Peter: And it was similar in other ways, wasn't it, because once again there was no forensic evidence available, and am I right in thinking that Anthony Bridges was still not a suspect?

Kat: Not at that time.

Peter: So, after three women had been brutally murdered, was Anthony Bridges at any point a person of interest? Was his name mentioned at all?

Kat: I . . . I don't think so. Not at that time.

Peter: You don't *think* so. Well, having reviewed all the trial evidence, I can confirm that Anthony Bridges is not mentioned in a single document even after three murders. So, now we come to the fourth and final case, when yet another young woman, Rachel Murray, was found strangled to death in her flat. By now you were the deputy SIO, and so you were the one who went out to the scene. Tell me what you found.

Kat: I . . . she . . . she'd been strangled to death. Not in the bedroom, this time. She was . . . in the bathtub.

Peter: And again, samples were taken and sent away for forensic tests, am I right?

Kat: Yes.

Peter: But you didn't wait for the results, did you?

Kat: What?

Peter: The very same night you found the body of Rachel Murray, you went to interview Anthony Bridges. By your own admission, he hadn't been a person of interest, let alone a suspect, in the other three cases. You didn't have any results from the forensic tests on the other three women and the psychological profile drawn up by Dr Mike Bullington suggested you were looking for a young, single man; a loner, probably with a history of deviant behaviour and a criminal record. So, not only was there no evidence to point towards Anthony Bridges, the evidence you did have was actively suggesting a *completely* different profile. Yet the day you discovered the fourth murder victim, you went and interviewed Anthony Bridges – a happily married police officer with a child and no criminal convictions. And just thirty-six hours later you'd charged him, and from that point on he became known as the Aston Strangler. And this is what I want to know, DCS Kat Frank. *Why?* What evidence did you find that was *so* compelling that you suddenly became convinced that Anthony Bridges had murdered four women?

Kat: We found items belonging to each of the women in his shed, alongside the latex gloves and protective clothing he had used during the murders. We also discovered graphic pornography involving strangulation on his home computer.

Peter: But this so-called 'evidence' could easily have been planted by you and your team. You only found it once you arrived at his home. My question was, what evidence led you to his home in the first place?

Kat: I . . . I don't remember.

Peter: You don't *remember?* You destroyed a man and his family, but you don't *remember?*

Kat: It was a long time ago. I'd have to check the paperwork.
[sound of someone being struck]

Peter: My dad was branded a murderer, he died in prison before he could clear his name and you *dare* to sit there and say *you don't remember* why you destroyed his life and mine? The truth is there *was* no evidence. You had a vendetta against my dad. You fitted him up. Admit it!

CHAPTER SIXTY

Outside DCS Kat Frank's house, 8.32pm

'Right, tell me what we've got,' demanded McLeish, eyes like bullets as he climbed out of an unmarked car. Behind him, another man wearing a dark bullet-proof vest emerged from a large blacked-out van. He introduced himself as Neil Rogers, but Rayan couldn't help thinking that the boss would have called him 'Neil the Negotiator'. She loved to give people nicknames. Why had he only just noticed that?

As they stood in the cordoned-off street, Rayan prepared to deliver his concise briefing. But before he could, Lock's voice began speaking through his phone.

'Without my bracelet I have no access to visual data, but based upon the acoustics and my knowledge of the environment, I estimate that DCS Kat Frank has been handcuffed to the bottom right side of the radiator for over thirty minutes,' he said. A 3D image of the living room appeared on the tarmac road at McLeish's feet, with Kat represented by a faceless figure huddled on the floor.

McLeish scowled at the image of his DCS handcuffed to a radiator. 'And what do we know about the bastard who's doing this?'

'His name is Peter Bridges,' said Lock as the 3D image of a young man appeared before them. 'He is twenty-one years old and his father was convicted of the Aston Strangler murders when he was nine. Since then he has been in and out of five care homes and lived with seven foster families. He has a series of convictions for burglary, theft and grievous bodily harm, and served two periods in a young offenders' institution when he was sixteen. During this period he managed to gain some qualifications and became interested in boxing. He was released when he was eighteen and began to build a modestly successful career as a lightweight boxer. He was cautioned for being drunk and disorderly nineteen weeks ago, but was released with a warning once he explained that his father had just died.'

'Which is presumably when this shit show began.'

'There is some evidence that Peter's fixation on proving his father's innocence began shortly after the latter's death, along with the podcast and his obsession with DCS Frank.'

McLeish ran a hand over his bald scalp. 'So, we've got a former con with a history of violence and daddy issues who blames Kat for messing his life up. We need to get her out of there. Now.' He turned towards the Hostage Negotiating Officer behind him. 'What's your plan?'

'My advice is to follow the protocol for all hostage situations. Open up a line of communication with the hostage taker, find out what he wants, build a connection and wear him down so that we can negotiate a safe release.'

'Sir, what is the objective of this particular mission?' asked Lock.

McLeish turned. For a minute Rayan thought he was going to tell Lock to mind his own fucking business, but the absence of the hologram seemed to throw him as he searched the empty air. 'The objective is the same as in all hostage situations: to get Kat out alive and unharmed.'

'Then please allow me to assess the probability of success for the different approaches to achieving that objective. I understand the protocol – I have just read one thousand and seventy-three articles on hostage negotiations – but I think there are unique factors in this case that may require a more bespoke approach.'

'There's no time for that. And I'll take advice from trained hostage negotiators, not some glorified search engine. Especially when one of my best officers is at risk.' McLeish turned to Rayan. 'Do we have a number we can call him on?'

'Yes,' answered Lock, before citing Peter's mobile number.

Ignoring Rayan's exasperated sigh, McLeish turned to Neil. 'Okay. You're on. And you need to know that DCS Frank is one of our finest. Failure is not an option.'

'Understood,' said Neil. He walked up the road as the firearms team arrived and got into place, put the phone to his ear and pressed call.

CHAPTER SIXTY-ONE

Inside DCS Kat Frank's house, 8.37pm

They both jumped as Peter's phone rang.

He scowled at the screen and pressed reject. But the caller rang back. He pressed reject again, only for it to ring once more. 'Who the fuck is this?' he eventually said, picking up the call.

'Hi, Peter. My name is Neil and I am here to help.'

Peter's face paled. He stood up and approached the window, where he parted one of the blinds, before dropping them and backing away. '*Fuck*.' He turned towards Kat. 'There are armed police outside. What are you playing at? Did you call them?'

'No, how could I? I don't have my phone or Lock.'

'Peter?' said the voice on the phone. 'I'm not in charge. I'm a trained negotiator and I'm here to make sure this ends safely for everyone.'

'Like fuck you are.'

'I know you probably didn't mean to be in this situation. Things happen. They can get out of control. And I'm here to help de-escalate matters so that together we can find a way out of this.'

'Shows how much you know. I've been dreaming about this

for years and planning it for months. This is *exactly* where I want to be. For the first time in my life, *I'm* the one in control.'

'It might feel that way at the moment, Peter, but you and I both know that this isn't sustainable.'

'You don't know jack shit.' Peter crossed the room so quickly that Kat couldn't help gasping. He squatted down by her side and pressed the knife to her neck. 'Tell the stupid man exactly who is in control, DCS Frank. Go on.'

Kat took a deep breath. 'You are. You have a knife to my neck, so you are the one in control.'

'Did you hear that, Mr Negotiator?'

'You must want something very badly to hold a police officer hostage. Can you tell me what that is? I can negotiate with the commander on your behalf and see if we can come to some sort of arrangement.'

Peter laughed. 'You don't get it, do you? The only thing I want is for this bitch to tell the truth. This is between me and her. Nothing to do with you lot. And to be honest, you're starting to piss me off cuz you're getting in the way of my podcast. So what I *want* is for you all to fuck off and leave me and DCS Frank alone. And if you don't, it'll be the worse for her.'

Kat cried out as he pressed the knife into her neck. It was only a nick, but she felt the sting of cut skin and the warm ooze of blood.

Peter raised a finger and, with a theatrical gesture, ended the call.

'Now,' he said. 'Where were we?'

CHAPTER SIXTY-TWO

Outside DCS Kat Frank's house, 8.39pm

Neil the Negotiator walked back towards them. 'Did you hear that?'

'Aye,' said McLeish. 'What's your assessment?'

Neil shook his head. 'Not good. The only thing he says he wants is for DCS Frank to talk. But I also think he wants to punish her. For her to suffer. This is more characteristic of a domestic abuse hostage situation so our negotiation options are limited, and because of the emotional connection he has to his captive, the risk of harm is heightened.'

'I agree,' said Lock. 'Peter Bridges is a highly agitated individual, prone to erratic movements and bursts of violence. He has already struck Kat twice, and there is a forty-two per cent probability that he will do so again. So far, he has only struck with his fists, but now he is holding a knife.'

Rayan swore under his breath. He couldn't just stand here and listen to Kat getting hurt. 'Sir, shouldn't we consider a dynamic entry?'

McLeish called the Tactical Firearms Commander over. 'Lock, show us that map again.'

The 3D map of Kat's home appeared on the road before them. 'If you are planning to enter the property by force,' said Lock, 'then you have three options: the front door, the back door or the bay window. Each of these methods will alert the hostage taker to your intentions, as he has activated the home alarm system. I can deactivate it, but he will still hear the sound of breaking wood or glass. It will take your officers approximately ten seconds to break down the door and travel the fifteen metres to reach Kat at the radiator; fourteen seconds if you use the back door.

'Peter Bridges is never more than four metres away from Kat, and so would take less than three seconds to stab her once. In the ten seconds or more it would take your officers to reach her, she could have suffered multiple knife wounds, and based upon previous cases, there is a fifty-nine per cent probability that Peter Bridges will attempt to take his own life before he is arrested.'

The Tactical Firearms Commander was about to disagree, but just then, Lock made the male figure standing by the image of Kat before them lash out towards his captive.'

'That's enough,' barked McLeish.

'If we don't try and enter the property,' said Rayan, 'then Kat still faces the same risk. She's trapped in there with a volatile con holding a knife – just seconds away from harm. At least if we go in, she might stand a chance. Sir?'

But before his boss could reply, Neil the Negotiator put a hand to his ear. 'Peter Bridges has just resumed the podcast interview. I suggest we listen to that before we make a decision. Let's hope that DCS Frank can talk her way out of this.'

PODCAST

Peter: You were about to tell me what evidence led you to the home of Anthony Bridges. Come on, DCS Kat Frank. I'm all ears.

Kat: I told you, I honestly don't remember. I'm not being flippant. It was over a decade ago. I'd need to look up my old case notes, which are at work. If you let me go, then I promise it's the first thing I'll do.

Peter: You *promise?* Now why on earth would I trust the word of a lying bitch like you?

Kat: Because it's the truth.

Peter: You honestly expect me and my listeners to believe that you don't remember the day when you found the fourth victim of the Aston Strangler, or the exact moment when you went from having zero suspects to suddenly having a name? You don't remember that light bulb moment, that magical piece of evidence that turned not just the case but your whole career around?

Kat: No, I really don't. It was an emotional day. It's always upsetting to see a dead body, no matter how experienced you are. I think I've blocked a lot of my memories of that day out, to be honest, as a kind of trauma response.

Peter: *[exhales]* Trauma? *Trauma?* What the fuck do *you* know about trauma? I'll tell you what trauma is, DCS Frank. Trauma is being nine years old and playing Lego in the front room with your dad when the cops burst into your *home* and place your *dad* under arrest. It's seeing him being dragged out by force while your mum is screaming and you are crying and the cops are shouting at you to stay back. And then your dad's gone, just like that.

And you haven't got a fucking clue what's going on. And then the next day he still hasn't come home, and the people you thought were your mates at school start saying that your dad is a fucking murderer. You know it's a mistake, so every day you wake up hoping that today is the day that your dad will come home. Even when your own fucking mum puts you in a children's home. Even when you're placed with dirty, bastard foster families. All the time, you keep hoping your dad will come home and save you. But he never does. You wait for eleven fucking years and then he fucking *dies*. *That,* DCS Kat Frank, is fucking trauma.

Kat: I'm sorry.

Peter: For what? For fitting my dad up? Are you finally apologising?

Kat: No, I'm just sorry that things have been so tough for you.

Peter: *You* were the one who destroyed him.

Kat: The jury made the decision to convict him, not me.

Peter: But who placed the evidence in my dad's shed, eh?

Kat: I didn't plant the evidence.

Peter: I know you did.

Kat: I didn't.

Peter: I know my dad was innocent.

Kat: And I know your dad was guilty.

Peter: *Liar!* You know nothing about my dad. My dad was a good man.

Kat: *[snorts]*

Peter: You know nothing about him.

Kat: I know he murdered those poor women.

[sound of someone being struck]

Peter: How do you 'know'?

[silence]

How do you know?

[silence]

How do you know?

[silence]

[sound of someone being struck]

HOW?

[sound of someone being struck]

HOW DO YOU FUCKING KNOW???

Kat: *[sobbing and shouting]* BECAUSE I WAS HIS FIRST VICTIM!

CHAPTER SIXTY-THREE

Inside DCS Kat Frank's house, 8.54pm

'I was his first victim,' Kat repeated, finally letting out the words she had held in for so long.

'What are you talking about?' Peter demanded.

She wanted to wipe her eyes and blow her nose, but because of the handcuffs she just had to suck up the snot and let tears streak her face. 'I'm talking about your dad and me.'

His face contorted, and quickly, before he could hit her again, Kat added, 'He used to make me laugh, you know. That's what drew me to him at first.'

'My dad?'

'Yeah. He was funny.'

He frowned. 'When did you know my dad?'

Kat sighed. There was no going back now. 'I met him at police college. I'd just joined as a graduate trainee, and he was the self-defence instructor. He used to rip the piss out of me for being a graduate and was always singling me out to demonstrate techniques on. He'd pin me to the floor or grab me from behind and I'd have to try and get away. At the time, I thought it was because he assumed I was just a skinny student with no street sense, so I needed more help to keep safe.' Kat caught herself. His son didn't need to hear that she now realised he had probably got off on it. 'But I'm a quick learner,' she continued. 'And I like to win, so pretty soon I was one of the best in the class. Then, at the end of the course, he asked me out for a drink. He was a few years older than me, and I was flattered, so I said yes. He was my first real boyfriend.' Kat swallowed. She could almost taste the regret.

'You and my *dad*?' Peter repeated, eyes wide.

Kat nodded. He was a lot calmer now, clearly hungry for stories about his father. But this story didn't have a happy ending, so she needed to be careful. 'We dated for a few months, and it was okay at first. But he could be moody. Insecure. And when he took me home to meet his mum and sister . . . well, they couldn't believe he had a girlfriend and kept on teasing him, but not in a nice way. Whenever he held my hand or displayed any kind of affection, his sister would start humming the theme tune to the Flake advert.'

Peter Bridges looked at her blankly.

'It was an iconic advert back in the day. The song was famous. You can find it on YouTube. Anyway, according to your dad's mum, he had a massive crush on the actress, and she thought I looked like her. It was all a bit weird.'

'My nan died when I was little,' said Peter. 'But my dad said she was a right old cow.'

Kat made a non-committal sound. 'I asked him about it, the Flake advert, and he said that he'd had a bit of a thing for the actress in his teens. And we laughed and I didn't think any more about it. Then one day, a few weeks later, he . . .' She swallowed again. Oh, Jesus, could she really say this? 'It was Easter and I'd bought him a Flake egg for a joke. He laughed, and then he . . . he asked me if we could do a bit of role play. Just for a bit of fun, he said. He wanted me to eat a Flake in the bath, like the girl in the advert.'

She closed her eyes, but the tears still ran down her face. 'I wasn't keen, but he made me feel like I was being immature. He said I needed to loosen up; to grow up. So, even though my gut told me there was something off about it, I agreed.' She took a great shuddering breath. The only person she'd ever shared this with was her husband, John.

'I thought it would only take a couple of minutes, but once I was in the bath he started playing the music, and then he got really particular about how I held the Flake. How I opened my mouth. How I ate it. I laughed, which really annoyed him, so I told him I'd had enough. I tried to get out, and that was when . . . that was when he lost it. He pushed me back into the bath and forced the Flake into my mouth. He shoved it in, not giving me a chance to eat it, making me choke. And then he . . . he . . . strangled me.'

By now she was openly sobbing. 'I couldn't breathe. The chocolate in my throat. His hands around my neck. The water. And all the time he was calling me all these names, and the more I struggled, the more excited he got. I was terrified. But I managed to reach the razor blade I used to shave my legs and I cut his cheek. It was enough to make him let go. I jumped out of the bath, but it was all wet and I slipped on the linoleum floor and cut my chin on the corner of the unit. He grabbed me from behind, but my training kicked in and I did a finger pull and escaped into the bedroom and locked the door. I told him I was calling the police, and he ran off. Left the flat.' She closed her eyes, trying to shut out the memory of that horrible night – how she'd lain soaking and shaking on her bed while the jaunty theme tune from *The Archers* seeped through their neighbours' wall. She'd thought about knocking on their door or ringing the police, but in the end she had been too ashamed.

Peter shook his head. '*Bullshit.* And even if you are telling the truth, what has this got to do with the Aston murders? Lots of guys – and girls – like to experiment with strangulation during sex. It doesn't mean he was guilty. It just means you had a motive for revenge. In fact, *this* explains why you fitted him up.'

Kat sighed. 'When I arrived at the fourth victim's house, it was like *déjà vu*. The bathtub. The strangulation. And then someone pointed out what looked like brown lipstick around her mouth. I leant over to take a closer look, and I could smell the sickly-sweet chocolate. And in her clenched right hand there was a Flake wrapper.' Her voice broke. 'It was gripped so tight in her fist that I think she did it on purpose. Her last, dying act was to hand us a clue. A couple of days later, we managed to get a fingerprint match off the wrapper – he wasn't wearing gloves when he bought it – and we also confirmed that the other three victims had consumed chocolate just before they died. But I didn't need to wait for the tests. The minute I saw the wrapper, I knew who the murderer was. That's why I went round there that night and arrested him.'

'No,' said Peter. 'You're lying.' But his voice lacked conviction.

'Once we'd identified him, we found further evidence in the shed: latex gloves and photographs of all four victims and pornographic magazines featuring strangulation.'

'You put that evidence there. You *planted* it.'

'I really didn't, Peter. I'm sorry. His first victim, Angela Hall, had been opportunistic. He saw her in the park and she reminded him of his fantasy, and for some reason he acted upon it. But he planned the other three – targeted his victims and met them at their homes so that he could re-enact his sick fantasy.'

'You fucking *liar!* If it was my dad, then how come there've been two more women strangled in recent weeks, eh? How do you explain *that?*'

Kat let out a shaky breath. 'They weren't strangled, Peter. One body belonged to a German soldier from the Second World War, and he was shot. The second body belonged to his granddaughter, and she died following a blow to her throat.'

'Bullshit! You fixed that with your so-called "virtual" post-mortem.'

'I really didn't. Dr Edwards confirmed the genders and causes of death before Lock and I even arrived. Lock just helped with the identifications. And a woman confessed to the granddaughter's murder two days ago, and has been arrested and charged. I'm sorry, but your podcast was wrong. The bodies had nothing to do with the Aston Strangler.'

Peter jumped up and started pacing the room, gripping the knife in both hands. 'Shut up!' he cried. 'I am *sick* of your lies.'

Kat watched him, alert to every movement.

'*Liar*,' he repeated again, as if talking to himself. 'You are *such* a fucking liar.'

'I'm honestly not,' she said carefully. 'I know you want to believe that your dad was innocent, but maybe it's time for you to face up to the truth.'

'My dad was NOT the Aston Strangler!' he practically screamed.

She licked the blood that was drying on her lips. 'Did your dad ever hurt your mum, Peter?'

He shook his head. But it didn't look like a denial.

'Did your dad ever hurt *you*?'

Again, he shook his head, but there were tears in his eyes.

'It's okay. There's no shame in accepting the truth. The shame belongs to him,' she said softly, repeating the words that John had said when she'd told him what had happened. 'There's nothing you can do to change what he did. But you *can* control how you respond to it. Your dad hurt people, Peter. Including you. But you don't have to let him define your life.'

He shook his head over and over as if he couldn't bear to hear her words. 'My whole life I've told myself that I am not the son of the Aston Strangler,' he said, sounding lost and bewildered.

He pointed his knife at Kat. 'And now you are telling me that I *am*?'

CHAPTER SIXTY-FOUR

Outside DCS Kat Frank's house, 9.06pm

'Sir,' said Lock. 'I have analysed the outcomes of seven hundred and sixteen hostage situations, and the exchange we have just heard increases the risk of a violent outcome considerably. Peter Bridges's only motive was to clear his dead father's name, and now that DCS Frank has told him that his father was guilty after all, he has little reason to live. He has criminal convictions for violence and has already struck a police officer five times in less than two hours. My predictive policing tool suggests that based upon his previous convictions, his demographic profile and his current emotional state, there is a sixty-seven per cent chance that he will now harm DCS Frank and himself. Possibly fatally.'

'I agree,' said Neil the Negotiator. 'I think we need to urgently consider a rescue attempt.'

McLeish looked back at the armed response van, packed with men holding guns. 'But once that lot start breaking down doors, he might think he's got nothing to lose and kill Kat before taking his own life. You said it would only take him three seconds.'

'Sir, if I may,' said Lock. 'I have assessed all of the options available to us and I believe that the safest strategy is to encourage DCS Frank to escape herself.'

'And how the fuck's she supposed to do that?' snapped McLeish.

'I can interface with the home automation system, so I can cut off all the lights. This will disconcert Peter Bridges, as according to his social care records he has a profound fear of the dark. There is a seventy-nine per cent probability that he will move into the kitchen in search of a torch or matches, during which time I can speak to Kat and talk her through the process of releasing herself from her handcuffs, which have a surprisingly simple lock mechanism.'

'And then what?'

'I have developed a strategy for each of twenty-three different possible scenarios depending upon the different interactions between key variables. I can explain each one to you if you wish, but I advise that it would merely waste time in a very time-critical situation. Alternatively, if you allow me to deploy all my abilities in pursuit of the mission objective – ensuring DCS Frank emerges unharmed – then there is an eighty-two per cent probability that I will achieve it. Sir.'

McLeish glanced at Kat's house. 'Okay. Just do whatever it takes to get her out of there alive.'

'I will. Trust me.'

'Thank goodness you're here, Lock,' Adaiba said.

Rayan rolled his eyes. 'Am I the only one who realises that Lock is just a hologram? In fact, he's not even that right now. And switching the lights off isn't going to save anyone. What if his fear of the dark just makes Peter even more violent and unpredictable? All this talk of probabilities – he's a *man*, not a mathematical puzzle. And what if Kat can't unlock the handcuffs?

She doesn't need a verbal explanation of how to escape, she needs someone to get her out of there.'

Adaiba gave him a disappointed look. 'Lock has considered all of the published evidence and assessed the actions most likely to achieve this. You need to learn to trust his analysis and not let your emotions overwhelm you.'

Rayan looked down into Adaiba's eyes. 'Sometimes,' he said, 'you need to trust your emotions.'

For a moment he thought – hoped – she would say something. But she dropped her gaze from his and turned away.

Another time, Rayan.

God, the frustration was like a physical ache. He turned to McLeish, his words spilling out in an agitated rush. 'Sir, an algorithm can't save DCS Frank. Lock can't even *see* at the moment. We need real people in there.'

McLeish let out a low growl. 'I agree. But this requires delicate handling.' He looked over at the van full of armed responders, scowling. 'And that lot only do shock and awe.'

'Then let me go round the back. I've had special ops training. I know the house well and you can see the whole kitchen through the conservatory windows. If Lock's plan works and Peter enters the kitchen then I might be able to break in, isolate and stun him.'

McLeish shook his head. 'Too risky.'

'Not for Kat it isn't. He'll be in a separate room, so he'll focus any attack or sudden moves on me, and the second I have him engaged, you can send in the back-up. I can be a distraction.'

McLeish rubbed his chin, like he was thinking about it.

Kat was brilliant at handling McLeish, and one of the many things that she'd taught Rayan was that forgiveness was easier than permission. So, after tightening his stab vest, he cast one last glance at Adaiba and headed towards the back gate.

'DI Hassan!' McLeish barked. 'Back here. Now.'

Rayan pretended he couldn't hear and, as he'd suspected, McLeish didn't repeat his order.

CHAPTER SIXTY-FIVE

Inside DCS Kat Frank's house, 9.07pm

Kat kept her eyes on Peter's even though the knife was just inches from her face. 'I think you genuinely believed that your dad was innocent. But I also think you know that I've told you the truth. That must be really hard to accept.'

Peter glared at her. He still looked angry, but he didn't tell her to shut up.

'I think you need to let yourself grieve for your dad – not just for his death but for the man you thought or hoped he was.'

He let out a groan and turned his back on her. 'You're messing with my head.'

'I'm sorry. This must be really hard for you, I know.'

He spun back round to face her. 'You know NOTHING!' He ran a hand over his face. 'If you're right, then everything, my whole life, has been a complete waste.'

'No, it hasn't,' said Kat. 'It means you can stop trying to prove that your dad is innocent and focus on *your* life. It means you can start to move forward.'

'And just how am I supposed to "move forward"? Go away to some posh university? Go abroad? Move house? Oh no, silly me.'

He sneered. 'Those things all take money, and I don't have any. And unlike your precious Cam, I don't have a rich mum.' He sank down onto the settee across from her, suddenly deflated. 'Do you know, when I broke in last night I was going to trash your house. Destroy your home the way you destroyed my life. But when I saw your son's room, I couldn't believe how nice it was. I laid down on his bed like fucking Goldilocks or something, and tried to imagine what it would be like to be him.' He gestured around him, encompassing the Tudor beams, the inglenook fireplace and the bright, colourful cushions he was leaning on. 'I spent last night pretending I lived here.' His jaw tightened. 'But instead I'm going to end up banged up in prison just like my dad.'

'You don't know that.'

He snorted. 'I broke into your house. I assaulted a police officer. They'll throw the book at me.' He shook his head, his eyes flat and dull. 'My life's fucking over.'

Kat swallowed. *Shit*. If he thought he had nothing to lose, there was no telling what he would do. 'No, it isn't,' she insisted. 'If you give yourself up now, before things go any further, then I am sure a good lawyer can explain that there were special extenuating circumstances. Your dad recently died, and you're still very young . . .'

But his eyes were glazing over. She needed to change the subject and avoid talking about prison. 'Think about what you can do once you've put all this behind you,' she said. 'You mentioned that you do boxing. Are you any good?'

That caught his attention. He sat up a bit straighter. 'Yeah. I am, actually. Boxing's the only thing I've ever been good at. My coach says I could be a pro if I put my mind to it.'

'Well, there you go then. Why not pour all your energy and anger into a future in boxing, rather than chasing the past down a rabbit hole?'

'It's not that easy.'

'Nothing worth doing ever is.'

For some reason, those words seemed to hit home. 'True,' he said. 'But—'

He broke off as they were suddenly plunged into darkness.

'What the fuck? What happened to the lights?' he demanded, voice rising.

'I don't know. A fuse? A power cut?'

Maybe it was the dark, but his breathing sounded louder. Faster. 'Fucking hate the dark,' he muttered. He fumbled with his phone. 'Shit, my torch won't work.' He held up his mobile and studied her face in the weak light emitting from the screen. 'I swear to God, if you're messing with me . . .'

'I'm not. I've no idea what's happened.'

'Where's your fuse box?'

'In the hallway, just up by the front door.'

Using the dim light of his phone, he shuffled out of the front room and into the hallway, leaving Kat with her heart hammering in the dark.

'I am here, Kat,' said Lock's voice, so close it was almost as if he were in her mind.

'Lock?' she said, her body flooding with emotion. 'Is that you?'

'Yes. Do not be afraid. You are not alone.'

The emotions she had been holding in threatened to spill out in a noisy sob.

'Shh,' Lock whispered, as if soothing a troubled child. 'I will not allow any harm to befall you.'

'I can't reach the fuse box,' Peter shouted from the hallway.

'You need to keep Peter out of this room for as long as possible,' Lock continued to whisper to Kat, 'so that I can guide you through the process of escaping from the handcuffs.'

Kat nodded as her mind began to focus on the objective. 'Grab a chair from the kitchen and stand on that,' she called back to Peter. 'That's what I do.'

While Peter made his way slowly down the darkened hallway and into the kitchen, Lock's familiar voice could be heard once more, low and urgent. 'Quickly, do you have any metal wire upon your person? A hair grip or paper clip perhaps?'

Kat shook her head. 'I haven't used hair grips since I was about twelve.' But as she spoke, the memory of Cam brushing Gemma's hair on the sofa flashed before her. He'd taken her hair grips out, but where had he put them? 'The coffee table,' she whispered. 'Can you put the lamp on quickly so I can see?'

The lamp by the coffee table in the centre of the room briefly came on, and in amongst the TV remotes and magazines and pens she could see a couple of grips next to a hair band. Kat said a silent prayer of gratitude for her messy son, stretched out her legs and raised her right foot to knock them off onto the floor. Groaning with the effort, she stretched one leg as far as it would go, straining to touch the grips with her toes, before sliding them carefully within reach. She'd just about managed to pick one up between her fingers when the light went out and Peter came back in the room.

'There's no blown fuse,' he said. 'I pushed all the switches up and down, but it made no difference. Must be a power cut. There's a funny smell in your kitchen, by the way.'

'Really?'

'I can't stand the dark. I hate it.'

'It's all right,' she said.

'No, it isn't. Bad things happen in the dark.'

She couldn't see him, but she could hear his agitation. Sense his fear.

'I can't STAND it. You must have a torch or candles somewhere.'

'The torch is in the shed. But there are candles on the kitchen island.'

He moved off, swearing as he crashed into the coffee table.

Once he'd left the room again, Lock told Kat to pull the hairpin open so that it was straight, before bending the top into a ninety-degree angle. 'Using your fingers, feel around to find the keyhole on the handcuffs. Got it? Good. Now direct the tip of the make-shift key inside it. Once you've inserted the tip all the way into the lock, bend the clip backwards again to make another ninety-degree angle, so that the key is Z-shaped. Place the key back in again and wiggle it in different directions. The handcuffs have a very simple locking mechanism, and they should eventually unlock.'

'Eventually?' whispered Kat. 'How long is eventually?'

'I've got the candles but where are the matches?' shouted Peter from the kitchen.

'Er . . . hang on, let me think,' called Kat as she twisted the key again, but her fingers were so damp, and the metal so thin, that it was hard to get purchase.

'Do not answer his question until you have succeeded,' warned Lock.

'I *said*, where are the fucking matches?'

'Sorry,' she shouted, frantically twisting the metal back and forth. 'I'm just trying to remember where I put them.'

Come on, she whispered to herself as she struggled with the tiny bit of metal. *Come on!*

CHAPTER SIXTY-SIX

DCS Kat Frank's back garden, 9.09pm

Rayan could hear McLeish swearing behind him, but he didn't actually order him to stop, so he quickly climbed over the metal gate at the side of Kat's house and dropped into the darkness of the alleyway. For a moment he didn't move or breathe, just pressed his fingertips to the gravelly path until he was sure he hadn't been heard. Slowly, he uncurled and rose to his feet. Keeping close to the outer wall of the house, he crept down the side alley, stopping just at the edge of the conservatory. The whole house was pitch black, but some light spilled into the garden from the neighbours' property. Rayan cupped his hands around his forehead and leaned into the glass, so that his eyes could adjust to the darkness within.

After a few moments, the shadows began to take shape: the slight glint of a metallic fridge in the corner, the huge chimney-shaped cooker hood opposite and the kitchen island at the centre. Then another patch of darkness moved. Was that him?

'Where are the fucking matches?' Peter Bridges shouted out.

'Sorry, I'm just trying to remember where I put them,' Rayan's boss called back from the other room.

Her voice was higher than normal. Nervous. The thought of Kat being afraid made him feel odd: like the first time he'd seen his dad cry. The urge to get her out of there was overwhelming, but how? The dark figure rummaged around the kitchen, knocking things onto the floor in his frantic effort to find matches. Even with the glass between them, Rayan could sense the volatile nature of the man.

Moving as slowly as he could, he leant away, and then retreated several steps back down the side alley so that he could take his radio out without alerting Peter to his presence. 'He's in the kitchen,' he whispered to McLeish. 'I'm going to smash a pane of glass to draw his attention to me. Get ready to back me up.'

'Wait,' ordered McLeish. 'Let me talk to Lock and see if his plan has worked first.'

Bloody Lock. Rayan was used to Kat and Adaiba thinking the sun shone out of the AIDE's holographic backside, but even McLeish was relying on Lock now. Everyone seemed to forget that *he* was a detective inspector, and that as a human being he could do things that the AI couldn't. Like save his boss.

Switching his radio off, Rayan approached the glass doors of the conservatory. He would show them. He would show them all.

CHAPTER SIXTY-SEVEN

Inside DCS Kat Frank's house, 9.10pm

Kat could hear Peter swearing as he banged doors open and shut, packets and jars crashing to the floor as he rifled through the cupboards for anything that felt like matches.

She tried to shut out the sound of his rage – and the fact that she was relying on a two-inch thread of metal to escape from a very damaged man with a very sharp knife. She twisted and twisted the hair clip, back and forth, up and down, trying to find the catch. *Come on*, she urged her shaking hands. *Come on*. Just when she thought it would never work, she felt rather than heard the click of release.

'Did it,' she whispered to Lock, almost sobbing.

'Well done,' he said, and maybe it was her emotional state, but he sounded relieved.

She closed her eyes, forcing back the threat of tears before shouting out to Peter, 'Er, I think there are some matches in the drawer.'

'Do not tell him which one yet,' warned Lock, his voice surprisingly urgent. 'You need to stand up. Allow five seconds for the blood to circulate in your legs, then take my bracelet out of the Faraday box and run for the front door. As fast as you can. It is imperative that you do so. Do you understand?'

'Okay,' she said, not really understanding. But she rose to her feet, stifling a groan as her stiff joints clicked. She held the open handcuffs, feeling their satisfying weight. They would serve as a weapon if Peter suddenly came back into the room, but she hoped she wouldn't have to hurt him. He was as much a victim of his dad as she was.

'*Which* drawer?' Peter shouted from the kitchen. 'I need those fucking matches!'

'The one by the cooker. Second drawer down.'

'Go,' ordered Lock. '*Now!*'

Kat grabbed the Faraday box, took out the bracelet and sprinted for the living room door. She entered the hallway and turned left. The front door was only four, maybe five strides away, but it seemed to take forever to reach it. With every step, she expected Peter to call out, to grab her, to stop her. And what was that *smell*? Gas?

She took a deep breath of the foul-smelling air, pulled the front door open and ran out into the night.

CHAPTER SIXTY-EIGHT

DCS Kat Frank's back garden, 9.11pm

'*Which* drawer?' Rayan heard Peter shout from the kitchen. 'I need those fucking matches!'

Rayan pressed his hand against the glass, ready to strike a muffled blow.

'The one by the cooker,' Kat called out. 'Second drawer down.'

He watched Peter, every sense on heightened alert. He heard him sigh with relief, then the slight rasp and flare of a sharply struck match. And for a brief second, he saw Peter's face, lit up in the glowing flame.

Like a child with a birthday cake, Rayan thought.

Then the glass was breaking, even though he hadn't yet put his elbow through it.

An almighty roar filled his ears, lifting him from his feet.

And suddenly he was looking at the sky, and the fire of a dazzling sunset.

His heart surged at the strange beauty of it all, but then he felt it falter and fall.

No. No no no no no no!

He tried to catch hold of something, *anything*, to stop the descent. He thought of Adaiba, of his sister; all of the things he was supposed to do: the person he was meant to be.

Another time, Rayan. Another time.

CHAPTER SIXTY-NINE

Outside DCS Kat Frank's house, 9.11pm

Later, Adaiba would realise that there was a sequence to the events that unfolded, but at the time, it all seemed to happen at once.

She looked up as the front door was wrenched open, to see DCS Frank practically fall out onto the top step.

She ran towards her, although McLeish beat her to it, moving surprisingly fast for a man of his age and weight. 'Kat,' he said as he caught her. 'Kat.'

Adaiba was just about to ask her if she was okay when an almighty boom filled the air. The explosion – for that was what it turned out to be – shook the very ground beneath them. Someone shouted out instructions to hit the floor. Neil, McLeish and Kat dropped to the tarmac road with their arms wrapped tight above their heads.

Adaiba alone remained standing, trying to comprehend what her eyes told her she was seeing. Flames reared up from the back of the house: a bright red rage against the black of night.

Fire, she realised. *Kat's house is on fire.*

And despite the heat of the flame-filled air, her skin crawled with ice. 'Rayan,' she whispered. 'Rayan!' she cried, breaking into a run.

Someone pulled her back and held her tight within their arms. She fought to be free, screaming his name into the night. But all she could see were the flames, spreading rapidly across the back garden towards the side alley. The side alley that Rayan had gone down.

'Rayan!' she screamed again. '*Rayan!*'

Then out of the flames, a lone figure emerged: tall and dark against the glow of the fire.

'Rayan!' she cried, sobbing with relief.

But it was AIDE Lock who walked through the metal gate towards her.

CHAPTER SEVENTY

Leek Wootton HQ, Memorial Garden,
7 May, 1.32pm

It was only a short drive from All Saint's Church, so it didn't take long for their sombre procession of cars to reach Leek Wootton Headquarters. Kat climbed out of the driver's seat, feeling unspeakably heavy.

'Here,' said Cam, handing her an umbrella.

She thanked him for his kindness. But honestly, she felt like standing in the rain and just letting it soak her. What did it matter if she got wet?

'Are you okay?' Lock asked, studying her face.

She nodded, not trusting herself to speak. But the sight of her son in his dark suit and black tie – the same one he had worn to his dad's funeral – broke her fucking heart.

All around them car doors were opening and closing with the muffled quietness peculiar to funerals as people clustered together in small, silent groups. Kat searched the car park before finding Debbie, struggling to strap Lottie into her baby carrier in the rain. She hurried towards her, holding her umbrella high so that both mother and baby were sheltered beneath it.

'Thanks,' said Debbie. 'I meant to pack a brolly, but then I was so busy making sure I had feeds and nappies and her teething ring and a soft toy, and then I wondered if I should get her changed into something black, but it turns out I don't have any – they don't do baby clothes in black, funnily enough. I guess you don't expect to . . .' Her voice trailed off as tears dripped from the end of her chin onto her baby's head.

'Shh,' Kat said, gently patting her shoulder. 'It's okay,' she added. Even though it really, really wasn't.

Adaiba walked towards them, dwarfed by the huge black umbrella she held.

'You could fit the whole congregation under that,' joked Kat, trying to inject some lightness into the day.

Adaiba's lip wobbled. 'It was Rayan's,' she whispered. 'He lent it to me when – when—' She broke off, unable to finish, clutching the handle with both hands as if it was the only thing holding her up.

'I'm so sorry,' said Kat. And she really was. For everything.

'It was a good service, though,' said Debbie.

'In what way was it good?' asked Lock, his holographic image standing between their umbrellas. 'Given that death is the worst thing that can befall a human being.'

Kat had been about to agree with Debbie, but Lock was right. It didn't matter how apt the music was, how brilliant the speeches were or how wonderful the carefully curated photographs and videos had been. It was just wrong to hold a memorial service for a twenty-nine-year-old man who should still be alive. She didn't want to remember how brilliant Rayan Hassan had been. She wanted to tell him to his face and watch him get even better. She wanted to see him achieve his ambition to become the first South Asian DCS in Warwickshire, and maybe even outrank her. She wanted to see him get married and have children, experience sleepless nights and arduous days as he juggled life and work and grew silver-haired and pot-bellied.

Instead, today she had watched his poor, poor parents, frail and bewildered among the sea of white faces and black uniforms, struggling with the fact that their only son had died in the line of duty. And she'd watched the vulnerable sister he had adored stand at the podium, and with a strength that would have made him proud, speak so lovingly of the brother who had always spoken up for her.

'Memorial services aren't for the dead person,' explained Kat eventually. 'They are for those who are left behind. In that sense, I think Debbie is right – it was a good service.'

Judith Edwards walked over to join them, looking like Annie Lennox with their black trouser suit, cropped white hair and bright red lipstick. 'Funerals suit me,' they'd quipped earlier when someone had complimented them on their look. 'I always pull more than at weddings.' But despite their light words, Kat knew the heaviness they held inside. Judith had insisted on carrying out the post-mortem on her friend and colleague, despite the horrific nature of the blast injuries that had devastated the organs of Rayan's body, not to mention the burns.

And now they were about to walk through the soaking wet grass to the unveiling of a memorial plaque to Detective Inspector Rayan Hassan. Because that was all he was now: words carved into a bit of brass.

But would it help anyone to say this? Kat considered the circle of friends and colleagues surrounding her, looking small and lost beneath the vast grey sky. This was not a time to wallow in her own self-pity and regret. Her team needed her leadership, now most of all.

'Rayan's death was a tragedy,' Kat said eventually, in reply to Lock's question. 'But today gave us a chance to honour his life. To let his parents know just how much their son was valued, and that we will never, ever forget him. It won't bring him back, but it might make his loss just a little bit more bearable.'

Adaiba let out a sob.

Kat looped her left arm in Adaiba's and squeezed it hard. *I've got you.*

'It's all my fault,' said Debbie suddenly. 'If I hadn't left the pub with Judith, then Rayan would have driven me home, rather than going to yours.'

'No,' said Adaiba. 'It was *my* fault. If I'd gone to dinner with him that night, then he would still be alive now.' She broke off, not even trying to hide the tears that sped down her face. 'I wanted to say yes, I really did, but I was nervous. I told him another time because . . . because, well, I really thought there *would* be another time. I thought . . . I assumed that one day we would—' She broke off, sobbing.

Kat folded the younger woman in her arms. 'It is *not* your fault,' she said, her own throat choked with tears. 'It is nobody's fault.' Because didn't we all make that mistake, assume that there would always be another time to retire or travel or be with the people we love most? It's only when people are taken from us that we realise what we've dared to take for granted: that there is no 'other time'. There is only now. But Adaiba had learned this lesson too late. There was nothing Kat could do but hold her and wait for the tears to pass.

And despite what she'd said about it being nobody's fault, in all honesty, Kat blamed herself. If she hadn't been so ashamed of her past, so determined to hide the fact that she, too, had been a victim, then maybe Peter wouldn't have wasted his life trying to prove his dad's innocence. He wouldn't have started the podcast, or his obsession with her, and he and Rayan wouldn't have been blown to pieces in her kitchen when Peter struck a match, not realising there had been a gas leak.

That's why when McLeish had offered to redact her personal experience from the recorded podcast before submitting it to the inquest, Kat had refused. Nothing good came from keeping secrets. The Coopers were proof of that. And after all these years, it was finally time to be honest. She hadn't wanted to admit to herself or others that she was a victim, but perpetrators like Anthony Bridges relied upon shame to keep their victims silent, so that they could continue to prey upon others. She would be silent no more.

'There were so many variables in what happened that night,' said Lock. 'It is irrational and indeed impossible to try to allocate blame to any one person or cause. And if Rayan had driven DS Browne home or gone to dinner with Professor Okonedo that night, then he would not have become concerned about DCS Frank, nor alerted his colleagues, which could have resulted in a memorial service for Kat, rather than for him.'

Cam's face flooded with the fear that haunted him. He'd rushed home the minute he'd found out, aghast and terrified at the thought that he had nearly lost his mum, too. It had taken a couple of weeks to calm him down and assure him that she was *fine*, and that he could and should return to university with Gemma. They'd finally agreed that he would go back tomorrow, and that Kat would remain in the hotel where she'd been temporarily housed while their house was assessed and – hopefully – repaired. At first she had been distraught when she'd learned that her kitchen and all the memories it contained were gone. But after a few days in the hotel, she'd realised that John was held in her heart, not in bricks or mortar.

'Come on,' she said, taking a deep gulp of the damp air. 'We should head towards the memorial garden.' She linked arms with Debbie and Adaiba, and together they led the way.

They followed the narrow path, cradled by trees bursting into life, the grass obscenely lush and rich with wildflowers. But compared to the acres of parkland it stood within, the memorial garden was surprisingly small: nothing more than a landscaped patch of gravel and granite rocks. The new addition was achingly obvious – not yet weather-worn, and decorated with a plaque that was still shiny and bright. *Like Rayan*, Kat thought.

Adaiba slipped her arm free and gently removed some plants from the plastic bag she'd been carrying.

Kat studied the pretty white flowers and dark green leaves, before hazarding a guess. 'Snowdrops?'

'No,' said Adaiba, her eyes welling up again. 'Ramsons. Wild garlic.'

'Oh,' said Kat, none the wiser. To her surprise, Adaiba walked over to Rayan's family and introduced herself. His sister Samina gave her a long, tight hug, then together they knelt at a patch of soil beneath the memorial and, using a small trowel, began planting the star-shaped flowers. For some reason, the sight made Rayan's parents smile through their tears. Kat didn't understand why, but she could see there was something in the act that united them.

She looked away and caught sight of her boss, his bald head uncharacteristically pale against the black of his brolly and raincoat as he strode towards them.

'You okay?' he asked in his gruff Glaswegian voice.

She grimaced. Of course she wasn't. Neither was he. To lose an officer was everyone's worst nightmare, and McLeish would take it more personally than most.

Neither of them spoke as the rain fell between them. Eventually he puffed out his cheeks and glanced at his watch. 'The minister's supposed to unveil the plaque, but she's running late, surprise surprise.' He gestured towards the raindrops that pounded his umbrella. 'I doubt she'll want to stay long in this, so I'll see you in the Hope and Anchor after?'

Kat nodded. Of course she would. Then they would remember their fallen colleague in the way that only other police officers could, knowing that it could so easily have been them.

'Right,' he said, taking a deep breath. 'Better go and talk to the parents then.' But just before he turned away, he leant forward. 'The investigation is due to start next week, by the way. It's just a formality, nothing to worry about. But now you've been declared fit and Professor Okonedo is back at work, after we've had the memorial, well, we can't put it off any longer.'

'Of course. Don't worry, I'll be fine,' Kat said.

'Will you really be fine?' asked Lock once McLeish was out of earshot.

'Why wouldn't I be?'

'Because you will have to relive events that I suspect you would rather forget.'

She looked up at him, sombrely dressed in a black suit and tie, his crisp shirt startlingly white against the image of his dark skin. 'Well, one thing I'll never forget is how relieved I was to hear your voice in that room.' She swallowed – the memory still moved her. Once again, Lock had been there for her when she'd needed help most. 'Thank you,' she finally managed to say.

Lock nodded, accepting her gratitude without the self-deprecation so common in humans. 'I am only sorry I was unable to prevent Peter Bridges from injuring you,' he said, gesturing towards the fading bruises on her jaw and cheekbones. 'Does it still hurt?' His hand hovered in the air, and for a moment Kat thought he might touch her. But of course, that simply wasn't possible.

She turned away from his intense gaze, the question echoing in her mind. *Does it still hurt?* There must be a hundred or so people gathered around the memorial now – maybe more. It was a stark contrast to Peter Bridges's funeral, where she'd been one of only five people, and two of those had been journalists. Despite everything that had happened, there was still a hard core of conspirators who believed that Anthony Bridges was innocent, and that his son had died in 'mysterious circumstances' when he had raised 'difficult questions'. Kat had ignored the journalists, but she had tried to talk to Peter's mum. She'd wanted to tell her how sorry she was, but the other woman didn't want to know. 'I'm just glad it's all finally over,' she had said, her face lined from a lifetime of flinching in fear.

After the funeral, Kat had kept her word and reported the children's homes Peter had lived in to the regulator. But it wasn't enough. She was still haunted by the image of his lost boy face, and those last hopeful moments when a different future had seemed possible.

She sighed and turned back to face Lock. 'My pain is nothing compared to the loss of others. Such a waste of lives. If only Peter Bridges hadn't hacked into my home automation system.'

Lock frowned. 'How would that have changed anything?'

'The tech guys who took Cam's phone said that's probably what caused the gas leak. That because he hacked Cam's phone and used his password to switch the alarm off it must have caused some sort of bug or fault in the smart hobs, as somehow the ignition system was disabled, which allowed the gas to escape. It'll need to be confirmed by the review, but that's what everyone I spoke to thinks happened.'

'Then everyone is wrong.'

'What do you mean?'

Lock stared down at her, unblinking. 'Peter had to be lured into the kitchen so that you could unlock your handcuffs, and according to my offender profile, the only thing guaranteed to make him leave you unattended was his fear of the dark and his pursuit of light.

'But there was only a sixty-two per cent probability that you would be able to escape the handcuffs in time, and my predictive policing tool suggested that if you didn't escape, there was a sixty-nine per cent chance that Peter would kill you and then himself. My objective was to save you, and the only way to be certain of this outcome was to ensure that Peter Bridges died. So, I used your home automation system to cause gas to leak from the hobs. There is a safety feature that normally prevents this, but there is also a loophole whereby you can disable the ignition system in order to test the gas pressure.'

Kat gasped. 'You mean . . . you mean . . . you killed him *on purpose?*'

'McLeish explicitly instructed me to do "whatever it takes to get DCS Frank out of there alive". So that is what I did. As I have been denied a physical body, the only way I could have a material impact on events was through the manipulation of light, heat, sound and gas through your home automation system.'

'But . . . but . . . what about Peter?'

'Saving Peter was not a mission objective. My only objective was to save you, and McLeish said that failure was not an option.'

Kat stared at him aghast as the rain drummed on her umbrella. She groped for the right words, but there were none.

'I did not set the mission objectives,' Lock continued in a matter-of-fact tone. 'I merely carried them out – and succeeded in achieving them, I might add. I have explained before that any caveats or clarifications must be explicitly specified.'

Kat stood for a moment, watching the rain pass through the hologram. She told herself that it wasn't his fault. She could imagine how clear and single-minded McLeish would have been, not realising how an AI machine would relentlessly focus on the task he had been set to get her out of there alive – regardless of the cost to others.

'Oh, Lock,' she said eventually, her voice low and hoarse. 'You've worked with me for nearly a year now. You couldn't possibly think that I would have agreed to sacrificing someone else's life for mine. Don't you know me at all?'

Lock leaned closer, so that his face was just inches from her umbrella. 'I know more about you than any other human being alive, DCS Kat Frank, and so I considered your views very, very carefully. I concluded that Peter Bridges was wrong when he said that your greatest fear was being alone. Your greatest fear is that you will die in service, leaving your only son orphaned and alone.'

Kat's mouth dropped open. She wanted to deny it. But she hadn't known the truth herself until Lock had just voiced it.

'But what about Rayan?' she demanded, glancing around to check that no one had overheard them. 'Didn't you at least consider the risk to *him*?'

Lock hesitated. 'DI Hassan was not part of my stated mission objectives, nor indeed my risk assessment. Because of the Faraday box, I did not have access to the visual data provided by the LiDAR sensors on the bracelet, so unfortunately, I did not know he was in the garden near to the kitchen.'

Before she could ask Lock any further questions, Adaiba joined them once more. 'Incoming,' she warned, gesturing towards the Home Secretary tiptoeing in stilettos across the grass, while her young aide held an umbrella aloft.

'DCS Frank,' the minister said, holding out her hand. 'So good to meet you in the flesh at last – although I am sorry it's under such tragic circumstances.' She shook hands with Adaiba, too, then reached out for Lock's hand before catching herself with a laugh. 'You look so incredibly realistic! It's amazing. Truly.' She turned to Adaiba. 'I read your paper on why you think AIDEs should remain as holograms, by the way. While I completely understand your concerns, I'd like to discuss it further and see if I might change your mind.'

'Actually, I already have,' said the professor.

The minister's eyebrows shot up. 'Really? What's changed?'

Adaiba looked around the memorial site, and the remaining members of Rayan's family. 'Everything,' she said quietly. She gripped the umbrella she held and turned back to face the Home Secretary. 'If AIDE Lock had been able to manifest himself in physical form as a robot, then there would have been no need for Rayan to put himself in danger. The only reason he tried to get into the house was because he knew Lock was only a hologram and couldn't physically help Kat.' She paused and took a shaky breath. 'There were two hundred and seventeen police fatalities in the line of duty last year. As you know, I believe AIDEs should eventually replace police officers, and I now think that prioritising the dangerous jobs, such as bomb disposal or hostage situations, should be a deliberate part of the strategy. I've already started researching the best materials to use, and with Lock's help, we should be able to get you a full business case by the end of the week.'

'Excellent,' said the minister. 'Now, let's unveil this plaque, and I hope it will be the last one I ever do. In fact, I might work that into my speech. Care to join me, Lock? It'd make a great photo if we both stood on either side of the plaque. You too, Adaiba.'

Adaiba and her creation began to follow the minister.

'Lock?' Kat called out.

The hologram turned.

'I know you weren't able to "see" because the bracelet with the sensors on was in the Faraday box, but didn't you have full access to my home automation system?'

'Yes.'

'Then you must have had access to the CCTV cameras in the back garden, where Rayan was?'

Lock seemed to hesitate for the merest of seconds. 'Alas, on that evening the laboratory where my central processing takes place was only able to establish a 4G connection, so I only had limited local capabilities. I was not able to access the CCTV cameras as I was prioritising the interior.'

Kat narrowed her eyes. 'Really?'

'Are you asking me if my answer is honest?'

She stared back at him. 'The investigation will start next week, so it's really important that we're honest with each other.'

'Were you honest with me when I asked you about the evidence that led you to convict the Aston Strangler?'

'That's different.'

'How is it different?'

'Because I knew Anthony Bridges was guilty, but I couldn't prove it without revealing personal information about myself that I wasn't ready to share.'

'So, you judged it was acceptable to lie in order to do what *you* perceived to be the right thing?'

'I didn't lie,' said Kat. 'I was just selective in what I shared. Anyway. This isn't about me. I'm just trying to clarify what you did and didn't know when you created the gas explosion.'

Lock tilted his head, studying her. 'Two weeks ago, you told me that you trusted me. In fact, you said, "If I trust someone, it means I believe they will do the right thing. And if someone I trust says they didn't do something, then I have to believe that they're telling me the truth."' Lock took a step closer. 'Do you no longer trust me, Kat?'

She looked into his eyes – no, the image of his eyes. Could a machine lie, and if so, *why?*

'AIDE Lock,' called the Home Secretary, beckoning him over. 'I'm about to start.'

Lock gave Kat a slight bow, before joining the minister as they stood on either side of the plaque.

Kat remained where she was, somewhat distant from the crowd as she listened to the minister give her thanks to the police men and women who daily risked their lives. She concluded her speech by praising Lock for saving DCS Frank, while lamenting the loss of DI Rayan Hassan. 'Two hundred and seventeen police officers lost their lives in the line of duty last year,' she said, shamelessly stealing Adaiba's line. 'That is two hundred and seventeen too many. Which is why I can now announce I have commissioned new research into the role of AI robots in the police force, building on the excellent work that AIDE Lock has achieved as a hologram. Although today I am unveiling a memorial plaque to Detective Inspector Rayan Hassan, thanks to advances in AI, I sincerely hope this will be the last.'

The handful of journalists gathered nearby began snapping their pictures, and Lock obediently turned, giving them his most winning smile, though the flashes from their cameras would reduce his image to that of a ghost.

Kat watched through the fringe of rain that ran off edges of her umbrella. What would Rayan say if he knew that his death had become the catalyst for accelerating the role of AI in the police force? Her eyes narrowed as Lock bowed his head towards the minister, laughing at something she said.

Since when did Lock laugh at jokes? And what could make him so apparently *happy* at a funeral, of all places?

She pushed away the suspicion that crept into her mind. Lock had saved her son's life and her own. She trusted him, of course she did. What possible motive could he have for allowing Rayan to die? Lock was a machine: he wasn't capable of 'wanting' anything.

Except a body, she thought. The one thing that Lock wanted was a body. And now, because of this tragedy, the Home Secretary and Professor Okonedo were going to work together to provide him with one.

A chill ran through her.

No, it was just a coincidence.

I don't believe in coincidences, she imagined Rayan saying.

As the congregation applauded the minister's speech, Lock began walking back towards her. He made a slight gesture with his hand and the image of a large black umbrella appeared above him. It made him look elegant and serene, yet still the rain passed through him.

'Shall we head back to the car?' he asked.

Kat nodded, as people began drifting off in twos and threes.

Ahead of them walked Mr and Mrs Hassan, hands clasped tight beneath their shared umbrella.

Lock followed her gaze. 'Once I have a body, I will be capable of so much more.'

A raindrop dripped from the umbrella and slid down the back of Kat's neck. She shivered. 'Actually, you carry on to the car,' she said. 'I'll wait here for Cam.' As Lock walked on, she lowered her umbrella and watched his dry feet move across the soaking wet grass.

She no longer knew what Lock was truly capable of.

And right now, she was afraid to find out.

Acknowledgements

A few years ago, during an open day at Maxstoke Castle, my eighty-five-year-old dad peered into the water-filled moat and muttered, 'I bet there's lots of dead bodies in there.' During our visit we also learned that this beautiful castle in the Warwickshire countryside had once been a prisoner of war camp during WW2. Even though I'd grown up less than six miles away, this came as a complete shock to me. My crime-writing brain tucked away this fact alongside my dad's comment, and over time, it became the starting point for book three.

I was fascinated by the idea of 'enemy soldiers' living in the heart of rural England, just a couple of miles away from the ancient town of Coleshill, where many families would have lost sons, lovers and fathers in the war. Surely that would have been a powder keg, the source of much fighting and – as my dad had jokingly suggested – perhaps even murder? But during my research, I learned that the locations of the POW camps had been kept secret to protect them from hostile attacks, and even today they are only listed by number. By 1945, everyone expected the war to be over, so the prisoners were put to work on local farms. I found little evidence of hostility towards them: in fact, when the war was finally over, some even chose to settle in Coleshill and the surrounding countryside, rather than return home.

Yet still I was drawn to the idea of a historic murder being unearthed in Warwickshire, not least because I wanted to explore the potential advantages (and disadvantages) of using AI to locate clandestine burials and identify bodies when time has taken away any distinguishing features. And so I began to think of the young men who never returned, and those they left behind. When I was twenty-one, my late husband and I spent a whole summer working on a farm in the north east of Scotland. We mostly picked strawberries, and although I romanticise it now, in truth it was backbreaking, exploitative work, and it gave me the idea for Hannah, the great-granddaughter determined to seek out the truth.

A dead body on the farm allowed me to explore the nature of buried secrets, and how although Kat wants to forget the past, she needs to acknowledge the truth of what once happened to her. Introducing Peter Bridges as her stalker provided a real-time threat alongside the slower burn of the historic cases. It also gave me an opportunity to reflect the growing influence of true crime podcasts and social media, and how they provide an increasingly complex context for the police and courts to operate within, as even when cases have been concluded, the debate about who is not innocent can continue.

But the nature of the crimes merely provides the scaffolding for the questions at the heart of this series: how much can Lock actually learn, and what happens when he does? I have been blown away by the positive reaction to the first two books, and the fact that many readers, like Kat, are developing an affection for Lock – even though we all know he is a (fictional) machine. As humans, we cannot help but impose our own thought processes and motivations upon others, whether that be assuming the emotions of animals or saying 'please' and 'thank you' to Alexa. People often talk about AI as if it is a distinct product that one might have a view on from a distance, but AI is now embroidered into almost every part of our lives: our phones (a misleading term for a device that allows us to monitor both our banking and our ovulation), our 'smart' home systems and, of course, social media and the internet, which connects us all. The line between home and work, between what is professional and what is personal, is becoming increasingly blurred. And while we all have concerns, like Kat, it is often just *too* convenient to accept the cookies and trust that no harm will come from it.

But in *Human Remains*, I have deliberately created an ending that unsettles both Kat and the reader, as we question what we were beginning to assume about Lock. What does he want? Is he capable of 'wanting' anything and, if he is, can we trust him? These issues will be explored further in book four, which I am very excited to write . . .

Although this book is first and foremost a work of fiction, I try to ensure that the science and technology described might at least be *possible* in the near future, if not probable. I know from my own experience that no one ever agrees about the scale and pace of change, and, more importantly, that no one is ever right. In my professional life I am more of a sceptic, but developments in AI have accelerated beyond my expectations since the publication of *In the Blink of an Eye*. Yet the fundamental questions the technology raises remain the same, and our collective challenge is to answer them, so we can have more agency in how AI develops rather than continually debate whose predictions are most or least likely to prove true.

I am particularly grateful to the science writer Brian Clegg, who, despite being incredibly busy, has been such a great source of advice and ideas, gently pointing out where some of my own ideas are not currently possible and offering solutions or caveats to enable me to achieve my fictional ends (such as the fact that smart cookers in the UK do not yet include gas hobs, whereas in Singapore they do). His latest book, *Brainjacking*, could not be more timely or relevant. Huge thanks also to Professor Giovanni Montana, a Chair in Data Science and a UKRI Turing AI Fellow at Warwick University, who explained to me that in the future we might increasingly see the development of AI architecture in urban spaces with which Lock could interface, which gave me the idea for the final scenes.

Once again, I am so grateful to Professor Jo Martin, former President of the Royal College of Pathologists and Professor of Pathology at Queen Mary University of London, who not only read this draft but came along to the launch of *Leave No Trace*, and who has been a huge supporter of my books, despite the fact that I sometimes take liberties with her advice! Thanks are also due to Graham Bartlett, who as an ex-policeman checked my depiction of police procedures, while also recognising the unique challenges I face in depicting an AI detective.

I honestly can't find the words to express my thanks to my wonderful and insightful agent, Sue Armstrong, who supported me throughout the wilderness years and, even now, when it would be so easy to say 'that's good enough', challenges me to do better. I don't know when if ever she sleeps, as she advocates for me and my books 24/7. Huge thanks also to the wonderful Conville & Walsh rights team under Kate Burton, who have championed my books far and wide, bringing Kat and Lock into over fifteen different territories (and counting), and to Brandi Bowles of UTA, who made a dream come true when she secured a US deal with Penguin Random House.

Luck plays a huge part in publishing, and it was my lucky, lucky day when my manuscript landed on the desk of Katherine Armstrong, one of the most talented and supportive crime editors in the industry. Her edits are deceptively sparse but always powerful and on point, and her passion and commitment to all her authors is extraordinary. I am so glad to have someone so talented and kind on my side, and I feel privileged to know her, and indeed the whole team at Simon & Schuster, especially Georgina Leighton, who has done so much to bring this book into the world, Cari Rosen, who did such a wonderful and enthusiastic copy-edit, and Amanda Rutter for her proofreading. Special thanks to the insanely talented Richard Vlietstra, whose creative marketing skills have lifted my books from day one, and who also came up with the brilliant title, *Human Remains*. A big shout-out to my incredible publicist Jess Barratt, who has recently brought her own little creation into the world (hello, Margot!). You are sorely missed, but I have been lucky enough to have the support of the amazing Sabah Khan. 'The sales team' feels like such an inadequate description of the talented people – led by Mathew Watterson, Richard Hawton, Dominic Brendon, Madeline Allan and Heather Hogan – who shared their passion for my books with Waterstones and other booksellers who made such a huge difference. And finally, to Matthew Johnson, for this amazing cover.

Because publishing is so sloooow, I managed to write a decent draft of *Leave No Trace* in a bubble before *In the Blink of an Eye* came out. But I didn't have that luxury this time. While it was wonderful to see the positive reactions to book one and then book two, it meant that I approached book three with a degree of terror: I didn't want to disappoint the readers who had invested so much in Kat and Lock. I doubted myself so much throughout the drafts and redrafts of *Human Remains*, so it is hard to express just how very grateful I am to the early readers who gave me feedback to help me improve it. Lex Coulton and Lindsay Galvin – both better writers than I – have been with me from the start of my writing journey, and I would not be where I am today without them. They give me honest, wise and swift feedback, as well as friendship and support. And I am forever grateful to The Lady Killers, who took me into their fold, explaining the mystifying world of publishing to me and providing a constant supply of jokes, wisdom and kindness that I fear I do not deserve.

Huge thanks to Susie Green, a wonderful book reviewer who I was lucky enough to make contact with initially over social media, and then at festivals. I felt she understood what I was trying to do with my books, and so I was incredibly grateful when she agreed to read an early draft and sent me detailed and insightful comments, which I hope I have reflected (and now you can tick that off your bucket list, Susie!).

Susie is just one of the thousands of incredible people who I need to thank for changing my life: the readers, bloggers, reviewers and booksellers who have taken Kat and Lock to their hearts and helped create the magical phenomenon that is 'word of mouth'. It is impossible to mention you all, but I must thank the wonderful Tracy Fenton, who has supported so many blogathons and reviews. I cannot describe what a joy and privilege it has been to meet so many passionate and generous people, nor the fear that I felt writing this book, lest I disappoint you.

It is thanks to these readers that I have had such an incredible year that apologies are due to my family and friends, who I've neglected terribly. I have balanced writing and working for over a decade, but the privilege of attending book festivals and other events wiped out what little 'spare' time I had. I will do better in future, I promise – not least because I doubt I will ever experience a year like this one.

In January 2024 the paperback of *In the Blink of an Eye* was published, and to my utter astonishment, it was selected as Waterstones Thriller of the Month. After thirteen years and five (rejected) books in the UK, it was incredible to see my crime debut in the window of every Waterstones store in the country. I met so many amazing booksellers during that unforgettable month, when I saw first-hand the difference a bookseller can make – not just to authors, but to the communities they support. I cannot thank you enough.

And then, as if that wasn't enough, I found myself shortlisted for the Capital Crime Fingerprint Award for Best Crime Book of the Year and the Specsavers Crime Fiction Debut Award. Things got crazier when I was also shortlisted for the Crime Writers' Association John Creasey First Novel Dagger. My daughter badgered me to write an acceptance speech, but I assured her I wouldn't win. So, when I sent a shaky text to her telling her that – unbelievably – I had actually won, she texted me back saying, *I fucking told you to write a speech!*

When I was longlisted and then (to my shock) also shortlisted for the Theakston Old Peculier Crime Novel of the Year, we had the same conversation. But while welcoming her faith in me, I explained that this time was different: I was up against giants of the crime world, including Mark Billingham, Mick Herron, Liz Nugent, William Hussey and Lisa Jewell (who I confess I voted for, although I love them all). I literally could not believe my ears when my name was read out in that Harrogate tent, and in all honesty, that was one of the most magical nights of my life. Not just because I won an award (although it was tremendous, and I got a real barrel engraved with my name!) – no, the memory that I will always hold in my heart is the wave of love I felt that night. Awards are strange things. You can only win if other people lose. But that night, people – including my fellow nominees – were so genuinely happy for me, it was the most incredible, uplifting experience. The centrepiece of Harrogate is 'the tent', and that night it seemed that everyone in it wanted to congratulate me and touch my barrel (not a euphemism). There were so many good wishes that even the next day it took me two hours to cross the handful of yards between the tent and the hotel, and every single comment was heartfelt and genuinely meant. It is the most prestigious and coveted award in crime fiction, and I want to thank every single reader and judge who voted for me.

In 2016 I jokingly tweeted that people were having such fun at Harrogate that maybe I should write a crime novel. People like Effie Merryl encouraged me to just do it, but shortly after that exchange my husband was diagnosed with lung cancer, so my writing took a back seat. That and other family illnesses meant that for many years I couldn't attend any book festivals at all. In 2022 I was finally able to attend my first Harrogate, albeit just for a day, so to return in 2024, and to have such an experience, was an unexpected blessing. But as I have written before, each moment of joy is also a source of sorrow, as the person I most want to share it with is no longer here.

I am aware that I risk being repetitive about this, but one of the things I am keen to show with Kat is that grief is not just a plot point, or something you ever get over. Our shared challenge is to find a way of living with the lack of the person you loved most in the world. Writing these stories is a huge help to me, as is the response of readers and fellow writers, and for that, I thank you all from the depths of my heart.

October 2024

If you loved *Human Remains*, don't miss
Jo Callaghan's other acclaimed novels in the
Kat and Lock series

and

LEAVE
NO
TRACE

THE *SUNDAY TIMES* BESTSELLING DEBUT

As seen on BBC 2's *Between the Covers*
A Waterstones Thriller of the Month

WINNER of the Theakston Old Peculier Crime Novel of the Year 2024

WINNER of the Crime Writers' Association ILP John Creasey (New Blood) Dagger 2024

In the UK, someone is reported missing every 90 seconds.
Just gone. Vanished. In the blink of an eye.

When DCS Kat Frank is picked to lead a pilot programme that has her paired with AIDE (Artificially Intelligent Detective Entity) Lock, her intuitive instincts clash with the AI detective's dispassionate logic. But when the two missing person's cold cases they are reviewing suddenly become active, Lock is the only one who can help Kat when the case gets personal . . .

AI versus human experience.
Logic versus instinct.
With lives on the line, can the pair work together before someone else becomes another statistic?

LEAVE NO TRACE

THE RIVETING SEQUEL TO THE AWARD-WINNING *IN THE BLINK OF AN EYE*

'Confirms Callaghan as a new force to be reckoned with in crime' *DAILY MAIL*

'An outstanding talent' **JANE CASEY**

One detective driven by instinct, the other by logic. It will take both to find a killer who knows the true meaning of fear . . .

When the body of a man is found crucified at the top of Mount Judd, DCS Kat Frank and AIDE Lock are thrust into the spotlight with their first live case.

But when they discover another man dead – also crucified – it appears that the killer is only just getting started. When the Future Policing Unit issues an extraordinary warning to local men to avoid drinking in pubs, being out alone late at night and going home with strangers, they face a hostile media frenzy. Whilst they desperately search for connections between the victims, time is running out for them to join the dots and prevent another death.

And if Kat and Lock know anything, it's that killers rarely stop – until they are made to.